BROTHERBAND

BOOK 7
THE CALDERA

Also by John Flanagan

BROTHERBAND CHRONICLES

THE RANGER'S APPRENTICE EPIC

RANGER'S APPRENTICE: THE EARLY YEARS

COMPANION TO THE BESTSELLING

RANGER'S APPRENTICE

BROTHERBAND

BOOK 7
THE CALDERA

JOHN FLANAGAN

PHILOMEL BOOKS

PHILOMEL BOOKS

an imprint of Penguin Random House LLC
375 Hudson Street, New York, NY 10014

Copyright © 2017 by John Flanagan.
Published in Australia by Penguin Random House Australia in 2017.
Heron illustration © 2011 by David Elliot. Map copyright © Mathematics and Anna Warren.
Penguin supports copyright. Copyright fuels creativity, encourages diverse voices, promotes free speech,
and creates a vibrant culture. Thank you for buying an authorized edition of this book and for
complying with copyright laws by not reproducing, scanning, or distributing any part of it in any form
without permission. You are supporting writers and allowing Penguin to continue to publish
books for every reader.

Philomel Books is a registered trademark of Penguin Random House LLC.

Library of Congress Cataloging-in-Publication Data is available upon request.

Printed in the United States of America.
ISBN 9780399163586
1 3 5 7 9 10 8 6 4 2
U.S. edition edited by Michael Green.
U.S. edition designed by Semadar Megged.
Text set in 13/18-point Centaur MT Std.

A Few Sailing Terms Explained

Because this book involves sailing ships, I thought it might be useful to explain a few of the nautical terms found in the story.

Be reassured that I haven't gone overboard (to keep up the nautical allusion) with technical details in the book, and even if you're not familiar with sailing, I'm sure you'll understand what's going on. But a certain amount of sailing terminology is necessary for the story to feel realistic.

So, here we go, in no particular order:

Bow: The front of the ship, also called the prow.

Stern: The rear of the ship.

Port and starboard: The left and the right side of the ship, as you're facing the bow. In fact, I'm probably incorrect in using the term *port*. The early term for port was *larboard*, but I thought we'd all get confused if I used that.

Starboard is a corruption of "steering board" (or steering side). The steering oar was always placed on the right-hand side of the ship at the stern.

Consequently, when a ship came into port, it would moor with the left side against the jetty, to avoid damage to the steering oar. One theory says the word derived from the ship's being in port— left side to the jetty. I suspect, however, that it might have come from the fact that the entry port, by which crew and passengers boarded, was also always on the left side.

How do you remember which side is which? Easy. *Port* and *left* both have four letters.

Forward: Toward the bow.

Aft: Toward the stern.

Fore-and-aft rig: A sail plan in which the sail is in line with the hull of the ship.

Hull: The body of the ship.

Keel: The spine of the ship.

Stem: The upright timber piece at the bow, joining the two sides together.

Forefoot: The lowest point of the bow, where the keel and the stem of the ship meet.

Steering oar: The blade used to control the ship's direction, mounted on the starboard side of the ship, at the stern.

Tiller: The handle for the steering oar.

Sea anchor: A method of slowing a ship's downwind drift, often by use of a canvas **drogue**—a long, conical tube of canvas closed at one end and held open at the other—or two spars lashed together in a cross. The sea anchor is streamed from the bow and the resultant drag slows the ship's movement through the water.

Yardarm, or yard: A spar (wooden pole) that is hoisted up the mast, carrying the sail.

Masthead: The top of the mast.

Bulwark: The part of the ship's side above the deck.

Scuppers: Drain holes in the bulwarks set at deck level to allow water that comes on board to drain away.

Belaying pins: Wooden pins used to fasten rope.

Oarlock, or rowlock: Pegs set on either side of an oar to keep it in place while rowing.

Thwart: A seat.

Telltale: A pennant that indicates the wind's direction.

Tacking: To tack is to change direction from one side to the other, passing through the eye of the wind.

If the wind is from the north and you want to sail northeast, you would perform one tack so that you are heading northeast, and you would continue to sail on that tack for as long as you need.

However, if the wind is from the north and you want to sail due north, you would have to do so in a series of short tacks, going back and forth on a zigzag course, crossing through the wind each time, and slowly making ground to the north. This is a process known as **beating** into the wind.

Wearing: When a ship tacks, it turns *into* the wind to change direction. When it wears, it turns *away* from the wind, traveling in a much larger arc, with the wind in the sail, driving the ship around throughout the maneuver. Wearing was a safer way of changing direction for wolfships than beating into the wind.

Reach, or reaching: When the wind is from the side of the ship, the ship is sailing on a reach, or reaching.

Running: When the wind is from the stern, the ship is running. (So would you if the wind was strong enough at your back.)

Reef: To gather in part of the sail and bundle it against the yardarm to reduce the sail area. This is done in high winds to protect the sail and the mast.

Trim: To adjust the sail to the most efficient angle.

Halyard: A rope used to haul the yard up the mast. (Haul-yard, get it?)

Stay: A heavy rope that supports the mast. The **backstay** and the **forestay** are heavy ropes running from the top of the mast to the stern and the bow (it's pretty obvious which is which).

Sheets and shrouds: Many people think these are sails, which is a logical assumption. But in fact, they're ropes. Shrouds are thick ropes that run from the top of the mast to the side of the ship, supporting the mast. Sheets are the ropes used to control, or trim, the sail—to haul it in and out according to the wind strength and direction. In an emergency, the order might be given to "let fly the sheets!" The sheets would be released, letting the sail loose and bringing the ship to a halt. (If *you* were to let fly the sheets, you'd probably fall out of bed.)

Hawser: Heavy rope used to moor a ship.

Way: The motion of the ship. If a ship is under way, it is moving according to its course. If it is making leeway, the ship is moving downwind so it loses ground or goes off course.

Lee: The downwind side of a ship, opposite to the direction of the wind.

Lee shore: A shoreline downwind of the ship, with the wind blowing the ship toward the shore—a dangerous situation for a sailing ship.

Back water: To row a reverse stroke.

So, now that you know all you need to know about sailing terms, welcome aboard the world of the Brotherband Chronicles!

John Flanagan

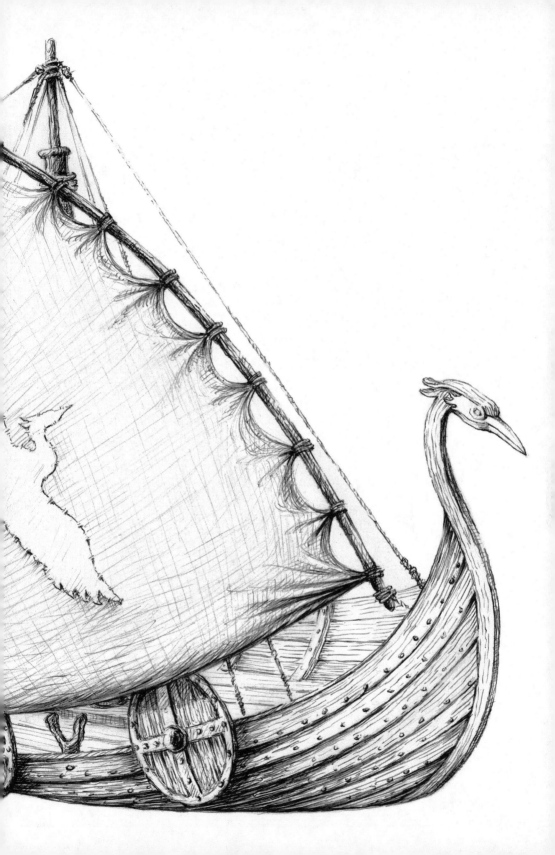

PART ONE

A FACE FROM
THE PAST

The heavy-set man came at Stig with a rush.

His arms were held out ahead of him as if ready for an embrace, his fingers curled and ready to grip. He was taller than Stig, and perhaps twelve kilograms heavier. His chest and upper body were thickly muscled. Stig could see a light sheen of oil covering his arms, and he had time to think that this was not quite in the spirit of the contest.

He braced himself, and their two bodies came together with a solid *WHUMP* of flesh meeting flesh. If his attacker had hoped to drive the wind out of Stig with the impact, his aim was thwarted. The young warrior had tensed his muscles ready for the hit. He stepped back half a pace, but otherwise remained steady.

Let him come to you, Thorn had told him. *See what he's got before you start.*

What he had was not particularly skillful or unexpected. He wrapped his arms around Stig's waist in a clumsy bear hug and, beginning to lean back, attempted to lift him off the ground so that he could apply pressure to the kidneys and lungs as Stig hung helpless in his embrace.

But Stig wasn't ready to be helpless—and he'd watched the man use this very tactic in a previous bout. As he felt the man's arms wrap around him, and was drawn in tight against him, Stig rammed his right hand, palm open, under the man's chin, locking his elbow tightly in a right angle and supporting his right arm with his left hand. The arm formed a rigid, unyielding barrier against the man's attempts to lift Stig's feet off the sand of the arena. In effect, as long as Stig could keep his right arm locked, the man was trying to lift himself off the ground along with his opponent.

The larger man grunted with the effort, trying to twist his chin away from Stig's iron grip. But Stig maintained the pressure and his opponent was caught in a stalemate. The more he heaved and strained, the more he exhausted himself. Yet he lacked the imagination or speed of thought to change the tactic. It had always worked for him before. It should work for him now.

Except, in previous bouts, his opponents hadn't been ready for the hold. And if they were, they had no effective counter to it.

The man tried to gather his strength for one last, superhuman effort to lift his rock-steady opponent off the ground. As he did so, he inadvertently released the pressure of his bear hug, expecting to resume it with even greater force. But Stig felt the momentary easing of pressure. In fact, he'd been expecting it. As the grip around his waist weakened, he released his hold on the other man's chin and spun in his grip so that his back was to him. He rammed his backside into the man's lower body to gain a little room, felt the hug release even further, then hurled himself backward, taking his opponent with him as they crashed to the sand, Stig on top, the force of the fall driving the breath from the bigger man's lungs with an explosive gasp.

The man's grip released as he struggled for air, and Stig swiftly rolled clear and leapt to his feet, crouching, hands held out ahead of him, arms bent in a classic wrestler's pose.

For a second, he considered hurling himself onto the other man to pin him. But he could see it wasn't quite time for that yet. There was one fall in these bouts and he knew he had to pick his time exactly for the ploy to be successful. If he went too early, he risked the heavier man throwing him off and pinning Stig in his turn. He had to be properly incapacitated before Stig could risk coming to close quarters on the ground.

Slowly, the other man came to his feet, eyeing Stig warily. So far, this bout hadn't gone anywhere like the way he had planned it. The younger, slimmer man was virtually unscathed. He had countered his most effective move easily, then sent him crashing to the sand in a rib-bruising fall.

For a few seconds, they faced each other. Then, as if by some prearranged signal, they hurled themselves at each other. Stig took a firm grip of the man's shirt around the shoulders and shoved mightily against him.

Instinctively, his opponent returned the shove, and in that instant, Stig gave way before him, stepping back with his left foot and dragging the other man after him. In the same movement, he brought his right foot up into the man's stomach and rolled backward. His opponent followed him, still propelled by the momentum of his return shove against Stig. Stig, his back curved, fell smoothly to the sand, his hands gripping the other man's shirt and his right foot buried in his stomach, knee bent.

As he rolled backward, Stig straightened his right knee in a violent movement, bringing his left leg up to assist the right in thrusting his opponent high into the air above him. At the same time, he maintained his grip on the shirt, so that as Stig's legs propelled his opponent through an arc overhead, his hands kept his upper body from following. At the last moment, Stig released his grip, and the other man flipped in the air, soared several meters and crashed heavily onto his back. Again, there was that explosive *whump* of expelled air, as the recently regained breath was driven out once more.

Stig rolled onto his hands and knees and sprang to his feet like a cat. This time, he realized that the other man was totally winded, after suffering two heavy impacts in quick succession. His opponent gagged and gasped as he struggled to fill his lungs with air, but before he could manage an inward breath, Stig pounced on him, lying across his upper body and pinning him to the ground.

The bout's referee, who had been watching with keen interest, fell to his hands and knees to check the man's shoulders, saw they were flat to the sand and slammed his hand down rapidly twice.

"One! Two! Pinned!" he yelled.

Stig drew back, coming to his knees, then his feet, and leaned down to offer his opponent a hand.

"Bad luck, Oren," he said as the other man came to his feet, still breathing heavily.

Oren shook his head ruefully. "Bad luck nothing," he said. "You were too quick for me. Too quick and too smart."

Stig shrugged. "Not sure about smart."

Oren wiped the sand from his face with the back of his hand. "Well, you beat me fair and square," he said, not sounding overly pleased with the fact. "That puts you in the lead, doesn't it?"

They were competing in the Maktig competition, the annual contest to crown the Maktig, or the Mighty One, in a series of physical contests. There were two events to go—a foot race over five kilometers, which Stig was favored to win, and a mock combat, where he was ranked second or first, depending on which wager-master you were laying a bet with. The fact was, Stig hadn't been expected to win the final leg of the wrestling event. Oren was bigger, heavier and stronger than he was. The unexpected win put Stig in an almost unassailable position. If he won the foot race, as everyone expected, the result of the mock combat would be immaterial. He was almost certain to come in second or third in that event and that would be enough for him to maintain his lead.

"I think it does," Stig agreed.

Oren nodded several times. "Well, good luck. At least then I can say I was beaten by the winner. That's something."

He raised a hand in farewell and turned away, limping slightly as the bruised and strained muscles in his back made themselves felt.

Stig felt a hand on his shoulder and turned to see the smiling face of his best friend and brotherband leader, Hal.

"Well done," Hal told him.

Stig grinned. He knew how important it had been that he should win the wrestling, against all expectations.

"Oh, it was nothing," he said lightly, then, seeing Thorn's bearded face over Hal's shoulder, he let the grin fade.

"Thanks for the tip about the rigid right elbow, Thorn," he said. "That caught him by surprise."

Thorn shrugged. "It shouldn't have. He's been using that bear hug throughout the tournament. He should have guessed someone would come up with a counter to it."

"Well, nobody else did. So thanks again."

Thorn nodded in acknowledgment. "That throw was neatly executed," he said. "Been practicing that, have you?"

Hal answered before his friend could, rubbing the center of his back with his right hand. "He certainly has," he said in heartfelt tones. "He's been hurling me all over the field behind Mam's place. I haven't got a square centimeter that isn't bruised."

Thorn made a little moue of surprise. "Is that so?" he said. "I never saw you."

Stig picked up his jacket and draped it around his shoulders. Now that the contest was over and the shadows were lengthening, there was a chill in the air.

"We practiced at night," he said. "Thought it might not be a good idea to let people see it in advance."

Thorn rubbed the side of his nose and regarded the young warrior with new respect.

"That's smart. It seems you're learning that the Maktig isn't just the strongest and fastest. There are brains involved as well."

Stig looked bashful at the words. "Well, it was Hal's idea. Not mine."

Thorn grinned. "That figures," he said. Then he clapped Stig

on the shoulder. "Being Maktig also means having smart friends."
The three of them laughed as they began to walk toward the fence
enclosing the wrestling ground.

"Well," said Hal, "I'd better get down to the beach to tell the
crew the good news."

"They didn't want to watch?" Stig said, smiling. "They thought
I'd lose, didn't they?" Now that he'd won, he could afford to
smile.

Hal hesitated awkwardly. "It's not that. They had work to do.
Heron needs repainting where that fishing boat hit us last week, so
I thought they might as well repaint the entire hull."

"And aside from that, they didn't think I'd win, did they?" Stig
persisted.

Hal allowed himself a small grin. "No. They didn't. But they'll
be glad to hear they were wrong."

"Will you come by my house later?" Stig asked. "We should
celebrate."

Hal gave a disappointed shrug. "We'll celebrate tomorrow. I
have to appear before the Navigators Guild this evening. They want
to discuss our last voyage."

Stig's cheerful look faded. "Should I come along? After all, I'm
your first mate." But Hal was already shaking his head.

"Best if you keep clear of it," he said. "If things turn nasty, I
don't want you involved."

"Nasty? Why should things turn nasty?" Stig asked.

Hal made an indefinite gesture with his hands. "There are
some old-fashioned thinkers in the guild. They think I should have
kept better notes on the voyage. Or any notes at all, come to that,"

he added. He grinned as he said it, but Stig noticed that the grin didn't reach his eyes.

"Don't concern yourself about it, Stig," Thorn interjected. "I'm going with him, and if necessary I'll straighten out some of those fuddy-duddies." He brandished the heavy, polished wooden hook on the end of his right arm. "I'll crack a few skulls if I have to."

Hal put a hand on Thorn's forearm, restraining the threatening hook. "I'm sure it won't be necessary."

Thorn grunted. "More's the pity," he replied.

eron was beached on the sand beside the main harbor. The crew had run her up the beach on rollers at high tide, then left her clear of the water as the tide receded. She was propped on either side with timbers to keep her on a level keel.

The previous week, she had been moored alongside the mole in her usual privileged position, astern of Oberjarl Erak's *Wolfwind*, when a fishing trawler in the harbor had dragged her anchor and drifted. The prow of the trawler smashed into *Heron*'s starboard side at an angle, pushing in and splintering two of the top planks along a section about three meters long.

Arndt, the trawlerman, was appalled at the damage his craft had caused to the smart little ship and had apologized profusely. Hal, after his initial anger, dismissed the matter and accepted the apologies. These things happened, he knew, when the weather was bad. Anchors could not be expected to be one hundred percent effective. They could drag, ships could come adrift and collide with others.

The damage was superficial, and the shattered planks were well above the waterline.

Arndt offered to pay for repairs to the smaller ship. "Take her into Anders's shipyard," he had said. "I'll pay all the bills."

But Hal had shaken his head. "I'll repair her myself," he said. "You can pay for the materials."

He was an accomplished shipwright. In fact, he had virtually built the *Heron* by himself, converting her from a half-sized wolf-ship that had been in the process of being built for a retired raider who had unexpectedly died of a heart attack. Much as Hal respected Anders's workmanship, he wouldn't trust his precious ship to anyone else. Accordingly, he had cut out the damaged section of the hull and assembled two new planks in place of the smashed ones. The joinery where new met old was so fine that an observer had to peer closely to see where the timbers met. The only giveaway was the fresh, unpainted timber among the seasoned, painted planks that formed the hull. Once the repair was smoothed and painted and calked, it would be virtually invisible. He also used the opportunity to repaint the entire hull, a project that had been on his mind for some weeks. *Heron* had done a lot of hard traveling in the past year, and the wind and salt and sun had peeled away sections of the blue paint that covered her hull. He decided to replace the light blue color with a dark sea green.

"It'll be more suitable if we're going somewhere we don't want to be too obvious," he told Stig, and his first mate nodded agreement. There had been several occasions like that in the years they voyaged together.

With Stig occupied in preparations for the Maktig contest, and Hal having agreed to help him train and prepare, the young skirl had summoned the rest of the crew and delegated the job of painting to them. Ingvar, Edvin, Jesper and Stefan all turned to and began repainting the ship, beaching her so they could scrape the barnacles and marine growth from her hull below the waterline.

Lydia lent a hand as well, taking on the task of retouching the finer-detailed parts of the ship—the oarlocks and tiller and the decorative scrollwork on the bow and sternpost. These she painted with gold leaf, an extravagance that Hal secretly derided. But he knew she meant to help, so he said nothing about the expense.

"After all," she had told him, "Arndt is paying, so we might as well let him spend his money on us."

Hal had to admit that when she had finished, the result was very pleasing to the eye. And he discovered that she had paid for the gold leaf herself. It was a gesture she wanted to make—to him and the rest of the brotherband—and the green color was a wise choice, he thought. It looked good, and seeing it now, he realized how dowdy *Heron* had become. But as well as looking good, the color had a more important function. He narrowed his eyes as he looked at his ship, trying to see her as she would appear on a dark, moonless night. She would be all but invisible, he thought, with the color merging into the gray-green of the sea itself.

Some might have thought that an all-black color scheme would be more effective. But Hal, aside from the fact that he refused to sail a black ship, knew that an all-black hull would appear as a solid mass and be more visible against the lighter tones of the sea.

Jesper glanced up from his work as Hal and Thorn approached. Wiping the excess paint from his brush, he rose from his stooped position under the hull and called a greeting.

"Hal! Thorn! How did Stig get on?"

As he called out, the others stopped their painting as well and turned to watch the new arrivals coming down the sand toward them. In answer to the question, Hal joined his hands together and flourished them above his shoulder in a winner's gesture. The crew were silent for a few seconds, then began to cheer.

"He won?" Edvin said, an incredulous note in his voice. "He beat that overgrown lump Oren?"

"Beat him solidly," Hal said with a broad smile as they came within comfortable speaking distance.

"How did he manage it?" Ingvar asked, and the crew gathered round their skirl and their battle master to get the full details of the bout. When Hal mentioned Stig's counter to the bear hug, with his right arm held rigidly under Oren's chin, Stefan gave a snort of admiration.

"Who taught him that trick?" he asked. They had all seen Oren over the past few weeks of competition, and his bear hug had been shown to be an almost unbeatable tactic.

"Who do you think?" Hal replied, grinning, as he gestured with his thumb at the shaggy-haired old sea wolf beside him. There was a chorus of praise for Thorn from the others. None of them, in retrospect, was surprised. Thorn had been Maktig three years in a row when he was younger—a feat unequaled by anyone before or since.

"What about Ulf and Wulf?" Jesper asked, with a grin. At the mention of the twins, smiles broke out across the faces of the crew.

"I haven't heard yet," Hal replied. "I imagine today's result will be the same as they've been so far."

Contestants for the title of Maktig were nominated by their skirls or brotherband leaders. The nominations were based on their proven ability in combat. Each nomination was assessed by a panel of judges, and if the nominee was found to have sufficient potential to win the title, he was approved as a contestant.

But there was another path to the title of Maktig. Anyone could nominate as a qualifier, and compete in a separate set of events with others of the same ilk. The qualifiers took part in the same events as those in the main competition: long-distance running, short-distance sprinting, mock combat with sword or ax, spear throwing, wrestling, and ax throwing. At the end of the qualifying competition, the winner—if the judges considered he had shown exceptional ability—was allowed to challenge the winner of the main event in those same disciplines. It wasn't often that a qualifier was permitted to challenge. And it was even rarer that he managed to win the overall contest, but it had happened.

Ulf and Wulf had nominated themselves in this part of the contest—or at least, Ulf had nominated himself first, whereupon Wulf had immediately followed suit.

"If he's going to try out, then I will," Wulf had said. "After all, everyone knows we're equal in all things—except that I'm a bit more equal than he is."

And therein lay a problem for the judges and organizers. The twins were equally matched in all physical aspects. Which meant that when they competed against each other, the result was always a dead heat.

Even in contests such as mock combat, the twins usually fought each other to an exhausted standstill. They had that uncanny knack, often shared by identical twins, of knowing what the other was thinking and planning. So when they fought against each other, each one always knew what his sibling was about to do, and was ready with an effective counter. When they competed against the other qualifiers, they were far more skillful and had eliminated all of the others in rapid succession. But to the chagrin of the judges who assessed their contests, neither could manage an ascendancy over his twin.

They had already fought two mock combats with blunted swords and wooden shields, and each had come to an inconclusive and exhausted end, after hours of swinging, hacking, blocking and ducking. They were currently engaged in a third, and hopefully decisive, combat. If no winner emerged, the contest would be rescheduled in two days' time, and the crew all planned to watch. They were fascinated by the strange bond between the twins. Ulf and Wulf would spend all day arguing and disputing with each other. They would argue that black was white and day was night. But if anyone else sought to argue with either of them, he would find himself confronting both.

Now the other Herons wanted to see if there would be a conclusive end to their combat. Most of them doubted it—although Jesper, as was his wont, had begun accepting wagers.

• • • • •

"Time!" called the senior judge, and the two brothers stepped back a pace. Their chests heaved with the effort of swinging and blocking, advancing and retreating, thrusting and feinting. The long wooden swords seemed to weigh twice as much as when they had commenced, forty minutes previously. The shields hung on their arms like blocks of stone.

They glared at each other as the three judges conferred.

"I make it eight points for Wulf," said one judge.

Per, the senior judge, interrupted. "Which one is he?" The twins were, after all, identical.

Woten, the judge who had spoken, gestured to the red scarf tied around Wulf's waist. "Red," he said briefly.

Per frowned. "Are you sure?"

His colleague shrugged. "Doesn't really matter what his name is, so long as Luda"—he jerked a thumb at his fellow judge—"has been scoring for the blue fighter." As Luda nodded to confirm that they hadn't been scoring for the same fighter, he continued. "Two arm strikes. Three body thrusts. Three leg strikes."

Wulf grinned triumphantly at his brother.

Per looked at the second judge, who was frowning unhappily.

"Um . . . I make it the same for Ulf—the blue fighter," Luda said.

Wulf's grin faded and he scowled at his brother instead. Ulf shrugged disarmingly. He had seen how his brother had assumed that he had won, so another draw was almost as good as a victory for Ulf.

The senior judge uttered a low groan. This was the way things had been going for two weeks, and they were no closer to finding a winner.

"We can schedule another bout," said the second judge. "Maybe we'll get a winner then."

But the senior judge scowled at him, then at the two contestants. "Why should it turn out any different? They've fought three times already with no result."

Woten, the first judge, nodded wearily. "We might as well let them settle it with berg-blad-trasa," he said.

For a few moments, nobody spoke, then Per replied thoughtfully, "Why not?"

Woten hastily made a negative gesture. "I was joking!" he protested.

But the second judge held up a hand to silence him. "It's actually not such a bad idea," he said. "Let's face it, either one is as good as the other. If we keep them competing, we may never get a result. We'll let them play a round of berg-blad-trasa. At least that way, we'll get a challenger. And since they're equally matched, it won't really matter which one it is."

The three judges all looked at one another. Per looked worried.

"Can we really settle a Maktig event with a children's game?" he asked doubtfully.

"Why not?" Luda muttered. "At least it will save us more hours of watching these two draw every contest."

"Besides, berg-blad-trasa is a traditional contest among Skandians," said Woten. "It has been part of our culture for hundreds of years."

Even he didn't sound as if he completely believed it himself. But slowly, all three men nodded. Then the senior judge beckoned Ulf and Wulf to come closer. The twins set down their practice swords and shields and moved to stand before the three judges.

"Are you familiar with berg-blad-trasa?" Per asked.

The twins exchanged a look, then Ulf answered.

"You mean rock-blade-cloth?" he said, and the judge nodded. That was the common-tongue name for the old game. Ulf smiled comfortably. "I know it. I've never been beaten at it."

The senior judge smiled contentedly. It seemed that they had found a way to decide the winner. At the same time, he thought it would be better if they didn't make it too public.

"Neither have I," Wulf said hurriedly, which should have warned the judges. But they were so intent on breaking this stalemate that they didn't consider the ramifications of the two answers.

"Very well, we'll reconvene at the obstacle course tomorrow afternoon at the fourth hour." The obstacle course, which was used to train brotherband contestants, was generally unoccupied at this time of year as it didn't feature in the Maktig contest. It would be a suitably discreet venue for the rather unusual competition the judges had decided upon. As the two contestants turned away, he stopped them. "And don't say anything about this to anyone. Clear?"

"Clear," said Wulf.

"As crystal," said Ulf.

The executive committee of the Navigators Guild was meeting in Oberjarl Erak's great hall, in a small annex to the side of the main hall itself.

They were all older men than Hal, who had been admitted to the guild only two years previously and was the youngest member. Erak, as Oberjarl and as a distinguished navigator in his own right, was present to oversee the meeting.

The six members of the committee were seated around a rectangular pine table, three on either side, with Erak at the head. There was an empty chair at the foot of the table for Hal. The members looked up as Thorn swung the door open—none too gently—and ushered Hal inside. One committeeman, Gerdt Smolensson, frowned at the sight of the shaggy-haired, one-armed warrior, who had taken a position standing behind Hal's chair.

"You're not a member of the guild, Thorn. What are you doing here?"

Thorn regarded the speaker for several seconds. He had expected that, if there were to be trouble, it would come from this man. Gerdt was notoriously arrogant and somewhat overconscious of his position on the guild committee.

"I'm here to observe on Hal's behalf and to make sure my friend is treated fairly and with the respect due to a member of the guild," he said.

"You have no authority here. You have no right to be here at all," Gerdt protested in a spiteful tone.

Thorn locked gazes with him. "As a former Maktig, three times over, I claim the right," he said in an even tone. Then he added: "I claim it three times over if necessary."

And there he had them. The position of Maktig carried great authority and prestige among the Skandians. A Maktig was entitled to speak on behalf of any citizen under questioning in Skandia's courts, and his opinion invariably carried great weight.

Gerdt, however, continued to bluster. He had forgotten Thorn's achievement. Most people had. In more recent years, after losing his right hand, Thorn had become a ragged, drunken wreck—until his association with the Heron brotherband, and Hal's mother, Karina, caused him to change his ways.

"This isn't a court of law," Gerdt said. "You have no special authority here. This is a closed meeting of the Navigators Guild committee."

"Closed?" Thorn said, raising one eyebrow. "Is there something secret and underhand going on here? Why do you need a closed meeting?"

"Thorn . . . ," Hal began. He was worried that his friend's belligerent tone might work against him.

But Thorn held up his left hand to stop the protest. "No, Hal. I'd be interested to hear Gerdt's thinking on this. What does he have in mind that needs to be kept so secret? Why can't a former Maktig—a *three-time* former Maktig—be present to observe and advise? Unless these men are planning something underhand?"

His gaze went round the people seated at the table. They avoided it, lowering their eyes. All except Erak, who allowed a faint smile to touch his craggy features and gave Thorn a small nod of approval.

Before Gerdt could reply, the Oberjarl spoke, in tones that invited no argument. "A Maktig's opinion is valued and respected by our law courts, and any legal case is a far more serious matter than a mere committee meeting. So I see no reason why this committee shouldn't give Thorn the same courtesy."

"But . . . ," Gerdt began, his face reddening. It was a brave or foolish man who tried to continue a protest when the Oberjarl had made such a definitive pronouncement. Erak's massive hand slammed down on the tabletop, the impact setting the solid table shaking and the noise echoing through the room.

"Thorn stays!" Erak roared. As Gerdt and the others actually recoiled in their chairs, he continued in a voice that was calmer but no less adamant: "Now get on with it."

Several seconds of confused silence followed, as the committeemen rearranged themselves in their seats and hurriedly consulted their notes. Finally, Paavo Nilsson cleared his throat.

"Perhaps I should start the proceedings?" he asked in a more conciliatory tone. He glanced sidelong at Gerdt, who had only just noticed that Erak's huge battleax was leaning against the wall within easy reach.

Gerdt nodded and his companion proceeded.

"Hal Mikkelson, when you became a member, you agreed to abide by the guild's rules and laws, is that right?"

"It is."

"And one of those laws is that all members should share new navigational information with one another?"

Hal went to reply in the affirmative once more, but Thorn dropped his wooden hook onto his forearm to stop him. In a pleasant, conversational tone, he said, "That's actually not a rule or a law. It's a custom."

"It's how we add to our knowledge of the world and to the overall body of navigational lore," Gerdt spat, his confidence returning as Erak had fallen silent.

Thorn looked at him as one might consider an unpleasant bug. "I repeat. It's not a law of the guild. It's a custom or a convention."

"It's an unwritten law!"

Thorn leaned in over the table, resting his weight on the polished wooden hook at the end of his right arm.

"If it's unwritten, it's not a law!" he replied calmly. "Otherwise I'll invoke an unwritten law that allows me to swat you with my hook when you behave like a boor and a bully."

"Now, now, Thorn," Erak said in a placating voice. "There's no need to threaten violence." He waited while Thorn stepped back a pace to resume his position behind Hal. "Nonetheless, Gerdt, he is right. There's no law that says Hal must share his navigational discoveries with the guild."

"But it is customary," protested Keldt Horgasson. The other three members of the committee shrugged, or indicated that they didn't see Hal's omission as a serious one.

Thorn was beginning to size up the meeting now. Gerdt and Keldt were both pompous men, full of their own importance. Their attempt to pillory Hal came more from a desire to humiliate him than a genuine desire for navigational information. Hal was a rising star among the Skandians, one of the leaders of the younger set of skirls and navigators. And Hal was known to be favored by Erak. He and his ship were often chosen by the Oberjarl for special assignments. Not just because Erak liked the Herons and admired their young skirl, but because he recognized that Hal had a special ability as a ship's skirl and navigator. If there was a difficult job to be done, Erak knew he could rely on Hal and his crew to do it.

This rankled men like Gerdt, who felt threatened by Hal's rising fame. It was some years since Gerdt had been chosen by the Oberjarl for any special mission. He resumed his attack now, with a sneering edge in his voice.

"As Keldt says, it *is* customary for a navigator to share new information. But perhaps we can't expect a foreigner to be aware of the importance of Skandian customs."

Hal shoved his chair back from the table and came to his feet. His face was flushed with anger.

"A foreigner?" he demanded. "You call me a foreigner." He felt the old, sickening rage—a sensation he had known as a boy growing up in Hallasholm—the pain and rejection that came with being regarded as an outsider. He hadn't encountered this attitude for years now, but it was obviously still there, just below the surface with some people.

Knowing how it would infuriate the young man if he didn't answer directly, Gerdt spoke to the table at large. "He's a foreigner. He can't help it. His mother was an Araluen slave, after all, so I suppose we can't blame him for th—"

He got no further. Thorn had elbowed Hal aside and leaned across the table. He twisted his wooden hook, which fortunately was blunt ended, into Gerdt's shirt and hauled him bodily out of his seat.

"Shut your mouth," Thorn said in an icy voice. "Don't you dare speak of Karina that way. Yes, she was an Araluen slave, but she was freed by my best friend, Mikkel Fastblade, one of our finest warriors. She has become a popular and valuable member of our community and is completely loyal to Skandia. She's always ready to lend a hand to anyone in need.

"And perhaps you've forgotten how, during the Temujai invasion, she organized the Araluen women among the slaves to make arrows for the archers who stopped the invaders? And how she took it upon herself to deliver supplies of arrows to the fighters, and exposed herself to the Temujai arrows?"

He suddenly untwisted his hook from Gerdt's shirtfront and shoved him violently back into his chair. The chair skidded half a meter on the pine boards of the floor. Gerdt opened his mouth to reply but, seeing the fire in Thorn's eyes, wisely shut it again.

"I'll also tell you this. On a personal level, I respect and care for Karina. And if you persist in slandering her like this and claim that she has no regard for our traditions or values, I will demand satisfaction—in the most traditional way possible."

Gerdt felt all eyes at the table on him, and his face turned scarlet with embarrassment. There was no way he would respond to Thorn's threat of challenging him to combat. Even with one hand, Thorn was still one of the deadliest warriors in Hallasholm—and they all knew it.

"I meant no disrespect to the lady," he finally managed to mumble.

Thorn's mouth curled in a sneer. "In a pig's ear you didn't," he declared.

One of the other Guild members, Seb Peckson, sought to bring the conversation back to less dangerous ground.

"The fact remains," he said tentatively, "Hal here has not shared knowledge of his recent voyage with the guild—as we might reasonably expect him to do."

Hal decided it was time he spoke for himself. "That's because there is no knowledge to share," he said. "We were caught in a massive storm off the north coast of Hibernia and driven to the southwest for weeks on end. When we finally sighted land, I had no way of knowing where we were. We were fighting for our lives in the storm and I didn't have time, or the opportunity, to take bearings or sightings. We saw no reference points—such as islands or reefs or shallows. I literally have no idea where we ended up."

"But you sailed back," said Holger Brayson. "Surely you kept a record of your course then?"

Hal shrugged. "We sailed back by using the prevailing winds, which were out of the southwest, keeping them on our starboard side and sailing on a reach. But I don't know where we started from, or how much leeway we made in the weeks before we reached Hibernia again. So our return heading has little value by itself."

There was a moment of silence as the committee digested this information. What Hal was saying made sense. But Paavo was reluctant to let the matter drop.

"Still, it's a shame you didn't bother to keep proper records," he said. "You made an important discovery—one that could benefit all of Skandia. You should have at least tried to ascertain where you ended up."

"Why?" Hal asked. "What value would there be to Skandia? The country had no deposits of precious metals that we saw. No gold or silver mines. It was simple farm country."

Paavo shrugged. "Land has its own value. Others could have sailed there and cultivated it. They could have grown crops there."

"There are already people growing crops there," Hal pointed out. "They might not want a bunch of Skandians wading ashore and taking their land from them. What right do we have to do that?"

In truth, Hal had not made any effort to chart the location of the land belonging to the Mawagansett. He had foreseen that people like Gerdt might one day choose to try to take the land. His friends among the Mawagansett tribe had agreed with him.

"What right did we ever have to go raiding in Gallica or Iberion?" snapped Gerdt.

Hal turned to face him. "Exactly. We had no right to do those things. Which is why we don't do them anymore."

"And that's the pity of it!" Gerdt spat, before he could think about what he was saying in front of the Oberjarl, who had banned raiding some years ago.

"You're getting onto dangerous ground there, Gerdt," Erak growled. "I suggest you drop the subject." He let his gaze scan the others, finishing on Paavo.

"Paavo," he said, "it seems to me that Hal doesn't have any knowledge that he needs to share with the guild. His voyage to . . . whatever he calls that country . . . was a complete accident. Nor is there any real value to us in knowing how to retrace his steps."

"Yes, but really, Oberjarl—"

Erak raised his voice and cut Paavo off. "If you disagree with my assessment of the matter, here's what you can do. Take your wolfship and go cruising off the north coast of Hibernia. Then wait for the mother of all storms to come out of the northeast and blow you thousands of leagues across the Endless Ocean. With any luck, you'll fetch up at the place Hal discovered. Alternatively, you might be blown clear off the edge of the world."

He paused and cast a baleful eye on Gerdt. "And if you choose to do that, may I suggest you take Gerdt with you. And good riddance."

Gerdt elected not to reply. Erak gave him a few moments, then rapped his knuckles on the table.

"As for now, this matter is closed. The meeting is adjourned."

W e'll need to tread carefully for the next few weeks," Thorn said as they strolled through the streets of Hallasholm toward Karina's popular eating hall, set on the outskirts of the town. The weather was still warm, even though autumn was nearly upon them, and young children played in the half-light in the streets and fields surrounding them. Their high-pitched shrieks of laughter brought a smile to Hal's face and, once, he had to catch and steady a young boy who came careering round the corner of a house, three of his companions in hot pursuit.

"Watch out there, Gordy," Hal said in a friendly tone.

"Sorry, Hal," the boy said breathlessly, looking up at him, eyes wide with hero worship. Hal was something of an idol to the young people of Hallasholm—which only served to increase Gerdt's animosity toward him. Gordy's comrades rounded the corner, shrieking, then fell silent as they saw the skirl and his legendary friend. There had been a time when little boys would tease Thorn as he shambled around the town in a drunken haze. That time was now long past. His exploits over the past several years, as battle master for the *Heron*, had made him a respected and admired figure—a real homegrown hero. Most of the boys hoped to emulate his example as they grew older.

Thorn was aware of this, and the knowledge warmed his heart. But it wouldn't do to show that to these boys. He scowled at them and brandished his hook.

"Cut out that infernal racket!" he yelled. "And stop racing about like mad things!"

"Yes, Thorn," the boys all chorused. They backed away a pace or two. They were reasonably sure that his anger was a pretense, but not sure enough to ignore it. As Hal and Thorn continued on their way, the boys waited till they had gone a dozen paces, then began to giggle and whisper among themselves.

Hal raised an eyebrow at his friend. "Boys!" he said. "Do they ever change?"

Thorn regarded him seriously. "Spoken with all the authority of a cranky old man. How old are you again? Sixty? Seventy? I suppose you can't remember when you were just like them?"

"Matter of fact, I can't," Hal agreed.

Thorn snorted derisively. "Well, I can. And it wasn't all that long ago."

Hal grinned at him. "Getting back to what we were talking about, what do you think Gerdt is likely to do?"

Thorn ran the fingers of his left hand through his tangled, untidy thatch of hair. That was as close as he usually came to combing it.

"Probably nothing, so long as we keep our noses clean," he said. "But he's not a man who likes to be contradicted. He'll be looking for any excuse to come down on us or—more particularly—on you. We just have to make sure we don't give him one."

Hal pursed his lips. Then his attention was taken by two familiar figures on the far side of the market square.

"There are Ulf and Wulf," he said, quickening his pace. "Let's see how they made out in their mock combat."

Thorn grinned. "I'm betting it was a draw."

Hal let out a piercing whistle, and the twins stopped and turned, looking for the source of the sound. They saw their two shipmates hurrying across the market square toward them and waved a greeting.

"How did the match go?" Thorn asked as they came within easy speaking distance.

"It was a draw," Ulf told them, then added, "although I was winning when they stopped the match."

"How could you be winning if it was a draw?" his brother asked scornfully.

Ulf assumed a haughty expression. "I couldn't expect you to understand the nuances of combat," he said. "But I was definitely winning."

Hal thought it might be best to head off this line of discussion. Ulf and Wulf, once engaged, could argue the most facetious nonsense for hours.

"So have they scheduled another match?" he asked.

Wulf shook his head. "They've come up with another way of deciding the winner." He paused for dramatic effect and then added: "Berg-blad-trasa."

Both Hal and Thorn burst out laughing, which somehow spoiled Wulf's intended dramatic effect.

"Berg-blad-trasa!" Thorn said. "They're going to decide a Maktig event using a children's game?"

Ulf drew himself up and said, with great dignity, "Berg-blad-trasa is an ancient ritual among our people."

"It's part of our culture," Wulf added, with equal dignity.

"It's a children's game," Thorn repeated. "Do the judges seriously expect you to play berg-blad-trasa in order to determine a winning qualifier?"

"Yes, they do. And I think it's a great idea," said Wulf. "After all, I've never lost at berg-blad-trasa."

"Neither have I," Ulf added hurriedly.

Thorn and Hal exchanged an incredulous glance.

"Well, I have to say, I can't wait to see it," said Hal, a grin spreading across his face. "When and where is this momentous event taking place?"

"Tomorrow afternoon at the obstacle course," Ulf said. Then, looking a little guilty, he added, "But we weren't supposed to tell anyone."

"I can understand why," Hal said, his grin becoming even wider.

"You're not planning on coming to watch, are you?" Wulf asked anxiously. Again, Thorn and Hal exchanged an amused look.

"Wouldn't miss it for the world," Thorn said.

"It's just . . . we weren't supposed to tell anyone," Wulf said as both twins remembered the senior judge's injunction for secrecy a few minutes too late.

Hal looked suitably concerned. "Oh, I see," he said. "Well, in that case . . . bad luck!"

He lost the concerned look and the grin reappeared. Ulf and Wulf looked downcast.

"We might get into trouble," said Ulf.

Thorn leaned forward and said in a conspiratorial tone, "Don't worry. If the judges turn nasty, we'll threaten to let the whole town know that they planned to choose a Maktig qualifier with a game of berg-blad-trasa. That should calm them down."

Which the twins had to admit was true. The judges would be a laughingstock if word about this particular contest got out.

"All right," said Wulf. "Just don't tell anyone else." He had a sudden, horrified vision of the entire Heron brotherband turning up to watch. He glanced at his brother and saw from the expression on his face that he was thinking the same thing.

"Not a soul," Hal lied cheerfully. "Not a soul."

The following day was gloomy and overcast, which fitted Wulf and Ulf's mood as they waited by the high beam at the obstacle course. The beam was a solid log set three meters above ground level, spanning a deep pit filled with oozing, sticky mud. At least during the brotherband season, it was filled that way. As the course had not been in use for some months now, the pit of mud had dried out. It was caked and cracked.

Ulf looked into it, remembering the days of their brotherband assessments. He had fallen from this beam several times, as had his brother.

"Glad we're not doing that today," he said.

Wulf considered the idea. "Might be preferable," he said. He glanced around as he heard footsteps approaching. The course was set at the top of a hill overlooking the town. Now three figures were appearing over the crest and he recognized the judges—Per, Luda and Woten.

He sighed with relief. "No sign of Hal and Thorn."

"Maybe they're not coming," Ulf said hopefully.

"Maybe," Wulf repeated, but with a lot less hope.

The judges hurried across the grass toward them. Ulf noticed they were looking round furtively, making sure there was nobody present to observe the proceedings. He realized that Thorn had been right. If any word of this somewhat unusual method of selection got out, the judges would be subjected to merciless ridicule.

As they came closer, Per, the senior judge, looked around one last time to make sure they were alone, and then rubbed his hands briskly together.

"Good. You're on time. Now, let's get this over and done with, shall we? Everyone ready?"

Obviously, Per wanted this done as quickly as possible. But Luda demurred.

"Shouldn't we run through the rules first?"

"Rules?" Per said with some asperity. "What rules? Everyone knows the rules for berg-blad-trasa! You berg, or you blad, or you trasa. That's it."

"But how many rounds? Who keeps score? Do they face away from each other to start and turn when they've chosen their call? Do I score for Wulf or Ulf? And how will I know which is which? I notice they've left their colored scarves behind."

"There's no scoring," Per said angrily. "First to win a round wins the contest. That's it. As for how they stand, they face each other with their hands behind their backs, I count to three, and they show their hands. Luda, you call out the choice for . . ." He was about to nominate one of the twins when he realized that he didn't know which was which. He grabbed Ulf by the shoulder and dragged him to one side, facing his brother. "This one," he continued.

Ulf grinned at him. "I'm Ulf," he said obligingly.

"Congratulations," Per said through clenched teeth. He man-handled Woten, the other judge, into position beside the remaining twin.

"And you call out the choice for this one. I assume you're Wulf?" he added.

Wulf smiled. "If you say so," he said. The twins liked to maintain a little uncertainty about their respective identities.

"I do," said Per. "So here's how it will go. These two face each other, hand behind their backs—"

"Which hand?" asked Woten.

"*IT DOESN'T MATTER!*" Per shouted. Then he made an effort to calm down. "I'll count to three and each contestant will immediately show his choice. You two will call the choices for your respective competitor, clear?"

All four nodded.

"And if either contestant hesitates, or doesn't show his hand until his opponent's choice has been revealed, he's disqualified. All right?" He addressed the last two words to Luda, who shrugged.

"Fine. I said we needed to establish the rules."

"Well, now we have. So if everyone's ready?"

"Ready," said Ulf.

"Ready," said Wulf.

"Ready," said Luda.

"Just a moment," Woten said, and Per heaved a sigh of exasperation. "Are you going to count *one, two, three* or *three, two, one*?"

For a moment, Per was speechless. Truth be told, he hadn't even thought about this. Now he decided. "I'll count *one, two, three*," he said, and Woten nodded sagely.

"Now . . . are we ready?"

"Ready!" said Luda.

"Ready!" said Woten.

"Ready!" called Ulf and Wulf together, facing each other, hands behind their backs and half crouching in anticipation.

Per took a breath to begin the count, when a cheery voice interrupted proceedings.

"Hello there! What's going on here?"

The tension went out of them all like air out of a punctured bladder as they turned in the direction of the shout.

Emerging over the top of the slope were three figures, outlined by the lowering sun. Per squinted against the glare and recognized Thorn, Hal and Stig approaching them. He looked balefully at the twins.

"You had to tell them, didn't you?" he said bitterly.

"We didn't tell them," Ulf began, then he amended the statement. "I mean, we didn't *mean* to tell them—"

"It just sort of slipped out," Wulf said.

"We just sort of said that we might be up here at the obstacle course," Ulf continued weakly.

If looks could kill, Per's glance would have dropped them both dead on the spot. He opened his mouth to speak but then realized the three interlopers were now within hearing. He glared at them instead.

"What are you doing here?" he asked coldly.

Hal grinned disarmingly at him. "We were out taking the air and we saw you all here," he said. It was an obvious lie, as the new arrivals couldn't have seen anyone before they actually came to the top of the hill. That was why Per had chosen the spot in the first place.

"I imagine you're working on a way to decide the tie between Ulf and Wulf?" Thorn said, smiling in his turn.

"That's right." Per's voice was tight and unwelcoming.

"Mind if we stay to watch?" Stig said. "After all, there's a good chance I might be competing with the eventual winner here."

Woten decided Per might need a little help. "It's sort of private," he said.

Stig turned a surprised look on him. "Private? I thought Maktig events were open to all to view."

Woten shrugged awkwardly. "Well, they are . . . but this one isn't."

"Because they're qualifiers," Luda put in.

Hal turned to him, his grin still in place, still wide and ingenuous. "What difference does that make?" he asked.

Luda made an uncertain gesture in the air. "The loser might be embarrassed," was the best he could come up with.

Thorn laughed. "Oh, I'm sure that's not a problem."

Hal looked around the obstacle course. "So, which of the events here did you decide to use as a tiebreaker?" he asked. "The high beam?" He studied the dried cracked-mud pool below it. "Not sure

I'd like to fall off into that. You could break a leg. Or were you thinking the rope swing?"

He pointed to another installation, where a thick rope hung above a wide pond. Contestants would leap for the rope and hope to swing across the water to the far side. Like the high beam, it hadn't been used recently and the pond was decidedly green and malodorous.

He waited for an answer, still smiling.

Finally, Per replied, "No. Neither of those."

"Then it must be the rock climb?" Stig suggested, indicating a short, but steep, sloping section of grass. Contestants had to carry heavy rocks from the bottom to the top in that event. It was a new one that had been added to the brotherband obstacle course. None of the Herons had contested it during their trials.

Again, Per shook his head in the negative.

"What is it, then?" Thorn urged.

Per glared at him. It was all too obvious that these three grinning buffoons knew what the contest was to be. He decided he might as well come clean.

"It's berg-blad-trasa," he said in a subdued tone.

Thorn made a pretense of not hearing correctly, cupping his hook behind his ear as if he couldn't quite hear him. "Say what?"

Per took a deep breath. "Berg-blad-trasa," he said firmly. And for one horrible moment, he thought that maybe they hadn't known, and that he'd given it away. Then he saw them smothering their smiles.

"Berg-blad-trasa?" Thorn said. "You're using a children's game to decide a Maktig challenger?"

"Yes. We are," Per replied obstinately, waiting for the inevitable argument. But instead, Thorn nodded his head several times and sat on a nearby log.

"That works for me," he said. "Go on with it."

"You're planning to stay and watch, are you?" Per asked.

Thorn nodded as Hal and Stig took seats beside him.

"Wouldn't miss it for the world." He winked at Ulf and Wulf, who looked as if they wished they were somewhere else—anywhere else.

Per realized he wasn't going to get rid of these three observers. He decided he might as well make the best out of a bad situation. He turned back to the other judges and the twins and said in a tight voice, "Right. You all know the rules—"

"What are they?" Stig asked.

Hal looked at him with mock annoyance. "Oh, come on, Stig! Everyone knows the rules of berg-blad-trasa. You berg, you blad or you trasa."

"But there might be special rules for a Maktig contest," Stig said. "If so, what are they?"

"You don't need to know them!" Per shouted at him. "We know them. Ulf and Wulf know them. That's all who need to know them. Now may we continue?"

Stig threw his hands in the air in apology. "Please! Don't let us delay you any further."

"Thank you," Per said in a voice heavy with sarcasm. Then to the others, he repeated, "You all know the rules, stand ready . . ."

Ulf and Wulf resumed their crouching positions, each with his right hand behind his back. Woten and Luda frowned in concentration. Per drew in his breath to signal the start of the bout.

"This is really very exciting," Hal said to his two companions.

Per turned on him. "Will you SHUT UP!" he yelled.

Hal half recoiled from his seat on the log. "Please. Ignore me. Go ahead with your little game."

Per gritted his teeth and decided not to rise to that bait. He turned back to the contestants. "Ready?" he called. The four others nodded. Then, because all the interruptions had confused him, he counted: "Three . . . two . . . one!"

Nobody moved. Ulf, Wulf, Woten and Luda stood frozen in place. Luda finally turned to Per.

"You said you were doing *one, two, three*," he said apologetically.

Per cursed under his breath. He could hear the three bystanders sniggering behind him. He whipped around and glared at them, and they hastily rearranged their features. The fact that they were trying so hard *not* to smile was even worse somehow than if they had guffawed like loons. He turned back to the contestants, who were still poised, tension obvious in every line of their bodies.

"Very well," he said heavily. "Here we go: one . . . two . . . three!"

Ulf and Wulf flashed their right hands out from behind their backs, their four fingers extended to indicate a sheet of cloth.

"Trasa!" yelled Woten and Luda simultaneously.

"That was sort of predictable really," Stig observed.

"Shut up," Per growled, without looking at him. He had hoped above all hopes that they would settle this on the first call. Now he saw that it would go to two rounds.

"Ready?" he asked.

Ulf and Wulf, staring at each other intently, nodded.

The judges replied in a chorus. "Ready!"

"Then here we go. One, two, three!" This time, the twins presented their fists clenched, to resemble a rock.

"Berg!" chorused Woten and Luda together.

Per looked at the sun, low in the west. He estimated there was only an hour of daylight left to get this done. He hoped it would be enough. But he was beginning to fear that it might not be.

"Again," he rasped. "One, two, three!"

"Berg!" the two judges called simultaneously, as both contestants chose the rock symbol once more. The twins scowled at each other.

"Stop copying me," Ulf said.

Wulf bridled at the accusation. "I'm not copying you. You're copying me!"

"Be quiet!" Per snapped. "We'll go again. One, two, three!"

Both hands flashed out. Both judges shouted simultaneously. "Blad!"

This time, Ulf and Wulf held their index and second fingers out in a V, to represent the shape of a pair of shears.

"Time out," said Per. He beckoned Wulf closer. "I thought you said you had never lost at this game?"

Wulf smiled at him. "No. My brother said that. I just agreed with him."

"Then what are you doing, messing around like this?"

"Well, neither of us has ever lost. But when we play each other, we don't win. We tend to draw."

"Every time?" Per asked, a terrible doubt forming in his mind.

Wulf considered, then nodded cheerfully. "Pretty much," he said.

Per groaned softly. He should have realized, he thought. He waved Wulf back to his position.

"We'll give it another half hour," he said. "If you're still drawn, we'll give it away for the day."

So they continued. By the end of the half hour, all three judges' voices were hoarse from shouting, and the twins steadfastly continued to draw every match. Finally, Per called a halt.

"That's enough!" he said. "We'll have to find another way to choose between you."

"Like what?" Ulf asked.

Per glared at him. "We'll probably draw straws," he said.

The twins nodded.

"That sounds fair," said Wulf.

"Not very exciting, but fair," Ulf agreed.

"We'll leave it for two days in case I get a better idea," Per said. "I'll let you know the time and the place."

The three onlookers rose to their feet. They had enjoyed the spectacle enormously. Somehow, it was edifying to watch someone else being annoyed by Ulf and Wulf's nonsense. The three judges stalked off without a word, trying to reestablish their dignity.

"Thorn and Hal are having dinner at my house," Stig said. "Would you two care to join us?"

"His mam is making spiced pork pie," Hal said. It was the one dish where Stig's mother's cooking excelled even that of his own mother, and his mouth watered at the thought of it.

Wulf shook his head reluctantly. "Better not," he said. "We should get some rest before the next contest."

"You're drawing straws," Stig pointed out, but Wulf simply nodded.

"I know. But Per might hold on to them really tightly."

Hannah Olafson's pork pie was every bit as delicious as Hal had expected. She smiled fondly at the three Herons gathered around her table, their chairs thrust back and their legs stretched out before them. Hannah enjoyed cooking for guests, but since she had been deserted by Stig's father years before, the opportunities to do so were infrequent.

She was always delighted when her guests included any of the Heron brotherband—but particularly Hal and Thorn. They had befriended her son when he was a spiky, belligerent teenager, always ready to take offense at the slightest hint of criticism, even when none was intended. His quick temper, coupled with his powerful build and athletic prowess, had caused the local inhabitants to steer clear of him. With Stig, you could never tell when an innocent jest might rub him the wrong way. Once that happened, things tended to get nasty very quickly.

Hal had been the first to befriend him and give the lonely boy the sort of company and regard that he craved. Hal was ostracized as a boy too, and he knew the bitterness of growing up fatherless and alone.

Thorn had entered Stig's life a few years later, when the Heron brotherband formed and he took on the position of mentor to the boys. Once Thorn had sworn off strong alcohol and become part of *Heron*'s crew, serving as the battle master, Stig saw a man he could admire and hope to emulate. Thorn returned the affection to the two boys. They were willing to give him a second chance in life, whereas many of his contemporaries hadn't been.

"More pie, Thorn?" Hannah said now. She indicated the remains of the magnificent pie that she had served up. "I could cut you another sliver?"

Thorn considered the offer. "Just a small piece, then," he said. As Hannah measured a slice with her carving knife poised over the golden flaky pastry on top of the pie, he added hastily, "Not that small."

Hannah adjusted the angle of her knife and looked at him inquisitively. He pursed his lips, and she moved the knife to form an even wider angle. He nodded.

"That's perfect. As I said, just a small slice."

She cut the slice and deftly balanced it on the flat of the knife blade, moving it to his plate, where a few small crumbs testified to the fate of his former helping. Thorn picked up a two-pronged fork carved out of walrus bone and attacked the slab of crusty pastry and fragrant pork mince. He stuffed a large forkful into his mouth and chewed, smiling rapturously.

"'A's very goo','" he said, which Hannah interpreted to mean, "That's very good."

Hal grinned. He was tempted to have another slice himself. But his belt was uncomfortably tight. He'd feasted on a large piece of pie, along with the creamy mashed potatoes that Hannah had served, and the perfectly cooked green beans, slathered in butter. Additionally, he'd noticed a dish of mulberries and a jug of thick cream on the kitchen bench, and he wanted to leave room for them. He leaned forward and poured himself another cup of coffee. All the members of the Heron brotherband were partial to the drink, and Hannah made sure she always had plenty on hand.

Hannah, seeing the movement, indicated the pork pie with the tip of the knife. "More for you, Hal?" she asked.

He made a defensive gesture with both hands. "No thank you. I'm saving room for dessert."

"Me too," mumbled Thorn, through a spray of pastry crumbs.

Stig eyed the massive second helping the one-armed warrior was hoeing into. "So I see," he said.

Thorn glanced at him and waved his fork over the rapidly diminishing piece of pie. "Restraint in all things," he said. Thankfully, he managed this statement without an accompanying blizzard of crumbs.

Stig was about to answer when there was a knock at the door. The four people seated round the kitchen table all exchanged glances. Skandians tended to hammer on doors with their clenched fists, but this knock had been light and almost tentative.

"Expecting anyone, Hannah?" Thorn asked.

Stig's mother shook her head, frowning. Thorn laid down his fork and slid his chair back from the table, loosening his saxe in its scabbard.

"I'll get it," Hal said. He was closest to the door. None of them were prepared to let Hannah open the door. Hallasholm was generally a peaceful town, but they were living in dangerous times and it was nearly ten o'clock, too late for social visitors.

Hal reached the door. It was fastened by a simple lift latch, which could be opened from the outside via a leather thong that ran through a hole in the wood. Inside, it was locked by a heavy brass bolt.

"Who's there?" he called.

"A friend," came the reply. It was a male voice, muffled by the thick wood of the door.

Hal turned back to the others. "Of course, anyone could *say* that," he said.

There was a slither of wood on wood as Thorn and Stig pushed their chairs back farther and stood, hands on the hilts of their saxes. Hannah made no move to rise. Hal thought he saw a glimpse of recognition and surprise on her face—as if she knew the voice.

"Step back from the door," he called. He heard a rustle of movement outside on the porch and slid the bolt back with his left hand. His right was occupied with his saxe.

He opened the door halfway, placing one foot against it to prevent it being shoved wide-open, and saw a man silhouetted on the porch. He was tall and broad in build, and Hal could see light glimmering off a cone-shaped helmet with a mail fringe hanging from the sides and rear to protect the wearer's neck. He wore a thick cloak that looked to be fur, thrown back from his shoulders to reveal a glint of metal studs on his waist-length jacket, and Hal saw the hilt of a sword at his left side. The newcomer started to move forward, but Hal held up his left hand, palm out, to stop him.

"Not so fast," he said. "Let's get a better look at you."

There was a small oil lamp hanging beside the door, designed to give light to the entrance at night. At the moment, it was turned low, and the man's face was in shadow under the eaves of the porch. Hal turned the wick up, illuminating the visitor's face more clearly.

It was broad, with prominent cheekbones, a strong nose and deep-set eyes under heavy eyebrows. A red-brown mustache and beard covered the lower half of his face. Hal thought there was something about him that looked vaguely familiar.

"I mean you no harm," the stranger said.

Hal heard a little gasp from Hannah behind him. Then he heard her rise from her chair and step across the room to stand just behind him, peering over his shoulder.

"What are you doing here?" she asked. Her voice was not particularly friendly.

The stranger lowered his gaze, looking rather shamefaced. For the moment, he didn't answer.

"You know this person?" Hal asked her.

Hannah nodded slowly. "Oh, I know him. This is Stig's father, Olaf."

Both Stig and Hal stared at the newcomer. Thorn had moved

from the table for a closer look and he shook his head in wonder as he made out the other man's features.

"So it is," he said slowly. Then, in a harder tone, he repeated Hannah's question. "What are you doing here?"

The stranger hesitated, then gestured toward the inside of the house. "May I come in?" he asked.

Thorn looked at Hannah, who nodded.

"Yes. You'd better," she replied. "Somebody might recognize you if they see you out there."

Olaf stepped forward into the room, and Hal closed it behind him.

"Lock it, Hal," Thorn ordered, and the skirl shot the heavy bolt closed.

Stig had moved from his position by the table to study the new arrival. A torrent of different emotions coursed through him: curiosity, anger, contempt and confusion all chased one another across his features. He felt once again the deep sense of loss he had experienced as a boy when his father deserted him. Part of him felt nothing but hatred for the bulky figure. But another part harbored a faint hope that, somehow, they might rekindle a father-son relationship that he only dimly remembered, and he might learn what it was to have a father to look up to and respect.

"Hello, son," Olaf said, conscious of Stig's penetrating gaze.

Stig opened his mouth to reply, but Hannah cut him off. "I'm not sure that you've earned the right to call him that," she said sharply. Olaf actually flinched under the lash of her tongue.

Hal's eyes darted from Olaf to Stig to Hannah and back again as he watched the tense scene unfold. Unlike the others, he had never seen Olaf before—though he had an instinctive dislike for the man, based on the way Olaf had abandoned Stig as a child, and left him and his mother to face the anger of his shipmates, whose loot he had stolen when he absconded.

Viewed now in the light of the kitchen, Hal thought Olaf was a somewhat exotic figure. He had shrugged off the heavy fur cloak and laid it over a chair back. The belted jerkin underneath it was a dull red color, heavily brocaded, and studded with brass scales to protect the wearer from sword or dagger thrusts. On each breast was a large plate-sized circle of hammered brass, adorned with foreign-looking engraving. The polished helmet, he could see now, was surmounted by a sharp spike some eight centimeters long, and the chain-mail fringe that hung from the rear half of the helmet was also highly polished, catching the light from the two lanterns and the fireplace and sending reflections rippling around the walls of the cozy little room.

Olaf's trousers appeared to be a light linen weave—certainly not suitable for the cold Skandian night. They were baggy, and the bottoms were tucked into red leather boots that came up to the knee.

His sword scabbard was made from the same red leather, chased with silver fittings. The blade was long and seemed to follow a slight curve. The brass-hilted dagger on the other side of his war belt was heavy and broad bladed, sheathed in an unadorned scabbard. That was normal. Warriors usually decorated their sword hilts and scabbards. A sword was a personal item, an expression of individuality. A dagger was a tool, more utilitarian.

Finally, Olaf answered the question that Thorn and Hannah had put to him.

"I'm in trouble," he said. "I need help."

Thorn snorted. "Why am I not surprised to hear that?"

Olaf seemed to think it was better not to reply. He held Hannah's gaze for a few seconds, then switched to look at Stig.

"I need a ship and a crew to sail it," he said.

Instinctively, Stig looked to Hal. If anyone were to provide a ship for his father, it would be the skirl.

"My ship and my crew?" Hal asked.

Olaf nodded. "I take it you're Hal Mikkelson?" When Hal nodded curtly, he continued. "I don't know if you realize it, but you have quite a reputation in my part of the world. You and your ship and your crew."

"Is that right?" Hal asked. His tone was flat, almost uninterested. If Olaf had intended to flatter him, it hadn't worked.

"Yes. Word started to get round after you fought a pirate called Zavac, off Raguza. And then later, you cleared out that nest of assassins in the Amrashin Massif of Arrida. You have a reputation as a skirl and a crew that gets difficult jobs done."

"And where exactly did you hear this? What is your 'part of the world'?"

Olaf hesitated. "I'll get to that in a minute. But word spreads quickly in the Constant Sea. Sailors talk among one another, and as they traveled from port to port, so did your reputation. So, when I found myself in need of a good ship and a good fighting crew, naturally, you sprang to mind—particularly as my son is one of your men."

Hannah snorted derisively at the last few words, but Olaf ignored her. Stig shifted uncomfortably. He was still unsettled by the sudden reappearance of his father. Olaf, for his part, didn't add another significant fact. He had no one else to turn to. He had no friends and no money to hire a ship.

Hal's expression remained neutral. He gestured toward the table.

"Sit down," he said. As Olaf started to pull back a chair, he added, "Take off that ridiculous helmet and your sword first."

Olaf complied. There was a red mark across his forehead where the leather-padded rim of the helmet had rested. He glanced around, saw a row of wooden pegs by the door and hung the helmet on one. Then he unbuckled his sword belt and removed it. Fastening it again, he hung it over the same peg, then sat down.

"All right," said Hal, taking a seat opposite him, "let's hear what you have to say."

I suppose I'd better start at the beginning," Olaf said. He glanced at the platter bearing the remains of the pork pie. "Haven't eaten all day," he said.

"Get used to it," Hannah said coldly. She pointedly gathered up the platter with the pie, and the dishes in front of her other guests. She placed the dirty dishes in a large washtub on the kitchen bench. The pie she covered with a cloth and placed in a cupboard.

Olaf shrugged. He'd expected no better. He gathered his thoughts.

"After I left here years ago—" he began.

Hannah cut in on him. "You mean after you ran away, leaving Stig and me to face the music?"

He took a deep breath and nodded. "If that's the way you want it."

She laughed harshly. "It's not the way I want it. It wasn't the way I wanted it then," she told him. Her face was red with anger, and there was a hint of tears in her eyes as all those years of bitter struggle came back to her. The years of being treated as an outsider because her husband was a thief who had betrayed his own crew and brotherband, the years of taking any menial work she could find to put food on the table for herself and her son, the years of not feeling able to raise her eyes to meet the gaze of her neighbors. The shame of those times was still fresh in her mind. It was only in recent years, when Stig had gained a measure of fame and respect in his own right, that the situation had improved and Hannah had been treated with more friendship.

Olaf flushed. He fell silent, seeking for words that would not trigger another scornful reply. Hal leaned forward and put his hand over Hannah's, squeezing it gently.

"Hannah, perhaps you should let him talk without interrupting, or we'll be here all night," he said in a kindly tone.

She looked at him, then dashed her free hand across her eyes. "You're right, Hal." She turned her gaze on Olaf once more. "Go ahead. I'll let you speak. For now."

"Thank you," he said. He glanced at Hal and nodded his gratitude for the intervention. But if he was expecting to find an ally there, he was disappointed. Hal simply wanted to hear what Olaf had to say. He had no regard for the man and no sympathy. Olaf had intimated that he needed a ship. More specifically, he needed the *Heron*. That meant Hal was involved. He would hear Olaf out and then make his decision.

Olaf took a deep breath and continued. "After I . . . ran, I put as much distance between me and Hallasholm as I could."

Thorn grunted sarcastically. "Wise choice," he said. Hal glanced sharply at him and he shrugged. "Sorry. I'll keep my comments to myself too. For the time being."

Olaf couldn't help but be interested in the byplay between them. Thorn was a senior warrior and Hal was a young man—the same age as Olaf's own son. Yet the young skirl seemed to carry himself with an authority and maturity far beyond what one would expect. And the others, both Hannah and Thorn, seemed to recognize it and defer to it.

"Go ahead," Hal said. "We don't have all night." The last words reminded Olaf that Hal might be prepared to listen to his tale, but he was not overly sympathetic to him.

"Very well," he said. "I wandered for several months, never staying in one place for too long—for obvious reasons," he added, before anyone else could. "I got a job on a guard ship traveling down the Dan. The river is infested with pirates, and merchant ships need to travel in convoys to—"

"We know." Hal cut off the explanation. "We've been hired as a convoy escort several times."

Olaf nodded. "We reached the southern end of the Dan and I headed east on a trader, ending up in Byzantos."

"Byzantos?" Hal asked, his voice showing interest now. The fabled city-state was something of an enigma this far north. He had heard of it, of course, and heard many stories about it.

Byzantos had been founded many years previously, when the Toscan empire had become too large and unwieldy to be controlled and ruled by one city. Accordingly, Toscana had split into east and west empires, with the western empire seated in the original capital, Toscana, and the eastern empire centered on the new city of Byzantos.

Its laws, traditions, language, religion and military organization were the same as those of the original empire. But whereas Toscana was old and corrupt and increasingly vulnerable to invasion from the north, Byzantos was new and energetic and well protected by its natural position, surrounded on three sides by water and secure behind high, thick walls built by its founding emperor, Constantus.

As a result, over the ensuing years, Byzantos had grown to be the stronger and more prosperous of the two capitals, while Toscana's internal politics and corruption had weakened the western empire, reducing its prestige and influence.

The old empire was still a powerful force in the world. But it had been outstripped by its younger, more vigorous sibling. Byzantos was a growing center of trade and political power, situated on the border between the eastern and western continents, with a foot placed firmly in both.

"It's an amazing place," Olaf said, sensing the young skirl's interest. "It's a major harbor and a very important trade center. But there are vested interests and factions everywhere. Many years ago, the then emperor founded a palace guard of foreign mercenaries, figuring they would not be influenced by the political tides in the new empire and would remain loyal to the man who paid them— the emperor himself.

"This palace guard has become increasingly powerful, due to the fact that the emperors felt they could trust the members of the guard implicitly—so long as they were paid."

"Where does he recruit these men?" Thorn asked.

Olaf turned to him. "Interestingly, the vast majority are Skandians—former wolfship crewmen who have settled in the empire. Our skill with weapons, and our loyalty to our leader, have become watchwords in Byzantos."

"You say 'our,'" Hal interrupted. "I take it this means you are a member of this palace guard?"

Olaf nodded. "I was recruited shortly after I arrived in the city. There's little surprise in that. Obviously, I sought the company of other Skandians—particularly those who knew nothing of my recent history. It was a logical step for them to offer me a place in the guard. I accepted because I needed the money."

"But you had the loot you'd stolen from your shipmates," Thorn said.

Olaf smiled sadly. "It's amazing how money evaporates when you're on the run," he said. "Everything costs more once people realize that you're a fugitive."

"And presumably you continued to gamble," Hannah said accusingly.

Olaf nodded sadly. "Yes. I'm afraid I hadn't learned my lesson there."

"And presumably you hadn't learned to gamble more skillfully," Thorn said.

Hal gave the two older people a warning glance. "Let the man talk," he said. He was intrigued to hear more about Byzantos. He was an avid traveler and was fascinated by new destinations, new parts of the world to see.

"Sorry," said Thorn, although his tone belied the sentiment. Hannah said nothing. Olaf glanced at the two of them and resumed his story.

"I rose through the ranks of the palace guard and became an officer. Then, eventually, when the old commander died, I was appointed in his place."

"You'd risen far," Hal commented. He noticed that Stig was looking at Olaf with new interest. Perhaps, he thought, there was finally something for Stig to be proud of so far as his father was concerned.

"That's true," Olaf agreed. Then he added heavily, "But the trouble with rising far is that it leaves a long way for you to fall."

"And presumably, you did just that," Hal said.

Olaf nodded. "It wasn't really my fault . . . ," he began. When Thorn muttered something under his breath, he turned to him. "No, really, it wasn't. I was sick in bed with a terrible stomach fever. I was barely conscious. Couldn't keep any food down. Even water set me to throwing up. I was like that for a week before the fever broke and I began to recover. It took another two weeks to get me back on my feet."

"And in that time, what happened?"

Olaf sighed. "The Empress's fourteen-year-old son was kidnapped by corsairs. He's being held for ransom. I was held responsible."

"But if you were so sick, how could they blame you?" Stig asked.

Olaf smiled wearily. "I was the palace guard commander. My guards let me down. I let the Empress down."

"You keep talking about the Empress," Hal said. "What about the Emperor? Where does he stand on this whole thing?"

"There is no emperor. He died some eight years ago, and his

son inherited the title. But the boy was only six years old, so his mother, Justinia, began acting as Regent. As time passed, she decided that she enjoyed the power and prestige and became more like a ruler in her own right, calling herself Empress."

"And people accepted this?" Thorn asked.

Olaf smiled at him. "She had the palace guard behind her. We're probably the strongest military force in the city. Of course, there were other factions who didn't want her as ruler. But they were divided. They couldn't organize a cohesive resistance to her plans and she took them on, one at a time, and destroyed their power." He smiled a little whimsically. "The fact is, she's a good ruler. She's efficient and intelligent—if somewhat vengeful. In any event, the corsairs, led by a man called Myrgos, kidnapped the boy, Constantus."

"How did they manage that?" Hal asked.

Olaf shrugged. "It might have been sheer happenstance. Or he might have been betrayed. He'd gone down the coast from Byzantos to a small coastal village. Myrgos and his ship, the *Vulture*, appeared off the village. The pirates stormed ashore and overwhelmed Constantus's guards and carried him off. I'd only just gone back on duty and was weak as a kitten. There was nothing I could do. His mother received a ransom demand within the week. Myrgos wants three hundred thousand reels of silver for the boy. And she was given nine months to gather the money and pay up."

"When was this?" Hal asked quickly.

"Three months ago," Olaf replied.

"Why did he give her such a long ransom period?" Hannah asked. She had been sitting listening, gradually being drawn into the tale and forgetting, for the moment, her animosity toward Olaf. The thought of that young boy being ripped away from his family and loved ones wrung her heart.

Olaf glanced at her. "Myrgos is a black-hearted, merciless killer. But essentially, he's a businessman. He knew it would take time for her to gather such a large amount of money in cash, and then transport it to him."

"And if she doesn't make the deadline?" Thorn asked. "Will he kill the boy?"

"He may. But it's more likely he'll increase the ransom amount. There's no profit in killing him. Unfortunately, the same doesn't hold true for me."

"How do you mean?" Hal asked.

"When the ransom demand was received, the Empress called me before her and told me that I was to blame for the situation. Therefore, it was up to me to remedy it. Either I return the boy to her before she has to pay the ransom, or my life is forfeit."

"You could always run," Hal said.

But Olaf shook his head. "No. I've had enough of that," he said. "And there's nowhere left for me to run to. I'd spend the rest of my life looking over my shoulder, waiting for her assassins. As I said, she's a very vengeful woman and she has a long reach. Besides, if I manage to rescue Constantus, she'll pay me a third of the ransom money. That could set me up for life."

"Then the answer is simple," Hal said. "Take some of your men, hire a ship and go find the boy. After all, you say this palace guard is a powerful military force. Surely you'd be able to take on a bunch of raggle-tail pirates." Hal had little respect for the fighting qualities or courage of pirates. As Olaf said, they were concerned mainly with profit. Most of them would fight savagely when they faced a weak or disorganized enemy. But a properly trained military unit should have little trouble dealing with them.

"I'd do that," Olaf told him, "but she won't release any of the guard to help me. The political situation in Byzantos is extremely unstable at the moment—and made even more so by this turn of events. She says she needs all her men to keep order. I'm afraid she's cut me loose. I'm on my own."

He turned to face Stig, holding the young man's eyes with his own.

"That's why I've come to you. I need you to help me find these pirates and rescue young Constantus. What do you say, son?"

H e says no," Thorn replied instantly. "You deserted him. You've left him to his own devices for years. Now when you're in trouble, you come running and sniveling to him and asking for help. Well, it doesn't work that way. I—"

But Stig held up a hand to stop the furious tirade. "Just a moment, Thorn," he said. When the old sea wolf fell silent, Stig turned to Olaf and gestured toward the door.

"Can you step outside for a moment? I need to talk with my friends."

"Of course." Olaf picked up his cloak, pulling the heavy fur around his shoulders.

"Stay clear of the light," Hal warned him. "If anyone passes by, we don't want them to recognize you."

Olaf nodded and, opening the door, stepped out onto the porch. They could hear the floorboards creaking as he moved away from the door and the little oil lamp set above it. After a few seconds, when he felt that Olaf was out of earshot, Thorn rounded on Stig in an angry whisper.

"You can't seriously be considering this, Stig!" he said. "Why should you give him any help? He has never done anything for you." He looked at Hal. "You tell him, Hal."

But Hal shook his head. He thought he could see how Stig was thinking.

"This is for Stig to decide, Thorn," he said quietly, and Thorn recoiled slightly, surprised by the tolerance in his skirl's words.

"He's my *father*, Thorn," Stig said. "He's my father and he needs my help. You're right, he hasn't been any part of my life so far. But this might be my chance to make a connection with him. To really become his son."

"You owe nothing to him, Stig," his mother said bitterly.

He smiled sadly at her. "I know that, Mam. But what about what I owe to me? This is an opportunity for me to get to know my own father, and to form a relationship with him. You understand that, don't you, Hal?" he appealed to his best friend.

Hal nodded slowly. "I think I do. I'd give a lot for a chance to get to know my father."

"You can't compare Mikkel with Olaf!" Thorn said, outraged.

But Hal raised a hand to calm him down. "I'm not comparing them. I'm saying I understand Stig's position. Besides, we're all forgetting that there's a fourteen-year-old boy who's been taken from his home and family, and who's probably terrified that at any moment, he'll be killed."

"That is a point," Hannah agreed.

"What about the Maktig contest?" Thorn asked as the thought occurred to him. "You're a certainty to win it. But we can't keep Olaf out of sight for the next two weeks! Someone's bound to see him and recognize him."

"Thorn's right," Hal said. "If we go, we'll have to go in the next few days. Time is running out for that boy, after all. You'll miss the last two events."

Stig shrugged. He'd already considered this aspect of his decision. "There'll be other Maktig contests," he said. "After all, there's one every year," he added, trying to smile.

Thorn shook his head in disgust. "I hope Olaf is worth it," he said.

Stig grasped his shoulder in a firm grip. "So do I, Thorn. But it's something I have to find out for myself." He turned to Hal. "So if I say I'll help him, you'll agree?"

The skirl nodded. "You're part of the brotherband. We support each other," he said simply.

"Will you give the rest of the crew a say in the matter?" Thorn asked.

"No. I'm the skirl and I decide where we go and what we do. We don't vote on matters like that," he pointed out. A ship's crew wasn't a democracy. They followed their skirl's leadership and obeyed his orders. Otherwise a ship could descend into chaos.

"Of course," Hal continued, "any crewman who has strong feelings about it can always opt out. I assume that's what you'll do?"

Thorn took a deep breath and looked at the ceiling above him. If he did refuse to go, it would mean leaving the brotherband. "No," he said. "I'm part of the Heron brotherband. I go where my brothers go—even when they're being foolish," he added with a sad grin.

Hal smiled at him and reached out to cover his left hand with his own. "Thanks, Thorn," he said.

Stig looked from one to the other. "So we'll help him?" he asked, a note of hope in his voice.

"We'll help him. And we'll get this boy away from the pirates," Hal said. "Better call him in and tell him."

Stig moved to the door, opened it and called his father in. Olaf had been waiting at the end of small porch. He reentered the room, stooping under the low doorframe, and looked at the four faces awaiting him. He stood silently, refusing to beg or plead any further. Finally, Hal gestured for Stig to speak.

"We'll help you," Stig said, and Olaf's shoulders, which he had been holding tensed, subsided in relief.

"Thank you," Olaf said simply. He looked at his wife. "Thank you, Hannah."

She shook her head. "It's Stig's choice, not mine."

He nodded, understanding. After all, he thought, she had every reason to resent him. "Fair enough," he said. "But thank you anyway."

"All right," Hal said briskly. "We'd better start making plans." He gestured for the others to sit round the table, glancing hopefully at the coffeepot on the stove. "Hannah, is there any more coffee?"

She nodded and fetched the pot, setting out another mug for

Olaf. She refilled their cups and he took a deep sip of his, reacting with surprise. Coffee hadn't been a popular drink in Hallasholm when he was last here.

"This is excellent," he said. "We drink this in Byzantos."

"So it can't be too barbarous a place," Hal replied. Then, changing the subject, he continued. "Right, we haven't any time to waste. Three months of the deadline have gone already. We're going to have to leave here within the next day or two." He looked at Stig. "Is the ship ready for sea?"

The first mate nodded. He'd checked on progress at the beach earlier in the evening. "The repainting is finished and the stores have been loaded aboard. Edvin may need to top up on fresh water, and fresh fruit and vegetables, but we can do that tomorrow."

"Or we can replenish down the coast," Hal said. "I want to get clear of Hallasholm as soon as possible. Tomorrow night will be ideal."

Thorn scratched his beard thoughtfully. "You're thinking about the guild?"

"That's right. They already have a set against me. If they find out we're harboring, and assisting, a wanted criminal, they're sure to make things ugly for us."

"Why would they do that?" Olaf asked, but Hal brushed the question aside.

"I've had a little run-in with them and they're looking for any way they can find to bring me down. But as long as you stay out of sight, there's no problem." He looked at Hannah. "Can he stay here for tonight, Hannah?"

She nodded assent. "I suppose so."

Olaf essayed a smile in her direction. "Be like old times," he said, but there was no answering smile. She regarded him, stony faced.

"No, it won't," she said. "You'll sleep out in the boiler-house."

Hannah supported herself by taking in laundry from other households in Hallasholm. The boiler-house was a large structure built in the vacant space behind the house. It contained two big wood-fired boilers in which she did the laundry—and a supply of firewood to feed them.

"You can keep one of the boiler fires burning," she said. "That should keep you warm."

"Sounds cozy," he said. He continued to smile, although his attempt to ingratiate himself with her wasn't having a lot of success.

She grunted. She didn't mention the fact that the floor consisted of hard flagstones. He could find that out for himself. She regarded the fur cloak he was wearing. That should provide enough softness for him, she thought.

"Stay in there," Hal admonished him. "I don't want you wandering around outside. There are still a lot of people in Hallasholm who remember you and might recognize you—particularly if they see you here, in this house."

Again, Olaf remarked to himself on the authority in the young man's voice and the confidence with which he issued orders. He might be young, he thought, but he was definitely a skirl, who was used to issuing orders and having them obeyed. He nodded meekly. He needed Hal's cooperation.

"I'll stay out of sight," he said. "It's only one day, after all."

"Hannah, are you happy to give him meals?" Hal asked, and she nodded.

"It'll be nothing fancy," she warned.

Olaf nodded toward the cupboard where she had put away the remains of the pie. "I'd be happy with leftovers," he told her.

She snorted derisively. "Well, don't get your heart set on them. Bread and cheese will be what you're getting."

"Are we going to tell Erak what we're doing?" Stig asked. Hal and his crew had a special relationship with the Oberjarl.

Hal considered the idea for a few seconds, then shook his head. "Better not," he decided. "Erak would feel duty bound to throw Olaf in the cells and bring him to trial. It would be awkward for him if he were seen to be helping us."

"He's not around anyway," Thorn told them. "He's taken *Wolf-wind* down the coast to Baskenholm. Sigurd Breathblaster has been lax with his tax payments and Erak thought he'd remind him of his civic obligations."

That was a common enough occurrence among the jarls of Skandia. They felt obliged to minimize the tax they paid to the Oberjarl. Erak, on the other hand, liked to remind them forcibly about such matters. Previous Oberjarls would have sent someone to collect the money. Erak liked to keep his hand in as a helmsman, and from time to time he'd take his ship and crew and, arriving at first light, would burst into the recalcitrant's lodge, bellowing and threatening.

"That's probably all to the good," Hal said. "I'll leave him a written message with my mam."

"You'll tell her, of course," Hannah said.

"Yes. She deserves to know. And she'll keep quiet until we're well away." Hal looked around the room, deciding that their business for the night was finished. "Right, Thorn and I will head for home. You get some sleep. And remember, stay out of sight. We'll go aboard *Heron* around the tenth hour tomorrow night. The tide will be turning then, so we'll ride it out."

Like any good skirl, he was always aware of the state of the tide. He and Thorn said their good-byes and headed out. Hannah, Stig and Olaf listened as the sound of their boots on the shingle path faded away. Then Hannah looked meaningfully at her former husband.

"Stig will show you the boiler-house," she said. As the two of them headed for the door, she relented on her earlier decision and dragged a large cushion off the settle along the wall and passed it to Olaf.

"You'd better take this," she said. "Those flagstones can get hard after a while."

he following morning, Hal called the crew together to brief them on the upcoming voyage. They gathered on the ship, which had now been launched and moored in its usual place beside the harbor mole.

Kloof, who had spent the last two days tied up beside Karina's woodshed, seemed happy to be on board once more. She prowled around the deck, nose down, tail up, sniffing for new smells and old familiar ones. Finally satisfied that she'd found them all, she flopped down beside the mast with a dull thud, curled up and went to sleep.

"I sometimes think that dog sleeps twenty-six hours a day," Jesper said, eyeing her with some envy. She did seem to know how to enjoy sleeping, he thought.

The crew were seated close by the steering platform. Hal mounted this so he could address them.

"We've got a mission," he said, and they all exchanged glances. There were a few muttered sounds of satisfaction. The Herons were young and adventurous, and it went against the grain to stay idle in port for too long.

"Is this for Erak?" Ingvar asked, glancing forward to the empty berth where Erak's ship was usually moored.

Hal shook his head. "This is a private matter," he said. "I'll tell you more when we're at sea. But I don't want people to know we're leaving, so we'll head out tonight, after dark. Don't talk about it in the marketplace or in any of the taverns. Of course, you can tell your close family, but ask them to keep quiet until we've gone."

The circle of faces were intent on him now, fascinated to know what their mission would be. They all nodded as he cautioned them on the need for secrecy.

Hal looked to Edvin. "How are we placed for supplies?"

Edvin frowned as he took mental stock of what was aboard and what would be needed.

"We've got plenty of dried and salted food," he said. "But I usually wait till just before we leave to buy fresh food—bread and vegetables and meat. Should I do that today?"

Hal shook his head. "Not if that's what you normally do," he said. "It will alert people to the fact that we're leaving. We'll get those things in Aspenholm."

Edvin nodded. Aspenholm was a small fishing port a day's sail away. There was a market there where he could buy everything they needed. And word wouldn't filter back to Hallasholm for several days.

"I'll need fresh water too," he said. "Always best to fill the water barrels as late as possible."

Water stored in the barrels belowdecks tended to develop an unpleasant taste and color if left too long. It was preferable to flush out the barrels and refill them with fresh water just before leaving.

"You can get that in Aspenholm too," Hal told him.

Edvin nodded agreement.

"How long will we be away?" Wulf asked.

"Two months. Maybe more," Hal told him.

Instantly, his brother had another question. "Can you tell us where we're going?"

Hal paused. It was a reasonable question. Their choice of gear and clothing and equipment would be affected by it.

"South," he said. "We'll be going down the Dan to the Constant Sea." There was no harm in telling them that, he reasoned.

Several of the crew smiled contentedly. South meant warmer weather. Had he said west or north, they might have expected a wet, cold trip, with freezing rain and sleet. South was preferable by far.

Hal paused. He'd decided to say nothing about the fact that they would be carrying an extra person on board. The less said about Olaf, the better; and if word got out that there was a stranger on board *Heron*, people might become curious. And there were still too many people in the town who had cause to remember him with bitterness. He would tell the crew when Olaf boarded that night.

He looked around the assembled faces. "Any questions?" he asked, then he smiled. "Not that I can answer too many at this stage anyway. I'll tell you more when we've left port."

Several heads nodded. He made a gesture of dismissal.

"Well, better get on home and get your gear together, and tell your families you'll be gone for a couple of months." There was nothing unusual in that. Most voyages took at least a month or two. As they stood and prepared to leave, he had one last word to add. "The tide is full at the tenth hour tonight," he said. "I want to go out on the last of the ebb—about half an hour after eleven. So be here and be ready well before then."

There was a general surge to the side of the ship as they clambered ashore, breaking up to head for their homes. Hal caught Stig's eye. The first mate hadn't made any move to leave.

"Best get home and get your own things ready," Hal said. "And make sure Olaf stays out of sight for the rest of the day. Bring him aboard just before eleven."

Stig nodded and turned to go. Hal realized that Ulf and Wulf had hung back when the others had departed.

"Did you want something?" he asked.

Ulf shrugged his shoulders diffidently. "Well, we were just thinking about the Maktig contest. What should we do about that?"

"Last I heard," Hal told him, "you were going to draw straws to see who won the qualifying round. And if that didn't happen, you were probably going to think of a number between one and ten to decide the contest. So do you really care what happens?"

The twins exchanged a look, then both of them grinned.

"Naah. Not really," Wulf said, and his brother nodded agreement.

"We were just filling in time, really," Ulf said. "It was fun driving the judges mad."

Hal regarded them curiously. "So when you kept drawing events, you were doing it intentionally?"

They shook their heads.

"Not at all. We don't need to do that sort of thing intentionally. It just happens," said Wulf.

"Try us out," Ulf suggested.

Hal thought for a moment, then said: "Think of a number between one and ten."

"Four," the twins chorused simultaneously.

Hal shook his head. "Remarkable. All right, think of a number between one and . . . three hundred." That should test them, he thought.

"One hundred and seventy-six," both twins said at the same time.

Hal looked at them with some awe.

"Was that right?" Ulf prompted him.

Hal shook his head. "I don't know. I hadn't thought of one myself. But you do realize that you just both picked the same number out of a possible three hundred, don't you?"

Wulf shrugged. "Well, of course we did. We always do."

Hal grinned at them. "I imagine the judges will be very glad when you don't turn up tomorrow," he said.

Dusk crept over the town and lights began to twinkle in the windows. In houses all over Hallasholm, the crew were making their preparations and saying their farewells to families. None of the latter were surprised or particularly concerned at the news that their sons—and in one case, Lydia—were heading off on another voyage. That was their life, after all. They were sea wolves, descendants of the fierce warriors who once raided all over the known world. Voyaging was what they were born to do, and what they loved doing.

Nor was there any surprise at the secrecy involved in their departure. In the past few years, the Heron brotherband had carried out several clandestine operations for the Oberjarl, and their families accepted the need for confidentiality without question.

As the night drew on and time for departure came closer, they began to straggle down to the harbor in ones and twos, carrying their kit bags slung over their shoulders and wearing their weapons. Their big round shields were slung over their backs, and once they boarded the *Heron*, they slipped them over the pegs that held them in place along the bulwarks, beside their rowing positions.

The muted rattle and clatter of equipment sounded across the harbor as the crew unstowed their oars from the brackets that ran from behind the mast to the afterdeck, and Ulf and Wulf untied the frappings around the big sails and unrolled the heavy bolts of canvas, laying them out ready for hoisting. Ingvar busied himself checking the Mangler and its ammunition locker, ensuring there was a plentiful supply of bolts for the big weapon. Lydia stowed her quiver of darts and a heavy canvas bag holding two dozen spares, in her screened-off quarters in the stern of the rowing well. She wasn't part of the sailing or rowing crew, although if required she could take a turn at the tiller. Her main contribution would come when *Heron* went into battle, at which time her darts would rain confusion and destruction down on the decks of any enemy ship they encountered.

It was just after the tenth hour when Stig shouldered his kit bag and shoved his ax through the retaining ring on his belt.

"Time for us to be going," he told Olaf, and the older man nodded, buckling on the war belt that held his sword and dagger. He slung the heavy fur around his shoulders and picked up his spiked helmet from the side table where he had left it.

"Don't put that on," Stig cautioned him. "It's a little exotic for these parts and it'll only draw attention if we're seen."

Olaf grunted agreement and looped the helmet's chin strap over the hilt of his sheathed dagger. Stig turned to his mother and embraced her warmly.

"Good-bye, Mam," he said tenderly. "Take care while I'm gone."

"Travel safely, son. Go in Thalga's care," she said. Thalga was the Skandian goddess of sailors and travelers, and this was Hannah's standard farewell when her son left home. But this time, she put extra feeling into the benediction. They held the embrace for several seconds, then Stig gently pushed her back and disengaged himself.

Olaf cleared his throat uncertainly. "Good-bye, Hannah," he said, shuffling his feet.

She regarded him coolly. "Good-bye, Olaf."

He noticed that she didn't invoke Thalga's protection for him. He took a half pace toward her, uncertain as to whether he should embrace her or not. She settled the matter by withdrawing a corresponding distance. He stopped and made an awkward gesture in the air, not sure what to say.

"You take care of my boy," she said.

He gave her a tentative smile. "Our boy," he corrected.

She snorted dismissively. "Not on past form," she said. Then she stepped closer and he could see the light of anger burning in her eyes. "If any harm comes to him, I will find you, wherever you are," she warned.

Olaf held up a hand, palm out, in a defensive gesture. Stig broke the tension of the moment.

"I'll be fine, Mam," he said reassuringly. "I'll have the Herons with me, remember?"

She switched her gaze to him and her expression softened somewhat.

"Just as well you will," she said.

Stig opened the door and ushered his father outside into the darkness. He nodded once more to his mother, who stepped out onto the porch. She would stay there until he was out of sight, he knew. He pointed to a path through the thick trees that led down to the bay.

"We'll go through the trees and along the beach to the harbor," he said. "No sense in chancing being seen walking through the town." Then he gestured to his father, standing uncertainly by.

"Let's go," he said.

T horn had taken over as first mate in Stig's absence, checking that the ship was ready for sea, that all mooring lines were ready to be cast off and that oars were ready in place at the rowing benches. Although, knowing Hal, he assumed that the young skirl would sail rather than row her out of the harbor. He glanced up at the wind telltale—a strip of ribbon at the sternpost. The wind was coming in over their port bow, a favorable direction for getting under way and making their exit through the harbor mouth.

He glanced aft as two tall figures hurried along the quay and dropped lightly onto the deck. Stig had obviously waited until the security patrol had moved to the far end of the quay. The young warrior pointed to the stern and gestured for Olaf to wait there, where he'd be relatively inconspicuous. Several of the crew noticed their arrival and glanced curiously at the bulky figure in the fur cloak crouching in the stern, behind the rowing platform.

Stig hurried forward to take up his duties as first mate. He nodded his thanks to Thorn.

"Everything ready?" he asked. The old sea wolf pointed fore and aft.

"Bow and stern lines are ready to cast off. Oars are unstowed." Stig glanced quickly at the telltale.

"He won't use oars," he said. "Not with this wind."

In the stern, Hal moved to his place by the tiller, untying the leather thong that fastened it and prevented it banging back and forth with the movement of the water. He nodded a curt greeting to Olaf.

Lydia, who was accustomed to standing close by him as they moored and unmoored, glanced at the figure, muffled in his fur cloak.

"Who's that?" she asked softly.

But Hal shook his head. "Later," he said.

She shrugged and leaned against the bulwark ahead of him. It had been idle curiosity that had led her to ask, and she realized Hal was preoccupied with getting the ship under way.

The skirl cupped his hands round his mouth and called to the crew. "Stig! We'll go out under sail. Ulf and Wulf, ready to hoist starboard! Stefan, tend the stern line."

He saw the dark mass of the starboard sail begin to rise a few meters as the twins heaved on the halyards, taking up the slack. Stefan left his rowing bench and ran aft. The stern line was looped around a large iron bollard on the quay and tied off at the ship. Stefan untied the knot securing it and held the rope firmly.

"Starboard sail!" Hal called, and as the yardarm went aloft

in a series of jerking motions, he called, "Release the bowline!"

Stig, who had prepared the bowline the same way Stefan had done with the stern line, now let the end of the rope run free. It snaked out as he did so, running smoothly round the quayside bollard as the wind caught the sail, setting the sail flapping and shoving the bow to starboard, away from the quay. Stig quickly gathered in the line and coiled it on deck.

"Sheet home! Hal yelled.

Ulf and Wulf hauled on the sheets, bringing the sail tight up to the wind. The ship was now swinging thirty degrees clear of the quay, held only by the looped stern line.

"Let go aft!" Hal said, judging angles and forces. Stefan released his end of the stern line, and it ran out over the bulwark. He gathered it in before it could fall into the water alongside.

At the tiller, Hal felt that familiar sense of exultation as the ship came to life. The tiller vibrated under his hand, and the rudder bit into the water as he hauled the bow back to port. Within a few seconds, *Heron* was sliding smoothly through the water, gathering speed until she was moving faster than a man could run and angling out into the harbor.

The two men of the harbor watch raised their arms in farewell as the ship accelerated away from them. Lydia, Jesper and Ingvar returned the greeting.

"Down fin keel!" Hal called now.

Thorn raised a hand in acknowledgment, then leaned his weight on the fin keel behind the mast, sending the bladelike fin down through the keel box and out into the water below.

Hal felt the ship's sideways drift check as the fin bit into the water. He glanced at the harbor mouth, bringing the ship's head a few degrees farther to port, judging angles and speed and drift until he was satisfied they would make it through the gap on one tack, without further adjustment.

He looked down and saw Lydia watching him, an expression of amused tolerance on her face. He grinned at her.

"Ah, Gorlog's eyebrows, I love this!" he said.

She couldn't help smiling in return. "That's pretty obvious."

Stig came aft now and joined their little group. They always stood this way when they were leaving port.

"That was pretty neat," he said. "The boys haven't got rusty while they've been ashore."

The dark bulk of the starboard mole loomed alongside them, only five meters away, then they shot clear of it into the open sea, heeling slightly as the wind, now unobstructed by the quay and the mole, hit them with increased force. Ulf and Wulf released the sheets slightly without being told. They knew their job. Hal used the extra power to bring the ship even farther round to port.

"Ship ahead!" called Stefan, who had taken up his customary position as bow lookout. Hal craned down to peer round the billowing sail as Stefan added more information.

"Off the starboard bow. Heading away."

Hal could make out the long, low shape in the water. The massive square sail above the hull told him whose ship it was. She was heading to cross their course at an angle and there was no risk of collision.

"It's *Wolfwind*," he said just before Stefan called again, confirming his identification. "She must be waiting for the tide to flood before she goes into the harbor," he added.

"We got away just in time, then," Stig remarked.

"Just in time for what?" Lydia asked, puzzled.

Her two friends replied simultaneously. "Later."

On board *Wolfwind*, the lookout called to the deck as he sighted the small dark shape sliding away from them.

"Ship to starboard!"

Erak and Svengal, standing by the tiller, both followed the direction of his pointing arm. They could only just make out the little hull as she slipped away into the darkness. But the triangular sail was unmistakable.

"It's the *Heron*," Erak said, frowning. "What's she doing leaving harbor at this time of night?"

Svengal glanced over the side at the racing water below them. "Taking advantage of the ebbing tide?"

But Erak continued to frown. "He could have done that tomorrow. What's the hurry?"

"Maybe he's testing his night sails," Svengal suggested. He saw Erak nod, and he smiled to himself as he waited for the inevitable comment, which came a few seconds later.

"Night sails? What are night sails?"

"They're sails you use at night so people can't see you so well," Svengal answered, allowing no hint of his grin to enter his voice.

Erak shook his head angrily. "Never heard of such a thing."

"People don't talk about them much—they're hard to see," Svengal told him. Erak glared suspiciously at his first mate, conscious that Svengal was always ready to pull his leg. Svengal's innocent look confirmed his suspicions.

"Idiot," Erak said. Then he turned away and bellowed a series of sail orders to the crew as he angled *Wolfwind* away from the harbor. They had half an hour to wait before the tide stopped flowing out and they had still water to enter port. He glanced over his shoulder but there was no sign of the little ship that had passed them.

"Night sails," he muttered disgustedly.

Svengal nodded. "Night sails," he agreed.

Hal waited until *Wolfwind* had been lost astern for some minutes, then he called the crew aft for a briefing. Ulf and Wulf tied off the sheets and joined the others as Hal kept the ship on a steady course.

"Take the helm, please, Stig," Hal said, and when the first mate did so, he stepped down from the steering platform and moved close to the assembled crew, noting the expectant looks on their faces.

"You've noticed we have a passenger on board," he began. Inevitably, all eyes turned to Olaf, who was now standing by the sternpost. Hal indicated him with his hand.

"His name is Olaf and he's Stig's father," he said.

That caused a ripple of interest and curiosity among the crew. They all knew the story of Stig's father, of course, and the shame he had brought upon their shipmate and his mother. The look they turned on the bulky, fur-cloaked figure changed from curiosity to dislike. Hal had expected the reaction, and he went on regardless.

"He's asked our help and we've agreed to give it to him. We're heading for the Constant Sea to rescue a young lad who's been kidnapped by a gang of Hellenic pirates."

The expressions of dislike changed once more to interest. The idea of fighting pirates and rescuing a hostage appealed to their sense of adventure. It was the sort of thing they had done on more than one occasion. Hal's next words increased the interest level.

"The boy is the son of the Empress of Byzantos. Olaf was the head of the Empress's personal guard and he's been tasked with rescuing him." He didn't elaborate on Olaf's being blamed for the boy's loss and threatened with dire consequences if he was not rescued from the pirates. But the reference to the Empress and the fabled city-state of Byzantos added an exotic touch to their task, one that stimulated the crew's imaginations.

"We're heading for the Dan, and we'll sail down it to the Constant Sea." He grinned. "So that's what we're up to. And that's why we had to leave port in such secrecy. Olaf isn't too popular with a lot of people in Hallasholm." He noted the way the crew looked at Olaf again, the expressions of enmity back on their faces. "I'll give you more details as I have them, but for now, everyone back to their stations."

As they turned away, he felt a hand on his arm and turned to see that Olaf had approached him. The burly warrior leaned closer to speak to him.

"I wonder if I could say a few words to the crew?" he said. "I'd like to thank them for helping me."

Hal raised an eyebrow and looked again at his brotherband as they made their way back to their stations.

"Not a good idea," he said shortly.

Olaf sighed at the rebuff. He guessed he was going to have to get used to that sort of thing.

· · · · ·

As they sailed into the night, the crew laid out straw-filled mattresses in the rowing spaces. Hal, as skirl, had a small enclosed space to himself under the rear deck. He handed the tiller to Thorn and beckoned to Olaf, leading the way to the hatch that led to the cramped space.

"You may as well take my sleeping space," he said. "I'll bunk down on deck. I don't like to get too far from the tiller when we're at sea."

Olaf shrugged. "I could always bunk down with the crew," he suggested.

But Hal shook his head. He thought it was best to keep Olaf separate from the crew. He wasn't a popular addition to their number, and there could be unpleasantness if they were in close contact during the trip.

"No. Better this way," Hal said.

Olaf raised his eyebrows, guessing the reasoning behind Hal's choice. He regretted it. He'd always enjoyed the close camaraderie of a ship's crew. *Right up until I robbed one,* he thought somberly, and nodded acceptance.

Kloof, seeing Hal move from the tiller, had ambled aft and pushed her nose toward him, her heavy tail swinging. She knew better than to distract him when he was steering. Absently, he fondled her big head and scratched her ears.

Olaf essayed a smile. "That's not a dog. It's a bear," he said.

Hal regarded him for a few seconds. Like any big dog owner, he had heard all the witticisms that people would come up with, each one thinking they were the first to say it. *That's not a dog. It's a bear. Have you got a saddle for him? He's so big he could pull a cart.*

"No," he said without a trace of humor. "She's a dog."

Olaf, rebuked, pushed out his bottom lip, then held his hand out, knuckles upward, for Kloof to sniff.

"Good dog," he said. "Come and have a scratch."

Kloof, sensing the somewhat strained atmosphere between her master and this stranger, sniffed perfunctorily at his hand, then turned away. She went a few paces for'ard and let her front legs slide out from under her, settling on the deck with a soft thud and a deep sigh. Then she curled her tail around her and went to sleep.

"Even your dog doesn't like me," Olaf remarked.

Hal relented a little. It must be hard, he thought, being confined on a small ship surrounded by people who disliked you and treated you with disdain.

"You just have to win her trust," he said, then added, "Same as the rest of us."

PART TWO

THE DAN

O n the fourth day of sailing, late in the afternoon, Jesper, who was perched on the crosstree on the bow post, keeping a lookout, gestured toward the water several hundred meters ahead of them.

"Brown water," he called.

Hal craned down to peer under the curved foot of the sail. He could make out the tumbling mass of brown water ahead of them where the tidal flow from the Dan River met the crosswind and waves of the Stormwhite Sea and created a seething, troubled mass. At the moment, the tide was running out, staining the sea brown and muddy for several kilometers offshore.

At the same time, he could sense a new smell in the air. The fresh salt smell was overlaid with the odor of mud and earth. It was only slight at the moment, but it was there. As yet, there was no sign of land.

Heron butted into the outflowing tide. There was no susceptible change in her speed through the water, but Hal knew the tidal flow would be reducing their actual speed by several knots. He had consulted the tide charts the previous evening, memorizing the times for the ebb and flow of the tide. When the tide shifted, they would ride the ingoing flow upriver for the seven or eight kilometers that the tide's effect reached, letting it boost their speed. For now, he knew, they had another hour to wait before the tide changed.

"Sheet home," he called to the twins, and they tightened the sheets, bringing the sail harder onto the wind and increasing the power in the sail. From time to time, a dull thud would reverberate through the fabric of the ship as she struck larger pieces of timber being carried in the current.

"Keep an eye out for tree trunks!" Hal called to Jesper, who raised a hand in acknowledgment. His eyes scanned from side to side, looking for larger pieces that might damage the hull.

"Really no need to tell him that," he said in an aside to Olaf. "He knows his job."

"They all do," Olaf said. He had been impressed by the smooth, unhurried teamwork of the Herons. They were obviously highly skilled and well trained. They went about their various tasks without too much prodding from Hal, often anticipating his orders as they kept the ship sailing smoothly to the south. They might be young, he thought, but they're an excellent crew.

Hal's reply mirrored his thoughts. "Yes," he said. "They're a good crew."

"They have a good skirl," Olaf ventured. Hal looked at him sidelong, one eyebrow raised over the gratuitous compliment. He said nothing, then looked back to the direction in which he was steering.

Olaf frowned to himself. That was clumsy, he thought. It made him appear that he was trying to ingratiate himself with this young man. Ruefully, he realized that that had been exactly what he was trying to do. It came from spending too much time with the sycophants and hangers-on of the Byzantian court, with their unctuous compliments and easy flattery. Skandians were more prosaic in their approach and didn't give themselves to false praise. He had forgotten that in the years he had been away from home. "Land ahead!" Jesper called from the lookout perch.

And slowly, a green-and-brown line began to spread itself across the ocean ahead of them. They had reached the mouth of the Dan.

They rode the inflowing tide when it turned, speeding inland under the combined thrust of the tide and the big triangular sail.

The river was wide and deep, and at this point ran in a south–north direction. With the prevailing wind out of the east, they could maintain a series of easy reaches as they sailed inland. The banks were heavily forested, with many small tributary streams leading off to either side. Olaf noticed a sense of heightened awareness among the crew. "Heads up, everyone!" Hal called from the steering platform. "Krall should be around the next turn!"

Krall was the prosperous river town that charged a toll for ships passing through. Its administrators had been known in the past to be in a loose alliance with the pirates who infested the river. They didn't actively help them, but they did little to discourage them. When *Heron* had first passed through the town, the authorities attempted to charge them with a murder. Hal and his men defeated that trumped-up accusation, but it cost them a serious delay in chasing Zavac and his black ship.

It left a bad taste in their mouths, and on subsequent trips down the Dan, they had avoided Krall. The port authorities here charged a hefty toll on ships passing through, but since *Heron* didn't plan to stop at the town, there was little they could do to make her pay.

There was always the chance, of course, that guard boats might be on the river, barring their passage. It was unlikely, but it was a possibility, which was why Hal had alerted his crew.

They rounded the bend and there was the township on the western bank, a sprawling mass of houses and warehouses, with a harbor full of ships and river craft.

The toll wharf was prominent along the waterfront, marked by its sign—a gold circle with two black bars through it. As *Heron* sailed past, several men came out onto the wharf by the toll office and waved at her. They weren't friendly greetings. They were peremptory demands for the little ship to come alongside the wharf and be assessed for a toll.

"Keep waving," Hal said as he maintained his course, staying well out in the center of the river.

Jesper, leaning on the bow post, made a rude gesture toward the shore. The men on the wharf reacted angrily. Fists were shaken and their voices carried faintly across the water as they demanded the *Heron* pull in to shore.

Most of the crew had their eyes on the angry figures. But Lydia was not one to be distracted from the main task in hand. She had maintained a watch over the river before them.

"There's a guard boat," she warned, pointing to starboard. Hal followed her pointing arm and saw a large rowing boat, pulling eight oars and crowded with armed men, shooting out from the eastern bank. His eyes narrowed as he measured her speed and marked a spot where she would intercept *Heron* if he maintained his current course.

"Stand by to tack starboard," he called softly. Ulf and Wulf sat upright on their benches, ready to act on his command, hands on the sheets and halyards.

"Come about!" he called, putting the helm over. *Heron* began swinging to starboard as the twins hauled down the port sail and began hoisting the starboard yardarm. *Heron* came smoothly about, racing for a spot behind the guard boat's stern. For a moment, there was confusion among the men on board the large open boat. As Hal had suspected, her crew weren't particularly skillful or well drilled. Belatedly, her helmsman shouted orders, and the port-side oars backed while the starboard-side pulled ahead. The big rowing boat lurched in the water and began to pivot, heading back to cut *Heron* off. But the maneuver was clumsy and poorly executed. Hal waited as the guard boat steadied on her new course, then called more orders.

"Down starboard. Up port!"

He swung the tiller back to port again as the twins answered his command, scuttling across the deck to the sheets that controlled the port sail. The sail filled and the ship leapt forward once more, speeding back behind the stern of the guard boat, leaving it no time or room to reverse course. The helmsman tried, but the result was a dismal failure and the boat wallowed in confusion, losing forward way as *Heron* shot past her. In the bow, Jesper and Stefan laughed aloud and shouted insults at the rowing boat's crew.

"Quiet," ordered Hal, and they fell silent immediately. On the longboat, they could see one of the crew fumbling with a short recurve bow, trying to nock an arrow to the string while his companions floundered around him. Lydia's hand dropped to the quiver of bolts hanging from her belt and she withdrew one, fitting the notched end into the handle of her atlatl.

"If he looks like shooting, let him have it," Hal told her.

She nodded, saying nothing. Her eyes were riveted on the bowman, waiting to see if he could manage a steady position in the wildly rocking boat.

Luckily for him—for Lydia rarely missed at such a short range—as he was about to raise the bow, one of his companions lurched and fell against him, knocking him off his thwart and sending the bow clattering into the bottom of the boat.

"We're clear," Lydia said quietly, unclipping the dart and returning it to her quiver. Hal glanced once behind him and nodded, satisfied. It always galled him to pay a toll for the simple act of sailing past a town. The people of Krall didn't own the river, he thought. There was no reason he should pay them to travel on it.

Stig was grinning, admiring the neat way his skirl had sidestepped the guard boat.

"They'll be expecting us when we come back," he said.

Hal shrugged. "They can expect all they like. I'm not paying them."

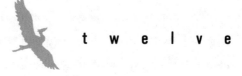

It was a different matter a day later when they reached the town of Bayrath. It was a major town on the river, much larger than Krall. And it was sited where the riverbanks came closer together, leaving a gap of barely one hundred meters between them.

Seeing an opportunity for profit, the town council had built a heavy boom across the river—a series of large logs lying nine-tenths submerged and held together by heavy chains. Two boom vessels were moored, one at either end, with windlasses and cables to pull the two halves of the boom aside, allowing ships to pass through.

Needless to say, this didn't happen until each ship had paid a substantial toll.

Stig watched his father leaning idly on the rail, studying the town as they approached it.

The young first mate felt somewhat conflicted about his father. Stig had spent most of his life wanting to know what it was like to have a father on hand to guide and advise him, to share his triumphs and adversities. He knew other members of the brotherband had this sort of relationship with their fathers and he envied them.

At the same time, he had grown up resenting this unknown figure, who had now suddenly reappeared in his life. Olaf had deserted him and his mother, and left them to bear the shame of his theft and his betrayal of his own crew. When Olaf reappeared, Stig hoped he might provide some reason for his actions, or at least show some sort of repentance. Yet when Olaf referred to the past, he showed no real sign of regret for what he had done. He mentioned it in more or less casual terms—*After I left here years ago.* He hadn't acknowledged the wrong he had done, to his shipmates and to his wife and young son. He hadn't apologized or shown any sign of remorse. He had alluded to the fact that his life on the run had been difficult, but the overall feeling was that this had been more the fault of others than due to any of his own actions.

Stig's expectation that he might finally get to know his father had been denied. Olaf showed no special interest in his son, other than to say he needed help and had nowhere else to turn. Since they had left Hallasholm Stig had waited, hoping that sooner or later Olaf might draw him aside and apologize for his desertion, that he might provide some compelling reason for having left Stig and Hannah behind. But such a moment hadn't happened. They'd had a few brief conversations during the trip so far but, overall, they had been inconclusive.

Now it occurred to Stig that perhaps his father was ashamed, and couldn't find a way to show it. Maybe it was up to Stig to make the first approach. Maybe then the floodgates would open. As it was, with each of them staying aloof and not offering any opportunity for a more open dialog, things would remain awkward and unresolved. So maybe the first approach was up to him.

Coming to a decision, he strolled over to the railing, trying to keep his manner casual. Olaf looked up from his perusal of the river and nodded a greeting.

"That's Bayrath," Stig said, nodding his head toward the sprawling buildings on the river bank. He forced a smile. "We had a lively time here the first time we came upriver."

Olaf looked only mildly interested. "Oh?"

Stig continued. "Zavac, the pirate we were chasing, had bribed the Gatmeister here to detain us. He was a nasty piece of work called Doutro—as crooked as a dog's hind leg, he was. He impounded the ship and had us all arrested."

Olaf raised an eyebrow. "That was careless of you all. Didn't Hal foresee that something like that might happen?"

Stig shook his head. "How could he? This sort of thing was new to us. We were pretty young and inexperienced. Maybe we were a little naive, in hindsight."

Olaf snorted. "A little? A lot, it sounds like. How did you get out of his jail?"

Stig's smile became more genuine now and he glanced down the length of the ship to where Lydia was sitting cross-legged on the central deck, setting new vanes on her atlatl darts.

"That was Lydia's doing. She was terrific."

"Really?" Olaf seemed determined not to be impressed by any

- 97 -

of this. "I suppose she used her feminine wiles to get you out." He regarded the dark-haired girl for several seconds. "Not that she seems to have too many of them," he added. "She dresses like a boy."

Stig straightened up, offended. Lydia was a good friend, and a member of the brotherband who had proven her worth on more than one occasion. He resented Olaf's sneering reference to her.

"Do you expect her to wear dresses and petticoats on board ship?" he asked. "She can look very pretty when she's dressed up. Very feminine," he added, feeling the inadequacy of the words.

Olaf laughed dismissively, holding his hands up as if to ward off Stig's anger. "Steady on!" he said. "I didn't mean to criticize!"

But he had, Stig realized. His father seemed to be unimpressed by anyone other than himself, and Stig felt obliged to make him understand just what Lydia had done in Bayrath.

"Sounded as if you did," he said, then went on. "But what she did was overpower her guard, escape through a third-story window, climb over the roof and jump across an alley to an adjoining building. Then she made her way to ground level, got on board the ship without being seen and fetched Jesper's lockpicking tools. Without her, we never would have got out of that jail."

Olaf refused to show any signs of regard for the girl's exploits. "Well, you shouldn't have been in there in the first place."

Stig moved a little closer, confronting him. "Really? And what would you have done?" he challenged.

But Olaf wouldn't be pinned down by his direct challenge. "I wouldn't have got myself arrested," he said.

Their gazes locked for several seconds, his disdainful, Stig's angry. Then the younger man turned and walked away.

Olaf shrugged. "What did I say?" he asked, of nobody in particular.

Hal brought the Heron up into the wind and heaved to. They lay rocking gently on the smoothly flowing river, studying Bayrath. Little seemed to have changed since they had last seen it.

"I wonder what became of our friend Doutro?" Thorn said.

"Didn't I tell you?" Hal replied. "Last time we came through here, I heard he had been betrayed by his assistant," Hal said. "He was killed in his bath and the new man took over." Men like Doutro—cunning, treacherous and corrupt—rarely stayed in power too long. There was always someone ready to supplant them, and as a rule, they had done little to win the loyalty of those under them.

"Can't say I'm sorry to hear it," Thorn replied. Doutro had arranged for Hal to be badly beaten when they were held prisoner and the one-armed sea wolf had always itched for revenge.

"Well, I'm sure the new man won't be any better," Hal said. "They rarely are in cases like this. But at least he won't hold a grudge against us."

Doutro, of course, had sworn vengeance on the *Heron* and his crew after his beautiful ship had burned to the waterline.

Thorn grunted. "He'll still try to gouge us and cheat us and overcharge us," he said.

Hal shrugged. "True. But it'll all be in the name of business. It'll be nothing personal."

"That's not much comfort," Thorn growled. His hand strayed to the hilt of his saxe.

Hal grinned at him. "We could always sail back the way we came and run the Wildwater Rift again," he suggested.

Thorn shook his head. "No thanks."

Stig, who had been an amused spectator to their conversation, now weighed in. "I second that," he said. The passage down the Rift, a wild, fast-flowing channel filled with rocks and rapids, had been a hair-raising experience.

"And I third, fourth and fifth it," Ingvar called from amidships.

Hal regarded his huge friend with amusement. "Can one person act as third, fourth and fifth in a vote?" he asked.

Ingvar nodded solemnly. "When they're as big as me, they can."

T hey've seen us," Jesper said from the for'ard lookout
position.

That was hardly surprising. A ship like *Heron*
could hardly expect to go unnoticed for long. After
all, she was the only craft of any size on the river at the moment.
Hal glanced toward the town. Several men had come out onto the
toll office dock and were watching them, using their hands to shield
their eyes from the glare of the sun. Like the toll officers at Krall,
they used their free hands to beckon the little ship in alongside the
dock.

They had also attracted the interest of the six-man crew of the
nearest boom vessel. Their main duty was to man the capstan that
opened and closed the eastern half of the boom. Another similar
ship was moored close to the western bank.

"We'll head for the boom ship," Hal said, pointing toward it. "Ulf, Wulf, Stefan and Jesper, oars, please."

The four designated crewmen clambered into the rowing wells and ran out their oars.

"Give way," Hal said quietly, and they leaned back against the shafts, feet braced against the hull ribs, sending the ship gliding through the water. Hal steered for the boom ship.

"Stig, be ready to pass a line," he ordered.

The first mate made his way to the bow, where he readied a line, coiling it in his left hand, preparing to throw it to the other ship. The boom ship's crew made several gestures, pointing to the toll dock onshore. But Hal ignored them. Judging his moment, he gave the order to cease rowing and the *Heron* ran on through the calm water, her speed gradually falling off until she stopped, rolling gently, a mere three meters from the other craft. Stig tossed the line he had ready, and after a moment's hesitation, one of the boom ship's crew seized it and hauled in, bringing the two ships alongside one another. Stig tossed a wickerwork fender over the bow to protect the side of the ship as the two hulls bumped gently together. Then he made the line fast.

"Edvin, stand by the tiller, please," Hal ordered. Then he gestured to Thorn and the four oarsmen, who had now run their oars in and stowed them along the line of the hull.

"You lot, get your weapons and come with me."

The five crewmen picked up their weapons—an assortment of swords and battleaxes, which were kept ready by the rowing benches—and scrambled onto the center deck after him. Hal was buckling his sword belt as he walked toward the bow. Thorn, who would normally go into a fight armed with the huge club Hal had made for him, was caught unprepared. He snatched up a sword belt and slung it over his right shoulder.

Even left-handed, he was a formidable warrior.

Olaf followed a few paces behind the skirl, his hand dropping to the hilt of the long, slightly curved sword that he wore on his left hip.

"Do you need me?" he asked.

Hal hesitated. He had no doubt that Olaf was a capable warrior, but he didn't know him and didn't know how he might respond to orders. The upcoming situation could be tricky. Hal had no intention of going ashore to pay the toll. If the new Gatmeister proved to be obstructionist or excessively greedy, they could be held here for days—or worse. Hal would pay the toll, but he wasn't going to be delayed and he was prepared to use force if necessary. He knew how his own men would respond to his commands if there were trouble. But Olaf was an unknown quantity.

"I'll let you know," he said finally. Then, as he was passing Lydia, he jerked his head toward the crew of the boom vessel, clustered curiously along the rail of their ship.

"Keep an eye on them," he said, and she nodded, fingering the atlatl handle at her belt. It always felt comforting to go into a potentially dangerous situation with Lydia guarding their backs. She could load and cast an atlatl dart in mere seconds, with devastating accuracy.

He reached the bow, held firmly against the side of the boom vessel, and stepped up onto the railing. The uptilted bow of the *Heron* was half a meter higher than the other ship. As he prepared to step down, one of the boom vessel's crew—presumably the captain—gestured for him to stop.

"Coming aboard," Hal said.

The other man looked flustered. "But . . . you can't. You have to go . . ." He fluttered his hands toward the shore and the toll office set on the dock there.

"Stand aside," Hal said. His tone didn't invite any discussion.

He stepped down onto the other ship's rail, then dropped lightly to the deck. The captain was forced to make way for him. Behind him, Hal heard the thud of feet as his men followed him aboard.

The captain backed up a pace or two, looking round nervously as he took in the situation. He had five men with him but they were unarmed, except for the knives they all wore at their waists. They were facing an equal number of armed men, who had swarmed aboard without any warning and without giving them a chance to resist. As he watched, Stig came aboard. Ingvar had hurried forward to hand him his ax, and the first mate now shoved it through the retaining ring on his belt. That made seven warriors in all, armed with a variety of axes, swords and saxe knives. And those seven were all Skandians, he could see—men from the north who were famous for their proficiency in battle. This group were young, except for the one-handed, bearded man, who had followed their captain aboard. But they looked capable enough.

"You have to pay the toll," he said weakly, trying to assert his authority but failing.

Hal nodded pleasantly. "And I'm prepared to do just that," he said. "How much is it these days?"

The Bayrathian captain shook his head several times. "No, no, no," he said. "You have to pay it at the toll office. You have to see the Gatmeister."

"That's not going to happen," Hal said firmly. "I don't have time to get mixed up with gatmeisters. They're usually crooked and spend all their energy trying to cheat sailors passing through. Plus, whoever he is, he'll probably hold us up while he haggles over a price. And I don't have time for that. We're in a hurry."

In spite of himself, the captain found himself nodding slightly. This Skandian's assessment of gatmeisters was a pretty accurate one, he had to admit.

Hal saw the movement of his head and seized the advantage. "Tell me the toll," he said, "and I'll pay you. Plus I'll pay you the usual . . . *commission* . . . the Gatmeister adds on." He hesitated meaningfully over the word *commission*. A more accurate term would be *bribe*. "You can choose to share that with him or not. It doesn't matter to me."

He saw a gleam of interest in the captain's eyes. As he had guessed, the bribes paid to the senior officials never filtered their way down the line to men like these.

"And if I refuse?" the captain asked, but Hal could sense his resolve was faltering since the mention of the commission.

He smiled disarmingly. "Well, we'll throw you and your men overboard, open the boom ourselves and sail upriver." He let that message sink in and then added in a deceptively mild tone, "And we'll burn your ship when we go."

A light of recognition shone in the captain's eyes. He looked back at *Heron* to confirm his suspicion, then said nervously, "You're *that* ship! The one who burned Doutro's ship." His tone said that he believed Hal's threat was no empty one.

Hal smiled grimly. "We have been back once or twice since then," he pointed out. "But yes, we might have accidentally set the Gatmeister's ship on fire when we were leaving."

Thorn smothered a short bark of laughter. If tossing a burning torch onto the decks of the ship constituted "accidentally" setting it on fire, Hal's description was accurate.

The captain glanced quickly at him, then back to Hal. He straightened his shoulders as he came to a decision.

"The toll will be eleven korona," he said. "You can pay here. No need to go ashore."

Hal smiled at him. "Price has gone up since last time," he remarked.

The captain shrugged. "That's what happens."

Hal untied his purse from his belt, opened it and counted out the money. Then he added a four-korona gold piece to the small pile in his hand.

"And this is for you and your men," he said. It was worth it to make sure they left no hard feelings behind. After all, for all his talk of throwing the boom vessel crew overboard and opening the boom themselves, they still had to come back this way, eventually. The captain grinned eagerly as he saw the extra payment, and Hal knew he had made a good decision.

"My men will appreciate it," he said, and there was a murmur of agreement from his crew. He swept the money into his own purse and reached out to shake Hal's hand.

"My name's Zigmund," he said. "When you come back down-river, if I'm not here, mention my name."

"I'll do that," Hal said, then he turned to his own crew, who were standing by expectantly. "Back to the *Heron*, everyone," he ordered, and they clambered quickly back on board. As they settled into their positions, one of Zigmund's crew was already rowing a small skiff out to the center of the river, where he unlocked the two ends of the boom. Once it was clear, he waved and began paddling back. The rest of the crew were manning the capstan, fitted with four long wooden bars. At Zigmund's order, they leaned their weight on the bars and began to tramp round in a small circle, turning the capstan and winding in the cable that opened and closed the boom.

The cable ran out to a buoy moored thirty meters upriver. As they wound it in, it pulled the boom to one side, opening a gap between the eastern and western sections. Hal took the tiller and ordered his men to the oars. As Zigmund tossed their bowline back on board, *Heron* backed water for a few meters to clear the boom vessel, then went ahead with the tiller over to port, swinging the slim bow to starboard and heading for the middle of the river. They slid smoothly through the gap in the boom and he waved a farewell to Zigmund on board the boom vessel. The man in the skiff was already paddling back to relock the boom as Zigmund's crew reversed the direction of the capstan, pulling the two ends together again.

"In oars," Hal ordered, glancing up at the wind telltale. "Hoist the starboard sail."

Ulf and Wulf were ready for the order. Hal felt the little ship gathering speed and adjusted his course toward a distant headland. The Dan here was broad and deep and relatively slow flowing. Lydia leaned on the sternpost beside Hal's steering position.

"That went well," she said.

"Saved us a lot of time," he agreed. "If we'd gone ashore, we'd probably still be haggling with the Gatmeister." He grinned. "He probably would have wanted to buy you as a housemaid."

Lydia smiled. "I doubt it," she said. "My references aren't too good in that department."

"I guess you're not cut out to be the demure housemaid type," Hal said.

She nodded, the smile fading. "Not on your life," she said. "I don't do demure."

chapter fourteen

The river was wide and smooth, the sun was shining and the wind was constant out of the northeast.

Heron bowled along easily, zigzagging on a constant port tack. The V-shaped ripples of her wake spread out on the glassy surface of the river behind her, eventually reaching the banks on either side, where they set the reeds and water grasses bobbing gently. From time to time, a waterbird, alarmed by the disturbance, would splash its way out onto the river, squawking in annoyance.

Ulf and Wulf sat at ease by the sheets and halyards. There was little for them to do. As Hal changed direction for each leg of the zigzag, they would haul in or ease the sheets as required. Then they could relax again.

The other crew members had even less to keep them busy. They passed the time by attending to small personal chores—repairing clothes or items of harness, sharpening weapons and so forth. Only Stefan was occupied, perched on the bow-post lookout, searching the banks either side for the first sign of a potential enemy.

Jesper, having completed his stint as lookout, was relaxing on deck near the twins, practicing his lockpicking skills. He had a canvas tool roll that contained picks of differing sizes and several examples of locks that he practiced on. As the twins watched, he inserted one of his tools into a large iron padlock on his lap and twisted it a few degrees. Then he slipped another rod into the lock and seemed to jiggle it slightly. Within a few seconds, there was a loud *click!* and the lock sprang open.

"That looked easy enough," Wulf said.

Jesper glanced up at him and smiled tolerantly, pushing the haft of the lock back into its recess and clicking it shut again.

"Looks can be deceiving," Ulf said loftily.

Wulf rounded on him. "You think so?" he challenged.

Ulf shrugged. "If it's as easy as it looks, I'd like to see you do it."

Wulf snorted derisively. "I could if I wanted to," he said. Since Jesper never lent his tools to anyone, he knew there was no risk that he would be asked to live up to his words.

Then, to his surprise, Jesper offered him the padlock and the two lockpicks. "Go ahead," he said.

Wulf went to reach out, then hesitated. In truth, he had no idea what Jesper had just done with the lock. He waved a hand in the air, refusing the proffered tools.

"Show me again," he said.

Jesper nodded and took the lock and the picks back. With Wulf watching like a hawk, he inserted the first pick, one with a flattened end, into the lock and turned it slightly. Then, as Wulf leaned forward to watch closely, he took the other pick—a slender rod shaped into a small half-moon at the working end—and inserted it into the key slot above the first tool. He gently worked it into the lock, moving it slightly back and forth. Listening carefully, Wulf heard three faint clicks, then the lock sprang open.

Jesper grinned. He removed the picks, pushed the lock closed once more and offered the three pieces to Wulf. "Go ahead," he said.

Wulf hesitated, then his brother cackled.

"Yes. Go ahead," Ulf said.

There was nothing for it. Wulf took the lock and the picks, handling them gingerly, and turned them round in his hands, studying them, not knowing what to do next. Ulf cackled once more. Wulf shoved the first pick into the lock, as he had seen Jesper do, and turned it firmly. He glanced up at Jesper to see if he was doing it correctly. Jesper's expression was noncommittal, so he proceeded with the second pick. He had seen Jesper slide the curved end section into the key slot, so he mimicked the action and jiggled it energetically.

Nothing happened. The lock remained closed. Jesper eyed Wulf with amusement as he jiggled some more, his actions becoming increasingly violent as the lock remained obdurate.

"Do you have the faintest idea what you're doing?" Jesper asked.

"Of course I do," Wulf snapped.

"Of course he doesn't," Ulf said at the same time.

Angrily, Wulf shoved the lock and the picks toward his brother. "Let's see you do better," he challenged.

But Ulf held up his hands in a gesture of refusal. "I never said

I could," he pointed out. "You were the one who said it looked easy."

"Well, it does . . . when he does it," Wulf retorted, indicating Jesper with his thumb, and still holding the padlock with the two picks inserted into its innards.

Jesper gave a short laugh. "I have had a bit of practice," he said.

Wulf handed him the lock and the tools and spread his hands in a defeated gesture. "Just what are you doing with all that jiggling and joggling?"

Jesper shook his head gravely. "Jiggling, maybe. But never joggling. Joggling has connotations of violence to it and you need to be gentle when you're persuading a lock to open."

"You have to jiggle gently," Ulf said in a pontifical tone, and Wulf glared at him while Jesper responded with a smile.

"Exactly," he said. "Here, take a look."

While he had been talking, he had taken a small screwdriver from his tool wallet. There were four screws holding the side plate of the lock in place. He undid them and removed the plate, exposing the inner workings of the lock. The twins leaned forward eagerly to see, Wulf angrily pushing his brother's head aside when he blocked his vision.

"See?" said Jesper. "The tongue of the lock is held closed by these three small tumblers. When you turn the pick slightly— about one-eighth of a turn—you align them with three sockets. You turned it too far," he told Wulf, looking up for a few seconds.

Wulf, for once, didn't argue when he was told he had done something wrong. He nodded, intent on Jesper's demonstration.

"Now," Jesper continued, "once those little tumblers are aligned with the sockets, you slide the curved tool in . . ." He proceeded to do so.

"Gently," Ulf said in a lofty tone.

"Shut up," Wulf told him, eyes locked on what Jesper was doing.

"You use the curved section to feel for each of the tumblers in turn . . ."

He did so, *gently* moving the curved surface of the pick over the metal tumbler. As it came into position, there was a faint click and the tumbler slid home into its recess.

"Then the second . . . ," he said. Another click.

"Then the third." A final click and the lock sprang open. Both twins nodded. He removed the picks, closed the lock once more and handed lock and picks to Ulf.

"Try it," he said.

Ulf took the lock and laid it in his lap, then he inserted the pick with the flattened end and began to twist.

"Not too far," Jesper warned him. "Now the curved pick."

With the tumblers and recesses aligned, Ulf slid the second pick into the lock and let it ride gently onto the first tumbler. He moved it slightly and the tumbler clicked into its recess. Repeating the action twice more, he had the lock open after twenty seconds of intense concentration.

"I did it!" he said triumphantly.

Wulf scowled. "I don't know why you bother with it," he said. "Why not just take the side plate off and open it that way?"

Jesper regarded him tolerantly. "This is a demonstration lock I keep for practice," he said. "Locks usually have the side plate riveted or welded in place. Not screwed."

"Oh," said Wulf, chastened.

Ulf, feeling a little superior about the fact that he had gotten the lock open in such a relatively short time, handed it to his brother. "Try it now," he said. He was unable to resist adding: "Jiggle it gently."

Wulf took the lock and the picks and began to work on it as he had seen Ulf do. But he was angry and that made his movements clumsy. He jiggled wildly for some time with no result.

"Take it easy," Jesper said eventually.

Wulf took a deep breath and slowed down. Within a few seconds, he had sprung the first tumbler. The other two followed in quick succession.

"Got it!" he said triumphantly.

"Took your time, didn't you?" his brother said.

Wulf scowled. There was no reply possible. It was obvious that he had taken far longer than his brother. Instead, he removed the picks, closed the lock and repeated his actions. This time, it took him less than thirty seconds to open the lock.

"That's pretty good," Jesper told him. But Ulf had already snatched the lock back and opened it even more quickly.

"D'you think this is such a good idea, Jes?" Hal asked. Fascinated by what was going on, he had left the tiller in Stig's hands and walked for'ard to watch.

Jesper looked up, a question on his face. "How's that, Hal?"

"You're teaching these two irresponsible idiots how to open locks when they don't have a key. Is that such a great idea?"

Jesper considered the question. "You may be right," he said. He took the lock back from Ulf and quickly reattached the side plate. "That might make things a little tougher," he said, and for the next half hour, the twins struggled to repeat their achievement. But they found it considerably harder when they couldn't see the workings of the lock. Ulf managed to open it once, with great difficulty. Wulf was still trying when Hal resumed the tiller and called them back to duty.

"Bend in the river!" he called. "We'll go about!"

Wulf placed the padlock and picks down in a safe spot and moved to the halyards, ready to come about on Hal's command. As one sail came down and the other soared up the mast to replace it, Hal muttered an aside to Stig, standing close by the steering platform.

"That's the first time I've seen one of them do something better than the other," he said.

Stig nodded. "Maybe they should have made lockpicking the tiebreaker in their Maktig contest," he said.

His friend grinned in agreement.

Heron settled on course for the next leg of the river—a stretch of wide water several kilometers long. The twins went back to their lockpicking exercise. There was a cry of triumph from Wulf as he finally managed to unlock the padlock, working blind. Instantly, Ulf snatched lock and picks back from him and went to work himself. Edvin, watching them critically, made his way aft. He shared Hal's reservations about having the twins learn how to open locked doors.

"Are you planning on putting in at Amalon?" Edvin asked.

Amalon was the next large town along the river, where trading convoys assembled for the run down to Drogha or the Constant Sea, past the notorious pirate haven of Raguza.

"I thought I would," Hal replied. "I'd like to have a word with Mannoc and check conditions on the lower part of the river." Mannoc was the skipper of a fighting ship. He organized armed escorts for the convoys, and the Herons had worked with him on several occasions.

"Do you need more supplies?" Hal added.

Edvin shrugged. "I could manage without them, but I always like to restock when we have a chance. Particularly coffee. We're always running low on that."

"That settles it," Hal told him. "We'll definitely put in."

From amidships, they heard another triumphant cry from Ulf as he sprung the lock.

"Perhaps we could drop those two off," Edvin said sourly.

"Oh, I don't know," Hal replied. "At least they're too busy to bicker."

And as he said it, a spirited argument broke out between the two sail handlers, as Ulf declared his superiority over his brother once more.

"Spoke too soon," Hal said morosely.

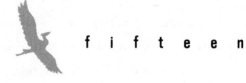

he harbor at Amalon was a mass of ships. The constantly moving forest of masts and rigging made it difficult to single out any one ship, and as *Heron* was escorted to a berth by a harried guard boat, Hal looked in vain for a sight of *Seahawk*, Mannoc's slender warship. Amalon was a large, busy river port, and he knew this was where Mannoc usually assembled his convoys for the trip downriver to Drogha.

As they finally made *Heron* secure at a berth between two traders, he hailed the guard boat's helmsman.

"Mannoc and *Seahawk*!" he called. "Are they in port?"

The helmsman paused, his face twisted in thought. "He's still here. He's taking a convoy downriver later this week. *Seahawk* is moored on the far side of the harbor." He waved a hand vaguely in the general direction. Then he gave an order to his oarsmen, and the boat pulled quickly away. There were more ships coming into the harbor, and secure berths had to be found for all of them.

"We'll catch up with him tomorrow," Hal said to Thorn. "I'd like to get a briefing on the situation farther down river, toward Raguza. Mannoc's always up-to-date on what the river pirates are up to."

The old sea wolf nodded. "Always a good idea to know what you're sailing into."

Hal glanced around and saw the ship was moored properly, fenders were over the side to protect the hull and the oars and sails stowed. "We'll go ashore," he said. He grinned at Edvin. "No reflection on your cooking, but I fancy a meal in a nice inn for a change—where the table stays still."

Edvin smiled in return. "I agree," he said. "Besides, food always tastes better when someone else cooks it for you."

"Whose turn is it to stand harbor watch?" Hal asked.

Ingvar held up a massive hand. "That'd be me," he said. "I'm happy to stay. And Kloof can keep me company."

"I'll stay too," Lydia said.

Ingvar smiled widely. He and Lydia were close friends and he enjoyed her company. For her part, she tended to be uneasy in crowded, noisy places like inns and taverns. She had spent a good deal of her early life stalking and hunting in the silence of the forests of her homeland.

Lydia indicated a food stall at the end of the jetty. "We can get a meal from there," she said.

Ingvar nodded. The stall was selling grilled meat on skewers, cooked over a charcoal fire. Even at a distance, the aroma was enough to set his stomach rumbling.

"Good idea. I could manage two or three of those kebabs," he said. Then he thought about it and added, "Or four or five, come to think of it."

As the sun sank below the western horizon, outlining the buildings of the town, the rest of the crew prepared to go ashore.

"Stick together," Hal cautioned them. Amalon wasn't a particularly lawless town, but a harbor front was a harbor front and they had no time to go chasing after any crew members who might get into trouble. They trooped down the jetty, with Hal, Stig and Thorn in the lead and the others following, talking animatedly. The chance to get ashore and have a good meal had put everyone in good spirits. Everyone except Olaf. He walked alone, a few meters behind the leading group and in front of the rest of the crew.

In spite of their earlier disagreement, Stig felt a surge of sympathy for Olaf, sensing the loneliness his father must be feeling. He nudged Hal with his elbow and jerked his head toward the lone figure. Hal turned and looked, frowned slightly, then stopped.

"Come and join us," he said. He really had no wish to make Olaf feel unwelcome. In fact, the sooner they established good relations between him and the rest of the crew, the better it would be. They were probably going to be facing some hard fighting in the near future and they would have to rely upon one another. Excluding him from the group didn't make sense. He was a skilled warrior—Thorn had told him that much—and he'd be a valuable ally in a fight.

But not if Olaf felt no loyalty or connection to the group as a whole.

Olaf smiled, nodded to his son and increased his pace to make up the gap between him and the three companions. He settled between them.

"So," Thorn said, clapping his left hand on Olaf's shoulder as the other man came level. "Tell us about the Emperor's palace at Byzantos. Pretty fancy, is it?"

"It's more a fortress than a palace," Olaf replied. "The whole thing is surrounded by massive stone walls—four meters thick at the base and two at the top. They run round three sides of the city, with the fourth side protected by the sea. There are towers and redoubts every forty meters, each one capable of covering its two neighbors with arrows and other missiles."

"How high are the walls?" Hal asked. He was always interested in tactical matters.

"Five meters at most points. Sometimes they drop down to four. But the *Empress*," he said, correcting Thorn's reference to the Emperor's palace, "maintains a large garrison and they can man the walls along their entire length."

"Sounds like a hard nut to crack," Thorn observed.

Olaf nodded. "Hasn't been done in over a hundred years," he said. "That's why the corsairs waited until Constantus was outside the fortress before they snatched him."

"What about the Empress's living quarters?" Hal asked. "I assume they're not as stark as a fortress?"

"No. She has a central building, with a huge meeting hall and suites of rooms. There's a central tower as well—eight stories of it—which provides an outlook over the entire fortress complex. And the fittings and furnishing are as lavish as anything you'll find anywhere. Beautiful wall hangings, satin and silk drapes and soft carpets. The servants are specially trained and the kitchen staff are all experts. All in all, it's a wonderful place to live." There was a note of sadness in his voice.

"Except for the Empress," Stig said.

His father nodded glumly. "Except for the Empress. She's prone to terrible fits of anger when things don't go her way. She's a hard woman to please and she'll punish a clumsy servant at the drop of a hat. Or the drop of a plate," he added, with a small smile.

"I thought this boy, Constantus, was the Emperor," Hal said. "Isn't she the Regent in his place?"

Olaf pursed his lips. "Technically, yes. But she chooses to call herself Empress. Nobody uses the term Regent in front of her."

"What would happen if they did?" Stig asked.

His father frowned. "I'm not sure. She's a very unpredictable woman and you don't want to get on the wrong side of her. Life in the palace can be pretty tense. You're always on tenterhooks waiting for her next outburst—and hoping it won't concern you."

"Sounds like fun," Hal commented.

Olaf shrugged. "There are compensations. The pay is good— very good, in fact—and living conditions in the palace are quite luxurious. We enjoy the best of food and wine and ale. The rooms are beautifully appointed and far more comfortable than the normal soldier's accommodation. It's a big step up from Ragnak's smoky old timber lodge in Hallasholm."

"It's Erak's now," Thorn told him. "He replaced Ragnak as Oberjarl after the Temujai invasion."

Olaf nodded. "Of course. I'd forgotten that."

"Here we are," Hal said, indicating a sign hanging above one of the buildings lining the wide main street. It depicted a side of beef being carved with a seaman's cutlass, the slices appearing to fall off the bottom of the sign. Below the illustrative sign was a name-plate—THE CUT OF BEEF.

They pushed open the doors and went inside. It was a big room, but it was crowded with customers and their noise. Hal looked around for an empty table and his face fell. He'd been looking forward to this meal, and now it appeared the inn was full.

He needn't have worried. The proprietor was a former trading captain whose ship had been saved from pirates by the *Heron* on a journey downriver. He saw the group standing uncertainly just inside the door and bellowed a greeting. He shoved his way through the crowded tables to embrace Hal and Thorn.

"Welcome, friends! Welcome! You're always welcome in Piko's Cut of Beef!" he roared.

Hal indicated the crowded tables around them. "You don't seem to have room for us."

Piko threw his arms wide. "I'll make room!" he declared. He looked around, saw a table where the occupants had finished eating and advanced on them. "You lot! Clear the table! I have honored guests who need to sit here."

"But we were here first!" the leader of the other group protested. He looked angry at the thought that he was being ordered to move.

Piko hesitated. He wanted to make room for Hal and his crew, but these men were regular customers and good spenders. He didn't want to offend them too much. Finally, he hit upon a solution.

"It's a fine night," he said. "I'll put a table outside for you. And there'll be a free cask of my best ale on it."

That swung the deal. The group evacuated the table swiftly,

and two of Piko's servers carried a spare table from the back room through the restaurant and set it outside the door, close up against the wall of the inn, much to the interest of curious passersby. A third servant followed with a cask of ale and a string of tankards, the sight of which evoked a loud cheer from the mollified patrons.

"If you're giving away ale, they can have our table!" cried a member of another group, and there was a general roar of laughter.

Pleased that he had saved the situation, Piko beamed at his new customers. "You'll be having beef, of course?"

"Of course!" they all chorused in reply, and more laughter followed. Within a few minutes, a smoking joint of beef was carried to the table on a wooden platter, and the proprietor began to swiftly carve slices from it. The crew helped themselves, then dished up the fragrant vegetables that followed—potatoes and sweet potatoes, baked onions, green beans cooked with small chunks of bacon, and crusty fresh loaves of warm bread.

Silence fell, broken only by the sounds of dedicated munching and the occasional sigh of pleasure as the hungry crew demolished the meal. When he was done, Thorn pushed back his chair and emitted a thunderous belch.

"Better not do that at the Empress's palace," Hal said.

Thorn waved the comment aside. "Belching is a high form of praise," he said with great dignity.

"Plus it could be handy for use as a foghorn," said a familiar voice from behind Hal. The young skirl leapt to his feet, turning to face the tall, broad-shouldered warrior behind him.

"Mannoc!" he cried. "It's good to see you!"

A delighted smile lit Hal's face, and he moved to embrace the other man. Mannoc returned the gesture, then stepped back and surveyed the table, where the rest of the Herons had risen to their feet. There followed several minutes of greeting, embraces and handshakes as Mannoc moved around the table to renew old friendships. He looked quizzically at Hal.

"I notice a couple of faces missing," he said. "I trust nothing has happened to Lydia, or that giant Ingvar?"

Hal shook his head and called to a passing waiter to bring another stool. "They're fine," he said. "They volunteered to keep an eye on the ship. How are things with you?"

Mannoc shrugged. "Much the same. The pirates keep trying to dash out of Raguza and capture merchant ships and we keep fighting them off. It's an endless cycle. Matter of fact, I'm taking a convoy downriver the day after tomorrow and I could use an extra escort. Any chance you'd be interested?"

Hal hesitated, frowning slightly. "We're on a tight deadline," he said. "We've got a job in Byzantos." He indicated Olaf, who was a keen listener to the conversation. "Olaf here commands the palace guard and he needs our help on a mission."

He thought it was simpler to say that Olaf was the guard commander still, rather than go into the detail of how he'd been dismissed and handed an ultimatum to rescue the boy emperor.

Mannoc pursed his lips, considering what Hal had said. "Well, you might make better time in company with us," he said. "It's a fast convoy—six traders and two escorts. So we wouldn't hold you up—and if you join up with us, we should be a big enough force to discourage most of the river rats. They've been particularly active this season."

"Maybe," said Hal, not yet convinced.

Mannoc continued. "On the other hand, if you travel alone, you're almost sure to be attacked—over and over again. And that could delay you a lot more than if you sailed with us. *Heron* could be damaged and you might have losses among your crew."

Hal glanced at Thorn and Stig to see their reaction.

Thorn shrugged. "He's got a point," he said, and Stig nodded agreement.

Hal turned to Olaf. "Olaf? What do you think? It's your mission, after all."

The former guard commander was already nodding. "Makes sense to me," he said. "Eight ships would make a pretty formidable force. Whereas if we're traveling alone, we could be attacked by every bit of riffraff on the river."

Mannoc nodded and added the clincher. "I'll pay you half again the usual rate."

The four Skandians exchanged looks. Hal could see by their expressions that the others were in favor of the idea. And the money would be useful. Escorting convoys paid well.

"All right. We're in," he said, and reached out to shake Mannoc's hand to clinch the deal.

Mannoc grinned in pleasure. "Glad to hear it," he said. "We're leaving in the morning, at the ninth hour, day after tomorrow. We'll assemble out in the river. It's too crowded in the harbor at the moment. Now," he said, looking round the table, "does Piko have any of that good ale left in his cellar?"

T wo days later, at mid-morning, *Heron* slipped out of the harbor at Drogha. The convoy preceded her by half an hour—a suggestion made by Mannoc when they had met at the Cut of Beef.

"Word will have gone downriver that we plan on leaving to-day," he said. "And that we only have two escorts. If you hang back a little, you might catch a few of 'em napping if they try to surprise us."

Hal agreed. *Heron* was a fast ship and, if pirates attacked the fleet, she could easily make up the distance and take the raiders by surprise.

"If we're attacked," the escort leader continued, "I'll shoot a signal arrow in the air. If you see that, come running. And have the giant crossbow ready for action."

A signal arrow was one that trailed a ribbon of colored smoke and was fitted with a high-pitched whistle. It gave out a visual and audible signal when shot straight up into the air—both of which would be obvious for at least a kilometer.

The wind was light and steady, and Hal turned the ship upstream. They were yet to reach the elbow bend where the river split, with the South Dan flowing south-southwest toward the Constant Sea and the North Dan—the arm they were currently on—flowing north to the Stormwhite. Once they made that turn, they would be traveling downstream, with the current. The river went downhill at that point, running down from the ridge where it had been traveling for a height of forty-five meters. A series of six barrages, or weirs, had been built to create a set of level pools as the river ran toward the Constant Sea. At the edge of each barrage, an open space, or sluice, had been left to allow the water to run downhill in a smooth and navigable slope. For ships traveling back upstream, there were wide paths alongside the bank, equipped with rollers and heaving tackles so that ships could be hauled bodily up the slope to the next pool.

On their first trip down the Dan, they had been denied the use of the sluices and had navigated the Wildwater Rift, a side stream that turned into a wild chute—making the downward passage on one wild swoop instead of a series of controlled descents.

"There's the turn," Thorn said quietly.

Hal put the ship about, swinging through the elbow bend onto the new arm of the river. At once, they felt the ship speed up, and the bank began to slip past them much faster, and the current now worked with them. They swung onto the first of the lakes created by the barrage. The open sluice was on the western bank, and Hal swung the ship toward it.

"Stig, Ingvar," he ordered. "Ready on the oars in case I need steerageway."

With the current behind them, there was always the chance that the water would move faster than the ship itself, rendering the rudder useless and making her unmanageable. As the gap in the barrage was no more than five meters across, Hal wanted to make sure she would respond instantly to the helm. The two oarsmen would provide extra thrust and, if necessary, they could haul the ship bodily onto a new course.

At first, there was no need for Stig and Ingvar to lend a hand. The ship continued to move faster than the river flowing around it and the rudder maintained its bite on the water. Hal lined up the gap in the barrage—a low wall of rocks and bare tree trunks—and gave the ship her head.

There was a sudden plunging motion as the bow dipped downward, and *Heron* accelerated into the gap. As the water course narrowed and the current moved faster, the rudder became ineffectual, and Hal had to shout orders to the two crewmen manning the oars, as they heaved on the shafts to keep the hull heading straight down.

The rest of the crew reached for handholds as the ship suddenly accelerated downhill. Then she was in the level water at the bottom of the chute. She hesitated for a moment in the eddy that formed there. Without needing orders, Stig and Ingvar heaved on the oars to pull her clear into the main river once more. The sail, which had been flapping uncertainly during the fast plunge, filled again with a dull *boom,* and the little ship accelerated away from the roiling water at the bottom of the chute.

Hal realized that his grip on the tiller had tightened during those few moments of wild, downhill plunging. He made a conscious effort to release the tension in his hands as *Heron* resumed her smooth, fast passage across the calm water.

They rounded a bend, switching to a new tack as they did so.

"There's the *Southwind,*" called Jesper from the bow lookout position. The *Southwind,* the last in line of the six trading ships, was two kilometers away. She had four oars out on each side and was maneuvering to run down the next chute.

"Ease the sheets," Hal called. "We don't want to get too close."

With the sail eased, their speed dropped a little, and he angled the ship across the river, steering a long zigzag course to let the convoy stay well ahead of them.

Olaf was standing close to the steering platform. He studied the heavily wooded banks of the river keenly.

"No sign of trouble so far," he remarked.

Hal shook his head. "They're unlikely to attack here in the lakes," he said. "The space is too restricted, with only the narrow chute if they need to make an escape. If they do attack, they'll do it farther downriver, where they have room to get away—and to take any prizes with them."

Olaf nodded and grunted agreement. Hal added, with a smile, "Mind you, it never hurts to expect the unexpected. Keep a good lookout."

"I'll do that," Olaf told him. Unconsciously, his hand touched the hilt of the curved sword at his waist.

Hal watched as *Southwind* negotiated the chute. He saw the hull dip, then accelerate forward. For a few seconds, he could see her tall mast above the barrage wall. Then that was gone as well. Judging that she had made it safely, he nudged the tiller and headed *Heron* for the gap. As they got closer, he felt the current quicken and the ship began to move faster.

"Ready oars," he said, and Stig and Ingvar prepared to row as he directed. They were a little off line for the chute, and Hal called his orders in a calm, but carrying, voice.

"Ingvar—three strokes. Stig, back water. Enough! Now, both together. Pull!"

As the ship straightened and she aligned with the gap, the two oarsmen heaved on their oars and she accelerated into the chute. Again, there was that momentary surge downward, and for a few seconds they all felt as if they had left their stomachs behind them. Then she flew down the chute, the water surface smooth and sleek with the speed of its passage. Again, there was a moment of hesitation at the foot of the chute.

"Both together!" Hal called, and the oars dragged her out of the uncertain current and back into the main river.

"This could get to be quite enjoyable," Olaf commented.

Thorn glanced at him. The guard commander didn't realize that Hal was making the passage of the chutes look a lot easier than it was. He had a deft touch on the tiller and a sure eye for angles and speed. A lesser helmsman could have let the ship's head fall off momentarily, in which case she would be swept broadside down the chute, with water pouring in over her downhill gunwales and the crew having to bail frantically.

"I'll be glad when we've cleared them," Hal replied. "Ulf! Wulf!" he called in a warning tone as the sail flapped briefly in an uncertain gust of wind. Instantly, the twins sprang to the sheets and hauled in, keeping the sail taut once more.

They saw *Southwind* again for a brief moment. Then she was lost to sight as a bend in the river intervened. When they reached the bend, there was no sign of the ships ahead of them. Hal scanned the river and pointed to the gap in the barrage wall. This time the chute was on the eastern side of the river, to accommodate a slight bend to the west.

"A couple more after this," he told Olaf. "Then it might get interesting."

They negotiated the next chute, and the next, then the final one that lay two kilometers downstream, without any trouble. As they emerged onto the calm waters of the river below the last chute, Jesper called from the lookout.

"The fleet's ahead. About a kilometer."

"Ease off!" Hal called to the twins. "We don't want to get too close."

Olaf was aware of a new tension in the ship, a new sense of expectancy among the crew. They had made this voyage several times in the past and they knew that this was the area of greatest potential danger. Several of them unconsciously touched their weapons, and all of them were alert, scanning the banks on either side of the river for the first sign of an attack.

As *Heron* slowed, the other ships gradually pulled away. The traders were formed up in two columns. *Seahawk*, Mannoc's ship, was ahead of them, leading them downriver. *Foxhound*, the other escort vessel, was stationed on the right side of the right-hand column, and just astern of the last ship.

"Ingvar," Hal ordered, "get the Mangler ready. Lydia, stand by in the bow, please."

Lydia gathered up her quiver full of darts and clipped it to her belt, checking to make sure that the atlatl handle was in place on the opposite side. Then she went forward, slipping past the twins at their sail-handling station and taking up a position in the bow. Jesper, still perched on the bow-post lookout, glanced down as he heard her soft footsteps and nodded a greeting.

"Nothing in sight," he said.

"Doesn't mean there's nothing there," she replied.

He nodded, resuming his scanning of the river ahead.

Ingvar had also made his way for'ard. He unlashed the thongs that held the canvas cover for the Mangler in place, folded the cover carefully and set it aside. Then he opened the ammunition locker beside the giant weapon and selected a heavy bolt. He set it down, leaned forward over the Mangler and took hold of the twin cocking levers. With a slight grunt of exertion, he heaved them back until the heavy cord clicked into place over the trigger latch.

Olaf was watching with interest. He had heard about the Mangler and had asked Hal about the large canvas-shrouded shape on the foredeck when they were crossing the Stormwhite. But this was the first time he had actually seen the weapon uncovered.

"Usually it takes two of us to cock it," Hal said, noticing his interest. "Ingvar is the only one who can do it by himself."

Olaf could see from the thickness of the two bow limbs that it would take a lot of strength to draw the cord back and put it in position over the latch.

"Thorn can't do it?" he asked, a little surprised. He knew Thorn's arms and shoulders were incredibly strong.

Hal shook his head. "He might just manage," he said, reluctant to sound as if he were criticizing his friend. "But without his right hand, he doesn't have the same leverage to work with. He has to crook his elbow round the right cocking handle."

Olaf nodded. "That makes sense."

"I don't like leaving it under tension for long periods," Hal continued. "But if we need it, we're going to need it in a hurry."

"That's usually the way it goes in a fight," Olaf said. "Better to be prepared in advance." He watched as Ingvar slid the heavy, iron-headed bolt into the loading groove on top of the crossbow.

"That'll make a mess of any pirate longboat that gets in the way," he opined, and it was Hal's turn to nod.

"That's what we've found in the past," he said. "One well-placed shot can sink a boat."

He glanced around and saw Edvin was standing close by. "You ready to take over if I have to do any shooting?" he asked.

His crewman waved a hand in confirmation. "Anytime you say."

Olaf regarded the skirl with interest. "You don't take the tiller in a fight?"

Hal shrugged. "I do when we get to close quarters," he said. "But I usually take the first shot myself. I'm the best shot on board," he added, without any sense of boastfulness. "And we find if we can make that first shot really count it gives us a big advantage. Stig and

Thorn are our boarding party, and Lydia stays for'ard and reduces the odds for us."

"Can she hit anything with those big darts?" Olaf said doubtfully.

Hal replied with a mirthless grin. "Don't let her hear you saying that. You might find out the hard way."

They were interrupted by Jesper. "Hal!" he cried, pointing. "Signal arrow!"

They were coming up to a wooded headland that jutted out from the eastern bank and obscured their sight of the river beyond. But, rising from behind the trees, they could see a thin trail of red smoke. And they became aware of a shrill, distant whistling sound.

"Looks like the guests have arrived," Hal said. "Time we joined the party."

A s they rounded the bend and came into the next reach of the river, they could see that a major battle was taking place.

No fewer than six pirate longboats were attacking the fleet. *Seahawk* was engaged with two, one on either quarter, held fast like leeches with grappling hooks and lines.

Hal studied her closely. Her decks were swarming with a struggling mass of fighting men, but as he looked, he could see that the pirates were slowly being driven back toward their boats. He could make out Mannoc's tall figure amidships, his sword flashing in the light as it cut through the boarders like a scythe through wheat.

There was no need to go to her aid, he decided. *Foxhound* was farther downriver, with a single pirate boat grappled alongside. She too seemed to be holding her own. Five of the six traders were in a tight bunch farther south again. Two of them had sandwiched a longboat between their hulls. Their crews were pouring rocks, spears and any other missile that came to hand down onto the raiders. The pirate longboat, crushed between the two hulls, was in a bad way. She had only a few centimeters of freeboard left. When they pulled apart, she would undoubtedly sink.

It was the sixth trader, *Southwind*, who was in trouble.

The pirate band had obviously planned to single out one ship and take it while they kept the escorts engaged elsewhere. *Southwind* had been last in line—a straggler—and she had been the chosen victim.

There was a large longboat grappled to her stern, and another rowing frantically behind her, racing to catch up. Hal's eyes narrowed as he measured the angle to the second boat, checking the telltale on the *Heron*'s masthead. They'd reach her in two tacks, he realized, well before she caught up with *Southwind* and her attacker.

Men were struggling on *Southwind*'s decks, but the crew was badly outnumbered. If the other boat were allowed to join in, her fate would be sealed.

"They're crazy," Olaf said. "They must know we'll reach her before they can get her ashore."

Hal shook his head. "They haven't seen us yet. But in any event, they don't need to run her ashore. They'll sink her in the shallows and recover her cargo after we've gone."

Olaf grunted in understanding. He half drew his sword, then rammed it home into the scabbard again in frustration. "Then we'd better stop them," he said.

Hal grinned mirthlessly at him—more a grimace than a grin. "That's what I plan to do," he said. He glanced round, saw Edvin standing ready and pointed to the tiller. "Take the helm, Edvin. I'll go for'ard and try a shot."

The pursuing longboat still hadn't registered that there was a third escort vessel bearing down on it. The crew, intent on the embattled *Southwind*, shouted curses and threats as they bent to their oars.

Edvin took over the tiller and Hal ran forward. Olaf, with no assigned battle station, followed him. Lydia was crouched in the bow, a dart clipped to her thrower. She glanced up as she heard Hal take his place behind the Mangler.

"Nearly in range for me," she said. Hal gestured for her to stand clear of the arc covered by the Mangler and move back behind the huge crossbow. She skipped lightly to the position he'd indicated, leaving him a clear field of shot, no matter which way the longboat turned. He crouched behind the Mangler, flicking up the rear sight for one hundred meters, and slowly wound the elevating wheel, watching the sight rise to cover the helmsman at the rear of the longboat. Then he changed his mind, and his target. Lydia could take care of the helmsman. He'd put a bolt through the side of the boat from the inside, smashing out the planks and opening the boat up to the river. He slowly raised the sights, traversing the Mangler with both feet on the deck, walking the weapon around.

"Take the helmsman," he said quietly to Lydia. She raised a hand in acknowledgment. He saw the movement from the corner of his eye.

"One of them has a bow." Olaf's voice interrupted Hal's

concentration, and he leaned back from the sights. Sure enough, one of the pirates, standing in front of the helmsman, was aiming a short, powerful-looking recurve bow in their direction.

"Lydia . . . ," he said.

"I see him," she replied, acknowledging that she would change her target. Hal bent to the sights again and flinched as an arrow slammed into the woodwork of the Mangler, less than a meter away from him. The archer on board was either a very good shot or a very lucky one. Hal realized he had to finish this quickly. Then, as he steadied his aim on the inside of the hull, and his hand tightened on the trigger, he heard a cry of pain from Lydia and saw her stumble back, falling to the deck.

Enraged, he checked his sight and pulled the trigger. But in his haste, he jerked the shot and the bolt whistled just over the row of oarsmen, plunging into the river five meters ahead of the boat.

He turned to help Lydia, a sick fear in his heart. But Olaf was already there, arms around her, dragging her into the starboard rowing well, where she would be safe from more arrows. There was an arrow through the fleshy part of her upper left arm. Olaf studied it and grinned fiercely at her.

"Nothing serious," he reassured her.

Lydia gritted her teeth. "It feels pretty serious," she said. Then she gasped as Olaf gripped the shaft and broke off the barbed head, then withdrew the rest of the shaft from the wound.

"Take it easy!" she shouted, adding a curse for emphasis.

Olaf shook his head. "Better to get it out quickly," he said, and she knew he was right. His abrupt action had been painful in the extreme. But if he'd hesitated and dillydallied over it, it would have hurt even more. She nodded her thanks to him as he tore off a strip of his sleeve and bound it round her arm.

Another arrow slammed into the Mangler close to Hal. He looked at the longboat. They were only twenty-five meters away now. He turned to Olaf.

"Look after Lydia," he said. "I'm going aft."

He rose in a crouch. Another arrow whirred close overhead, punching into the sail. Then he ran for the steering platform, where Edvin was ready to hand over the tiller.

"Lydia's hit," Hal told him. "Go for'ard and take care of her. And keep your head down."

As he spoke, he saw Ingvar's head jerk up at the mention of Lydia's injury. The huge youth muttered a curse and reached for his long-handled voulge. He half rose from his position in the rowing well, but Hal stopped him.

"She's okay," he said. "Stay where you are." He didn't want to present the archer with any further targets. He raised his voice, addressing the rest of the crew. "Everyone stay down. I'm going to ram."

Stig stepped up beside him, his large round shield on his left arm, holding it to cover Hal in his exposed position on the steering platform. Hal nodded his thanks as another arrow thudded into the oxhide and wood of the shield. With no targets visible in the bow, the archer had changed his aim to the exposed steering position. Stig's protective action had been just in time, Hal thought.

"Haul in the sheets!" Hal shouted to Ulf and Wulf. "And stay low!"

The sail tautened, and *Heron* began to surge faster through the water. Peering around the sail, Hal could see the river rats redoubling their rowing efforts. After a few seconds, they realized they couldn't outdistance the ship behind them. Belatedly, the helmsman tried to avoid the axlike bow bearing down on him.

It was a mistake—a fatal one. As he tried to swing away from the *Heron*, he presented the broadside of his hull to her. Hal swung the tiller and easily matched the turn. Then the bow smashed into the rowing boat, caving in the side and spilling men and oars into the river. The ship seemed to hesitate. Then she gathered speed again and rode up and over the shattered hull. The longboats were large but they were flimsy in construction and the bulwarks were no match for the hardened oak of *Heron*'s bow. The pirate boat was cut in half. *Heron* shuddered at the impact, almost seeming to shake herself like a wet dog, then began to gather speed again, leaving the two halves of the longboat, and her crew, in her wake.

Two of the pirates, with reactions faster than their companions, sprang for the *Heron*'s bow and scrambled aboard, weapons ready. They saw the injured Lydia, with Edvin and Olaf crouched over her, just a few meters away. One of them let out an animal-like growl and, raising his jagged-edged sword, advanced on the three figures.

Dimly, he heard the metallic hiss of a sword clearing its scabbard, then Olaf's curved blade flashed around in a horizontal stroke and almost cut him in half. Shocked and horrified, the pirate looked down, disbelief in his eyes. Then his knees gave way and he toppled to the deck.

The second pirate hesitated as Olaf came to his feet. The former guard commander had dispatched the first man while he was still kneeling. Now the second boarder took a half step back, seeing the rage in the other man's eyes.

He never saw Ingvar. The huge youth came rushing down the deck, his voulge held ready like a lance. The spear point took the pirate in the middle of his chest, shattering his leather breastplate, picking him up bodily and hurling him back over the bow of the ship into the river.

"Are you all right?" Ingvar demanded of Lydia. His voice was hoarse and his face was twisted with worry.

She smiled weakly and waved a hand at him. "I'm fine," she said.

Ingvar looked to Edvin, who was tending her wound. The healer glanced up, caught his gaze and nodded confirmation.

"It's a flesh wound," he said. "Olaf stopped the bleeding before she lost too much blood."

Ingvar looked at Olaf with a new regard. "Thank you," he said simply.

Olaf inclined his head. "Glad to be of service."

They were interrupted by Hal's shouted orders from the tiller. "Ingvar! Get back here on your oar! Ulf, Wulf, lower the sail!"

The river rats on *Southwind*, after seeing the fate of their comrades, had swung the trading ship up into the eye of the wind and run out her oars. Now they were pulling strongly for the shore. The captured trader was already pulling away. *Heron* could sail close to the wind, but not directly into it. Hal was going to have to run her down by rowing. And for that, he needed Ingvar's massive strength.

The sail was useless heading into the wind and would only serve to slow them down. Accordingly, he had the twins drop it to the deck. A few seconds later, *Heron*'s oars ran out. Thorn, manning the oar opposite Ingvar, gestured for Olaf to join him.

"Grab hold," he said.

Olaf frowned in surprise. "Two of us on one oar?"

Thorn nodded. "Between us, we might just balance Ingvar's rowing," he said.

Then Stig called the stroke and they all leaned on their oars. Olaf, not yet in position, felt the ship leap forward, and slew to the side under the uneven thrust of Ingvar's mighty strength. His eyes widened in surprise, and he grasped hold of the oar handle alongside Thorn, putting all his strength into the next stroke.

"I see what you mean," he said.

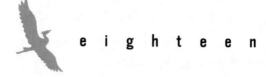

chapter eighteen

With the extra thrust of Ingvar, Thorn and Olaf at the oars, *Heron* skimmed the calm river water, gaining ground on *Southwind* with every stroke. After a few minutes, Hal could see they were going to be up with the captured trader before she reached the shallows close to the bank.

But when they caught her, he realized, he would face a problem. Normal procedure would be for Stig and Thorn to form a boarding party and smash their way through the enemy. But the moment he ordered them forward to do so, the *Heron* would slow down as they left their oars and the pirates would pull away once more.

Plus there was still the problem of the archer on board *Southwind*. Another arrow slammed into Stig's shield, which Hal was now holding on his left arm to protect him from the projectiles. The shield jerked sideways under the impact and he only just managed to get it back in place as another arrow thudded into it. This time, the barbed point bit right through the wood and oxhide and protruded on the inside of the shield.

This bowman was getting to be a nuisance, Hal thought.

As he had the thought, he saw Lydia, her upper left arm heavily bandaged, haul herself up onto the center deck in the bow, crouching behind the protective bulk of the Mangler. In her right hand, she held her atlatl, with a dart already nocked in position. The bowman saw the movement and let fly with another shaft, which ricocheted off the front of the Mangler and whined overboard.

It was now a race against time, with two expert shooters each desperate to get a missile away before the other.

The bowman had an arrow nocked and half drawn when Lydia's shot came streaking over the gap between the two ships and hit him in the chest. He was hurled backward, crashing heavily onto the deck, his half-drawn arrow flipping feebly into the air.

"Good work!" Hal shouted, and the slim girl acknowledged him with a wave of her right hand. Then she loaded another dart and let fly once more. The captured ship was very close now. They were only five meters behind her.

Hal shouted to Edvin, who was still in the bows with Lydia. "Edvin! Grapple them!"

Edvin nodded his understanding and stooped to take the iron grapnel from the forepeak. It was a triple-barbed hook that would bite into the other ship's timbers and hold her fast. The grapnel was attached to *Heron* by a long hemp rope. The first four meters of the grappling cable were iron chain, to prevent the enemy from cutting the hooks loose.

Lydia's flashing darts would add a further incentive for the pirates to leave the grapnel untouched.

Edvin drew back his arm and threw. The heavy iron hooks sailed across the intervening space and thudded onto the stern deck of *Southwind*. The moment the grapnel hit the planks, both Edvin and Lydia seized the rope and hauled on it as hard as they could. The hooked grapnel slid back across the deck, then bit into the base of the steering platform at the stern. The two Herons heaved once more to set the hooks solidly, and *Heron* was sliding along in *Southwind*'s wake.

The minute she saw the hooks were set, Lydia retrieved her atlatl and began to pepper the captured ship with darts, sending the pirates scattering for cover.

Edvin, meanwhile, led the rope in a turn around the base of the mast and, with the extra purchase this provided, began hauling the *Heron* closer and closer to *Southwind*. Hal turned to call to Stig and Thorn, but he had only just drawn in breath to do so when he heard a furious roar, like that of a wounded bull, and saw Olaf sprinting forward along the central decking.

His sword was drawn, and with his left hand he held a small metal shield—about the size of a large platter, with a protruding bowl-shaped section in the center, surmounted by a long spike. He barely paused in his headlong rush along the deck, leaping onto the upward curving bulwark in the bow and springing across the three-meter gap to the deck of *Southwind*.

One of the pirates had seen him coming and thrust with a spear at him as he was in mid-leap. Almost contemptuously, Olaf flicked the spear aside with his sword while he was still in the air. Then, landing as sure-footed as a cat, ready immediately to fight, he slammed the deadly spike on his shield into the defender's mid-section. The pirate grunted in shock and pain and fell back, dead before he hit the deck planks. Two more defenders took his place and Olaf dispatched them with the same ease, cutting left then right with his curved sword, now red with the blood of his enemies, and dropping them to the deck as well.

The other pirates, seeing his deadly speed and skill, began to abandon their oars and clamber forward toward the bow of the ship, shoving one another out of the way in their efforts to escape him.

He pursued them relentlessly, striking left and right with the sword and sending his enemies sprawling into the scuppers, wounded and dying.

In the space of thirty seconds, he accounted for a further six of the pirates, his sword barely seeming to stop, forming a continuing glitter of red-tinged steel as he fought his way down the deck.

On board *Heron*, Hal watched in awe as Stig's father spread fear and havoc among the pirates. Already, several of them had decided discretion was the better part of valor and hurled themselves over-board, striking out for the shore. As the young skirl watched, more and more of the boarders joined their companions until the river was seemingly full of heads bobbing and arms and legs thrashing the surface to foam in their panic to escape.

Hal had moved forward into the bows of *Heron* and now he leaned his hip against the railing where it curved upward and in-ward to form the prow. Edvin and Lydia joined him, watching the solitary figure cutting, slashing, kicking and thrusting, driving the pirate crew back before him.

"He must have been outnumbered ten to one," Lydia said quietly.

"More like twenty to one," Edvin corrected her, and she nodded agreement.

"You can see where Stig gets it from," Hal commented, and
glanced around as his friend joined them in the bows, with Thorn
a few paces behind him.

"He's quite good, isn't he?" Stig said, slightly awed by Olaf's
prowess. Once again, he found himself conflicted. He had been
offended by Olaf's attitude some days prior. Now he found himself
impressed by his father's skill and power.

"He was always good," Thorn said. "Now he's a whole lot
better."

Olaf had reached the bow of *Southwind* now, where the surviving
members of the crew were being held captive. Seeing the one-man
juggernaut coming at them, their captors turned and ran, climbing
onto the railings to leap overboard. As soon as they did, their former captives seized the weapons they had dropped and went after
them. They had lost good shipmates in the attack on their craft
and were in no mood to be merciful now. They lined the rail, hurling spears, axes and even swords at the bobbing heads in the water.
Soon, the air rang with the cries of those river rats struck by the
flying missiles that peppered the water around them. Eventually,
they grew silent, either because their former captives had run out
of weapons to throw or because there were none of them left within
range.

"He sort of spoiled your fun, didn't he?" Hal grinned at Thorn.
He knew how much the one-handed sea wolf loved a fight, and how
much he loved to smash into pirate crews.

Thorn nodded morosely. "At least he didn't say *let's get 'em*," he
said.

. . . . .

Once the crew of *Southwind* were back in control of their ship, Hal took stock of the situation with the others in the fleet.

Seahawk had sunk one of her attackers, leaving its crew struggling in the water. They didn't cry for help. They knew there would be none forthcoming. Like their comrades, they struck out for shore, hoping to make it before the crew of *Seahawk* could muster enough bows and spears to prevent them.

The other pirate longboat, badly damaged and low in the water, crabbed awkwardly for the bank under an uneven spread of oars. It was doubtful that it would make it, Hal thought. Before too long, its crew would be swimming as well.

Foxhound, likewise, had sunk her lone attacker. One of her crew had hurled a small cask of oil into the longboat, following it up with a burning torch, while his comrades fended the longboat off with spars and oars. The battered, burning hulk was drifting slowly downriver. It was a race as to whether she would burn to the waterline before she sank. Either way, she posed no more danger to the fleet—or to any future traders.

The longboat that had been sandwiched between two of the traders was gone as well. There was no sign of her crew in the water. Trading ships' crew showed little mercy to pirates once they gained the upper hand. The boat was sunk and her crew were killed.

As *Southwind* and *Heron* set sail to rejoin the rest of the fleet, Olaf leapt nimbly across the gap between the two hulls and joined Hal at the steering platform. He had taken a long scarf from one of the dead river rats and he used it now to wipe his sword blade clean.

"That was pretty impressive," Hal told him, and several of the crew joined in with words of praise.

Olaf grinned at them all. "All in a day's work," he said. His grin widened when Stig moved up and held out his hand in congratulation. Olaf took it and gripped it firmly, looking deep into his son's eyes.

"Well done," the young warrior said sincerely.

Olaf gestured toward the escaping river rats from the first boat as they straggled ashore.

"What do we do about them?" he asked.

Hal shrugged. "We leave them," he said. "We haven't room to take them prisoner, and there's always the chance that they'd rise up against us if we did."

"Mind you," Jesper put in, "with Olaf, Thorn and Stig on board, they'd be mad to try it."

There was a general chorus of agreement and the awkward emotional moment was past. Hal gestured to the twins.

"Raise the sail," he said. "Let's rejoin the fleet."

The little fleet continued its journey downriver with no further interference. They passed Drogha and the pirate stronghold at Raguza, where Hal was sure he felt dozens of baleful eyes turned on them. But he told himself this was fanciful thinking. None of the Raguza pirates felt inclined to try their luck against such a powerful fleet. The three escort vessels cruised close by the traders, setting themselves between the five ships and the port itself.

Two days later, they reached the point where the South Dan flowed into the Constant Sea and the traders dispersed, heading for their individual destinations. The three escorts heaved to close together while the traders sailed past in line astern, waving and cheering the men who had kept them safe on their voyage down the Dan.

When the traders were hull down, with only their masts and sails visible above the horizon, Mannoc ran his ship close alongside. Lines were passed across, and the two ships were drawn together. The tall captain stepped lightly across from one bulwark to the other and greeted Hal and his men with a wide smile.

"Well done—as ever," he said. "It's always a pleasure to sail with you Herons—good to know you have our backs. This is for you."

He passed across a canvas sack that jingled suggestively. Hal weighed it in his hand and raised his eyebrows. It was a lot heavier than he had expected. Mannoc saw his look of surprise.

"The skipper of *Southwind* contributed a little extra," he said. Then he amended the statement. "In fact, it was a lot extra. But it was well worth his while."

"It was a good idea to have us shadow the fleet," Hal said. "We caught two of the river rat boats napping that way."

Mannoc nodded. "I'll bear it in mind for the future," he said. "But to do it, you need a fast, well-handled ship. And it helps if the rats don't know how many escorts there will be."

He paused, studying the neat little ship and its crew. "What's your plan from here?" he asked.

"We'll head for Byzantos and see what information we can pick up there," Hal told him. "We need to find out where Myrgos's base is, and when he goes raiding."

Mannoc nodded thoughtfully. "Wish I could help you. I know

Myrgos has a base on an island in the east Constant Sea. But the actual location is a well-kept secret. I guess if you're going to find out more, Byzantos is as good a place as anywhere to start."

Inadvertently, Hal glanced at the sun. It was already high overhead. Half the day was gone, and like all sailors, he was loath to lose a moment if the winds were favorable. Mannoc saw the look and smiled, reaching out to grasp hands once more.

"Daylight's wasting," he said. "And you have a long way to go. Travel safely, Hal, and thanks again for your help. You're welcome to sail with us anytime."

"Our thanks to you, Mannoc. It's always good to give those pirates a beating."

Mannoc shook hands quickly with Thorn and Stig, then stepped back across onto his own ship. The two crews lined the rails, calling farewells to one another. Then Jesper and Stefan released the lines holding the ships together and they began to drift apart. As the gap widened, Hal made a hand signal to Ulf and Wulf and the twins hauled the big triangular sail up the mast. It filled with a *whoomp,* and *Heron* began to move faster through the water, heading in a long curve to the east.

And Byzantos.

The harbor at Byzantos was huge—many times larger than any port Hal had ever seen.

They crossed the Golden Reach, the large waterway that ran north from the Constant Sea to Byzantos, separating the western landmass from the eastern, and sailed through the harbor entrance, set between two headlands about a hundred meters apart.

Inside, the harbor opened up before them—an immense span of protected water filled with shipping. Fishing boats, traders, warships, ships of all shapes and sizes, all crisscrossed the harbor, setting up an erratic chop as their wakes met from a dozen different directions. *Heron* bucked and plunged in the disturbed water, and the crew stared openmouthed at the vast mass of shipping moored inside the protective walls.

Hal heaved on the tiller to swing *Heron* clear of a small trawler that seemed intent on dragging its nets under *Heron*'s bow.

"Drop the sail and run out the oars," he ordered, gesturing for Stig to take his position at the stroke oar. Ulf and Wulf complied with his order, with Jesper and Stefan assisting them to bring the large sail down and gather it in, quickly bundling it up and lashing it to keep it from billowing in the wind that blew across the harbor. *Heron* rocked awkwardly in the chop for a few minutes as the oars were run out, manned by Stig, Stefan, Jesper and the twins. As they settled into their rhythm, *Heron* began to slip through the water and the plunging, rocking effect of the cross chop was reduced.

"Do you want me rowing?" Ingvar asked. He enjoyed rowing. Secretly, he was amused that when he took an oar, the ship tended to swing off course due to his powerful heaving. As a consequence, Hal rarely called on him to row.

The skirl shook his head now. "We don't need speed here," he said. "We need control." He heaved the tiller over as a four-oared wherry cut under their bow, missing them by mere centimeters. "Particularly with idiots like that around," he added, yelling an insult after the other craft. He turned to where Thorn was standing behind him, surveying the scene that surrounded them.

"Have you ever seen anything like this?" Hal asked.

The old sea wolf shook his head. "Never," he said. "I thought Raguza was one of the busiest harbors I'd ever seen. But this—this is something else altogether."

Olaf had joined them and Hal addressed his next question to the former guard commander.

"Is it always this busy?" he asked.

Olaf nodded. "Pretty much," he said. "Ships put in here from east and west. It's a major trade center, so there's a lot of shipping passing through. Plus there's the local fleet, which numbers in the hundreds—fishing vessels, trading vessels and the Empress's warships, of course."

He indicated one such—a high-sided galley with two banks of oars down either side. It plowed through the assembled shipping in the harbor, turning neither left nor right. There was a heavy ram visible just below the waterline at her bow, and the timbers themselves were reinforced with brass plates. A sailor stood in the bow, blowing constantly on a braying horn to warn other ships to stay clear.

"Imperial ships have right of way, no matter what. And they tend to enforce it. Don't get in front of one," he said.

Hal eyed the heavy warship as it continued its undeviating way toward the harbor mouth. "I'll remember that," he commented.

Olaf glanced up at the wind telltale. "Remember not to get downwind of one either," he said. "The rowing slaves don't have the best personal hygiene."

Even as he spoke, a stray gust of wind carried from the galley to where they stood. They all turned their heads away from the stench of unwashed bodies, and worse. The four rowers responded by redoubling their effort, pulling *Heron* clear of the drifting miasma.

Hal looked around, bemused by the mass of shipping moored all around the huge harbor front, and at buoys and pontoons out in the deep water. Above their bobbing, tossing masts, the walls of the fortress city towered—gray and ominous and impregnable.

"Where should we moor?" he asked.

Olaf pointed across the water to a large wharf with the universal symbol of a gold circle with two black strokes through it. "There's the harbor master's office," he said. "Head for that and they'll assign us a berth."

"But where?" Hal asked, shaking his head as he peered around at the huge number of moored ships. It seemed that every centimeter of space available was in use. "It all looks full."

Olaf smiled. "You'd be surprised. They'll find room for us."

They were lucky. A berth along the main waterfront, close by the commercial district and the serried ranks of inns, taverns and restaurants, had just been vacated by a departing fishing vessel. Since *Heron* was a small ship, it was an ideal fit for her. There were several larger traders waiting to find moorings, but none of them would fit in the newly empty space. Hal brought the ship in, bow toward the waterfront. At the last moment, the rowers backed water to slow the ship down and he guided her into the space, as easily as threading a needle. Thorn, ready in the bow, leapt ashore and fastened the hawser to a bollard. He leaned his weight against the hawser as *Heron* drifted in the final few meters, taking the last of her speed off her. Two fishing boats rode in their moorings on either side of the little ship. Jesper sniffed, wrinkling his nose, as he tossed the wicker fenders over the side to protect the hull.

"Ugh. Old fish guts," he said. "Wish they'd sluice those ships down from time to time."

Stefan grinned at him. "They'd only be covered in more fish guts and scales within a day or two," he pointed out.

Jesper grimaced. "Still, it'd be nice to have a day or two without that stink."

They stowed the oars and furled the sail properly, making the ship neat and tidy for her stay in port. Hal had paid three days' mooring fees. He, Thorn, Olaf and Stig sat cross-legged on the stern deck, holding a council.

"What do we do now?" Stig asked.

Hal indicated the thronging harbor foreshore close by. "Go ashore and see what we can find out," he said. "We'll see if there's been any further word of this pirate, and what he's up to." He smiled. "Who knows, he may have had a change of heart and handed young Constantus back to his mother."

Olaf nodded agreement. "I know a few tavern keepers who might be able to bring us up to date," he said. "Tavern keepers tend to hear most of the gossip around a port."

"Good idea," Hal said.

But Thorn interposed, frowning. "Will it be safe for you to go ashore?"

Olaf shrugged. "I don't see why not."

Thorn continued. "You've said this Empress is a little unpredictable. Maybe she had a change of heart while you were gone and decided she needs to teach you a lesson."

Olaf made a small moue. "I doubt it," he said. "There's no reason why she should have done that."

"Empresses don't need a reason to be difficult," Thorn said.

Hal nodded agreement. "Thorn may be right," he said. "We'll go ashore and check things out. You might be better to stay on board—and out of sight—until we see how things lie."

Olaf wasn't happy with the idea. After all, he knew this harbor, and the city. He felt he would be quicker to gather information about the missing boy emperor, and the whereabouts of the pirates who had taken him, than a group of Skandians unfamiliar with the city—and unknown by its inhabitants.

"I think you're being too careful," he said. "I'm sure it's safe for me."

Hal paused for a few seconds, then came a decision. "No," he said firmly. "Let's wait until *I'm* sure it's safe. Thorn and Stig and I will go first and check things out. You stay on board until we know it's safe for you."

Olaf shrugged resignedly. "If you say so."

"I do," Hal replied. He wasn't sure why he felt there might be a problem for Olaf going ashore. But he'd heard enough about the unpredictability of the Empress, and her impulsive mood swings and temper, to feel an indefinable sense of danger for Stig's father, in spite of his Olaf's confidence that all would be well.

As their meeting broke up, Edvin came to Hal with a list of supplies that he wanted to purchase. He was always looking to buy fresh supplies whenever they came into port. "Salted and smoked food will keep a crew alive," he was known to say, "but fresh food keeps them happy and well fed."

Hal quickly scanned the list Edvin had prepared and nodded his agreement.

"I don't know why you feel you have to ask me every time," he said. "You know I trust your judgment. And you have control of the ship's purse."

Edvin shook his head doggedly. "I've heard of too many ships where the purser or cook got too greedy. This way, I know someone's keeping an eye on me."

Hal laughed. The idea that Edvin would cheat his shipmates

was so implausible. He touched his finger against a few items at the bottom of the list: willow bark, warmweed extract and linen bandages.

"Medical supplies?" he asked.

Edvin nodded. "Plus I expect they'll have items here we haven't heard of. I'll spend some time at an apothecary and get some advice."

Hal glanced at him warmly. Some healers he had seen assumed that they knew it all. Edvin, on the other hand, was always ready to learn new ways and new techniques from foreign sources. That willingness to learn was what made him such a good healer. That train of thought reminded him of something else.

"How's Lydia's arm?" he asked. "Should she go ashore and find a local healer?"

Edvin inclined his head. "I'll ask her," he said. "But it seems to be healing pretty well."

As it turned out, Lydia agreed that there was no need for a second opinion on the wound she'd sustained during the battle on the South Dan. She flexed her left arm experimentally, although Hal noted that she did flinch slightly at the end of the movement.

"It's healing cleanly," she said. "Maybe a little stiff still, but if I keep working it, that'll take care of itself."

"Do you want to come ashore with us?" Hal asked.

She looked doubtfully at the thronging waterfront a few meters away, then shook her head. She was uncomfortable among crowds, and Byzantos was more crowded and noisy than anywhere she had ever seen.

"Maybe tomorrow," she said.

Hal glanced around. The rest of the crew were sprawled

comfortably on the deck, some dozing, others repairing items of kit. Like all sailors, they took every opportunity to rest when they weren't at sea. Ulf and Wulf, he noticed, were busy practicing with the padlock and the lockpicks that Jesper had lent them. As he watched, he saw Wulf spring the lock open and grin triumphantly at his brother.

"You're getting good at that," Hal said.

Wulf beamed with pleasure, but Ulf snorted sardonically.

"I'm better," he said. He snatched the lock from his brother, slapped the hasp shut, then inserted the lockpicks into the key slot. In a few seconds, there was a loud *CLICK* and the lock sprang open. Instantly, Wulf snatched the lock back and closed it again. Hal turned away. This could go on all day, he realized.

"Stig and Thorn and I are going ashore. Stay on board until we've checked things out. If everything's clear, you can all go ashore tonight."

The others nodded. They'd be glad to have a few idle hours with no duties to take care of.

Hal started toward the gangway that led to the dock, then hesitated, taking up his sword belt and swinging it around his waist. Stig, seeing the action, buckled on his own weapons belt, slipping his ax through the iron ring at his side. Thorn was already wearing a short sword in a scabbard. The three of them stepped up on the bulwark, then Hal stopped as he heard a pleading whine. He looked for'ard. Kloof was standing expectantly, her heavy tail swinging from side to side, her head inclined hopefully.

"Oh, all right," he said, clicking his fingers, and she bounded forward gleefully to join them.

The broad thoroughfare that ran along the waterfront was, as they had noted, crammed with taverns, bars and eating houses, all of them crowded, with customers spilling out into the road.

In some cases, customers weren't just spilling, they were being ejected onto the footpath, to go staggering farther down the street in search of a tavern that might let them in. Some were so confused that they attempted to reenter the place that had just thrown them out. The second time, they were treated far less gently by the tavern keepers and their staff.

Hal frowned at the noisy scene. "Let's get away from the waterfront," he said. "I can hardly hear myself think here."

They took a narrow cobbled path that wound uphill away from the harbor, bringing them to another large street running parallel. This was similarly furnished with taverns and inns, but they appeared to be of a higher quality, and the clientele was less rowdy.

They walked slowly past the establishments on offer, peering at the menus displayed outside the doors. They paused at one, where the mouthwatering smell of grilling meat drifted out to them. The three shipmates exchanged a grin.

"This seems like a likely spot," Stig said happily. The smell of cooking meat always put him in a good mood.

Hal smiled indulgently. "You think grilled skewers of lamb and good information go together?"

Stig nodded emphatically. "That has been my experience."

They went in through the open doorway, stooping under the low-hanging lintel. Inside, they paused, allowing their eyes to become accustomed to the dimness, after the bright sunlight outside. Kloof wagged her tail experimentally and emitted a little whine. Like Stig, she enjoyed the smell of grilling meat.

They were met by a waiter, recognizable as such by the long white apron tied round his waist and extending down to his shins. He glanced doubtfully at Kloof. Most taverns and inns had no restrictions on dogs in the bar, but this was a very large dog indeed.

"Is that dog of your likely to cause trouble?" he asked suspiciously.

Hal smiled winningly at him. "Bless you, no. She's as peaceable as your old granny."

The waiter's frown deepened. "My old granny is always starting fights," he said. "She set off a riot in here last month. Cracked the skull of one of the watch with a chamber pot."

"Well, Kloof is hardly likely to do that. She doesn't have a chamber pot," Hal told him. He gestured for Kloof to sit and she did so, lolling her tongue out the side of her mouth and grinning disarmingly at the waiter.

"As you can see," Hal continued, "she's full of love and kindness."

"Hmmm," said the waiter, unconvinced, but weakening. "I'll sit you near the door here. But any trouble and you're out."

"If your kitchen could spare a big beef bone, that'd ensure she remains peaceable," Hal suggested.

The waiter nodded. "I'll see what I can do. I suppose the rest of you want something less basic?"

"Oh yes," Stig replied happily. "Bring us a dozen lamb skewers to start." He paused and looked at his friends. "Did you two want something as well?"

Hal sighed. "Better make it two dozen skewers," he said to the waiter, who made a note on the slate that hung from his waist.

"One beef bone, two dozen skewers. Any ale?"

"Coffee," Thorn said. "For all of us."

The waiter made another note, then turned away toward the kitchen. The three friends relaxed. Kloof remained sitting by Hal's side and he fondled her ears idly. She inclined her head to his touch and rumbled with pleasure. There were few things Kloof enjoyed more than the undivided attention of her master.

One of those things was a bone, however, and when the waiter returned with a massive shinbone, she sat up a little straighter and trembled with expectation. The waiter eyed those massive jaws tentatively, then offered the bone to Hal.

"You give it to her," he said. "I need all the fingers I've got."

Hal accepted the bone and showed it to Kloof, who drooled alarmingly. He held up an admonishing finger.

"Be nice," he said, and offered the bone to her. She took it delicately, then, with the bone clamped firmly in her massive jaws, she allowed her front paws to slide out from under her until she was lying on the floor beside the table. She turned her head to one side and gnawed blissfully on the bone, her eyes closed in pleasure. The waiter shivered slightly at the sound of jaws grinding bone.

"You've made a friend for life," Hal told him.

He shook his head and turned back to the kitchen. "I'll bring your skewers," he said.

Stig grinned. "Then you'll have made two friends for life."

A serving girl brought them a coffeepot and three mugs, and Stig filled them and passed them around. The three friends pushed back from the table a little, stretching their legs and relaxing. It was good to be ashore after weeks on board ship.

Hal glanced around at the neighboring tables. There were four men seated at the next table, finishing off a large platter of skewers and a green salad. Hal nodded a greeting and their leader, a man with his hair in four thick pigtails, nodded back.

"New in town, are you?"

"Just got in from the South Dan," Hal replied.

The man studied them for a few seconds, taking in their leather and sheepskin vests, the sealskin boots and heavy woolen trousers—and their weapons.

"Skandians, are you?" he asked. He seemed to have a habit of making a statement, then following it with "are you?" to turn it into a question.

"That's right," Hal said. "You?"

"Gallicans," the man replied briefly. "We're waiting on a cargo of coffee for Toscana. Been waiting eight days." He leaned forward slightly. "If you don't mind my offering a piece of advice, you'd be best to keep a low profile at the moment. Skandians aren't too popular with the Empress—may the gods bless her name." He added the last in an ironic tone.

Hal raised his eyebrows. "Oh? Why's that? We'd heard she preferred hiring Skandians for her palace guard. Thought we might see if we could get a job with them."

"At the moment, she's a good woman to steer clear of," Pigtails told him. "She's unpredictable and dangerous at the best of times, but since her son was taken by the pirate Myrgos, she's worse than ever. Apparently, the commander in charge of the detail guarding her son when he was taken was a Skandian." He glanced at one of his companions. "What was his name again, Aristide?"

The second Gallican looked up from the remains of his meal. "Whose name?"

"The Skandian guard commander. Remember, that tavern keeper was telling us about him the other night?"

"Oh, him. Yes. It was Olin or Odin or something like that." He frowned, thinking. "Olaf!" he said as he remembered. "That was it. Olaf someone-or-other. She's put out a reward for him."

The three Skandians exchanged a worried glance. This was an unpleasant surprise.

"Why didn't she just order him to get the boy back?" Hal asked, choosing his words carefully, and trying to sound indifferent.

Pigtails shrugged. "Well, she did at first. But when that didn't bring any immediate results, she lost patience. I'm told she does that quite frequently," he said with a grin. Then he frowned slightly. "You don't know this fellow, do you?"

The three Herons hastened to deny any knowledge of Olaf.

"Probably a good thing," he said. "The way she is, she'd probably have his friends arrested as well. Or instead of. She's put posters up all over the city, offering a reward for his capture."

"We'll bear it in mind," Thorn said, and looked up as the waiter arrived with their platters of sizzling grilled skewers. He turned his attention to the food as it was laid in front of him. "Nice talking to you," he said to the Gallican, who nodded sociably and turned back to his own friends.

As he leaned forward to take a couple of the skewers, Stig spoke in a lowered voice. "Maybe we'd better—"

Hal cut him off with a quick hand gesture. Stig's lowered voice could carry to the four corners of the room if he wasn't careful.

"Eat your meal. Then we'll be on our way," he said, a warning expression on his face as he let his eyes glance quickly around the crowded room. Stig followed his eye movement and nodded, understanding. This was not the place to discuss Olaf's predicament. He applied himself to the food, eating quickly. Even his concern for the new situation didn't stop him from appreciating the meal. He polished off half a dozen skewers in rapid order, then took a deep draft of his coffee, smacking his lips in appreciation.

After five minutes, Hal judged that they had eaten enough of the meal to leave without drawing undue notice to themselves. He signaled to the waiter for the reckoning, counted out a handful of silver coins and pushed back from the table. Kloof rose reluctantly from her position between his feet, the huge bone clamped firmly in her jaws.

Nodding farewell to the pigtailed man, who raised his shoulder in a typical Gallic gesture, Hal led the way out into the street. The three friends formed a circle, leaning in close together to make sure they weren't overheard. Hal cast a swift glance back to the tavern to make sure the Gallican wasn't watching them. If he saw them engaged in an urgent discussion like this, so soon after learning about the predicament facing their countryman, he might put two and two together and decide that they knew Olaf, and his where-abouts. But the Gallican had remained inside, obviously having no further interest in them.

"This is unpleasant news. Just as well you told Olaf to stay on board," Thorn said.

Hal nodded. "I'm not sure why I did. I just had a premonition. We'd better get back to the ship and make sure he stays out of sight."

As they hurried back downhill toward the harbor, Thorn sud-denly stopped and pointed to a large sheet of parchment pasted to a stone wall. They moved closer. The sheet contained a rough, but reasonably recognizable, sketch of Olaf, and a notice of the reward of one thousand crowns for his arrest.

"Not a bad likeness, unfortunately," Hal said. He glanced down the street and noticed several other similar notices. "He said they were all over the city."

"Didn't see them on the way up," Stig said.

Thorn shook his head. "We weren't looking for them then."

They redoubled their pace, moving down the winding street at a jog. Hal felt a sense of relief as the ship came in sight. He'd half expected to see crowds of soldiers milling around it, calling for Olaf to surrender. But everything seemed normal.

But everything was definitely not normal. As they approached down the quay, Edvin saw them coming and sprang ashore, run-ning to meet them.

"We've got trouble," he said. "Olaf went ashore shortly after you left and he's been arrested."

twenty-one

A rrested?" Hal asked, his voice rising in disbelief.
"Where? How?"

"He decided to go ashore after you'd gone—"
Edvin began, but Hal interrupted him.

"I told him to stay on the ship! Who let him go ashore? Gorlog's
teeth, doesn't anyone do what they're told these days?"

Edvin spread his hands in a defensive gesture. "Don't kill the
messenger, Hal. I'm simply telling you what happened. I reminded
him that you'd said he should stay aboard, but he ignored me.
What did you want me to do, tie him up?"

Hal calmed down and raised a hand apologetically. "Sorry,
Edvin. Not your fault. If someone's determined to be an idiot, they
will be one. So what happened?"

"He said there was a tavern along the waterfront where he'd be
able to get good information about the pirate—Myrgos. The tavern

keeper was an old friend and he always had his finger on the pulse, Olaf said. He waited till you were out of sight, then he took off."

"Why didn't he simply tell us about this tavern keeper? We could have questioned him."

Edvin shook his head. "I suggested that. But he said the man wouldn't talk to strangers."

Hal shook his head in frustration. Edvin continued. "I sent Ulf and Wulf after him to keep an eye on him. Just in case there was any trouble."

"Good thinking, Edvin," Hal said. "And I take it there was trouble?"

"Yes. They were almost at the tavern when a brawl broke out. Half a dozen thugs started beating up a young man who was out with his girlfriend. Olaf intervened and the thugs turned on him."

"At least his heart's in the right place," Thorn remarked.

Hal turned to him. "Even if his brain's not," he said. Then, seeing Stig's concerned expression, he added, "Sorry, Stig."

The first mate waved the apology aside. "I tend to agree with you."

"Anyway," Edvin continued, "someone called the watch and a patrol arrived and arrested everyone involved, marching them off to the watch house."

"At least it has nothing to do with those posters offering a reward for him," Hal said. That had been his first concern when he heard about the arrest.

Edvin raised his eyebrows. "A reward? For what?"

"The Empress has had time to reconsider her position," Hal told him. "She's now convinced that Olaf is to blame for her son's capture and she wants him arrested."

"Well, that could be awkward," Edvin said. "But so far the arrest has nothing to do with that. As far as I know, he wasn't recognized."

Hal was glancing around the ship, studying the crew who were standing by, listening keenly. He realized that Ulf wasn't present.

"Where's Ulf?" he asked, a nasty suspicion forming in his gut.

Edvin sighed. "I'm afraid he was arrested too. He tried to drag Olaf out of the fight and he got caught up as well. They're both in the watch-house jail with the others. They'll be brought before a magistrate the day after tomorrow."

"At which time he'll probably be recognized," Hal said. A watch-house jailer might not recognize the former guard commander, but a magistrate most likely would. "Is there any chance we could break him out before then?"

Edvin looked doubtful. "It's a pretty solid building—made of stone with only one entrance. There are half a dozen guards in the upper room. The prisoners are all in one big cell on the ground floor."

"Hold on, how do you know that?" Hal asked.

Edvin indicated Lydia, leaning against the ship's rail. "I sent Lydia in, pretending to be Ulf's fiancée, asking if she could bail him out. The corporal on the desk was quite polite, but he told her it was impossible. That's when we learned about the magistrate and the date of the hearing."

"That was good thinking, Edvin," Hal said, and Edvin shrugged.

Hal moved over and sat on the central decking, his feet dangling into the rowing well. He put his chin on his hand and thought for several long minutes, waiting for inspiration. None came. The crew watched expectantly. They had sublime trust in their skirl and his ability to always come up with a plan of action.

"Maybe . . . ," said Stig slowly, and all eyes turned to him. He flushed slightly, then continued. "Maybe Jesper could get himself arrested . . ."

"Oh, thank you very much!" said Jesper heatedly.

Stig made a mollifying gesture. "Just for something minor. And you could take your lockpicks and open the cell door. That way you could set the prisoners free and overpower the guards."

"That's not bad," Hal said.

But Edvin was already shaking his head. "Won't work," he said. "They'd search him and find the lockpicks on him."

"And watch-house guards would recognize them for what they are," Jesper said. He sounded relieved that he would not have to get himself arrested. After all, he'd spent most of his former life as a thief attempting to avoid such an eventuality.

"They search anyone who goes in?" Hal asked, although, in truth, it wasn't unexpected that they would do so.

Edvin nodded. "They even searched Lydia. They had one of their serving women go over her to make sure she wasn't carrying any weapons."

Hal grunted, aware that the crew were watching him intently. He found he was looking steadily at Wulf. The sail handler noticed his skirl's scrutiny and shifted uncomfortably. A thought was forming in Hal's fertile mind.

"What was Ulf wearing?" Hal asked suddenly. The question was an unexpected one, and for a second or two, nobody replied.

Then Wulf, aware that Hal was still watching him, indicated his own clothes. "Much the same as me," he said. "A linen shirt, sheepskin vest and woolen pants over his sea boots. And his watch cap, of course," he added, indicating his own woolen watch cap, emblazoned with a white heron symbol.

Hal nodded. Wulf had described the de facto uniform worn by most of the Herons, with a few individual variations.

"What have you got in mind, Hal?" Stig asked. He was intrigued to know. He sensed that his original suggestion had sparked Hal's current train of thought but he couldn't see what his friend was planning.

Hal looked at him and a slow smile spread over his face. "I'm thinking that they search everyone who goes in, but they wouldn't bother with someone who's already inside."

"Well, of course not," Stig said, still mystified.

But Thorn was starting to grin, as he saw where Hal was going. "Or somebody they *think* is already inside."

Hal glanced at him. "Exactly," he said. He switched his gaze back to Wulf. "How's your lockpicking coming along?"

Wulf considered the question. Being Wulf, he was tempted to exaggerate his skills. But he sensed this might not be a good time to do so. He shrugged diffidently.

"Not too bad. I'm getting faster," he said.

Hal looked to Jesper for confirmation. The former thief nodded agreement.

"He's pretty good, for an amateur," he said. He couldn't help differentiating between his own ability and that of the sail handler. "Ulf is faster," he added.

Wulf turned angrily toward him. "Not anymore! I've caught up with him! I can . . ." He sensed Hal's steady, unamused gaze still on him and subsided. "Well, maybe he is," he admitted.

"Thank you," Hal said. Then he looked back at Jesper. "Jes, I want you to practice with him for the next hour. I assume we'd be looking at a pretty old-fashioned lock in the watch house?"

"I'd be surprised if we weren't," Jesper said. "It doesn't look like the most modern jail in the world."

"I can vouch for that," Lydia put in. "The place looks as if it's at least a hundred years old."

"I suppose Olaf could confirm that, if he were here," Thorn said.

Hal looked at him, a grim expression on his face. "And there lies the problem," he said. "All right, Jes." His manner became brisk and businesslike again. "Get to work with Wulf for the next hour. Then we'll get moving. Wulf has work to do."

"What am I going to do?" Wulf asked, a little nervously.

Hal smiled at him. "You're going to break into the jail."

Corporal Junius Dall, commander of the watch-house garrison, looked up from the requisition form he was painstakingly filling out as the outer door to the watch house creaked open on its rusty hinges.

A figure slipped tentatively through the gap, silhouetted against the glare of the sunlight outside, and made his way across to the raised counter behind which the corporal sat. As he came closer, and the light stabilized, Junius realized that he was vaguely familiar.

"Please, Captain," the young man said in a whining voice, "can I go back to my room now?"

"I'm not a captain," Junius began brusquely. Then he stopped and studied the person before him more closely. "Just a minute!

Aren't you . . . weren't you in . . . ?" He looked to the heavy wooden door that led to the large detention cell. "How the blazes did you get out?"

Wulf shrugged, looking nervously around him. "Someone didn't lock the cell door, so I sort of . . . left," he said. "But then I thought I might get into trouble, so I decided to come back and report myself."

Wulf superbly played the part of a nervous prisoner seeking to avoid further punishment. After all, he and his brother had spent their lives fooling and confusing people who couldn't tell them apart, and they were past masters at prevarication.

Actually, not to put too fine a point on it, they were expert liars. He stood now before the corporal, eyes down and hands fiddling with his watch cap. Junius recognized that cap. He had admired it when the prisoner had been arrested several hours previously. He had even been tempted to requisition it for himself. But he felt a surge of panic as Wulf waited, eyes cast down. If what he said was true, and the door had been left unlocked, there was only one person who might have left it so—and that was Junius himself. He shuddered as he thought of the punishment that might have been meted out to him if the unlocked door had gone unnoticed. The Empress was not lenient when it came to punishing men who had neglected their responsibilities. Thank the gods for this simpleton before him, he thought.

Junius rose and came out from behind the counter, seized Wulf by the elbow and hastened him toward the door leading to the cells. Wulf stumbled along awkwardly. The corporal opened the door and shoved Wulf through. Ahead of them was a large open-fronted cell. The wall facing them was constructed from iron bars, with a large, barred door in the center. Thankfully, Junius saw, it was firmly closed.

"It's not open now," he said.

"I closed it behind me," Wulf told him, then, raising his voice, he shouted out in Skandian. "Stay out of sight, brother! They think I'm you!"

Junius rounded on him suspiciously. They had been speaking the common tongue and he had no knowledge of Skandian.

"What was that?" he asked.

Wulf shrugged. "It was a prayer of thanks to our god Loki," he said. The Skandian god of deception was, in fact, Wulf's favorite god, and he and his brother were two of Loki's favorite disciples.

Inside the large cell, surrounded by at least a dozen other prisoners, Ulf slipped furtively behind the bulk of Olaf as he saw his brother being shoved unceremoniously through the barred door. The door slammed shut with an echoing clang. Junius waved a fist at the returned prisoner.

"And this time, stay there!" he ordered.

"Yes, Captain. That's what I plan to do," Wulf told him.

From the rear of the cell, he heard his brother's unmistakable snigger.

chapter   twenty-two

A s Corporal Dall shoved Wulf inside, the sail handler
pretended to stumble and fetched up against the
burly form of Olaf, standing a meter or so away from
the door. He looked up and, facing away from the
jailer, he grinned.

Behind him, he heard the door clang shut and the lock turn.
This time, the guard shook the door several times to make sure it
was securely locked, then he turned on his heel and headed back to
the outer room.

Ulf stepped out from behind Olaf, his face wreathed in a smile.
"What are you doing here, brother?" he asked.

Olaf shook his head doubtfully. "Looks like you've decided to
be a prisoner too," he said.

Around them, several of the other prisoners, noticing the fact that Ulf and Wulf were identical in every respect, started to mutter in surprise. Wulf turned to them, his finger raised to his lips in an unmistakable sign for silence.

"Be quiet, if you want to get out of here," he demanded.

Olaf raised an eyebrow. "Get out? How do you plan to do that? You've only just got in."

But Wulf continued to grin at him as he undid his belt and pulled up the tail of his woolen shirt. Underneath it, strapped to the small of his back with a length of material, was a small canvas wrapper. He rolled it out to reveal the lockpicks that Jesper had been instructing the twins with.

"Oh, wonderful!" Ulf cried as he saw the two small pieces of metal. Then he held his hand out, clicking his fingers in an imperious gesture. "Give them here."

But Wulf snatched the picks away from his brother's outstretched hand. "I'll do it," he said pugnaciously.

Ulf's smile faded. "Better if I do it. I'm quicker than you."

"So you say," Wulf replied. It was amazing how the twins could work together in such easy harmony when they wanted to confuse the jailer, yet how quickly they reverted to bickering when their common enemy had gone.

"Come on! Let me do it!" Ulf said, his voice rising, and the anger showing in it.

"I'll do it," Wulf repeated stubbornly.

Finally, Olaf had had enough. He grabbed them each by the shoulder and pulled them close to each other. "One of you had better do it," he said roughly. "Or I'll bang your heads together."

They didn't know Olaf well enough to judge whether this was

an empty threat or not. The two brothers exchanged a look and decided to give him the benefit of the doubt.

Ulf nodded to his brother. "All right. Go ahead," he said.

Wulf shook off Olaf's hand and moved to the door. He reached through the bars with the first piece of the picks and tried to insert it into the keyhole. Then he stopped, frowning.

"It's all back to front," he said. He glanced at Ulf. "Could you do the turning part while I feel for the tumblers?" He felt it would be easier if he had to concentrate on only one part of the lockpicking process. Ulf stepped up beside him, took the flat-ended piece of metal and reached through the bars, bringing it back to the keyhole. Like Wulf, he hesitated.

"You're right. It's back to front. It'd be easier if we were on the other side of the door."

"If we were on the other side of the door," Olaf put in, his voice heavy with sarcasm, "we wouldn't need to pick the lock."

Ulf didn't notice the sarcasm. He nodded agreement. "Quite true," he said. Then, frowning with concentration, he inserted the pick into the lock and turned it slightly.

He grinned at his brother. "You just have to think backward," he said.

"Something I'm sure you're good at," Olaf said.

But they ignored him, engrossed now in the problem of picking the lock backward. Wulf took the curved pick and reached through the grille beside his brother, inserting it in the lock. It was easier for him as he didn't have to turn it one way or the other. He slid it along the top of the bolt, holding it with his thumb and forefinger as he raked it lightly across the tumblers. The other prisoners had begun to mutter in anticipation of being set free, and Wulf turned angrily on them.

"Be quiet!" he ordered. "I have to be able to hear."

"Hear what?" demanded one of the prisoners, a shifty-looking type who had undoubtedly seen the inside of this cell on numerous occasions. The man next to him, a rough-looking thug with a scarred face, added a scornful comment.

"What's to listen to?" he demanded. "It's a lock, for pity's sake, not a tin flute."

Wulf shook his head in exasperation and looked to Olaf for help. The big former commander took a step toward the two prisoners.

"If the lad says he needs silence, he needs silence," he told them. They eyed him nervously. He was big and well muscled and was an obvious warrior. They edged away.

"I was just saying . . . ," Scarface began, but Olaf's big hand shot out and grabbed the collar of his jerkin, twisting it quickly to cut off the man's breath. Scarface struggled for a few seconds, his face growing red as he tried to breathe. But Olaf twisted harder still, and the man found himself choking.

"I'll use words you might understand," Olaf said in a grim tone. "Shut . . . up. Is that clear now?"

The man, deprived of breath, gurgled incoherently. But he managed to nod desperately until Olaf relaxed his grip. The prisoner drew in a long, shuddering breath, then hastily waved his hands in apology.

Olaf turned to Wulf. "Go ahead."

Wulf went back to the task. Ulf, who had relaxed his twisting force on the flat pick, turned the lock slightly. As before, Wulf held the curved piece lightly, running it across the tops of the tumblers.

Almost immediately, a faint *click* could be heard, and he grinned triumphantly at his brother.

"Got one!" he said. But if he was expecting praise, there was none forthcoming.

"Then get the other two," Ulf told him.

Wulf curled his lip at him before going back to work. Thirty seconds passed, and there was another small click. Then, within seconds, Wulf, now more familiar with the feeling of the lock, tripped the third tumbler and the door swung open.

Immediately, there was an excited surge for the door from the other prisoners, but Olaf barred the way.

"Stand back!" he ordered. His voice was low, but it carried to the back of the cell and was filled with undeniable authority. The movement toward the door ceased.

"How many guards are there, beside the one at the counter?" Olaf asked the group in general. One of the prisoners held up a hand, and the Skandian signed for him to speak.

"There are usually a dozen or so," he said. "They're in a guard room on the first floor."

"But there's just the one turnkey outside?" Olaf asked.

The man shrugged. "Usually, yes. So far as I know," he added hastily. He didn't want the big Skandian to blame him if he was wrong.

Olaf nodded and looked to Wulf. "All right. Go out there and bring him in. Tell him the door has unlocked itself again."

Wulf nodded, grinning. He enjoyed confusing the gray-haired jailer.

As he stepped to the door leading to the outer room, Olaf waved the other prisoners back.

"Make sure there's no one else out there," he told Wulf.

Wulf nodded and eased the door open a crack, peering into the large receiving room. He could see a staircase in the far corner, obviously leading to the guards' room on the next level. Junius Dall was relaxing at his counter, his chair tilted back and his feet propped up on the scarred wooden surface. There was no one else in sight. Putting on his meekest look, Wulf slipped through the door and approached the counter.

"Please, Captain," he said in an apologetic tone, "it's happened again."

The corporal came awake at the sound of his voice, letting the front legs of his chair drop back to the floor.

"Gods of Chaos!" he said. "Not you again!"

Wulf gestured to the door behind him. "The cell door came open again, sir. It wasn't my . . ."

Before he could finish the sentence, Dall had risen and come out from behind the counter, hurrying toward the door and grabbing Wulf by the arm to drag him along.

He threw the inner door open and stepped inside, seeing the cell door hanging open and the prisoners gathered back against the far wall. For a moment, he wondered why they hadn't come out of the cell. Then a hard-muscled arm slid round his neck from behind, cutting off his air and making it impossible to breathe. He struggled briefly, but the grip was relentless and unbreakable. Gradually, his struggles grew weaker and his eyes slid shut.

Olaf lowered the guard's unconscious form to the floor. He glanced quickly into the outer room, an idea forming. Then he waved the prisoners out of the cell.

"Come on," he said. "Get out of here while you can!"

As they surged out of the cell, he grabbed Ulf and Wulf and shoved them through the door, dragging them behind the high-set counter where Junius Dall usually held court.

"Get down out of sight," he told them. The three of them crouched underneath the counter, unnoticed by the other prisoners, who shoved and struggled as they fought to be first out the door. The thud of footsteps and the clatter of running feet from the street outside was clearly audible in the guard room upstairs.

"What's going on down there, Dall?" a voice came from above.

Olaf waited until the last three prisoners were shoving one another aside in their efforts to get out the door, then shouted out, "Help! The prisoners are escaping!"

As he said it, he ducked under the counter, where the twins crouched in hiding. There was a small nail hole in the front of the counter and he put his eye to it as he heard a clatter of booted feet on the stairs.

The first of the guards appeared as the last of the prisoners escaped through the main door. The guard yelled to his companions to follow. He was buckling his sword belt around his waist as he ran after the escapees. Another ten guards followed him, in varying states of preparedness—some armed, some half dressed, all carrying an assortment of weapons. Like the prisoners, they bunched together in their efforts to be first out the door. They shoved and jostled one another, cursing their companions for getting in their way. Then, after a few brief hectic moments, they were out the door, running after the fast-disappearing prisoners.

"Split up!" Olaf and the twins heard a voice call. "Some of you go after that bunch. The rest with me!"

Obviously, the escaping prisoners had the presence of mind to head off in different directions. The three Skandians heard the shouts and curses of the guards as they ran after the escapees.

"Stop!" one of them shouted. "Come back!"

Beneath the counter, Olaf shook his head in wonder. "Why do they always say that?" he asked, of no one in particular. "Do they really expect them to stop and come back to jail like good little boys?"

He waited another fifteen seconds as the shouting and the sound of running feet receded into the distance. Then he crawled out from behind the counter, the twins following him.

His sword belt was hanging from a peg behind the counter, as was Ulf's belt with his scabbarded saxe. The guards confiscated weapons carried by prisoners and sold them in the market. It was one of the perks that came with the job. Olaf swung the sword belt round his waist with the ease of long practice, and passed Ulf his saxe knife.

"All right," he said, "I think we can go now."

He slid the door open a few centimeters and peered out at the street outside. There was no sign of guards or escaping prisoners. A few passersby glanced at the three Skandians with idle interest as they exited onto the street and set off at a brisk pace for the harbor. A whistle came from the alley opposite the jailhouse, and they saw Hal, Thorn and Stig waiting in the shadows. They crossed the street quickly, and their companions handed them long, flowing robes they had bought in the market—the type of clothing worn by the locals.

"Put these on," Hal ordered. "And let's get out of here."

chapter   twenty-three

eron was ready for sea. Her slim bow was facing the
open water of the Golden Reach and there was
only one mooring rope, looped round a bollard on
the pier.

"Get aboard," Hal said tersely. "Ulf, Wulf, take your
positions."

The twins scrambled for'ard to their workstation beside the
mast and sail. Stig hurried to the stern rope, ready to cast off. The
other crew members stood ready. One or two of them nodded to the
twins, in recognition of the fact that the escape plan had worked.

"Starboard sail," Hal called, and Ingvar, Jesper and Stefan
heaved on the halyards with a will, sending the starboard yardarm
and sail soaring aloft. The yard thumped into the retaining bracket
at the top of the mast, and the sail began to fill with the wind
coming in over the port bow.

"Sheet home," Hal called, and the twins brought the sail under control, so that it formed a smooth, bellying curve. Then he turned to Stig. "Let go aft."

Stig let the mooring line run through his fingers, gathering in the loose coils as it slid free. *Heron* surged away from the dock, going from a standstill to full motion in a matter of seconds. Hal felt the pressure on the tiller against his grip, and noted that the ship was making considerable leeway. He waved to Thorn by the mast.

"Let down the fin," he ordered. Thorn leaned his weight on the bladelike fin keel and slid it down into the water. Instantly, Hal felt the increased grip on the water, and *Heron* stopped crabbing sideways. She pitched and buffeted her way through the uneven chop set up by half a hundred wakes going in different directions, then steadied on her course for the open sea.

A six-oared boat from the harbor patrol was moving diagonally to cut across their course. The rowers cursed as they realized that they had underestimated the departing ship's speed and redoubled their efforts.

Hal made a gesture to the twins. "Ease off a little," he said, and they let the speed fall off so that the guard boat could run alongside them. The skipper of the guard boat, who was manning the tiller, shouted across the gap between them.

"You're leaving port," he shouted, and Hal nodded. "Do you have your clearance papers signed?"

"Darned bureaucracy," Hal muttered. "We've paid harbor fees for three days and we're leaving after one. What's their problem?"

"They're pen pushers," Thorn said. "They have to justify their existence somehow."

Hal nudged the tiller so that they ran a little closer to the patrol boat. Wedging the tiller under his arm, he cupped his hands and called to the other skipper.

"Just testing some new rigging," he said. "We'll be back in an hour."

The other helmsman seemed satisfied by this explanation. "Report in when you come back," he said.

Hal waved acknowledgment. "I'll be sure to do that!" he shouted, adding in an undertone, "Whenever that may be."

The guard boat sheared away from them, the rowers gratefully reducing their pace. Hal signaled for Ulf and Wulf to tighten the sheets and *Heron* accelerated, heading for the wide gap that led to the open sea. He realized that Edvin had been standing close by for some minutes, obviously waiting for an opportunity to talk to him. He raised an eyebrow.

"What can I do for you, Edvin?" he asked.

"Just thought I'd let you know, I didn't have time to replenish a lot of the stores we need. The main market day is tomorrow and I was going to do it then. We've plenty of water and enough dried and salted food to live on. But I like to give the lads fresh food whenever I can."

Hal nodded. "We'll put in to an island in the next couple of days," he said. "You can stock up then."

Edvin nodded. "That's fine. You know I hate to miss an opportunity to lay in fresh supplies."

Hal grinned. "I do know," he said. He looked around, saw Olaf standing nearby, looking over the stern at the rapidly receding city. He frowned. There was still something he had to do. He gestured to the tiller.

"Take over for a few minutes, will you, Edvin?" he said, and the purser-cum-healer hurried to comply. "Just keep her steady on this course. I won't be long."

He stepped down from the steering platform and moved closer to Olaf. Olaf glanced curiously at him, then Hal jerked his thumb for'ard.

"Come with me," he said tersely. "We need to talk."

They made their way to the bow. Jesper was on the lookout post and Lydia was leaning idly on the rail, watching the staggering variety of craft passing them. She had never seen so many different types of ships and boats in one place. The water fairly teemed with them. She glanced curiously at Hal and Olaf as they made their way for'ard.

"Give us some privacy, please, Lydia," Hal said. He was very calm and his speech was measured, but she knew him well enough by now to realize that, beneath the calm exterior, he was seething. She nodded and started aft. Hal glanced up at Jesper.

"You too, please, Jes," he said. The lookout slid down and hurried after Lydia, leaving Olaf and Hal alone in the bow.

Olaf, sensing what this was about, heaved a long-suffering sigh. "All right," he said, "I'm sorry. I shouldn't have—"

"Shut your mouth," Hal snapped at him. He kept his voice low. He didn't want the crew overhearing. But the lack of volume didn't negate the tone of command in his voice. "Shut your mouth and listen."

Olaf had spent the last five years as a commander of the Empress's guard. He was accustomed to giving orders, not taking them. He opened his mouth to demur, but something in Hal's eyes stopped him. He shrugged, pretending an indifference that he didn't really feel. Hal waited and locked his gaze on that of the older man. After a long pause, Olaf dropped his eyes.

"You may think I'm young and inexperienced—someone you can ignore when it suits you. But if that's the way you're thinking, let me tell you how wrong you are. I'm the skirl of this ship and the leader of this brotherband. I've fought pirates and invaders. I've helped liberate two cities. When a raider stole the Andomal some years ago, I led the crew on a journey across the Stormwhite and down the Dan after him. We caught up with him at Raguza and we fought his ship—one twice as big as this and with three times as many men. And we beat him. We sank his ship and left him to drown."

He paused, letting this sink in. Then he continued.

"Since then, I've carried out special missions for Oberjarl Erak on half a dozen occasions. He apparently doesn't think of me as a boy. I've fought slavers in Arrida and a death cult in the eastern desert. Last year, we sailed to the far side of the earth and I led the crew in a pitched battle against a tribe of murdering raiders there.

"All in all, my men and I have fought battles, single ship engagements and personal combats all over the world while you've been nursemaiding a pampered young emperor—and apparently not doing such a great job of it."

Olaf bristled angrily at those words. He straightened his shoulders to reply, but Hal continued before he could.

"We're here to help you, Olaf, not because we have any particular regard for you. We're here for Stig's sake. Because we all admire and respect him and you're his father. As far as most of us are concerned, your record isn't an impressive one. You're a thief who betrayed his brotherband and robbed them, then ran off in the night, leaving your wife and son to pick up the pieces."

Olaf's hand dropped to the hilt of his sword. Hal matched the movement, letting his hand rest on his saxe.

"Go ahead," he said evenly. "You'll be dead before your sword is halfway clear of the scabbard. Trust me. That's no idle boast."

Olaf was an experienced warrior. And that experience was borne of an ability to look at potential opponents and gauge their determination and skill. He saw no sign of hesitation or uncertainty in Hal's eyes. He saw instead a calm assessment of his own confidence and ability. The lad facing him had a wealth of experience in combat. This was no unskilled river pirate. He'd been trained by Thorn, and Olaf knew Thorn to be a superlative warrior. And Hal was young—with the speed that goes with youth. His hand moved away from the sword hilt.

Hal's shoulders relaxed slightly. "That's better. Now listen, and listen carefully, because I won't be saying this again. This is your first and only warning. From now on, if I give you an order, you will obey it, without question. Is that clear?"

Olaf hesitated, then he dropped his eyes. He knew that the young man facing him was right. He was the skirl and his orders were to be obeyed—promptly and to the letter.

"It's clear," he said finally.

Hal studied him for some time, gauging the level of conviction in his words. Then he nodded briefly.

"It had better be," he said finally. "Because here's the other side of the coin. If you ever, *ever*, disobey one of my orders again, you will be off this ship so fast your ears will ring. I'll put you ashore on the first piece of land we come to, even if it's four square meters of bare rock that only reaches a few centimeters above the high-tide mark. I mean it."

Olaf took a deep breath. He needed this ship and this crew to help him rescue the boy emperor. And that meant he needed this skirl as well. He couldn't afford to alienate Hal again.

"I understand," he said softly. Then he raised his eyes and met Hal's steady, unwavering gaze with his own. For a few moments, their eyes were locked together, then Hal made a dismissive gesture with his hand.

"All right," Hal said. "That's settled. Now we need to find a port where Edvin can replenish his precious stores."

"And where we can get information about Myrgos," Olaf added.

Hal agreed. He gestured toward the stern, stepping aside to allow Olaf to precede him. "Let's go look at the chart. You know this part of the world better than I do."

"Here." Olaf stabbed a blunt forefinger at a small island to the southwest of the Golden Reach. Hal leaned over and studied it. Thorn, Hal, Olaf and Stig were grouped around a small folding chart table close to the steering platform. Lydia was currently handling the tiller, and the ship was swooping gracefully over the clear waters of the Adrios Sea—an adjunct of the Constant Sea.

"Cypra," Hal said, reading the name. "Why there?"

Olaf shrugged. "It's a crossroads. There's constant traffic there, so it has a well-stocked marketplace. And constant traffic means a good possibility of information."

"What are the people?" Thorn asked.

"They're a mix of Ottomans and Hellenese. About equal numbers of each."

"I thought they hated each other," Thorn said.

Olaf nodded confirmation. "They do. They're constantly fighting, always at each other's throats. But they tend to agree when it comes to cheating foreigners. Tell Edvin to haggle like mad when he's buying supplies. Even then, he's liable to pay too much."

Hal took one more look at the chart, then checked the wind telltale. It was an unconscious gesture, but one that sailors made constantly. He touched a point on the map that he calculated to be their current position, then placed his sun compass on the chart. He had recalibrated the instrument only that morning, so it showed an accurate reading for north. He laid off a straight edge between their position and the island of Cypra.

"Maybe a day and a half away if the wind holds," he said.

"No reason why it shouldn't," Thorn put in.

His young friend grinned at him. "No reason why it should either," Hal said. "Particularly when we need it to."

"You're a fatalist," Thorn told him, matching his grin.

"I'm a realist," Hal replied. He turned to call to Lydia. "Bring her around four points to starboard." Then, raising his voice, he addressed the twins beside the mast. "Trim the sail for the new course."

Heron heeled sharply as she came round. Spray cascaded over the bow, showering them all with warm salt water. The sheets creaked as Ulf and Wulf hauled in and allowed her to settle on her new course.

"Better tell Edvin to get his haggling shoes on," Hal said.

PART THREE

THE CALDERA

There was no harbor as such at Cypra, just an open bay with a long crescent of beach where ships were drawn up above the high-water mark. There were no piers and no infrastructure. The constant feuding between the two indigenous groups meant that there was no civil administration on the island. Neither side would trust the other to take control, hence nobody did.

On the positive side, that meant there were no harbor fees or mooring charges. Ships arrived, found a space and beached themselves.

Hal cruised along the beach under oars until he found an open space between a fishing boat and a small freighter unloading a cargo of oil in clay amphoras.

"Beaching!" he called. He swung the bow of the ship toward the gap between the other two boats.

Stig peered over his shoulder as he rowed, then, judging his moment, he called to the other oarsmen. "Easy all!"

They stopped rowing, bringing their oars inboard, and *Heron* slid smoothly onto the beach, her curved bow letting her run up onto the sand. As she came to a halt, she tilted to one side on her keel, and Jesper sprang over the bow onto the wet sand and ran farther up the beach to set the anchor. The rest of the crew began stowing oars, furling the sail properly and coiling the various ropes and halyards that were no longer required now the ship was immobile.

Kloof went for'ard and reared up with her forepaws on the bulwark, peering at the land, with her tail wagging heavily. She was a good seadog but always preferred to go ashore when there was dry land nearby. Hal glanced at Thorn and nodded toward the beach.

"Let's stretch our legs and give Kloof some exercise," he said. Stig, as first mate, would oversee the general tidying up and stowing of gear. "Rig the awning," Hal told him. "It's going to be a hot day."

Stig nodded. The tentlike awning would shade them from the sun as they lay on the beach. Without the breeze of their motion, it would soon become insufferably hot on board. Ingvar and Stefan were preparing to drop over the side with props to level the ship on the sand—after a few hours, it became tiring to stand and sit on a sloping deck. Ingvar's enormous strength would allow him to heave the ship upright while Stefan placed props under the hull to keep it level.

Lydia, without any task to do, saw Thorn and Hal moving to the bow.

"Going ashore?" she asked, and when Hal nodded, she added, "Mind if I come with you?"

Hal grinned. Unlike the rest of them, Lydia hadn't been brought up around boats and the sea. She was always keen to go ashore—except in places like Byzantos, where the mass of people and buildings crowded in on her. By contrast, the long, open beach was an inviting sight.

"Can't wait to get off our little floating home?" he asked.

She smiled in return. "It's nice enough. But it gets smaller with every day we're aboard."

"Ships will do that," Thorn chipped in. "Even the biggest ones shrink after a week at sea."

Kloof had heard them coming and she turned now, still propped up against the rail, her tail wagging faster and an expectant look on her face. Hal clicked his fingers and gestured overside.

"Go on," he told her.

Without hesitation, she scrambled her back legs up onto the bulwark, then sprang down to the beach. Feeling the soft, giving sand under her paws, she streaked off in a huge semicircle, her tail streaming behind her, her ears flapping madly with each bound. A fisherman from the neighboring boat, sitting cross-legged on the sand mending his nets, smiled at the big, lolloping dog.

"He's happy," he said to Hal as the skirl dropped lightly over the side and onto the sand.

"He's a she," Hal corrected him, but he kept his tone friendly. "And she does love to get ashore."

Kloof, seeing her humans had climbed down to the beach, came rocketing back to them and dropped belly down in the sand, her hindquarters tensed, ready for a game. Hal leaned down to ruffle her ears.

"Calm down, you big idiot," he said fondly. Kloof raised herself, then moved over to sniff the malodorous pile of fishing nets. Hal could see what was about to happen and scolded her quickly. "Get out of that!"

"She's all right," the fisherman said tolerantly. He liked dogs, and this one was obviously good-natured. "She can't do any damage."

"Maybe not," said Hal, "but she's liable to roll in them and it'll take me weeks to get the stink out of her. Nothing worse than a wet dog who smells of dead fish."

Reluctantly, Kloof moved away from the nets, giving Hal a reproachful look. The fisherman studied her with interest. He'd never seen a dog like her before.

"She's a big one, isn't she?" he said, reaching out to fondle her ears. Sensing a friend, Kloof angled her head to one side, allowing him to scratch under her chin and around her ruff, her eyes half closed with pleasure. "What is she?"

"She's a mountain dog," Hal told him. "We're from Skandia, way north of here. She's big, but she's very friendly."

"Best keep her away from that lot, then," the man said, nodding his head to the eastern end of the beach.

Following the direction he'd indicated, Hal could make out a long, low-slung black ship. It was nearly three times as big as *Heron*, and pierced for fifteen oars a side. There was a square-rigged sail furled on the cross yard of its single mast.

"Who's that?" Hal asked, although instinct was beginning to

tell him who it might be. The fisherman's next words confirmed it.

"She's the *Vulture*," he said. "Myrgos's ship." The dislike in his voice was all too obvious. Lydia, Hal and Thorn exchanged a look.

"Myrgos?" Hal said. "He's the famous pirate captain, right?"

The fisherman leaned over and spat in the sand. "Infamous is more like it. He's started his summer cruise, which is why I'm ashore, mending nets while he's in the area."

"Why would he bother a fisherman?" Thorn asked, his tone friendly. "Last I heard, you people aren't exactly rolling in riches."

"He does it because he can," the fisherman replied. "He'll sink, burn and destroy any ship he sees, just for the sake of it. He's an evil, cruel swine of a man."

"But you say he likes dogs," Hal said. It seemed at odds with the description of the man.

The fisherman shook his head. "He doesn't like them. He breeds them for fighting."

Hal screwed up his lips in a gesture of distaste. "Kloof here's not a fighter," he said. "She'll protect any of our crew if they're in trouble, but she won't start a fight."

"That's why he'd want her. He looks for big, powerful dogs— but dogs that aren't aggressive. And he uses them to train his fighting dogs. He trains his dogs to kill, you see. So a dog like yours would put up a good resistance, but it would lack the killer instinct that his fighting dogs have been taught."

Thorn made a sound of disgust, and Hal looked at his dog. She had discovered something under the sand and was pawing with her left foot to reveal it, her head cocked to one side. She sensed his glance and looked up at him, tongue lolling and tail wagging.

"I don't know how anyone could mistreat a dog," he said quietly.

The other man shrugged. "He's been doing it for years. I suppose if you're prepared to kill and torture people without mercy, dogs don't really rate a second thought. Best keep her where he can't see her. If he does, he'll offer to buy her. And if you refuse, he'll take her anyway."

"He could try," Thorn said grimly.

The fisherman looked at him, assessing him. His gaze took in the missing hand and the wooden hook. For all that loss, the bearded Skandian looked like he'd be a tough nut to crack.

Meanwhile, Hal had sensed this was their opportunity to get more information about Myrgos. It was a heaven-sent coincidence that they had chosen to beach beside this particular ship.

"You said he's started a summer cruise," he said. "How long does that last?"

"Two, maybe three months if the pickings are good. He'll range around the Adrios, up to the edge of the Golden Reach. Then he'll head back to the mouth of the South Dan to see what's happening there. He stays out to sea. The pirates at Raguza don't make him welcome—they don't like competition. Then he'll make his way through the smaller islands, sinking and burning anything he can put his hands on, before he returns to his base."

The Herons exchanged a quick glance. This was the sort of information they were looking for, and now—thanks to Kloof's friendly nature—it seemed to have fallen into their laps. The fisherman, intent on his nets, didn't notice their reaction.

"Where's that?" Thorn asked, keeping his tone casual, and the man waved a hand in a general southwest direction.

"An island called Santorillos," he replied. "It's a huge caldera that forms a natural lagoon."

"Caldera?" said Lydia. She had never heard the term before.

The fisherman glanced at her. She was a warrior, he thought. But a real beauty as well.

"It's an old volcano that blew up about a hundred years ago. It formed a huge circular lagoon when it did. Some of the walls have collapsed since, but it's an amazing sight. The island—at least the eastern side of it—clings to the cliff tops, which drop away into the lagoon. The lagoon itself is deep—too deep for an anchor to find bottom. Myrgos has his base on the top of those cliffs. He moors *Vulture* in against the base of the cliffs and has a lifting device to get him and his men up the sheer drop."

"And what's at the top?" Hal asked, storing all this information away for later use.

"He has a fortified villa there. A walled compound with his living quarters inside. He has a crew of seventy to eighty men and they live there."

"You seem to know a lot about it," Thorn said.

The fisherman shrugged. "There's good fishing in the lagoon. If the fishing's poor elsewhere, I sometimes sneak in there when they've gone raiding."

"Do they all go?"

The fisherman paused, looking curiously at Hal. The young man seemed to want a lot of information about Myrgos and his movements, he thought. Then he shrugged mentally. It was none of his business, and if these tough-looking Skandians managed to give Myrgos a bloody nose at some time in the future, that would be all to the good. He shook his head.

"The *Vulture* carries a crew of fifty. The others remain behind, guarding the compound."

Hal rubbed his jaw thoughtfully, trying to picture the layout of Santorillos. He realized there was one piece of information missing.

"So the compound is at the top of the cliffs on the eastern side of the island. What about the western side? That's not another callidera, is it?"

"Caldera," the fisherman corrected him. "No. The land slopes away to the west for about three kilometers to a normal coastline." He took his fishing knife and traced a quick outline in the damp sand beneath their feet. One side formed a deep curve, obviously the site of the lagoon. He pointed to it.

"This is the lagoon. The cliffs here are eighty to ninety meters high. Myrgos has his compound here." He touched the knife to a point beside the deep, curving cliffs. "Then the island slopes away here through cliffs and broken rocky ground to the west. There's a small village on the western edge of the island, but nothing between them."

"Would it be possible to reach the compound from the western side?" Lydia asked, forestalling Hal with the question.

The fisherman shrugged. "It wouldn't be easy. The cliffs are steep and the ground is rocky. And of course, guards at the compound would see you coming long before you got to the top. They'd be waiting for you."

He studied the three strangers as they all stared intently at the sand map. They were definitely planning something, he thought.

"There's another thing," he said, and they all looked

expectantly at him. "The villagers on the west coast know which side their bread is buttered. If they saw you heading inland, they'd most likely raise the alarm and warn the pirates you were coming."

"I imagine they could do that with beacon fires and signal rockets," Hal mused.

The fisherman leaned back and spread his hands in a conclusive gesture. "It's a pretty difficult spot," he said. "On one side you've got sheer cliffs eighty meters high. On the other, you've got several kilometers through broken ground and more cliffs—with the added fact that if you're seen, the alarm would be raised."

Thorn nodded soberly. "Sounds like the sort of place we should avoid."

The fisherman looked at him keenly. "I'd say so," he said. But he would have been willing to bet that avoiding Santorillos was the last thing these Skandians had on their minds.

The Herons split up that evening as they headed into the town looking for somewhere to eat. Hal reasoned that if eight or nine of them turned up at the same establishment, the chances of getting a table would be slim. The beach was crowded with ships, and the small town buzzed with people. Accordingly, they broke up into two groups.

Hal, Thorn, Stig, Olaf and Lydia went one way. Ingvar, Stefan and Jesper branched off in a different direction. Ulf, Wulf and Edvin remained on board as a harbor watch. Edvin had replenished his stores that afternoon. His last stop had been the fish market, and now he was baking a large snapper in the coals of a fire on the beach. The fisherman had readily agreed to join them when invited. Edvin had rubbed the fish with olive oil and salt, and stuffed olives and slices of lemon into the cavity. The smell of the fish cooking was mouthwatering. As they left, Thorn looked regretfully at the fire in the sand.

"Maybe we should eat here," he said.

Edvin glanced up at him. "I bought a fish, not a sea monster," he said. "I've seen how much you can eat."

Normally, Kloof would have remained with the ship. But Hal felt she'd been cooped up for a long period and let her come with him. She trotted obediently beside him, and the tavern they selected for their meal made no objection to her presence.

She lay quietly under the table while Hal spread out the sheet of parchment on which he'd reproduced the sketch of Santorillos. They'd chosen a table where there was no one nearby to overhear them.

"Sounds like the cliffs here are the best way to approach the compound," he said. "And the odds are that's where Myrgos is holding young Constantus prisoner."

"How will you get up the cliffs?" Thorn asked.

Lydia made a moue with her lips. "Cliffs can be climbed," she said. "I'll climb to the top and let down a rope."

"You haven't seen the cliffs yet," Olaf pointed out.

Lydia shook her head dismissively. "I haven't seen a cliff I couldn't climb," she told him.

He raised an eyebrow at that. "If they were that easy, somebody would have done it before this."

Lydia gave him a long, piercing look. "I didn't say they'd be easy," she said. "I said I could climb them. And who's to say someone hasn't already done so?"

"I just——" Olaf began.

But Hal interrupted them. "It's a moot point anyway," he said. "Kostas said there was some sort of elevator at the mooring. We'll use that." Kostas was the name of the fisherman who'd befriended them.

He sensed the waiter approaching with their food and hastily folded the chart that he'd drawn. The fewer people who knew of their interest in the caldera at Santorillos, the better.

The waiter set their food down on the table between them. There were two sizzling shallow iron bowls, set in wooden platters. On each was a generous helping of baby squid, with the bodies separated from the tentacles and sliced into rings, and the two parts grilled on hot iron griddles set over charcoal. The squid was generously seasoned with garlic, lemon juice, red flakes of chili and olive oil. The pieces spat and sizzled on the hot plates.

A second waiter placed a large bowl of green salad, dressed with a sharp mixture of lemon juice and more olive oil. Olive oil seemed to be an essential ingredient for just about everything in this part of the world, Hal mused. A platter of fresh flatbread loaves rounded out the meal.

The first waiter returned with a large bowl of raw beef pieces, which he set down for Kloof, who was stretched out on the floor beside Hal's chair. She wagged her tail gratefully, then rose and leaned forward to sniff the meat. Hal held up an admonishing forefinger.

"Wait," he said, and Kloof fixed an anxious gaze on him. Every dog knew that if you didn't eat beef the moment it was set before you, it had a tendency to escape. "All right," he said, taking pity on her, and she thrust her snuffling muzzle into the food.

In the meantime, Lydia had placed a generous portion of the squid and salad onto Hal's platter, and now he attacked it with vigor.

"Delicious," he mumbled, through a mouthful of squid and salad. Then he added "Ow!" as the hot squid burned his incautious tongue.

"They certainly know how to cook in this part of the world," Stig agreed. Prior to this, he had always disdained squid as a form of food. But there was no doubt about it. This was delicious. He tore off a chunk of bread and mopped up the oil and juices from his plate before spooning another large portion of squid onto it.

"The cooking down here in the south is one of the big attractions," Olaf told them. He'd had dishes similar to this one before, but that didn't make it any less mouthwatering.

The table went silent as they fell upon the rest of the food, rivaling Kloof for the speed with which they demolished it. Like Stig, the others finished their meal by tearing off strips of bread and sopping up the oil and juices with it. Thorn eventually thrust himself back and patted both sides of his belly, emitting a loud sigh of pleasure.

Kloof emptied her bowl of beef scraps and licked it experimentally, the expression on her face showing that she wondered where the food had escaped to. When the waiters cleared the platters away and brought jugs of coffee and pottery mugs, Hal heaved a sigh of contentment.

"It's occasions like these," he said, "that make all the cold, wet nights at sea worthwhile."

The others mumbled agreement, helping themselves to the

bowl of dessert that had been placed beside the coffeepot. It was a sweet, gelatinous substance, colored pink with rosewater and cut into small squares.

Hal took a deep sip of coffee, set down the cup and reached inside his jerkin for the chart once more. He laid it out on the table but, before he could unfold it, Thorn placed his hook over the parchment, keeping it shut. His eyes were fixed on the entrance, and Hal twisted in his chair to look in the same direction.

A momentary silence, followed by a soft buzz of conversation, had run around the room, greeting the entrance of the two new-comers who stood just inside the door, surveying the tables and their occupants.

Some instinct told Hal that he was seeing Myrgos, the pirate captain, and one of his subordinates. A low muttered comment of "Myrgos" from one of the nearby tables confirmed his guess. The single word contained a mixture of fear and dislike, and Hal glanced curiously at the man who had uttered it. Obviously a sea-man, judging by his clothes, the speaker rose hurriedly, tossed a few coins on the table and headed for the rear door of the tavern.

The man who had entered first, and was obviously the leader, was short in stature—barely a meter sixty in height. But he was barrel-chested and broad shouldered, with a powerful physique to make up for his lack of height. His arms were unnaturally long for his body. His head sat on a thick neck and was surmounted by a mass of unruly gray-black hair that seemed to grow in all direc-tions. It fell over his shoulders and down the back of his neck. The face was broad, with flat cheekbones and a large hooked nose that had obviously been broken, set, then re-broken, several times. His wild beard matched the volume and unruliness of his hair. It grew long and untrimmed, framing a mouth of discolored, misshapen teeth.

But it was the eyes that were the most striking features. Set under wildly growing eyebrows, they were dark obsidian, almost black, and were wide-open and staring, giving the man a manic, unpredictable look. The man's gaze darted round the room, settling on the Skandians at their table for a few seconds. Then Myrgos, for Hal had no doubt that this was he, turned and muttered something to his companion.

This man was a study in contrasts compared with his leader. He was completely bald, his head shaven and gleaming with oil. He was tall and broad in build, towering over this leader, and most of the men in the room. He sported a gold ring in the lobe of his right ear and, as if to compensate for the lack of hair on his head, he affected a long, drooping mustache.

Both the newcomers were dressed in black leather—sleeveless belted vests over stained white shirts and black leather trousers shoved into knee-high boots of the same material. And both wore long, slightly curved swords in scabbards that were adorned with silver facings and decoration.

The taller man replied to Myrgos's comment, nodding his head. Then, at a gesture from the pirate captain, they both started across the room toward the table where the Herons were seated.

The room was crowded and there wasn't a lot of space between the tables. But Myrgos and his henchman didn't deign to thread their way carefully between the benches. They shoved roughly past the seated patrons, causing them to spill food and drink as they came. As one man remonstrated loudly over the wine spilled down his shirt, Myrgos paused and uttered a brief word.

The man hastily backed away, rising awkwardly from his bench, and the two pirates continued on their way.

Hal swiveled his chair so that his back was no longer to the approaching pair and his way to stand was clear. The others shifted in their seats, coming a little more upright, their bodies and legs tensed for quick action. Only Olaf wore a sword, but the others all had their saxes, and in a confined space like this, they could be more effective than a long-bladed sword.

Kloof, sensing the tension in her master and his companions, stopped searching her empty food bowl and sat up, her hackles flaring. She grumbled a low warning growl deep in her chest.

"Be still," Hal told her. She looked quickly at him, then back at the two approaching men.

They stopped a meter away from the seated Skandians—just a little too close for politeness, their proximity issuing an unmistakable threat and a challenge. Hal looked calmly up at the wild-haired man.

"I'm Myrgos," the newcomer said, and jerked a thumb at his companion. "This is Demos."

"How pleasant that must be for you," Hal said, not offering his name. He noticed that while Myrgos's gaze had roamed the table, assessing all its occupants, Demos was staring fixedly at Olaf. Maybe it's because he's the only one armed with a sword, Hal thought. But a tiny worm of worry began to eat away at the back of his mind.

Myrgos scanned the table quickly to see if any of the others were laughing at Hal's words. They had been said without a hint of sarcasm, merely as a statement of fact. He looked back at Hal.

He's been briefed by someone, Hal thought. Usually, on first encounter, strangers assumed that Thorn, the oldest member of the group, was the leader. But Myrgos had singled Hal out immediately. The pirate reached into his leather jerkin and produced a heavy purse, which he dropped on the table. It clinked musically—the unmistakable sound of gold hitting wood.

"That's a good-looking dog," Myrgos said, his voice harsh and grating. "I want to buy her."

A low, rumbling growl emanated from Kloof's massive chest. Her lips peeled back momentarily to reveal her fangs. Hal soothed her with a hand in her mane of hair.

"Problem with that," he said evenly. "I don't want to sell her."

He picked up the purse and held it out to Myrgos. The man made no move to retrieve it, so Hal shrugged and let it drop to the floor. All eyes around the tavern followed it, listening greedily to that repeated chink of gold coins—lots of them.

"I could simply take her from you," Myrgos said.

Thorn moved his chair slightly to one side. "You could certainly try," he replied.

Myrgos's eyes darted to him, then his hand dropped to the hilt of his sword.

But Thorn moved with blinding speed. One moment he was seated, the next, he was standing facing Myrgos, a full head taller than him, and his wooden hook had dropped over the pirate's sword arm at the wrist, twisting sideways to lock the man's hand in a solid, relentless grip.

Stig was a heartbeat behind Thorn. Watching them, Olaf was impressed by their speed. His son had his saxe out—the *shriing* of steel on leather ran around the room. Its razor-sharp point was at Demos's throat, even as the tall pirate was thinking of reaching for his own sword. The pirate's eyes widened with surprise and fear. He had barely seen the young Skandian move. They faced each other now, as tall as each other. Demos's eyes were still startled. Stig's were calm and confident.

Demos moved his hand away from his sword, spreading both hands wide in a gesture of submission. Stig withdrew the point of the saxe a few centimeters. Demos looked again at Olaf, a memory stirring somewhere.

"Who are you?" he said. "I know you."

Olaf shook his head. "We've never met," he replied, but Demos seemed unconvinced.

Throughout all this, Hal hadn't moved from his seat. Now he rose casually and, placing a hand against Myrgos's chest, moved him back a pace. He felt a recurrence of that thrill of worry that he'd experienced earlier. Had Demos recognized Olaf as the former commander of the guard? He decided to muddy the waters a little.

"Well, now you have. Demos, meet Grundig." He smiled at Myrgos. "Now if you'll excuse us, we should get back to our ship."

"I'll kill you," Myrgos said savagely. "I'll take your dog and I'll kill you all."

Hal studied him for a few seconds. "Not a wise thing to say when my friend is in a position to break your arm," he said, and as he did so, Thorn twisted and applied more pressure to Myrgos's trapped wrist and forearm. The small bones in the arm grated together, and Myrgos uttered a low grunt of pain.

"All right, Thorn, let him go," Hal said after a few more seconds.

Thorn released the twisting grip on Myrgos's arm and shoved him back.

"Now get out of here," Hal told the two pirates, and they backed away toward the entrance, their faces black with rage. As they reached the door, Myrgos called across the now-silent room.

"I'll kill you for this, Skandian. All of you!"

Then he flinched violently as a meter-long dart slammed into the doorjamb by his head and sat there, quivering. Lydia smiled grimly at him.

"So you keep saying," she said.

Myrgos looked at the savage missile, its steel head buried in the hardwood doorjamb. He paled, then turned and hurried out, Demos close behind him.

"I think we'll use the rear exit," Hal said.

chapter   twenty-six

T he rest of the night passed without further incident—
although Hal set a double guard for the night, with
one sentry on the beach watching for potential enemies approaching landward and another in the stern
of the ship, keeping an eye on the bay.

The following morning, the crew were sitting down to breakfast when Thorn nudged Hal and pointed to the edge of the beach.
A troop of armed men, carrying spears and shields and with swords
at their waists, were marching in a double file down the sand toward them.

They wore no uniform as such, with each man equipped with
a different form of armor and helmet. Some wore brass-studded
leather vests and others had shirts of chain mail. Some helmets
were simple flat-topped metal caps; others were more ornate, cone

shaped or spiked and, in some instances, with metal wings flaring out to the sides.

But each man wore a yellow armband round his upper arm, embossed with a symbol of a black dolphin.

Hal rose from the circle around the cooking fire and took a few paces toward the approaching men. There were ten of them in two files, he saw, with an eleventh marching three paces ahead of them. This man held up his hand in an unmistakable gesture as they drew closer to the interested circle of spectators round the breakfast fire, and the men halted.

Their close-order drill was rather ragged and they obviously didn't practice too often. But they handled their weapons with a familiarity that indicated that their marching had no bearing on their fighting efficiency.

The leader regarded Hal for several seconds, sizing him up. Then he barked a question.

"Your name?"

Hal returned the look, letting his eyes rove over the two files of men halted behind the speaker. He didn't like the peremptory tone the man had adopted.

"Who's asking?" he said finally, his tone as challenging as the other man's had been. But the newcomer showed no sign of apology.

"Fergil Drommond," he said. "I'm a commander in the Citizens' Vigilance Committee."

Hal raised an eyebrow. "Never heard of them," he said, although the name smacked of the sort of unofficial organization that looked to assert an authority to which they had no legal right.

Their fisherman friend from the day before had seen the men approaching and he joined Hal now. "They're the nearest thing we have to a guard patrol here," he said quietly.

Hal glanced at him curiously. "I thought there was no elected body with jurisdiction over the town?"

The fisherman shrugged. "There isn't. But some years back, the merchants and tavern keepers recruited an unofficial force of armed men—usually foreign mercenaries—to more or less keep the peace. At least, the sort of peace that the merchants and tavern keepers want kept."

"I see," said Hal. It made sense, he thought. There would have to be some sort of semiofficial body to patrol the streets and stop fights when they broke out. Otherwise, with so many sailors of varying nationalities swarming ashore every night, Cypra would be in a constant state of anarchy. He turned back to the patrol leader now. "So what do I call you? Captain? Colonel? Committeeman?"

"Commander will do," the man said stiffly. He sensed a certain lack of respect in Hal's attitude and he was right to do so.

Men like this, in Hal's experience, often were no better than thugs and vigilantes, open to bribes and corruption and answerable to no official oversight.

"And you can call me skirl," Hal said. He saw the brief flash of incomprehension in the other man's eyes. "It means 'captain,'" he explained.

"Very well . . . Captain. Were you and some of your men in the Blue Lizard tavern last night?"

Hal nodded. "We were," he said. "I can recommend the baby squid grilled on a hotplate . . ."

The commander brushed that information aside impatiently.

"And you were involved in an . . . incident with Captain Myrgos and one of his men, correct?"

"If you mean the pirate Myrgos and his bald henchman, yes, we were. They were extremely unpleasant and made various threats to our well-being." He turned back to Stig, who was still seated on the beach with the others. "As I recall, he threatened to kill us all, didn't he?"

Stig nodded. "That's how I heard it."

Drommond glanced quickly at Stig and the other Herons. Then he returned his attention to Hal.

"Well, I'm afraid the committee doesn't take kindly to that sort of thing going on. You'll have to leave Cypra. You have an hour to stow your gear back aboard your ship and shove off."

"*We* have to leave port?" Hal said, a note of incredulity in his voice. "They threatened to kill us and we're the ones being tossed out?"

"That's your side of the story," Drommond said. "Myrgos and his man tell it differently. And the tavern keeper said you were quite belligerent."

"I often am when someone threatens to kill me," Hal replied.

But the commander was unapologetic. "Myrgos is a regular visitor to this island. He has a large ship and crew, and they spend a lot of money here."

"When they're not sinking ships in the waters around Cypra," Hal said, and the fisherman beside him snorted in agreement.

The commander, however, shrugged the comment aside. "I know nothing about that. It's not in my jurisdiction. But I know you're strangers."

"And there's only a round dozen of us," Hal said.

The commander was unmoved. He wasn't here to win friends. He was here to give orders and make sure the peace was maintained, no matter who might be in the right or wrong of it all.

"As you say. You have an hour. I suggest you stop wasting time."

"And of course, once we've put to sea, there's nothing to stop Myrgos and that ugly black ship of his coming after us and sinking us just as soon as we're out of what you call *your jurisdiction*," Hal said.

Drommond shook his head. "I'll hold them in port for twenty-four hours after you've gone. That should see you safely on your way."

Hal looked at his friends and shrugged. They had little choice in the matter.

Thorn stood up, dusting the beach sand from the seat of his trousers. "Money talks," he said. "It always does."

The other Herons began to gather up the gear they had brought onto the beach. Drommond watched for several minutes, then issued a curt order to his men. They came to a rather sloppy attention preparatory to moving out.

Hal stepped in front of him. "Just make sure you enforce that twenty-four-hour restriction on the *Vulture*," he said.

The commander met his gaze evenly. "Of course," he replied, although Hal had little confidence that he would do as he said.

Hal turned his back on the man pointedly, dismissing him, and called to his crew.

"Let's get her launched and under way," he said.

. . . . .

Within half an hour, they were at sea, bowling smoothly along before a gentle breeze. Thorn and Stig had joined Hal at the steering platform. Stig craned out now to look beyond the sternpost at the rapidly receding shape of Cypra as it sank below the horizon.

"No sign that they're following," he said. "Maybe that jumped-up vigilante kept his word."

Thorn snorted derisively. "I doubt it," he said. "I can't see a stuffed shirt like that telling friend Myrgos what to do and what not to do."

"Well, keep an eye out for them," Hal said. "I'm sure we'll see them before too long." He glanced up at the telltale. "In light winds like these, we might have an advantage over them."

"Fifteen oars a side," Stig reminded him.

He shrugged. "I know. But right now, we've got other decisions to make." He glanced for'ard to where Olaf was leaning on the rail amidships, staring over the side at the wake as it constantly formed, dispersed, then regenerated. "Olaf! Can you join us, please?"

The big former guard commander moved aft to join them, matching his gait to the rolling and gentle plunging of the deck beneath his feet. It was good to be afloat again, he thought, after so many years ashore. He looked curiously at the other three as he joined them.

"Problem?" he asked.

Hal shook his head. "More of an opportunity," he replied. "It strikes me that this might be the ideal time for us to rescue young Constantus from Santorillos."

He paused and looked at his companions. They all nodded as he expanded on his thought.

"Our fisherman friend told us that the *Vulture* stays on her cruise for two months or more. And Myrgos has at least fifty men on board. His total strength is seventy, so that leaves just twenty of them to guard his compound, and the young emperor. We may never have a better opportunity to raid the place and set Constantus free."

His words were met by murmurs of agreement.

"It make sense to me," Thorn said.

Olaf rubbed his jaw thoughtfully. "Me too," he said. "In addition, he'll have taken his best men along on his cruise. So we're likely to be contending with the leftovers at Santorillos."

"Mind you, we've still got to find a way up the cliffs," Stig pointed out.

"Lydia seems confident she can climb them," Hal said.

Stig shrugged doubtfully. "She hasn't seen them. And we don't know if they're guarded or not. She's assuming a lot. Confidence is a good thing, up to a point. But overconfidence can be fatal."

"That's true. But we won't know the answer to that until we've had a chance to reconnoiter the site," Hal said. "And the sooner we do that, the sooner we'll be able to form a plan to rescue Constantus."

"So, the sooner we head for Santorillos, the better," Olaf said.

Hal nodded. "Santorillos lies more or less southwest of our current position," he said. "Let's come about and head that way. I'll check the charts for an exact course once we've turned."

"Maybe we'd better wait," Thorn said. He'd moved to the sternpost and was peering aft over their wake. "We appear to have company."

chapter **twenty-seven**

T
hey all turned and looked astern at his words. There was small white square just visible above the horizon—the sail of a large ship.

Like them, she was running before the wind and making excellent speed. It was the best point of sailing for a square rig, Hal knew. Within an hour, the other ship was hull up on the horizon—and the black hull told them it was definitely the *Vulture*.

"She's gaining on us," said Lydia. She had come aft to watch the progress of the ship behind them.

"Not by much," Hal said. He glanced at the sun, now almost overhead. "If we can hold her off until dark, we can give her the slip then." He looked back at the other ship once more. She was almost dead astern. "We'll come about to starboard and get the wind on our beam."

They all knew that was *Heron*'s best point of sailing.

Thorn issued a warning, however. "If we turn, she can cut the corner and make up ground on us," he said.

Hal acknowledged the point. "But we'll be faster on that leg," he said. "And that should make up for any distance she gains."

"Why starboard?" Olaf asked. "Santorillos lies to port."

"That's why we'll go starboard," Hal told him. "No point in giving him any hint that we're heading for his base."

Olaf shrugged, a little annoyed with himself for not seeing that. "Of course," he said.

Hal gestured for Stig to take the helm and walked forward to address the rest of the crew. They had overheard the discussion from the steering platform but the earlier conversation—about Santorillos—hadn't carried for'ard.

He stopped amidships, by Ulf's and Wulf's position. The others all moved closer to hear what he had to tell them. Kloof padded slowly from her customary position by the mast and stood beside him, as if she too would understand what he was about to say. He smiled at her and ruffled her ears.

"This is all your fault," he said in a mock accusatory tone. Kloof tilted her head to his touch and closed her eyes in pleasure. Then Hal looked up at the crew. "You've probably realized that the *Vulture* is behind us, and obviously trying to catch us," he said. There were a few nods, and several of the Herons leaned out to glance astern at the other ship. When he had their attention again, he continued.

"We're going to come about on the starboard tack. We should make up some distance on her that way. We'll keep ahead of her through the afternoon, then we'll give her the slip once darkness falls."

"How do you plan to do that?" Jesper asked.

"I'm a cunning devil. I'll find a way," Hal told him cheerfully. "Once we're shot of her, we'll reverse course and head for the island of Santorillos. By tomorrow morning, Myrgos should be leagues away from us and continuing on his raiding cruise. We figure there'll only be twenty or so men left at his base at Santorillos, so this is an ideal opportunity to snatch young Constantus away from them."

"That make sense," said Ingvar. The others muttered agreement.

Stefan had been watching the other ship while Hal talked. He pointed now. "He's still gaining on us," he said.

Hal looked and could see that the pirate was noticeably closer—although not enough to worry about. "That'll change when we get the wind on our beam."

Stefan looked doubtful. "She's a big ship—nearly twice our length."

They all knew that the longer a ship's waterline was, the faster her potential hull speed would be. But Hal hoped that advantage would be outweighed by *Heron*'s more efficient sail plan—and the fact that the light wind would favor the smaller ship. He said as much now and Stefan looked mollified.

"So long as the wind holds," he said.

Hal inclined his head. "Why wouldn't it?" he replied. Then he added in a more serious tone, "The thing is, we don't have a big margin to play with, so all our sail drill, all our tacks, must be as fast and as efficient as we can make them. No mistakes please. No tangled sheets, no twisted sails. Clear?"

"Clear," they all chorused. They were a well-drilled crew and they rarely made mistakes. But it was worth making the point to keep them on their toes. Hal looked at each of them in turn, then nodded.

"All right. As soon as I'm back on the tiller, we'll come about. Let's show Myrgos how a Skandian ship can move."

There was a low growl of assent and he walked quickly back to the steering platform, taking the tiller from Stig. He twitched it once or twice experimentally, then called out to those for'ard.

"Stand by . . . coming about to starboard . . . NOW!"

As he shouted the last word, he put the helm over and *Heron* swung her sharp prow to starboard. They had been sailing under the starboard sail and now the crew for'ard released it, sending it sliding down while the port sail and yardarm soared upward. For a moment, there was the usual scene of apparent confusion as the new sail flapped and shook in the wind. Then, on his order, Ulf and Wulf heaved on the sheets and brought it under control. With barely a check in her movement, *Heron* accelerated onto her new course, moving noticeably faster through the water.

"What's *Vulture* doing?" Hal asked Stig. His own attention was on the trim of the sail, making sure it was set to the most efficient angle and tautness possible.

"Nothing so far . . . ," Stig said, shading his eyes to peer astern. "Now she's turning! She's coming about to starboard as well. Thorn's right. She's cutting the corner to pick up ground on us."

This was *Vulture*'s chance to make up ground. As *Heron* steadied on her new course, the black ship could aim to intercept her by swinging even farther to starboard, drawing a giant imaginary triangle on the face of the ocean between the two ships.

"She's head-reaching on us," Stig warned. That meant the pirates were gaining ground across the triangle. If they continued in this way, they would intercept the *Heron* at a point farther along her course. Hal studied the set of the sail. It wasn't quite to his liking.

"Sheet home . . . that's enough."

The adjustment sent *Heron* flying through the water even faster. He judged now that he was getting maximum speed from her and glanced at Stig.

"How is it now?"

Stig crouched down, closing one eye and lining the pursuing ship up with the sternpost as a reference point. He waited half a minute or so, then grinned.

"That's done it," he said. "She's falling behind."

There were grins all around as the crew heard him. Some of them had been sitting or standing tensely at their posts. Now they relaxed.

It was a strange feeling as the sun passed overhead and the afternoon progressed. It wasn't altogether comfortable to be sailing with a pursuing enemy in plain sight behind them. But *Heron* managed to keep the other ship at bay. And, after an hour, she began to draw away.

"We're gaining on her," Olaf said, a note of triumph in his voice.

Hal nodded. "The wind's easing," he said. The lighter winds would favor the smaller ship and the more efficient sail rig that

Heron carried. In addition, the *Vulture* was now on a beam reach to match *Heron*, and it was not her fastest point of sailing.

"We should be out of sight by nightfall if it keeps on this way," Lydia said. She had taken over from Stig monitoring the relative positions of the two ships.

Thorn glared at her reproachfully. "Never tempt fate like that," he said, and she looked suitably chastened. When it came to wind and weather conditions at sea, Thorn was highly superstitious. He felt the gods were always waiting for men to become overconfident. Then they would punish them for their hubris.

"Old wives' tale," Hal said, to ease Lydia's embarrassment.

Half an hour later, the wind died.

The sail flapped several times, then hung loosely from the yard-arm. *Heron* continued to carve through the water for another fifteen or twenty meters, but the way fell off her and eventually she lay becalmed, rocking gently on the swell. The crew didn't need Hal's urgent shout. As the wind died, they scrambled to unstow their oars and ran them out through the oarlocks. There was a rattle and clatter of wood on wood as they did so, then Stig called the order.

"Ready? Stroke!"

Six oars went back as one, dipped into the water, then heaved the ship forward once more—albeit at a fraction of her previous speed. Hal, watching astern, saw the flash of light on the *Vulture*'s oar blades as the pirate ship ran out her own oars, then they rose and fell in a deadly rhythm. He recalled hearing how the Toscans referred to a galley's oars as its wings. Now, watching the constant, rhythmic beat of the twin banks, he understood why.

He looked round at his own rowers, willing Stig to increase the pace. But his first mate kept the beat steady at a three-quarter rate, and Hal realized it was the best way. This calm might last a few minutes—or a few hours. If they rowed flat out, they would soon be exhausted and, even though they were losing ground now to the bigger ship, they would lose it even faster if they wore themselves out. In a race between six oars and thirty, they were always going to lose. All they could do was delay that inevitable end as long as possible.

He sprang up onto the railing beside the steering platform, steadying himself on the backstay, and peered across the water for some indication that the wind was returning.

But there was nothing, although the sky to the north was dark with clouds, foretelling a change in the weather.

The question was, would it arrive in time to save them?

He looked back to the *Vulture*. It was bearing down inexorably, seeming to grow larger even as he watched. He scanned the sea to starboard, and his heart leapt as he saw a patch of darker water. It was the sign of little waves caused by a ruffle of wind. As he watched, the disturbance in the surface moved closer to them.

Now was the time to use their last reserves of strength, he knew.

"Full speed, Stig!" he yelled, and he heard his first mate increase the tempo of the rowing, felt a little shudder run through the ship as she accelerated. He looked at *Vulture* once more. She was still gaining, but not as quickly as she had been. Standing on the rail like this, he had his foot hooked through the handle of the tiller. He shoved it over now and the ship swung to starboard, heading for that beautiful patch of disturbed water, that life-saving wind.

"Ulf! Wulf! There's a wind to starboard, bearing down on us. Be ready to leave those oars as soon as it hits!"

There was no reply. The twins were using all their energy to row. But looking quickly at them, he could see they understood and were ready. He looked astern again. *Vulture* was still there, still getting closer.

The first gust hit them and the sail flapped wildly, then hung loose again, then flapped once more. Ulf and Wulf shot to their feet, dragging their oars inboard and leaving them lying any which way as they lunged for the sheets. Somebody else would stow them. Hal dropped lightly to the deck, and as the sail filled, he felt the tiller come alive and he hauled the bow around to port, while Ulf and Wulf trimmed the sail.

Heron accelerated away, a triumphant shower of spray bursting over her starboard bow and drifting down onto the crew. Smiles broke out as they saw the big black ship beginning to fall behind again. They might have thirty oars, but they had been rowing hard too and were tiring. Myrgos made the mistake of staying with his oars for a few minutes too long, then realized he was losing ground and yelled orders for his crew to raise the sail and sheet home. The hairs on the back of Hal's neck prickled. They were so close he could hear the pirate captain's frantic orders.

They plunged on, regaining the distance they had lost while they had been becalmed. The wind was steady now, and *Heron* smashed through the oncoming waves, sending silver showers of spray high on either side of the bow, to hang there for several seconds, then drift back down onto the crew. The oars were stowed, and the crew stood ready for Hal's orders. The skirl continued to peer to the north, where dark lines of clouds were gathering on the horizon.

It seemed only a few minutes before the first of the dark clouds rolled down upon them. *Heron* heeled over as the wind suddenly strengthened. Ulf and Wulf eased the sheets, and she came upright once more. Then the rain squall was all around them, blotting everything from sight. There was no sign of *Vulture*. Their ship was engulfed in sheets of cold rain and dark cloud.

Thorn moved close to the steering platform. "Are you going to turn?" he asked. "Myrgos can't see us now."

But Hal shook his head. "We'll see how long this squall lasts. We could be in the clear any minute."

Within a few minutes, they had burst clear of the rain and heavy wind, into the late afternoon sunshine again. Looking behind, they could see no sign of *Vulture* until she too nosed out of the squall. They had increased their lead over the pirates still farther. Hal looked ahead. Another dark squall line was bearing down on them.

"I'll keep on this heading until the sun sets," he said. "Once it's dark we might have a chance of shaking him. Until then, I want him to think this is where we want to be going."

The second squall hit them, even more violently than the first, and again they were surrounded by the howling wind and driving rain. Ulf and Wulf re-trimmed the sail. Having the ship heel over under the pressure of the wind might give an impression of speed, but it was a false one. *Heron* moved faster when she was more upright. Hal held the tiller lightly, gauging the speed of the ship as he felt the trembling in the rudder.

Once more they burst clear of the squall, and once more all eyes turned astern to see how *Vulture* had fared. The black hull shoved clear of the rain a few minutes later. There was a low cheer from the crew. They were even farther ahead.

"Only a few minutes of daylight left," Thorn remarked.

Hal glanced to the west, where the sun was a giant, glowing orb just touching the horizon. Then it sank beneath the waves with a peculiar green flash of light.

chapter　twenty-eight

In the sudden darkness, it was difficult to see the black shape behind them—but just as difficult for Myrgos to see the *Heron*.

Perhaps more difficult, in fact. The *Vulture*'s hull, being darker than surrounding sea, showed as a black shadow in the night; whereas *Heron*'s deep green color scheme tended to blend in with her surroundings.

"Stefan!" Hal shouted. "Get for'ard and warn me when the next squall is about to hit."

Stefan nodded and scrambled toward the bow. Hal turned to Lydia, who was close by, unconsciously fingering one of the darts for her atlatl where it sat in her belt quiver.

"Lydia, you keep watch aft and tell me the minute you lose sight of *Vulture*."

Stefan and Lydia had the two sharpest pairs of eyes in the ship. Hal now called to the other members of the crew gathered amidships.

"Sail handlers! On my call, be ready to go about to starboard!" That would put the ship on the port tack.

Jesper and Ingvar, who were tasked with bringing the yardarms up and down, waved acknowledgment. The twins crouched over the trimming sheets, ready to act.

"Squall coming!" yelled Stefan, then the wind and rain hit them.

A few seconds later, Lydia called out, "No sign of *Vulture!*"

"Come about starboard!" Hal yelled, his voice cracking with anxiety. A mistake now could be disastrous.

But the maneuver went ahead smoothly, with Ingvar and Jesper running up the starboard yardarm and Ulf and Wulf sheeting it home, so that *Heron* shot through the water on the new tack with barely any slackening in pace.

Although now she was running at an oblique angle to her former course.

They came out of the squall into the dark night. The moon was a slender crescent riding high above the driving clouds, alternately casting a dim light, then allowing the darkness to blanket the ocean, seeming even darker after the few minutes of light. All eyes were on the black line of the squall as it fell behind them. Then Jesper let out a muted cheer, hastily muffled as Ingvar threw his hand across his mouth.

Vulture emerged from the squall, still on her original course, and now twice as far away as she had been before. It took several minutes for her crew, searching the horizon desperately, to sight the dim form of the *Heron*, slipping through the waves. As they did, Myrgos, who had taken control of the tiller, tried to bring his ship around to starboard, tacking across the wind as *Heron* had done. But, like many a square-rigger captain before him, Myrgos discovered too late that it wasn't easy to match *Heron*'s agility. It had been an instinctive action to try to follow the other ship, but it nearly brought him to grief. The wind caught the huge square mainsail as the ship came up into the wind, driving it back against the mast and stopping *Vulture* dead in the water. Then she began to gather sternway, and the mast and shrouds creaked alarmingly. Furious, Myrgos shouted a series of commands to his men. He was fortunate that, with a large crew, he had the necessary numbers to carry out the tasks he ordered.

The square sail slid down the mast, releasing the back pressure on the ship. Simultaneously, half a dozen oars on either side slid out through their oarlocks, the starboard-side oars backing water furiously, the port six driving ahead. And at last, the ship came round onto the new heading and the sail was reset.

Myrgos was an experienced sailor, and he recovered from his initial mistake quickly and efficiently. Even so, it had cost him time and distance while he lay stopped.

All the while *Heron* was driving away upwind.

"Squall coming!" Stefan shouted, and Hal looked off the port bow to where another dark line of wind and rain was bearing down on them. An idea was beginning to form in his mind, and he shouted to the rest of the crew. "Get those shields down off the bulwarks!"

The hull was dull green, but the line of regularly spaced shields were lighter in color, each one decorated with its owner's choice of symbol. They would be easy to spot in the darkness and he wanted them down. The Herons grabbed them from the pegs that held them in position and dropped them into the rowing wells.

"Got something in mind?" Thorn was an interested onlooker.

Hal shook his head, loath to reveal his thinking just yet. He had his own superstitions and one was to avoid talking about a plan too soon, in case it all went wrong. He checked the onrushing squall, then glanced astern at *Vulture*. She couldn't lie as close to the wind as *Heron* and she was angled off to starboard.

The squall hit them.

"She's gone!" Lydia cried as she lost sight of their pursuer.

"Hard aport!" Hal yelled into the storm, and the sail handlers went to work once more, swinging *Heron* back the way she had been heading before, bringing down one yardarm and sending another soaring aloft. Ulf and Wulf, crouched low, scuttled across the deck to the opposite side and began trimming the sheets. *Heron* steadied, then smashed into a rogue wave, drenching everyone on deck with spray and solid water, then shook herself like a wet dog and accelerated away again.

Anxious eyes watched for *Vulture* to emerge from the squall. When she did, there was an involuntary cry of disappointment from several throats.

Myrgos had outguessed Hal. Seeing that the *Heron* lay slightly to port of his own course, it had been a logical assumption that Hal would turn that way, going back to the starboard tack—with the wind coming over his starboard side. Accordingly, while he had been hidden by the driving rain of the squall, Myrgos had worn ship, swinging her on a two-hundred-and-seventy-degree arc to the right, until the wind was on her starboard side once more. As a result, she was on the same tack as *Heron* and had even made up some distance. Hal estimated that she was at least a hundred meters closer than she had been.

But even as he had the thought, he realized she was falling away to port, unable to keep the same heading that *Heron* could manage. The two ships raced on, on slightly diverging courses.

"Squall coming!" Stefan warned.

Hal thought quickly. Once to the right. Once to the left. And Myrgos had outguessed him the second time. Which way this time? His fingers drummed nervously on the tiller, then he yelled his instructions.

"We're going straight through this time!" he yelled. Let's see if Myrgos sees that coming, he thought to himself.

The wind and rain hit them again, laying the ship over under its increased force. Lydia called out that *Vulture* was out of sight, but this time Hal ignored the information. Ulf and Wulf eased the sheets, but Hal sensed they had let them go too far.

"Sheet home!" he called urgently. Then: "Steady there!"

The sail tightened. The deck heeled a little farther, but *Heron* moved fractionally faster through the water. The twins raised their eyebrows at each other. They were expert sail trimmers, but nobody had the feeling for this ship the way Hal did.

The ship burst into the clear again, the bow riding high on a wave, then knifing down into the trough, and sending twin arcs of silver spray high into the air on either side of the bow. Ulf and

Wulf adjusted for the slackening of the wind, and *Heron* flew across the dark sea.

All hands faced aft, waiting and watching for *Vulture* to emerge. Then the black shape slid out of the murk, and Jesper, Stefan and Edvin raised an ironic cheer. This time, Myrgos had been too clever. He had turned left once more, and now *Vulture* was well out of position and well behind them.

Hal glanced for'ard. He could see the dark line of the next squall approaching them. But it was several minutes away. He called out to the crew.

"Ulf and Wulf, stay at your positions! Everyone else come aft."

The crew hurried aft to group around the steering platform, waiting to hear what he had in mind. When he told them, several hearts beat a little faster. He was taking an awful risk.

"We can go on ducking and dodging like this all night," he said. "Myrgos has guessed wrong twice now and he'll be anxious not to miss again. This time, just as we go into the squall, I'm going to start a turn to the left. Lydia, warn me just before *Vulture* is out of sight. I want her to see us start that turn."

The girl warrior nodded.

Hal continued. "Then I'm coming back to our original course. When I do, I want you, Ingvar and Jesper, to drop the sail."

"Drop the sail, Hal? Are you sure?" That was Ingvar, the worry obvious in his voice.

Hal nodded firmly. "Drop it. We're going to stop. The two most visible things about us are our sail and our wake through the water. If we drop the sail and heave to, Myrgos won't be able to see either. But be ready to hoist it again in a moment if we're spotted.

If we're lucky, Myrgos will turn one way or another and sail on past us. Even if he keeps on straight ahead, the odds are good he won't see us. Once he's past, we'll hoist sail and reverse our course. I'll keep the squall between us and him and we'll simply sail away— with any luck."

With any luck, he thought to himself.

"Lydia, you stand by here and, if we're spotted, let fly. Try to kill the helmsman. It might even be Myrgos himself. But if not, it'll buy us a few seconds." She nodded grimly and Hal turned to his first mate. "Stig, tell the twins what we're doing. Make sure they understand."

The Herons started to turn back to their stations, and he stopped them again. "One more thing. When we stop, everyone keep down. Don't look. Your pale faces will be too visible in the gloom. Anyone looks up, I'll throw him overboard."

"Including me, Hal?" Ingvar said. The grin was obvious in his voice, and Hal nodded emphatically.

"Especially you, Ingvar. That moon face of yours will be seen for miles."

He dismissed them with a wave of his hand, and they returned to their posts. He kept a long, dark scarf hanging by the chart table for wild and windy weather and he picked it up now and wound it round his neck and face. Then he pulled down his watch cap so only his eyes were showing.

Thorn waited to study the effect. "You look beautiful," he said, then he went for'ard to his post by the mast. He sat down beside Kloof, one arm around her, ready to muzzle her if she should make any noise. The dog thumped her tail at his touch.

"Squall's coming!" Stefan warned.

Hal glanced at Lydia. "Warn me just before we lose sight of them," he said, and she nodded, then fixed her eyes on the pirate behind them.

They sailed into the first few meters of disturbed air and rain.

"Now!" Lydia called.

Hal instantly pushed the tiller to the right, letting the bow swing to port.

After a few seconds, Lydia called again, "Gone!"

He straightened their course back to where it had been. He allowed a minute to pass, then shouted his orders. "Down sail. Everyone flat on the deck!"

The sail, the biggest and lightest-colored item on board—and so the most visible—slid down the mast, and Jesper and Edvin gathered it in. Then all the crew threw themselves flat, facedown on the deck.

The ship, slowing gradually, ran on for another twenty to thirty meters, then the way came off her and she pitched and rolled in the violent wind and sea of the squall. Hal crouched down, one hand still on the tiller, although *Heron* had no steerageway on her. He strained his eyes aft and to port, searching for the first sign of *Vulture*, fearful that she would spot them and turn toward them.

For'ard, the crew lay flat, faces pressed to the deck. Stig found himself studying a rough line of splinters a few inches from his nose, where a dropped piece of equipment had gouged a scratch in the deck planking. Have to take care of that when this is over, he thought.

Heron, without any forward motion, pitched and rolled awkwardly in the uneven seas. At the steering platform, Hal held his breath, as if the sound of it rasping in and out might carry to the other ship. Then he heard her. He heard the creak and groan of her rigging as she shouldered her way through the turbulent waves, heard Myrgos's harsh voice as he called orders to his men—although Hal couldn't understand the language.

This time, despite the *Heron*'s feint left, Myrgos had elected to keep going straight ahead, and his decision brought him terribly close to the *Heron*, which lay silent and unmoving, seeming to crouch in the darkness.

Then *Vulture* slid into view—a black shape, darker than the surrounding night, moving swiftly through the water and barely fifty meters away. Hal's heart pounded in his chest as he waited for the shout that would tell him they had been discovered.

But it never came. The pirates were scanning the sea ahead of them, looking for the first sign of *Heron*, for the lighter-colored triangle of her sail. They didn't see her, lying still and silent and barely a stone's throw away. And as Hal peered carefully out from the narrow space between his watch cap and the wound scarf, the black ship slid out of sight into the darkness and rain that surrounded them.

"They missed us," Lydia whispered from her position a few meters away. He scowled at her, although the effect was lost behind the scarf and cap.

"Quiet," he warned her, in a low voice. He crouched, waiting, straining his ears to hear the receding ship. He could still hear Myrgos's voice, and the sound of her passage as she thrust her way through the waves. But the sounds were getting fainter, and eventually they faded altogether.

"Hoist the sail!" he called softly.

Ingvar, Stefan and Jesper grabbed hold of the halyards and sent the sail sliding up the mast. Ulf and Wulf sheeted home without the need for further orders, and *Heron* began to glide through the water again, accelerating to her normal cruising speed. The wind and waves buffeted her, but Hal swung her to port until the wind was dead astern and she was traveling in the opposite direction to the big black ship.

If he'd guessed correctly, when they emerged from the squall, the line of dark cloud and rain would be behind them and *Vulture* would be on the far side, with both ships hidden from each other.

"Let's get out of here," he said.

chapter   twenty-nine

T he weather cleared an hour before dawn. When the sun finally made its appearance above the horizon, the *Heron* was alone on the sea. The sky was clear and blue, the swell gave the ship an easy, rolling motion and the wind was strong enough to let them run at a good speed, without having to plunge and fight the waves.

As the light came up across the sea, Hal scrambled onto the bulwark beside the steering platform, balancing himself with a hand on the backstay, and scanned the horizon through a full circle. In the bow, Stefan did the same.

There was no sign of the *Vulture*. They had run all night on the direct opposite course to the one they had last seen her on. Assuming she had stayed on that course to search for them—and there was no reason to think she hadn't—she would be at least fifty or sixty kilometers away by now.

They had traveled southwest throughout the night, and Santorillos lay somewhere to the northwest of their current position. Now that he knew what island they were looking for, Hal quickly found it on his charts. Hal gestured to Edvin to take the helm and stepped to the chart table. He placed his sun compass on the map to gauge their current direction, making a mental note that he would have to recalibrate it soon. Sun compasses needed to be calibrated every three or four days.

Stig and Thorn joined him as he studied the chart, marking the spot where he estimated they had been the previous night. He set a straight edge from that spot heading southwest and marked what he thought their current position should be. His sailing notes said there was a northerly current in this part of the sea that would have taken them north of the line he had measured, so he adjusted accordingly. Stig and Thorn watched with interest as he did all this. Navigation was a mystery to them. It was a combination of knowledge of local conditions, measurement of speeds and distances, and a generous helping of instinctive reasoning. Hal, they knew, was a master of the art. After several minutes studying the chart, he straightened and marked a spot on the map with a thin piece of charcoal.

"We're there, more or less," he said. As ever, he checked the telltale before estimating how long it would take to reach Santorillos. "Maybe a day and a half or two days' sailing."

The others nodded. That much they could work out for themselves, once he had ascertained their current position.

"If the wind holds," Thorn said.

Hal grinned at him. "You're always saying that."

His friend shrugged. "Winds come and go. Only a fool would assume otherwise."

"We'll come about and head northwest," Hal said, stepping up to take the tiller from Edvin. The rest of the crew, seeing him resuming command, readied themselves for the change of course.

They came about and bowled along on a constant tack to the northwest. In spite of Thorn's pessimism, the wind stayed steady for the rest of the day and night. Early in the afternoon of the next day, Lydia called from the for'ard lookout that she could see land off to starboard. The vague shadow that they saw at first gradually altered into a hard outline.

Hal frowned to himself. He'd wanted a perfect landfall but he'd been off by about ten degrees. The perfectionist in him was dissatisfied, although most navigators would have been more than pleased with the result. He nudged the tiller and brought *Heron* around to starboard, heading for the land.

He consulted his sailing notes, purchased several years before from a Phyllirican trader. He could see three prominent spurs of rock on the spine of the island.

"That's Santorillos, all right," he said, and the crew studied the approaching island with interest.

They were approaching from the south, which was the side opposite the huge caldera. From this angle, they would see a rocky coastline with only a few suitable landing places. As with so many of these islands, there was no harbor. Ships would run ashore on the sandy beaches that were interspersed along the rocky coastline. The largest and most accessible of these was the site of a village on the island. Hal headed for it now. There were half a dozen small fishing boats drawn up on the sand, and inland was a haphazard cluster of whitewashed buildings, mostly single story, gleaming in the sun.

Behind the settlement, the island rose steeply. The ground was rocky and inhospitable, with little in the way of trees to provide shade. Several kilometers in from the shore, it was broken up by a steep rocky escarpment. At the top, Hal could make out several buildings, whitewashed as seemed to be the custom here. A rock wall joined them, creating a fortification at the crest of the slope.

"That'll be Myrgos's lookout," he said, studying the buildings and the lay of the land. "Be pretty hard to get close to that without being seen."

"Maybe it'll be easier from the lagoon side," Stig said.

Hal nodded. "Maybe," he said doubtfully. Then he set himself to the task of running the ship up onto the sand.

Once they were aground and the hull propped level, he turned his attention to two locals who had watched their approach. They were middle-aged men, clad in flowing white linen robes, with head coverings made from the same material and hanging down at the back to shade their necks.

"Good afternoon," he said in a friendly tone. "What island is this?"

The first of the two locals, a grossly overweight man, regarded him with a less-than-friendly attitude.

"Who's asking?" he said bluntly.

It occurred to Hal that these villagers carried on their daily lives under the umbrella of Myrgos's protection. Presumably, the village supplied the pirates with meat, vegetables and fish. Hal leaned over the railing and smiled at the man.

"This ship is the *Heron*," he said. "We're from the north. My name is Hal Mikkelson."

The fat man turned to his companion, who was of average height and build.

"Skandians," he said, his tone making it clear that he was not an admirer of northerners.

"Raiders, more like," his companion said, but Hal held up a hand.

"We're not raiders," he said. He indicated the crew gathered on the deck. "As you can see, there are just a dozen of us. We'd need more than that to be raiding. We're carrying a cargo of amber and we're looking to trade." Amber was a product of the north and it didn't take up a lot of room. So a small ship like *Heron* could well be an amber trader.

"Hmmmph," said the fat man, unconvinced. "You'd better not be raiders. This village is under the protection of Lord Myrgos. And we're not interested in your amber."

A pirate to protect them from pirates, Hal thought. He'd been right. There was obviously a cooperative relationship between the village and Myrgos.

"Well, I wouldn't want to make him angry," Hal said. "Where would I find him?"

"He's at sea—" the fat man began, but his companion nudged him savagely, cutting off his words with a grunt.

"He's around," he said firmly. "And you'd better not make him angry. His ship would trample this little cockleshell underfoot." He cast a disparaging look at the neat shape of the *Heron*.

"I'll make sure we don't get offside with him," Hal said. "In the meantime, we need to buy fresh food and stock up on water and firewood. Where can we do that?"

The unkindly looks vanished. Greed and the desire for profit trumped suspicion any day, Hal thought. The thinner man jerked a thumb toward the untidy village.

"You can do that here. Market is open tomorrow," he said.

"Well then," said Hal, "we'll make camp here on the beach for the night, if that's all right."

The fat man waved a magnanimous hand. "Make yourselves at home," he said. Then he spoiled the apparent welcome. "But stay clear of the village tonight. We don't like strangers causing trouble."

"We'll be no trouble," Hal promised. "As a matter of fact, we might even anchor offshore for the night." He turned to Stig and added in a low voice, "Wouldn't put it past the villagers to come calling while we're asleep."

Stig nodded. The thin man's next words seemed to confirm Hal's suspicions.

"No need to go to that trouble. You're welcome to camp here," he said. He glanced angrily at his companion, sensing that his unfriendly tone had alienated the newcomers.

But Hal waved his objections aside cheerily. "It's no trouble. The sea's calm and the cove is sheltered. It'll save us the trouble of making camp."

"Suit yourself," the thinner man said. But there was a tinge of disappointment in his voice.

Hal ordered Stig to prepare the ship for unbeaching, then turned back to the two locals. "My charts say there's a caldera on the far side of the island," he said. "I'd quite like to see that."

The thin man yawned. He was losing interest in the new arrivals. "Go ahead," he said. "But you'll need to come back here for the night. The lagoon is far too deep for anchoring and there are no moorings on that side."

"Still, now that we're here, we may as well take a look," Hal said, feigning no more than a casual interest.

The villager grunted and gestured to his friend. The two of them turned away and began to make their way back up the beach. A few meters on, the fat one turned around and called:

"Remember, the market is tomorrow."

Hal waved acknowledgment, saying in an undertone, "And I'll bet you take a healthy share of the profits."

Thorn looked at him and grinned. "That's the way of the world."

"True enough," Olaf put in. After years in Byzantos, he was used to the system of bribes and kickbacks that prevailed everywhere. Skandians eschewed such behavior. They tended to expend their energies avoiding making payments—particularly when it came to taxes.

Stig had the *Heron* ready for unbeaching. As they climbed back aboard, he and Ingvar put their shoulders against the prow of the ship and heaved, their feet finding purchase in the loose sand. The ship resisted for a second or two, then the hold of the sand released and she began sliding backward into deeper water. With a final shove, Stig and Ingvar reached up and hauled themselves up and over the bulwark. Stig hurriedly took his place on the rowing bench. Ingvar, now that there was no danger in sight, was relieved from rowing duties. His massive strength tended to send the ship off line.

They backed the ship for twenty meters, then, with one set of oars going ahead and the other astern, they turned her in her own length.

"Oars in," Hal called, and the oars were stowed with their usual clatter. "Port sail," he ordered.

As the yardarm ran up, he turned to Lydia, who was standing nearby. "Now, let's take a look at this caldera."

The lagoon was huge—an immense circle measuring nearly ten kilometers across, with precipitous cliffs rising from the sea.

Originally, the circle had been continuous, but over the years sections had crumbled and collapsed into the ocean, leaving large gaps in the rock wall that bounded the caldera. Now there were five entrances to the lagoon that Hal could see. But the eastern wall, covering nearly two-thirds of the circle, was virtually complete.

They sailed into the huge lagoon. Almost immediately, Hal ordered the sail down and oars out. "We'll stay close to the cliffs," he told Thorn. "That'll make us harder to see if there is a lookout up top."

Craning to look up at the massive cliffs, they could see no sign of habitation. But after they'd cruised halfway round, staying no more than thirty meters from the shore, they spotted a small build-ing clinging to the top of the cliffs. There was no sign of a lookout, no sign of anyone moving up there. Hal kept the ship hugging the rocks and they rowed on in silence.

"There's a cable," Lydia said as they came closer to the white-washed building high above. She pointed and they could all see the thin black line stretching down to the cliff's base. It emanated from the building, but where it ended they couldn't as yet see.

Then it became obvious. There was a narrow inlet in the base of the cliffs, concealed from sight until they were almost upon it. It was ten meters wide and forty deep. It had probably begun as a natural fissure in the rocks and had been dug out and widened by hand, and a timber dock had been built there. The black line of the cable was fastened at the end of the dock. Now they were closer, they could see it was a double line, forming a loop around what appeared to be a windlass or a winch of some sort.

Lydia, shading her eyes, was peering intently at the cliffs.

"There's a basket of some sort up there, attached to the cable," she said eventually. "Looks big enough to hold three or four people."

"That'll be the elevator," Olaf said. "They must moor the ship at the dock, then ride up and down in the basket."

Hal steered for the narrow inlet, calling to the rowers to keep a dead slow pace. At his order, Jesper came aft with a hawser ready to throw over one of the bollards they could see on the dock. As he did, he took the strain, gradually taking the way off the ship until she bumped gently against the rough timbers.

"Let's take a closer look," Hal said, stepping onto the planking of the dock. "Maybe we can ride their elevator up to the top to fetch Constantus down."

But they couldn't. As they examined the windlass, the reason for the lack of a lookout became obvious. The handle to the windlass was missing.

"They must take it with them when they go to sea," Stig observed.

Hal nodded absently. He was busy examining the axle of the windlass, over which the winch handle would fit. He'd hoped it might be a regular square-shaped piece of iron, which might have allowed him to rig a replacement handle. But it was a complicated shape, in the form of a five-armed cross. The arms of the cross were thick and blunt. The winch handle was obviously shaped to fit over them and turn the geared wheels that would bring the cable, and the elevator basket, down to the dock.

"No need for a lookout up there," Stefan said, looking up at the top station of the elevator. They could see now that it was an open-sided shed that held a large wheel, around which the cable was wound. "Without the winch handle, nobody can go up or down."

He was interrupted by a deep rumbling noise out in the lagoon. Startled, they all turned to look and saw what appeared to be a giant bubble breaking the surface. A low wave, perhaps two-thirds of a meter high, emanated from the spot, traveling in a circle. It washed onto the narrow inlet, setting the ship rocking wildly and grating against the dock. The fenders squealed noisily and the planking under their feet shook. Eventually, the disturbance eased and the unsettling movement ceased.

"What was that?" Ulf asked. Nobody answered.

Finally, Thorn put forward a theory. "They say this used to be a volcano," he said. "Maybe it's not totally extinct."

"Is there any such thing as 'a little bit extinct'?" Lydia asked. But nobody was in a mood for jokes.

Nervously, they waited to see if the phenomenon would be repeated, scanning the surface of the lagoon. After several minutes, there was no sign of a further disturbance and Hal shrugged.

"Whatever it was, it's finished now," he said. He turned his attention back to the problem of the winch handle, chewing his lip thoughtfully as he studied the five-armed cog.

Thorn moved closer to him and asked in a low voice, "Can you rig a replacement?"

Hal looked doubtful. "Maybe," he said. "The original will have been cast in iron or bronze to fit over that axle. I'll have to use wood to make a replica. But it might work."

He stepped a little closer to the windlass, studying the axle intently. In his mind's eye, he could see a hardwood winch handle, shaped to fit over the central axle and the five arms. He'd need to reinforce it with metal strips, he thought. And he'd need to use the hardest wood he had.

"It might work," he repeated, with growing conviction. He called to Edvin, who was still on board. "Edvin, bring me one of the wax tablets you use for writing, will you? I'll take an impression of this thing."

Edvin kept a supply of wooden frames filled with wax. He used them to make notes and lists, wiping them clean when he was finished. He selected one now and stepped onto the dock, bringing it to Hal.

The skirl positioned the tablet over the windlass axle and gently but firmly pressed it inward, making sure to keep it at right angles to the axle. When he withdrew it, he checked and saw that the shape of the axle was clearly imprinted on the wax. He grunted with satisfaction.

"All right, let's get out of here," he said. "It'll take me most of the afternoon to make a wooden replica for this."

Lydia was still gazing up the cable to the top station of the elevator. "I could always climb up the cable," she said. "There's sure to be another windlass at the top and I could let it down from there."

Olaf shook his head, following the direction of her gaze. "I doubt they'd go to the trouble of removing this winch handle and leaving another one at the top," he said. "After all, I think they'd foresee the possibility that someone could climb up and let the elevator down."

"Maybe." Lydia looked unconvinced. "But I could always climb up and see."

Hal vetoed the idea. "It'll take too long. And Olaf is probably right. Let's get back to the other side of the island, and I'll get started on a winch handle."

Reluctantly, Lydia agreed. They reboarded the ship and poled her out of the narrow inlet into open water. Hugging the cliffs still, they rowed back the way they had come. Once they were out of the caldera lagoon, Hal had them hoist the sail for the trip back to the village.

They beached the ship again. In spite of his stated intention to anchor out in the bay, Hal wanted to work onshore. He would need a good hot fire to work and shape the metal components of the handle, and they couldn't have such a fire on board ship. He set up a workbench on the sand, and carried his tools and a selection of pieces of timber ashore. He found a length of flat iron and took that as well. He could use it to form an iron tire around the axle piece, to strengthen it.

"Light a fire for me, Ingvar," he said, gesturing to a spot on the beach. If he was going to work the metal, he'd need to heat it. He had a small leather bellows and he placed that by the fire. Then he selected a thick piece of hardwood and cut it into a circular shape. Once that was done, he marked the shape of the axle on it and began to chip it away with a mallet and a razor-sharp chisel. The others watched for some time. He was a master craftsman and they could see the shape growing in the piece of blank wood. He measured as he went, referring to the wax impression to make sure he had the dimensions right. As he got closer to the end, he continued to make tiny alterations.

At this stage, the crew grew somewhat bored. It was interesting to see him shaping the outline at first. But as the work became a series of fiddling adjustments and alterations, it grew less fascinating. They drifted away and left him to it—all except Ingvar, who was tending the fire and building a bed of red-hot coals for Hal, ready for the time when his skirl would need to work the iron into a hoop.

Hal had been working for about two hours when the two locals reappeared to see what he was doing. Edvin called a low warning as the mismatched figures strode down the beach.

Hal glanced up. "Keep them away," he said to Stig. He had no idea if they would recognize the shape he was forming, or if they had ever seen the windlass handle. But there was no sense in taking the chance that they might.

The tall first mate, who was sitting in the sand, his back against the ship's hull, rose gracefully to his feet and strode out to meet the visitors. Thorn followed after him, trotting to catch up with Stig's long strides, then falling in beside him. They stood shoulder to shoulder, blocking the path of the two new arrivals, and effectively screening their view of what Hal was doing.

"What are you up to?" the shorter man demanded. His manner was as abrupt as it had been earlier in the day.

Stig smiled disarmingly. "Bit of minor repair work," he said. "Our rudder has a split in it, and Hal is making a replacement."

From where the local stood, it didn't look like a rudder that Hal was working on. He craned to one side for a closer look, but Thorn stepped to block his view, smiling as well—although the smile only went as far as his mouth. His eyes were definitely not amused.

Or friendly.

"We've got workshops in town that could have taken care of it for you." The taller man had a more approachable tone.

"Aye. I'm sure you do. And I'm sure they would have charged us for the privilege," Thorn replied.

The tall man shrugged. "A craftsman is worth his wages."

Thorn nodded agreement. "True enough. And Hal is as good a craftsman as any carpenter."

The words had barely left his mouth when they sensed, rather than heard, a deep rumbling underground. The surface of the beach seemed to heave, and they all staggered. The crew, who had been relaxing on the sand, sprang to their feet nervously.

"What in Gorlog's name was that?" Thorn said, addressing the two locals.

The taller man shrugged. He and his companion seemed unconcerned about the sudden movement under their feet.

"It's just the island," he said in a superior tone. "It does that from time to time. It used to be a volcano."

"Seems like it still is," Stig said, his voice tight with nerves.

The Santorillans dismissed his concern.

"It's been doing that for years," the shorter man said. "Sometimes, it lets steam out through the fissures in the rock." He paused to scan the rocky slope leading up to the escarpment, then pointed to a spot below the rim. "See there?"

They followed the direction he was pointing and could see several spots where thin jets of steam spurted from the rock face. After a few minutes, the white clouds dissipated.

"And it doesn't bother you when it does that?" Thorn asked.

The two men exchanged a look, and the shorter one screwed up his lips in a disparaging expression. "It's never done us any harm," he said. "It's nothing to get excited about."

There was an awkward pause as the four men stood facing one another, neither side showing any inclination to continue discussing the phenomenon. Finally, Stig broke the silence.

"We won't keep you any longer," he said. His tone left no room for discussion. After a few seconds and a quick exchange of looks, the two locals turned and departed back up the beach.

Thorn watched them go, then pointed to a large pile of firewood heaped into a beacon at the edge of the village. "I'd say Hal's right about them working hand in glove with Myrgos's men," he said. "I'll wager if we started up the hill toward the escarpment, that beacon fire would warn the people at the top."

Stig nodded agreement and Thorn continued. "And look there. That's a heliograph, for sure." He was pointing to a tripod-mounted piece of equipment covered in canvas. "There'll be a polished metal reflector under that cover. They can send messages up to the top with it during the day."

The sound of a hammer ringing on metal distracted them. Hal had finished shaping the axle seat and was bending the flat piece of iron into a hoop to fit over it. As he formed the shape, he heated the two ends until they glowed red hot, then began pounding the heated metal to seal them together.

With that accomplished, he placed the circular hoop into the fire and had Ingvar work the bellows until the entire piece glowed red-hot. Then, carefully handling it with a pair of tongs, he slipped it over the carved wooden cog wheel he had shaped. The metal smoked and burned against the wood until Ingvar doused it with a bucket of cold seawater. As he did, the iron ring contracted and sealed tight around the timber cogwheel, holding it firmly in position.

Hal looked up at them and smiled, wiping a grimy hand across his forehead and leaving a stain of ash there.

"Let's get my gear back aboard. Once this has cooled properly, we can head back around the island and see if it works."

Stig hesitated. "You want to do it tonight?"

Hal nodded emphatically. "Those two locals are suspicious already. If we give them too much time to think, they're likely to pass the word on to the pirates that we're up to something."

"So you want to strike while the iron's hot?" Lydia put in, with the ghost of a grin.

Hal rolled his eyes at her and glanced at the still-smoking iron rim.

"Actually, I thought I'd wait till it's cooled a little," he said.

They repeated their trip around the island to the huge lagoon. As before, once they entered the calm, enclosed waters, Hal had the crew bring down the sail and man the oars—two a side. He steered a course close to the base of the steep cliffs, keeping the ship hidden from any possible eyes at the top.

"Lydia," he said quietly—the location seemed to demand lowered tones—"keep your eyes peeled on that top station. Let me know if you see any sign of movement there."

She nodded and sprang up onto the railing, holding on to a mast stay to maintain her balance.

"No sign of anyone up there," she said.

"Keep watching," Hal told her. "Stefan, you watch the lagoon. Let me know if there's another one of those infernal bubbles."

Wordlessly, Stefan nodded and found a vantage point on the

bulwark opposite Lydia. Under reduced power from the oars, *Heron* glided into the narrow inlet. As before, Jesper ran a line round one of the bollards, gradually tightening it to take the way off the ship. She bumped gently against the timbers of the dock and he made the line fast, then ran forward to take another line ashore from the bow. *Heron* nestled gently against the dock.

Edvin looked around nervously. "It's a little creepy mooring up here in *Vulture*'s spot," he said. "I keep expecting to see her rounding the point there." He gestured to an outcrop of rock that blocked their sight of the entrance they had taken to enter the caldera.

"If she does, we'll be trapped here," Jesper pointed out, ever the bearer of glad tidings.

Edvin regarded him with a disparaging look. "That's why it's creepy," he said.

Jesper made a small moue and went about coiling a spare rope.

It was impossible to put Jesper down, Edvin thought. He had a hide as thick as a bull walrus.

Hal picked up the cumbersome winch handle he had fashioned and laid it over his shoulder. He stepped to the side and dropped down onto the dock.

"Let's get moving," he said. "We've wasted enough time . . . Loki's beard!"

The last two words were torn from him as the dock lurched under his feet, sending him staggering for several paces.

"I wish it would stop doing that!" he said angrily.

Stig made a calming gesture. "Those two locals said it happens all the time," he pointed out.

Hal glared at him. "I'm aware of that. But it doesn't make it any less unpleasant." He waited to see if the movement would repeat, but everything seemed calm. He strode out toward the windlass. Thorn, Stig and Ingvar followed him. The others stood by the oars, at his orders. He agreed with Edvin. There was a certain naked feeling about being moored here in *Vulture*'s dock. He wanted to be ready for a quick getaway if it became necessary. Then he shook off the unpleasant feeling. *Vulture* was hundreds of kilometers away, he told himself, intent on the business of taking and sinking other ships. There was no reason why she should suddenly appear back here in her home base.

"Burn her," said Myrgos. In spite of his harsh tones, his face creased in a cruel smile as he anticipated the sight of the tubby merchant ship burning to the waterline.

Although, he knew, once he withdrew the *Vulture*'s ram from the side of the ship and exposed the massive rent in her hull that the ram was currently plugging, it would be a race between the flames and the inrushing seawater to see which finished the ship off first.

They had spotted the trader just after noon, almost hull down on the horizon. At the sight of the long, low black ship, she had turned away, hoisting her clumsy square sail and fleeing downwind.

The ship was built to carry large amounts of cargo, not for speed. It had taken them barely an hour to run her down. Once they did, Myrgos attacked without any preamble or mercy. He brought down the sail and had his men run out the oars. Then, at double speed, they had swept in on an oblique angle from the ship's starboard quarter. The nine crewmen on board watched in horror as the bronze-plated ram rose and fell above the surface, speeding inexorably for the unprotected planking of their ship.

At the last moment, the trader's helmsman tried to avoid the ram, swinging the tubby ship to port. But Myrgos was ready for the maneuver. He heaved on the tiller and swung *Vulture* to starboard, then, having regained his attacking angle, he swung back to port and sent the ram crashing into their quarry.

"Grapple her!" he shouted, and his men hurried to fasten their ship to the other. He wanted to keep the ram plugging the hole as long as possible. That would give his men time to search the trader, and strip her of her valuables. His men swarmed aboard, hacking and chopping at the unfortunate crew, even though they showed no sign of resistance. After half a dozen of them had fallen bleeding into the scuppers, the remaining three retreated to the bow of the ship, where they cowered anxiously, eyes wide, watching the pirates, fearing for their lives.

"Leave them for now," Myrgos ordered. Even with the ram deep in the other ship's vitals, he knew they had only a limited amount of time before she filled with water and sank. The pirates, yelling triumphantly, levered the hatch covers aside and dropped into the hold, hurling the cargo out onto the deck. Myrgos stepped across the gap between the two hulls and strode to the stern, where the master's quarters would be.

And where the ship's strongbox was most likely to be found.

All traders like this carried a strongbox. Usually, it held substantial amounts of gold and silver in different coinage. Traders needed money to buy new cargoes. And they usually kept it in the same sort of predictable hiding place. It would be in the master's cabin. There would be no sense placing it anywhere where the crew could access it and pilfer the money. The most common spot was under a trapdoor in the deck, usually concealed by a rug or by the master's sleeping cot.

This time, there was no rug visible. Myrgos shoved the cot aside with one booted foot and was rewarded by the sight of a square outline cut into the deck, with a brass ring inset in it. He hauled the trapdoor open and peered down. There was an iron-bound box in there. He lifted it out, pleased to feel its considerable weight, and laid it on the rough table that the master took his meals on. The light was dim in the cabin, and the headroom was low, so that Myrgos couldn't stand upright. He glanced around the cabin and saw an iron spike in one corner. He jammed it into the crude padlock on the strongbox and jerked. The lock sprang open on his third attempt, and he eased the lid back.

His ugly face lit in a smile of satisfaction as he saw the dull gleam of gold and silver within. Even without the cargo, he thought, this would have made the trader a worthwhile capture. He slammed the lid shut, closed the hasp and hoisted the chest under one arm, making his way out into the sunshine again.

Demos saw him coming and raised his eyebrows in a question. Myrgos nodded and smiled. He slapped a hand on the black box under his arm.

"There's a small fortune in here," he said. "Either she's been trading very profitably or she hasn't got round to spending any money so far."

Demos grunted in satisfaction. "What do you want done with the crew?" he asked.

Myrgos looked forward. Sometimes, he liked to take his

pleasure in torturing and killing the men he captured. But today, the weight of the strongbox had him in a good mood.

"Leave them to drown," he said. "They can go down with the ship."

Demos nodded. "The cargo's a good one," he said. "Some olive oil and a lot of excellent furs. I've had them taken to the *Vulture*. We're almost ready to go." He paused. "You're sure you don't want to take any of the crew as hostages?"

And as Demos said the word *hostages*, the answer to the question that had been plaguing him on and off throughout the past several days suddenly came to him. Ever since the meeting in the tavern on Cypra, he had been trying to remember where he had seen the bearded Skandian before. Not the one-armed man. He knew he'd remember him if they'd met previously. But the other older one. His face had been familiar, but Demos couldn't place him. And the more he'd tried to remember where they had met before, the more the memory evaded him.

Then, as so often happens, while he was concentrating on something else, a chance word had triggered the elusive memory. The word *hostages* reminded Demos of the young boy being held for ransom on Santorillos, and he remembered where he had seen the Skandian before.

"He was the commander of the guard!" he said suddenly, as memory dawned on him.

Myrgos stopped and looked at him, puzzled by the abrupt outburst. "What? Who was?" he asked, unable to follow his sub-ordinate's train of thought.

Demos spoke quickly now, the words tumbling over one

another. "That Skandian we saw the other day. The older one."

"The one-armed man?" Myrgos asked. In truth, Olaf had hardly impressed himself on Myrgos's memory. He'd said very little during their encounter.

But Demos was shaking his head emphatically. "No. The other one! The one who was sitting to the side. I knew I'd seen him before!"

"All right, where did you see him?" Myrgos asked, with only faint interest. The strongbox was getting heavy, and he wanted to get back aboard *Vulture*.

"When we kidnapped the boy—Constantus. The Skandian was the commander of his bodyguard. I remember seeing him when we were scouting the location where we took the boy. He was ill, in a litter, which made our task a lot easier. But it was definitely him."

"So what was he doing on Cypra?" Myrgos asked, his interest fanned now. The two pirates exchanged a long glance.

"He's got a ship and a crew. And he's left Byzantos," Demos said slowly. Then realization dawned on both of them at the same moment.

"It's the boy!" Demos said.

"They're heading for Santorillos to snatch him!" Myrgos exclaimed.

Demos rammed a fist into his palm in frustration. "I knew it!" he said. "I told you the other night that they'd doubled back on us!"

After the *Vulture* had lost sight of the little ship in the squalls and darkness, they had argued the point fiercely. Eventually, Myrgos's viewpoint prevailed—as it usually did. Now he uttered a curse as he realized how he'd been duped. He started toward *Vulture* at a run, still clutching the heavy strongbox to his chest. He leapt awkwardly over the gap between the two hulls, staggering as the weight of the box unbalanced him.

"Get back aboard!" he yelled at his crew. "We're heading for Santorillos!"

Puzzled by the unexplained turn of events, the crew hurried to obey. Myrgos pointed wildly at the grappling lines holding the two ships together.

"Cut those lines! Back her away! We've got to get moving!"

Three men ran to cut the grappling lines while the others dropped into the rowing benches and ran their oars out. At a word from Demos, they backed water together, trying to wrench the ram out of the shattered hull.

For a moment, it was jammed and there was no movement. Then, as Myrgos screamed at them to redouble their efforts, *Vulture* began to slide backward, the ram disengaging from the trader's hull with a splintering, tearing sound. As it came clear, *Vulture* moved more freely, and the sea began to rush into the massive wound in the trader's hull. The three surviving crewmen cried out in fear as the hull tilted wildly beneath them, but Myrgos paid them no heed. He was already issuing orders to have *Vulture* turn to the southwest. The oars backed on one side, went forward on the other, and as the hull pivoted, other crew members ran up the sail.

She gathered speed quickly, heedless of the little trader sinking beneath the waves in her wake. Within minutes, she was heading at full speed to the south.

And Santorillos.

chapter   thirty - two

H al lifted the replica windlass handle and carefully aligned the socket he had made with the five-pointed axle. The wooden fitting slipped neatly into place. He tested it for movement. There was less than a centimeter of free play, then the shaped socket locked on to the axle. He beckoned to Ingvar.

"Take the strain here, Ingvar. I'll check and make sure there's no restraining brake."

It would be useless to haul on the windlass if it was locked in position. He crouched and peered under it, but there was no sign of any lock.

"Give it a turn—gently now," he ordered, and Ingvar moved the handle through an arc of about twenty centimeters. At first, nothing happened as the cable stretched. But then the windlass began to turn.

It was a gradual movement as Ingvar used just enough force to set it in motion. But the cable began to come in, a few centimeters at a time.

"Easy," Hal said, barely daring to breathe.

Ingvar pushed on the handle again, as gently as he could, and the line began to move. An ominous creaking sound came from the wooden socket fitted over the axle.

"Slow down," Hal said.

Ingvar rolled his eyes. "I'm going as slowly as I can," he protested.

But Hal was unmoved. "Just keep the minimum force on it that you can," he said. "If it breaks, we're finished."

Ingvar strained once more. The handle moved through a quarter of a turn, and the axle creaked and groaned alarmingly. But the rope was moving. Hal peered closely at the winch handle. Was there a small split forming in the wood where it fitted over the axle? Or was that just a natural seam in the wood that had been there all the time? He didn't know. But he prayed it was the latter. Ingvar, seeing him inspecting the handle, stopped turning and held it steady. He glanced interrogatively at Hal. Hal made a slow winding motion with his forefinger.

"Go again. But gently, for Loki's sake!" he said.

Another eighth of a revolution. A few more centimeters of rope recovered. Now that they were used to the creaking and groaning of the windlass handle, they relaxed a little. It protested but, so far, it had held.

"The basket's loose," Lydia called.

Hal looked quickly up to the top of the cable. The carrying basket had come free of its retaining cradle and it was now dangling from the cable, a few meters down from the top station.

"How does it feel?" Hal asked Ingvar. The big lad was sweating profusely—from tension rather than effort. He shook his head to clear a few drops of perspiration from his eyes.

"Awkward," he said at length. "But it feels solid."

"It should be easier now," Hal told him. "The weight of the cradle will be working for you."

Ingvar nodded. "Of course, on the way back up, it'll be a lot harder." He turned the handle again—tentatively, a few centimeters at a time. More cable came in to wind around the drum of the windlass.

"I think you've done it," Thorn, his voice full of admiration.

Then, with an ugly cracking sound, the wooden cogwheel split into four pieces.

Ingvar lurched as the cogwheel collapsed and lost its grip on the axle. The handle came away in his hands and the cog itself dropped to the planks of the dock, totally ruined. Hal stared at the split pieces of wood. He drew in his breath to curse but could think of nothing vile enough to suit the situation. There was a concerted groan from the watching Herons as they realized what had happened.

"Can you fix it?" Stig asked, hoping against hope.

Hal turned a scornful look on him. "Are you kidding?" he said bitterly. The cog was beyond repair. And even if he could have patched it up, it was obvious that a wooden cog wouldn't be up to the task. He picked up two of the splintered pieces and studied them gloomily. Then, with an expression of disgust, he tossed them aside.

It had been a long time since one of his ideas had failed. In his younger days, his inventions and devices had a fifty percent record of success—like the running water system he had devised for his mother's kitchen, which had collapsed spectacularly, flooding the kitchen and nearly knocking Stig unconscious as the components flew in all directions.

But since then, he had become accustomed to success. And the crew had become accustomed to expecting him to succeed. It was a bitter pill to swallow now as he stared morosely at the bare axle protruding from the windlass. Myrgos had outthought him, and he didn't like contemplating that idea.

Thorn seemed to sense his feelings and dropped his left hand on Hal's shoulder in a consoling gesture. "I guess you can't get it right every time," he said.

Hal looked at him bleakly. "It would have been nice to get it right *this* time."

Thorn shrugged. There was nothing he could say to that.

"So what do we do now?" Olaf asked.

Hal glanced angrily at him. "I don't know, Olaf," he said. "What do you suggest?"

Why does everyone depend on me for ideas? he thought. Then he pushed the bitterness aside. They looked to him for ideas because he was the skirl, because he was the leader of the brotherband and because he could usually come up with a way to solve most problems that faced them.

"Maybe we could haul it up by hand," Stig suggested, "if we all tailed onto the rope?"

But Hal shook his head. "The cage is too heavy," he said. "We might get it down, but it would be too difficult to haul it up again, even with one person in it. And we need two people at a minimum. That's why the windlass is so heavily geared," he added.

Lydia had been pacing the dock, looking from the windlass to the rope cable wound round its drum, to the *Heron* moored alongside.

"Could we row it up?" she said finally. They all stared at her.

"Row it?" Hal said. "You want to put oars on the cage?"

She shook her head. "I mean if we cut the rope and tie it to the ship, couldn't we row the ship out into the bay and haul the basket up and down that way?"

Hal opened his mouth to dismiss the idea, then stopped. Maybe it would work, he thought.

Thorn grinned at the serious-faced girl. "You're a genius," he said. "Why didn't you tell us sooner?"

She flushed, thinking he was making fun of her. "It was just an idea. But maybe it's not such a good one."

"It's a great idea!" Hal said, and she looked at him in surprise. "With eight rowers on the oars, that should be enough to lift you and me to the top. We're probably the lightest, apart from Edvin. And the oars will give us the extra leverage we need."

Olaf stepped forward. "I'll need to go too," he said. "You'll need me to help find Constantus."

Hal nodded agreement. "You can come in the second trip," he said. "It'll be one less rower, but it'll be a lighter load with just one in the cage."

Stig was scratching his chin thoughtfully. "If we cut the rope to bring it down, how do we get it up again?" he asked. "The loose end will go back up the cliff."

But Hal had already considered this. "We'll lengthen the loose end," he said eagerly. "We've got a sixty-meter anchor cable and heaps of spare rope for rigging. Plus there's maybe ten meters wound round the drum. That should give us enough rope to reach to the top. Then we change ends over and row out again."

He stepped quickly to the windlass, reaching for his saxe as he did. "Take the ship out and turn her around," he said. "We'll attach the rope to the sternpost. It'll be better if we row her forward, rather than in reverse. Then get to work splicing the anchor cable with as much of the spare rigging as you can find."

Stig and Ingvar boarded the ship and, with the twins' and Stefan's help, unmoored her and poled her out into clear water, where they could turn her around. Then Stig backed her into the dock. At the same time, Edvin, Jesper and Olaf raised the hatch to the cable locker and brought out the long, heavy anchor cable and half a dozen coils of rope intended for use as rigging. When they traveled across the world as they did, they needed to take plenty of ship's stores with them.

Once the ship was back at the dock, now facing outward, they sat on the planks and began to splice the various lengths of rope together to form one long cable. While this was being done, Lydia and Hal experimented, hauling on the cable to see if they could bring the cage down. Hal grinned in satisfaction as the weight of the elevator worked for them, and the cable came in hand over hand as the cage came sliding down the cliff face. They avoided using the windlass drum, letting the cable pile up on the dock behind them. Olaf and Ingvar, who weren't required for the work of splicing, joined them. Within a few minutes, the elevator cage was resting on the dock, ready to ascend.

Hal cut the cable under the windlass drum and unwound the extra eight meters of rope that it held. Then Stig brought him the new length of spliced rope and they tied that to the loose end, leading the long rope back aboard ship. Once that was done, they fastened the other end of the cable to the sternpost of the ship. Hal and Lydia collected their weapons. For a moment, as he buckled on his sword belt, Hal considered taking his shield, but then dismissed the idea. His sword and crossbow should be enough. Lydia, of course, had her quiver of darts and her atlatl, along with her long-bladed dagger.

"I'll wave when we're a few meters from the top," Hal told Thorn. "Keep an eye on us and slow down when you see me wave. We don't want to go crashing full tilt into the stops."

Thorn nodded his understanding, and Hal and Lydia climbed aboard the cage.

The skirl caught Olaf's eye. "We'll send the cage back down and you come up next," he said.

The burly guard commander nodded. "I'll be right behind you."

"Will three of you be enough to get the job done?" Thorn asked. He hated the idea of missing out on a fight.

Hal shook his head. "We can't spare anyone else from the oars," he said. "Besides, with twenty of the enemy up there, we're going to be using stealth, not force."

Reluctantly, Thorn agreed that he was right.

Hal continued with his plan. "Once Olaf is at the top with us, we'll wait for nightfall, then go looking for the boy. Keep an eye on the top station. We'll signal with a flint when we want to come down."

Striking a flint might create only a small spark, but it would be a brilliant light, visible from a long distance. Hal caught Stig's eye and gestured toward the ship.

"Get the crew aboard and on the oars, Stig. Let's get going while there's still light."

It was late afternoon and the sun was close to the horizon. There would be light on the cliffs for the next thirty minutes or so, Hal estimated. That should be enough for two trips up and down.

Stig hesitated, feeling he should say something to his friend. Then he shrugged and ran lightly across the dock to the waiting ship. The rest of the crew were in their rowing stations, waiting for him. All the oars were manned and Edvin was on the tiller.

"Out oars!" Stig called. "Let's send them up the cliff."

The oars dipped into the calm water, and on Stig's command, they all bit as the rowers heaved. For a moment, the ship didn't move. Then the combined force of eight rowers sent her nosing out of the inlet.

Behind her, drawn by the cable, the elevator cage began to glide smoothly up the cliff face.

chapter   thirty-three

G liding up through the late afternoon shadows was a fascinating experience. The cage rode at an angle from the cliff, rather than rising vertically. The dock dropped away rapidly below them, and when they looked down, they could see the little ship surging out into the bay, the oars rising and falling as one.

Hal could see Thorn in the stern, facing back to watch them. His face was a pale oval. Hal was about to wave when he realized that the old sea wolf might take that as a signal to stop. Hastily, he lowered his arm.

"This is quite a rush," Lydia said, grinning, and he realized she was enjoying the ride. She had no fear of heights, and the smooth upward passage created a breeze that stirred her fine hair. Hal returned the smile and turned to look upward. The top station was approaching rapidly. He narrowed his eyes, gauging speeds and distances, then held up a white scarf he had brought along for the purpose of signaling. He waved it in a wide circle.

Below, Thorn growled an order to the rowers and the ship slowed. The white cloth continued to wave from the elevator cage, now moving slowly up and down, then cutting to one side.

"Hold her there," Thorn said. The rowers leaned on their oars, resisting the tendency for the cage to begin sliding down again.

Thorn saw Hal wave the scarf one more time in a rapid up-and-down motion.

"One more stroke," Thorn ordered, and as the ship surged ahead, he saw the elevator ride up and over the bull wheel at the top and slide into the dock. "Easy all," he called, and the rowing stopped. He waited a few seconds, checking to see that the cage was secure and there was no need to counter its weight again with the oars.

Then he saw the flash of white cloth again, now waving horizontally. He and Hal had agreed on the simple signaling code while the crew had been busy splicing the additions to the cable. A horizontal movement meant the cage was ready to come down again.

"Switch the ends, Stefan," he ordered. As they had hauled the cage to the top, they had drawn in a long section of cable, which was now loosely coiled on the deck. As the cage began to descend under the power of gravity, they would pay this out again, using a bight around the sternpost to control the speed of the cage's descent. With the weight of the cage bringing it down, there was no need for the oars, other than to give them extra braking power over the cage.

"Bring her in a few meters," he told the rowers. They took two reverse strokes, and the cable began to run.

"Steady!" he ordered, and the rowers leaned on their oars to slow the descent, while Stefan put his weight against the cable round the sternpost, using the friction to keep the cage under control.

Within a few minutes, both the ship and the elevator cage were back at the dock. Thorn signaled for Olaf to board the cage.

"Up you go," he said.

The former guard commander scrambled aboard the elevator. He looked a little nervous about the whole thing. He didn't have Lydia's head for heights, and the cage seemed awfully frail.

Thorn sensed his unease and grinned. "Enjoy the ride. And don't forget to hang on."

"I'm not likely to," Olaf said through white lips. Then Thorn gave an order to the rowers, and both ship and cage moved away from the dock. Olaf's knuckles turned white on the cage railing as the elevator soared upward. But the motion was smooth and there was little jerking. Before long, he began to feel more secure. He could make out Hal's face leaning over the rail at the upper station, watching his progress. Then, as the white scarf waved again, Olaf felt the cage's progress slowing.

He grunted nervously as the reduction in speed caused the cage to rock from side to side. Previously, there had been little lateral movement, and now he felt as if the elevator were trying to shake him loose. He gripped tighter on the railing.

"Give me your hand." Hal's voice surprised him. It was only a couple of meters away. He raised his eyes and saw that the cage was almost at the top of its run. Hal was leaning out, stretching a hand to him. Lydia, he noticed, was hanging on to Hal's belt to anchor him. He took the proffered hand and felt a slight bump as the cage slid over the top of the hoist and came to rest on the solid floor timbers of the upper station. Hastily, he scrambled out, glad to feel firm ground under his feet once more.

Only to lurch awkwardly as the ground beneath him trembled. He grabbed at the timber frame to steady himself.

"Gorlog's teeth!" he exclaimed.

Hal shook his head sympathetically. "It keeps doing that," he said. "Look over there."

Following the direction of his pointing arm, Olaf saw a sudden violent jet of steam erupt from a split in the rocks. A few seconds later, he coughed as the smell of sulfur assailed his lungs.

He wiped his brow. "Just what I need. A ride on a spider's web and the ground shaking and quaking beneath my feet."

"Don't tense up," Lydia advised him. "If you stay loose, you stay balanced, and it won't throw you off your feet."

The ground shook again. This time there was a deep rumble that they could feel rather than hear beneath their feet. Olaf staggered, inadvertently tensing as he felt the movement.

"That's easier said than done," he said. "How long before we can get moving?"

If they had something to do, he wouldn't have to concentrate on the feeling that the earth was shaking itself to pieces beneath him, he thought. But just standing around waiting for it to heave and quake wasn't his idea of a good time. Hal pointed out to sea, where the sun was balanced on the rim of the horizon.

"Sun will be down in a few minutes. We can get going then and see what we're up against."

The transition from light to dark was surprisingly rapid. Once the sun sank below the horizon, deep shadows fell over the cliff top. The inlet below was already in darkness and they could only just make out the shape of the *Heron*, nestled into the dock.

Hal waited a few minutes after the light was gone, then gestured toward the entrance to the elevator hut.

"Let's get going," he said. He motioned for Lydia to lead the way. She was a skilled hunter and he knew she'd find the easiest route, and the best cover, across the cliff top. He gave her a twenty-meter start, then followed her, ghosting through the outcrops of rock and stunted, spiny trees. Olaf followed behind him, keeping the same interval between them.

The ground rose from the elevator hut to a small ridge fifty meters inland. Lydia stopped at the ridge, crouching behind a pile of boulders. She waited until Hal and Olaf dropped into cover beside her, then pointed across the flat plateau.

"There's their compound," she breathed.

Hal wriggled forward on his elbows and knees to see what she was pointing at. From the shallow ridge behind which they were concealed, the land rose slightly, until it reached the bottom of a low wall, perhaps three meters high. He scanned along its length but could see no sign of a gate or any break in the wall. He felt Olaf scramble forward to lie beside him, and the three of them surveyed the pirate compound.

The wall was patrolled by sentries. In the fifty-meter section that lay in front of them, Hal could see two men pacing. They carried heavy spears over their shoulders, the points gleaming occasionally in the last of the daylight. Both of them wore helmets. The parapet behind which they were pacing came up just past their waist height. Neither man seemed particularly alert, but there was very little cover between the spot where they lay, concealed by the slight ridge, and the base of the wall where the sentries were.

"We'll have to wait till it's fully dark," Lydia whispered.

Hal nodded agreement. "I'd like to give it a couple more hours after that, and let the sentries get bored and tired."

Olaf grunted impulsively. "Why wait?" he said. "Let's just fight our way in and find Constantus. This hanging around is giving me the heebie-jeebies."

Hal regarded him sardonically. "You're not big on subtlety, are you?"

Before Olaf could answer, Lydia chipped in. "Or brains. There are twenty to thirty men on the other side of the wall. We don't know where they are or what they're doing. If we go blundering in there now, we're liable to find out—the hard way."

Olaf flushed. He didn't like being criticized by people younger than he was—particularly when one of them was a girl. "Well, I say we attack now."

Hal eyed him coldly. "And I say we don't. And in this crew, it's what I say that counts, remember?"

Olaf snorted. He pointed to the nearest sentry. "Look. He's facing away from us now."

"And he'll be facing back toward us by the time you're halfway to the wall," Hal said. "Stay where you are."

Olaf glared at him and began to gather his hands and feet under him, preparatory to rising. Lydia's calm voice stopped him.

"You make one move toward that wall and I'll drop you with

a dart," she said. The tone of her voice left him in no doubt that she meant it. Reluctantly, he allowed himself to sink back to the rough ground. Then he started as the earth a few meters in front of him emitted a sudden gush of steam and sulfurous smoke. The ground shook. In response to the sound, the sentry on the wall turned and peered in their direction.

"If you'd moved, he would have spotted you," Hal pointed out.

Olaf reacted angrily. "I can't help it if the ground keeps snorting and belching every five minutes."

Hal exchanged a look with Lydia and rolled his eyes. You just couldn't win with some people, he thought.

As darkness fell and they lay hidden among the rocks, they became aware of the loom of a fire behind the wall, and heard the occupants shouting and laughing—and then singing. Sparks flew in the air, rising high above the wall. After some time, they could smell the fragrant scent of roasting meat.

"Sounds like some kind of celebration," Lydia said.

"Good!" said Hal. "We'll wait till it settles down and they're all either drunk or asleep. It'll make it easier to find our way around the compound."

The singing and feasting continued for several hours. Watching the moon slide across the sky, Hal estimated that it was well past midnight. The ground around them continued to heave and tremble with increasing frequency. Geysers of steam and sulfur smoke shot into the air from fissures in the rocks.

"That's getting worse," Lydia said after a particularly violent upheaval.

"It certainly isn't getting better," Hal replied. "Although it doesn't seem to be bothering them inside the compound."

Eventually, the noise of revelry began to abate, and the glow of the huge bonfire died down, so that sparks could no longer be seen beyond the wall. The singing grew more ragged, and there were fewer voices joining in the songs, until eventually, only one voice, slurred and wavering, could be heard, and that eventually died away into a hiccupping silence.

By contrast, the rumbling and trembling of the ground, and the eruptions of steam and sulfur, seemed to grow more frequent and more powerful. After one particularly violent outburst, Hal and Lydia eyed each other anxiously.

"I think the sooner we're out of here, the better," Hal said.

Lydia nodded, although she gestured toward the wall, where one helmeted head was still visible.

"Sentries are still on patrol," she said. "Although he's not looking our way now."

The celebrations inside the compound had one favorable result. The sentries hadn't been relieved in hours, although from time to time their friends had brought them jugs of wine. As a result, they were half asleep and definitely not alert.

Hal studied the nearest sentry. "Even so, there's still a good chance he'll see us if we start to move."

Lydia bared her teeth in a grin. "He won't see me," she said, and selected a dart from her quiver, fitting it to the atlatl handle.

"You're going to kill him?" Hal asked. Whether the sentry was a pirate or not, Hal wasn't altogether comfortable with the idea of killing a man in cold blood.

But Lydia was shaking her head as she held out the dart for him to see.

"It doesn't have a broadhead, just a knob of hardwood," she said. "It'll knock him out, not kill him." Before he could comment, she explained further. "If I used a broadhead, he might yell out in pain before he died."

Hal couldn't resist smiling at the serious way she said it. "For a moment there, I thought you were getting softhearted."

Lydia shook her head. "Me? Never. Wait here while I take care of him."

And so saying, she rose into a crouch and crept toward the wall.

L ydia moved in a crouch, using the scudding shadows of the clouds as they passed across the moon, moving with them, staying inside their concealment, then dropping to the ground as the shadows pulled away from her. There was a regular spurt of steam coming from a fissure in the rocks now, and she also timed her movement to coincide with that, using the noise to blanket any small sound she might make.

The trick is not to rush it, she thought to herself, avoiding the temptation to dash quickly forward. When she was thirty meters from the wall, she stopped and rose to a half crouch, the dart back over her right shoulder, ready to throw.

She rose to her full height and some part of the movement must have alerted the sentry. He turned and looked in her direction. But the uncertain light and the jugs of wine that he'd consumed over the past five hours combined to make his vision uncertain. He *thought* there was a slim figure standing out there among the rocks below the wall. But maybe it was a tree. He leaned forward, peering owlishly at it. Then it moved.

"Who—" He began the normal challenge, *Who goes there?* but never managed to articulate the last two words. Something came hissing out of the night and slammed into his forehead, just above the midpoint between his eyes.

His legs gave way beneath him and he collapsed, unconscious, to the planks on the walkway behind the wall. His spear fell from his nerveless hands, clattering briefly on the planks, then falling silent. Lydia paused anxiously, her hand automatically selecting another dart. This one was a broadhead, she knew—a leaf-shaped, razor-sharp iron point. If another sentry had been alerted, he was going to be out of luck.

But there was no further sound from the parapet and she ran lightly forward, signaling with her arm for Hal and Olaf to follow.

They arrived with a rush, making a little more noise than she thought was necessary. She made a shushing sound, with her finger to her lips, and Hal had the grace to look embarrassed.

"Sorry," he muttered.

"So you should be," she told him. "Now give me a boost up the wall."

He put out a hand to stop her. "You're not going up. I am."

She opened her mouth to argue, but he cut her off. "No argument. You've done your bit. Now stand back."

She heard the steel in his voice and shrugged mentally. Once her blood was up in a situation like this, she was keen to keep going. But she recognized the sense in what he was saying. He was a skilled swordsman, and all she had was a dagger. If there was trouble waiting on top of the wall, he was better equipped to deal with it.

Olaf obviously had the same thought. "Maybe I should go," he said.

But Hal waved him back. "You're too big for me to boost up the wall."

Olaf had to agree he was right. He stepped close to the wall and made a stirrup with his hands, lurching as the ground trembled under him, then recovering his balance and gesturing for Hal to put his foot in the stirrup. Hal slung his crossbow over his shoulder, checked that his sword was loose in its scabbard and stepped up into Olaf's clenched hands, immediately straightening his knee as the burly warrior heaved him upward.

He shot up the face of the wall, using his hands to push himself over the top and landing catlike on both feet. His knees bent to soften the impact, and his right hand dropped to his sword hilt, drawing the gleaming blade clear with the usual warning *shriing!* of metal and leather.

He faced left, then right, searching for any sign of danger. A few meters away, the unfortunate sentry lay sprawled on the walkway. But there was no sign of anyone else. In the compound itself, all was still. A few comatose bodies lay by the dying embers of the fire, but it appeared that most of the inhabitants had taken themselves off to bed. There was no sign of the second sentry they had seen earlier. Hal advanced down the wall a few paces and saw him, huddled in a shadowy corner, a wine jug cradled in his lap. His snores rivaled the sound of the volcanic disturbances that erupted every few minutes.

Hal returned to the point where he had scaled the wall and leaned over. "All clear," he called.

Lydia was waiting with a length of rope she had carried, looped over her shoulder. She tossed it up to him and he made it fast round one of the crenellations, then stood back as Lydia came up hand over hand, moving quickly and sinuously. Olaf followed, making heavier work of it, grunting and snorting as he hauled his bulk up the wall. The two Herons leaned over and grabbed him under the armpits for the last couple of meters, swinging him up over the wall like a hooked fish.

"Just as well you didn't come up first," Hal said with a grin.

Olaf, for once, acknowledged the fact. "Not as young as I used to be," he said.

Lydia regarded him with a serious expression. "I've never understood why people say that," she said. "None of us is as young as we used to be."

Olaf opened his mouth to reply but Hal held up a hand to stop him. "Let it pass," he said. "Let it pass."

Lydia, still puzzled, shook her head. "Sometimes I don't understand Skandians," she said to herself.

Hal pointed to a set of steps ten meters away, leading down from the wall into the compound.

"Looks like everybody's out for the night," he said. "Let's find the boy."

He paused at the top of the steps to take stock of the compound. Within the wall, there were eight buildings—all constructed in the whitewashed stucco that was standard for this part of the world. The roofs were covered in red clay tiles, each one shaped like half a pipe in the Toscan style.

Three of the buildings he discounted immediately. They were too large for a prison. Two of them had no windows on their long sides, and he guessed they were storerooms or warehouses. After all, he reasoned, Myrgos must need somewhere to stow the proceeds of his raiding. He indicated them to the others.

"We'll burn them if we get the chance," he said softly. The idea of destroying Myrgos's loot was an appealing one.

"To create a diversion?" Olaf asked.

Hal shook his head. "No. To really get up Myrgos's nose. I'd guess that's where he keeps his booty."

"Oh," Olaf said.

Lydia said nothing, but she flashed a fierce grin at her skirl. She liked the idea as well.

The other large building had five windows spaced along its sides. They were open spaces, with wooden covers hinged at the top that could be lowered over them in the event of bad weather. At the moment, the covers were open, held up by wooden props.

"Bunkhouse?" Hal asked the others, and they nodded. It was the most likely purpose for the building.

That left the four smaller structures, each about six meters by six. One stood close to an outdoor cooking pit, with a roasting spit set in place over a wide, open fireplace. Smoke drifted up from the bed of coals that glowed dully in the night air.

"Kitchen," he said softly. The other three buildings were on the far side of the compound, and he could make out no details from his current position. Carefully, he led the way down the stairs to the flat ground of the compound itself. A corsair, dressed in a flamboyant mixture of garments he had undoubtedly stolen from a victim at some previous time, lay snoring on the dirt beneath the steps. Hal inspected him closely, ready for the man to stir and waken. But he was out cold. There was a rumbling in the ground and the earth shook violently. Hal noticed a small crack appear down the outer wall of the compound. Still the pirate didn't stir.

"That was a big one," Lydia said nervously. She was right—the tremor had been stronger than most of its predecessors, and it had continued for much longer. Hal estimated that it had gone on for at least fifteen seconds—a small enough time in reality, but seeming like an age when the ground was shaking and lurching beneath your feet.

"Come on," he said. They took cover in the shadows beside the building he had guessed to be a bunkhouse, crouching double as they passed the open windows in case anyone was awake inside. The sound of loud storing reached them, confirming that his guess had been correct.

At the end of the bunkhouse, they would have to cross an open space with no cover to reach the remaining three buildings. Hal crouched in the deep shadow of the wall, trying to ascertain which one to try first. But there was nothing to distinguish them. They were all similar in size and construction. Each one had a door in one wall and a window in each of the others. The back wall, so far as Hal could see, was blank.

"Might make a good prison," he muttered.

Olaf nodded. "Problem is, which one do we try first?" he whispered.

"Might as well try the nearest one," said Lydia.

Hal glanced at her. "Always practical, aren't you?"

She shrugged. "If it's the right one, it'll save us a walk."

"Have you two finished chattering?" Olaf said tersely.

Hal gestured for him to lead the way across the open ground to the hut. He felt naked and exposed in the moonlight as he followed the burly warrior, sensing that a dozen eyes could be on him watching his progress. His skin crawled as he waited for a shout of alarm, or the thud of an arrow between his shoulder blades. The moonlight, which was no more than average in strength, felt like broad daylight as he ghosted along toward the hut. He heaved a sigh of relief when he was concealed in the shadows of the narrow porch by the door. They paused, listening carefully. From inside the hut, they could hear the gentle noise of snoring. Olaf grimaced and drew his saxe, transferring his sword to his left hand.

He slid the slim blade of the saxe into the narrow gap at the edge of the door and worked it slowly up and down, feeling for the latch. Most doors had a simple drop-latch device—a wooden piece attached to the edge of the door, which swiveled up and down to fit into a corresponding bracket on the doorjamb. He found it now as it blocked the saxe's downward path. He removed the blade and reinserted it in the gap, some ten centimeters lower. Then he gently raised it.

There was a moment of resistance as it came into contact with the lower edge of the bar. Then he increased the upward pressure and it popped free. The door swung inward five or six centimeters before he managed to hook his fingers around the edge and stop it. He paused a few seconds, then slowly swung the door open.

There were three bunks in the room, each one occupied. The heavy breathing indicated that the occupants were deeply asleep. Olaf edged into the room, with Hal a few paces behind him. Lydia remained outside, keeping watch on the compound.

There was a door in the far wall, opposite the front door of the building, obviously leading to another room. It could well be where they were keeping the boy, Hal thought. He indicated it and raised his eyebrows. Olaf nodded. Hal drew his sword, taking care to make no noise, and Olaf started across the room, moving between the bunks toward the door.

There was another falling bar-and-bracket latch, but this one was on the side of the door that faced into the main room. Olaf raised it gently, slid the door open and peered inside.

The room was no more than a large closet. There was a small barred window high in the wall that let in a minimal amount of light. As his eyes grew accustomed to the dimness, Olaf realized it was unoccupied. It was piled with old clothes, armor, weapons and assorted gear. He stepped back into the main room, easing the door shut behind him and lowering the latch into its bracket. He turned to see Hal's questioning look and shook his head.

"Who are you?" The nearest of the three sleeping men sat up groggily, his voice thick and slurry with the wine he'd drunk that night, peering at the large figure looming over him.

"I'm the boogerman," said Olaf, and threw a short, hard right-handed punch that dropped the man back onto his pillow, out cold. Then he jerked his head toward the door and followed Hal outside into the shadow of the small porch.

Y ou realize," Hal said in a whisper, "you've probably undone all the good work that man's mother did."

Olaf frowned at him, not understanding. "What are you talking about?"

Hal couldn't help grinning. "She probably spent years convincing him that the boogerman didn't exist. Now you've gone and ruined it all."

Olaf's frown deepened. "Don't be ridiculous."

Hal shrugged and turned to Lydia. "He's not big on humor," he said.

But she shared Olaf's frown. "I'm with him. Now if you've finished nattering, can we get on with it?"

Hal held up both hands in a gesture of resignation. "I was just trying to lighten the mood."

"Well, don't," Lydia told him. "The mood's fine as it is." Then she gestured to the next hut, which looked identical to the one they had just entered. "Let's go."

Once again, Hal felt alarmingly exposed as they crossed the open ground between the buildings. But, as before, there was nobody keeping watch to raise the alarm. They clustered together in the shadow thrown by the small porch, Hal and Lydia deferring to Olaf, who went to work with his saxe again, searching for and opening the latch. As the door began to slide open, the ground heaved to a larger-than-normal tremor. Hal was caught unprepared and thrown off balance against the stucco wall of the hut.

"They're getting worse. Let's get out of here as soon as we can," he muttered.

Lydia made a sign for silence. The upheaval was so severe it may well have woken the sleeping occupants of the hut. But Hal was right. The tremors were becoming more frequent, and stronger. It definitely seemed as if the volcano was building up to something— and that something was liable to be very unpleasant.

Even as she had the thought, there was a sharp splitting noise and a large crack opened in the ground of the compound ten meters from where they stood, zigzagging back and forth and letting clouds of steam escape. It was at least six meters long and, at its widest point, half a meter across. The three exchanged alarmed looks.

Inside the hut, they heard a voice call out. "What was that?"

"The volcano. It's been acting up all night," said a second voice. "Go back to sleep."

"It hasn't been doing that all night. I'm taking a look."

Olaf turned from the door and caught Hal's eye. He made a gesture indicating that he was going in, and Hal nodded agreement. He drew his saxe. It would be more effective in the confined space of the hut. Then he signaled for Olaf to go ahead.

The big man paused for a second, then slammed his weight against the unlatched door, sending it flying back on its hinges. He plunged into the room, closely followed by Hal. This time, Lydia joined them.

There were four men in the room, all of them awake. Two were still wrapped in their blankets on their cots. The other two were on their feet. Olaf slammed his shoulder into the nearest, sending him flying back against the stucco wall. The hut shuddered with the impact, and the man slid slowly down the wall to lie in a heap on the floor. The second man was looking wildly around for his weapons when Olaf's fist caught him on the side of the head and he went down as well.

By this time, one of the others had untangled himself from his blankets and came at Hal with a long knife. Hal parried the stroke with his saxe, thankful that he'd chosen to use it over his sword. The sword would have been too cumbersome at these close quarters.

The man lunged again. Hal beat the knife blade down, then grabbed the man's wrist with his left hand and jerked him forward. As he staggered, Hal brought the brass pommel in the hilt of the saxe down on his head. The man gave a little groan and fell facedown.

The fourth man decided he was outnumbered. He threw his blankets aside and broke for the door, beginning to yell a warning as he went. Lydia shot out a foot and tripped him. He crashed full length on the wooden planks. Half dazed, he attempted to rise. Lydia hit him with the edge of her open right hand, aiming for the point where his neck and shoulder intersected. This time, when he went down, he stayed down.

The three raiders looked warily around, waiting to see if any of the noise from the hut had alerted the other pirates. So far, there was no reaction, no noise other than the constant hiss of steam escaping from the zigzag crack in the ground.

"That'll have them all awake before too long," Hal said. He gestured to the far door. The hut was the same design as the one they had just searched. But this time, the inner door was fastened with a padlock through a metal hasp.

"This must be it," Hal said. "If they're taking the trouble to lock it, there must be something valuable in there. Or someone," he amended.

Olaf moved quickly to the door and pounded on it with a big fist. They heard a startled cry from the other side—a young, high-pitched voice.

"Constantus? Are you there, my lord?" Olaf called.

For a moment, there was silence, then a small, wavering voice replied, "Olaf? Is that you?"

Olaf flashed a smile of triumph at his two companions. Lydia began to search the cluttered table in the middle of the room for the key to the padlock. But Olaf was in no mood to wait for a key. He jammed his sword blade down inside the hasp, twisted it so the blade was edge on and jerked back violently.

The screws holding the hasp to the wooden door gave way and

the wood splintered as the hasp came free. Olaf staggered back a pace, then recovered and grabbed the edge of the door, dragging it open. A small figure darted out of the inner room and engulfed him, hurling his arms around the heavy-set Skandian. Olaf folded his massive arms around the boy.

"I knew you'd come for me," Constantus said, his voice muffled against Olaf's jerkin. Olaf patted his back, a surprisingly gentle gesture for such a big man.

"Of course I came for you," he said softly. "I'm your bodyguard, after all."

Constantus was pale haired and blue eyed. He was at that age in his early teens when his limbs were thin and gawky and his body hadn't caught up with his rapidly growing height. He was a good-looking boy, as Hal and Lydia could see when Olaf gently disentangled his grip and held him back at arm's length.

"Are you all right?" he asked. "Did they hurt you?"

Constantus shook his head, dashing one hand across his eyes to wipe the tears that were forming.

"I'm fine," he reassured his bodyguard. He was smiling with relief when the ground shook once more with yet another tremor—even bigger than before. His smiled disappeared, wiped away by fear.

"Why does it keep doing that?" he asked.

Olaf shook his head. "The mountain is angry," he said. "Now we have to get out of here before it gets any worse."

Lydia was at the door, holding it half closed and surveying the compound.

"It's all clear for the moment," she said. "Let's get going." She ushered Olaf and the boy out the door, pointing to the hut they had searched previously. "Head back the way we came," she told them. "Make for the stairs up to the parapet. We'll be right behind you."

Gripping Constantus firmly by the arm, Olaf ran out into the open space, crouching as he went, and headed for the nearby hut. After a brief pause, Hal followed him, with Lydia behind him. He didn't argue when she gestured for him to go first. It made sense for Lydia to act as the rear guard. She had her atlatl and darts to discourage any potential pursuers. He had his crossbow, of course, but it took over thirty seconds to reload, whereas with the atlatl Lydia could lay down a regular storm of darts in the time it took him to reload.

They paused for a few seconds at the first hut, then Olaf and Constantus led off again for the long bunkhouse. Hal followed and, as they drew closer, he became aware of raised voices coming from inside. The thundering and crashing volcano had woken the pirates. Crouching to stay below the level of the windows, the four of them ran along the side of the building to the far end, where they could strike out for the warehouses.

But as they drew level with the door, it flew open and three men emerged, in varying stages of undress, but all of them armed. They stopped in shock at the unexpected sight of three strangers. Then one of them noticed the small figure being hurried along by the leader of the group.

"It's the boy!" the pirate shouted, turning his head to call back into the bunkhouse. "He's escaping. Get—"

He got no further. Olaf's fist caught him in a wide backhanded swing, and he staggered and went down. The second aimed an ax blow at Olaf, but Hal stepped between them and parried with his sword, deflecting the heavier weapon down to one side. As the man was off balance, Hal kicked out flat-footed, catching him in the center of the chest and hurling him back through the half-open door. His companion swung a wild roundhouse sword stroke at the stranger in front of him. Hal dropped to one knee, and the blade whistled over his head. In almost the same movement, he pushed off with his left leg and lunged with the point of his sword, taking the pirate in the side. The man looked down, horrified, at the blood gushing from the wound, then slid sideways to the ground, supporting himself against the rough stucco wall and groaning in pain.

Hal jabbed his sword at two more men who were impeding each other in the doorway. Unable to defend themselves, they both reared backward into the hut and Hal slammed the door after them. Lydia appeared beside him with a long bench and jammed it against the door, holding it closed. The men inside hammered on the door with their fists, then threw their shoulders against it in a series of violent assaults. But the bench held firm.

"Run!" Lydia told him. "Any minute now they'll start coming out the windows."

Together, they sprinted across the heaving, quaking compound, after Olaf and Constantus. In the last few meters before they reached the steps to the parapet, Lydia turned and skipped backward, watching the bunkhouse. As she did, she saw a leg emerging over one of the windowsills, followed by the doubled-over body of one of the men inside. As he dropped to the ground, she notched a dart to her thrower, aimed and let fly. The dart hit the man as he was recovering from the drop. He straightened up, then felt the staggering impact of the missile against his chest. He fell back against the wall, dead before his body slid to the ground. One of his comrades, intent on following him, had his head and shoulders out the window. He saw his comrade hit by the massive dart and threw himself back inside, landing on the ground in a heap.

Lydia turned and ran for the stairs. It would be a few minutes before anyone tried the windows again, she reasoned.

The other three were waiting for her at the foot of the stairs. She gestured for them to go up. They could hear people shouting now from all parts of the compound as the word quickly spread that Constantus was escaping. But nobody knew where he was or where he was heading, and they cast around blindly to try to find him.

Olaf, Constantus and Hal dashed up the stairs, with Lydia bringing up the rear. The staircase was in deep shadow under the walkway, but as they emerged at the top, they were bathed in moonlight.

"There they go! On the wall!" One voice cut above the confusion of shouted questions.

Lydia and Hal shoved Olaf toward the parapet, where the rope still hung down. The sentry Lydia had hit with her blunted dart remained crumpled on the planks.

"Get down!" Hal yelled. "I'll pass the boy to you."

Nodding in understanding, Olaf threw a leg over the parapet, paused, then launched himself off the wall, landing on the ground three meters below and rolling to absorb the impact. Covered in dust, he regained his feet and held out his arms to receive the boy emperor. Hal grabbed Constantus by both wrists and urged him over the parapet. Behind him, he heard Lydia release a dart and, a few seconds later, heard a cry of pain and shock from inside the compound as it found its mark.

Constantus scrambled over the battlements, and Hal lowered him to full arm's length down the far side till he had barely a meter to fall. Then he released him, and Constantus dropped into Olaf's waiting arms.

Hal turned back to where Lydia was scanning the compound below the wall. He unslung his crossbow and, placing his foot in the front stirrup, hauled back the cord until the cocking mechanism clicked. The he laid a bolt in the groove on top of the bow and knelt beside Lydia.

She pointed to a row of barrels stacked by one of the store huts, barely forty meters away. "They've taken cover there," she said.

He nodded, licking his lips to moisten them. "We'll wait till they break cover, then shoot together," he said. "You throw two darts, I'll shoot a bolt. If we knock three of them down, that should discourage the others."

The ground quaked and the walkway heaved. Hal swore he could see the planks buckle in a wave-shaped motion that ran along the parapet.

"That's if we can hit anything with the ground leaping around like this," he added.

"They're coming," Lydia said calmly as half a dozen of the pirates broke from cover behind the casks and rushed the stairs. Hal brought his crossbow up to his shoulder and centered the sights on a target in the middle of the group. That way, if he missed, he had a chance of hitting someone else.

"Now," Lydia said in the same unexcited tone. Hal led his target carefully, aiming ahead of the running man so that his bolt and the man would arrive at the same spot simultaneously, and squeezed the release lever. The crossbow bucked in his grip and the bolt sped away. Lydia allowed for her lead instinctively, as she had done thousands of times while hunting. Then she released another dart within a few seconds of the first.

All three missiles found their marks. Lydia's first target was dead when he hit the ground. The other man, and the one Hal had shot, fell to the ground badly wounded, clutching at the cruel missiles that had transfixed them and howling in agony. The remaining three scrambled for cover.

Hal rose to his feet. "That should hold them for a few minutes," he said. "Let's get out of here."

H al ran to the parapet and grabbed the rope, swinging himself up and over the waist-high barrier. He turned to face the wall and went down the rope rapidly, using his feet against the rough surface as he went.

Lydia, following after him, saw that he had the rope. She put her legs through one of the gaps in the crenellations, sat on the edge and launched herself into space. She hit the ground and rolled to absorb the shock. Hal reached the ground a few seconds after her and waved urgently at Olaf and Constantus, who were crouched, waiting for them, at the base of the wall.

"What are you waiting for? Get going!"

The four of them ran, intent on reaching the shelter of the ridge before any of the pirates made it to the parapet. Hal swerved wildly as a huge eruption of sulfurous steam burst from the ground right in front of him, hurling a shower of small rocks high into the air. They came clattering down a few seconds later, peppering the ground around him. One landed heavily on his shoulder. He grunted in pain, but kept running.

Gratefully, he dropped into the cover of the ridge, where the ground sloped down to the cliff's edge some fifty meters away. Olaf and Constantus were a few meters from him, also lying in the cover provided by the sloping ground. Lydia had turned as she neared the ridge. A dart was ready in her atlatl and she paced easily backward, watching the parapet for the first sign of their pursuers.

Hal crawled the few meters to where Olaf crouched. He gripped his shoulder to get his attention.

"Take the boy and ride the elevator down with him. Then get Thorn to send it back up for us," he said. Then, remembering his earlier conversation with Thorn, he asked, "Have you got a flint?"

Even though he knew he didn't have a flint, Olaf slapped at his pockets in a reflex action, as if one would suddenly appear in his hand. Before he had finished, Hal produced his own and handed it to him.

"Strike it a couple of times to let Thorn know you're coming," he said. Then he added: "And remember to leave it in the shed. I'll need it too."

Olaf nodded and stuffed the flint in the side pocket of his jerkin. Then he gripped Constantus's arm and urged him to his feet.

"Come on!" he said. "And stay low!"

Crouching to stay in the cover of the ridge, the two of them ran, scrambling over the rough ground, weaving to avoid the sudden geysers of steam that shot out of the rocks with increasing frequency.

Olaf felt the ground trembling beneath his feet. "Sooner we're out of here, the better," he muttered.

Constantus looked at him fearfully. "Is it going to blow up?"

Olaf tried to grin reassuringly but he felt it was a pale effort, more a grimace than a grin. "Not with me here."

They reached the upper station of the elevator and ran to the edge, where the cage was ready to go down. He lifted Constantus over the railing and set him down inside the basket. Then he took Hal's flint and struck it several times against his dagger.

The Herons had waited through the night. Thorn had set a roster for lookouts to keep watch for some sign of activity at the top of the elevator cable.

"The rest of you might as well get some sleep," he'd told the crew. "We could be here for a while."

"What do you think's holding them up?" Ulf had asked.

Thorn shrugged. "Hal may be waiting for Myrgos's men to settle down for the night," he said. Even this far away, they had heard snatches of song from the cliff top as the wind varied.

"Maybe he's waiting for the volcano to settle down," Edvin said. There had been as much upheaval down here as on the top of the cliff. From time to time, the surface of the bay heaved with the force coming from below. The resultant waves would surge into the inlet, and they had been hard put to fend *Heron* off the jetty and the rocks.

"I don't think that's going to happen soon," Thorn had told him.

Now, as the sky was beginning to lighten, Stefan saw the brilliant flash of the flint and steel from inside the shadows of the elevator house.

"Thorn! Look!" he called.

A moment later, it was repeated. This time, Thorn was watching.

"They're coming down," he said. "Tail on to that rope to stop them getting out of control." He struck his own flint with his saxe several times, to signal they were ready.

The elevator would come down under its own weight. And without some form of control, it would move faster and faster as gravity took over. Stefan quickly woke the rest of the crew, and they all caught hold of the loose end of the cable. They felt it start to move as Olaf pushed it off from the top station and it began to slide down, gathering speed as it did.

The rope started to run faster, and Thorn gestured to Ingvar, who was at the head of the line.

"Take a turn round that bollard to slow them down," he said. Ingvar nodded and quickly looped the rope round one of the wooden bollards on the jetty. The added friction as the rope went round the bollard took some of the strain off the rope handlers. The cage was coming down smoothly, but not too quickly.

As it drew closer to the jetty, Thorn could make out the two figures riding in it.

"It's Olaf!" he called. "And he's got the boy!"

In spite of their preoccupation with the rope, the crew let out a muted cheer. They had got what they had come for. But their sense of triumph was tinged with caution. Hal and Lydia were still somewhere up the cliff.

Ulf let out a shocked yell as a large piece of rock broke off from the top of the cliff and plummeted into the inlet, raising a mighty splash only ten meters from the jetty.

"It's shaking itself to pieces!" he said. Nobody answered, but they all agreed with his assessment.

The cage thudded into the jetty. Distracted by the falling rock, they had let it run almost unchecked for the last five meters. Now willing hands reached forward to help Constantus and Olaf out of the cage.

Olaf grinned in triumph. "We got Constantus!"

But Thorn wasn't ready to celebrate yet. "Where's Hal?"

Olaf gestured back up the cliff. "He and Lydia are coming down next."

"Thorn!" It was Edvin calling, pointing up to the cliffs, now wreathed in smoke and steam. "Hal's signaling!"

A series of brilliant flashes emanated from the hut at the top of the cliff. Thorn looked around. The cage was empty, so it would be easier to haul it up by hand. And he sensed that there wasn't time to use the ship to take it up.

"Everyone on the rope!" he ordered. "Pull your hearts out!"

Everyone on the jetty, including Olaf and Constantus, grabbed hold of the rope and began to haul it in, running back along the jetty to get it moving faster.

"Time for you to earn your keep, Ingvar," Thorn said through gritted teeth as he heaved on the rope.

The big crewman said nothing but heaved with increasing force. Lydia was up there and she was relying on them to get her down, he thought. His feet gripped the rough wood of the jetty planks, and he leaned his body almost horizontal to the ground with his efforts. The others on the rope felt the difference. The elevator shot upward and they couldn't help looking at the massive lad in awe. They had never seen his strength demonstrated so forcibly.

"Here they come," Lydia said calmly. She was keeping watch over the rough ground between the ridge and the elevator hut. The first of Myrgos's men had just appeared over the ridge, moving cautiously, waiting to see if they'd be met by a hail of darts and crossbow bolts.

"Let's not disappoint them," Hal said grimly. He had taken the opportunity to reload his crossbow and now he settled his sights on a warrior in the middle of the line. Half a dozen of them were emerging over the ridge, moving with increasing confidence, as there was no reaction from the elevator hut.

"Let 'em have it," Hal said, and released the crossbow. The bolt streaked across the intervening space and hit the pirate in the center of his body mass. He doubled over, reeling back with the force of the shot, then dropping to the ground with a cry of pain.

In the same few moments, Lydia hurled three darts. Each of them claimed a target, and suddenly the remaining two pirates weren't so sure it was a good idea to charge the elevator hut. They turned and ran back to the ridge, dropping to the ground and yelling to their comrades who were coming up behind them to keep low and stay in cover.

Hal allowed himself a nod of satisfaction. "That's slowed them down," he said.

But as he spoke, the entire hut lurched violently as another tremor shook it. The beam supporting one corner splayed out to the side, and a corner of the roof crashed down into the interior.

The floor sagged at an angle. The hut wasn't going to last much longer, Hal thought.

Then the elevator cage thumped into the railing and the edge of the bull wheel.

Hal found the flint where Olaf had left it and struck it twice rapidly with his saxe. The brilliant flashes were seen from below, and he and Lydia clambered over the railing into the cage. He shoved off, pushing them away from the sagging, quaking hut and setting the cage sliding down the rope. As they went, they felt the crew hauling on the rope to check their speed.

"Look out!" Lydia shouted, grabbing his shoulder and pulling him down behind the railing. Three huge rocks had broken away from the top of the cliff, the largest smashing into the cage, setting it rocking wildly. A few seconds later, he heard an enormous splash from below as it plunged into the water of the inlet.

Hal looked back up the cliff, and his mouth dried in fear. There were cracks forming in the rock below the elevator station, huge splits that gushed steam and smoke into the night air. As he watched, they spread wider and wider across the cliff face below the hut.

"It won't last much longer," he said.

Lydia looked up at the spreading spiderweb of cracks and splits. "We only need a couple of minutes."

"I don't know that we're going to get it," he said as the rock shelf forming part of the mounting for the bull wheel cracked and fell away. The basket lurched wildly. The platform that held the upper end of the lift in place was hanging by a thread. One more decent tremor and it would collapse.

"Faster!" he yelled down at the heaving, toiling crew. But his voice was lost in the thunderous cracks and explosions of steam.

Rocks clattered down the cliff face in a constant shower now, hitting the water below and churning it to foam. The only thing that kept them safe was the fact that the rope moved out at an angle—it didn't run vertically down from the top station. Had that been the case, they would have been buried under the falling rocks and boulders.

Another section of the top platform gave way, and the cage swung wildly to the side. Hal felt a cold hand clutch his heart as he saw a massive rent in the rock wall beginning to zigzag up toward the elevator platform. When it reached the top, the entire structure would give way. He looked down. They were still twenty meters from the water in the inlet.

He gestured to the massive crack in the rocks. "Get ready to jump," he said. "When that goes, the cage will drop vertically. We'll have to jump out to get clear of it."

Lydia nodded, grasping the situation immediately, and began to haul herself up onto the railing.

"Not yet," Hal warned her, his eyes locked on the crack as it slowly inched its way up through the rock. He wanted to wait as long as possible to reduce the height they would have to fall. Then, suddenly, the crack accelerated toward the elevator hut, and he vaulted up onto the rail as well.

"Go!" he shouted.

Lydia pushed off, hurling herself out into space as far as she could. A second later, he felt the cage give its last death tremor and he launched himself after her, toward the black water fifteen meters below them.

The shock as he hit the surface of the water was stunning—far worse than he had imagined.

The impact jarred his feet and knees and punched the air out of his lungs as he went under. Involuntarily, he gulped in several mouthfuls of salt water before he could stop himself. He was still going down, in a welter of foam and bubbles, when the cage hit the water several meters from him. The shock was transmitted through the water and punched him like a massive fist. Again, he gulped and swallowed more water. He flailed weakly, desperately trying to make it back to the surface before his tortured lungs collapsed and he breathed in more water. In his dazed mind, he knew that if he did that, it would spell the end for him. He had no idea where Lydia was. He hoped that she was all right.

Then, when his lungs were ready to burst, he exploded to the surface, coming out up to his waist and gasping desperately for air, filling his lungs and then collapsing in a fit of coughing and retching as he tried to breathe in and, at the same time, expel the water he had swallowed.

He thrashed desperately at the surface, trying to prevent himself from going down again. A few meters away, he became aware of a dim shape. It was Lydia, floating facedown in the water. He swam weakly to her, grabbing her from behind, rolling her onto her back and pulling her face clear of the water. She groaned, and he felt a surge of relief as he realized she was alive. He tried to call for help, but his voice was nothing but a weak croak. He went under again and swallowed more seawater. He thrashed feebly, desperately striving to get back to the surface. But he was weakening and his efforts had no effect.

Thorn sized the situation up immediately. He turned to Stig and yelled:

"Come on!"

Then he leapt feetfirst into the water of the inlet and struck out for his skirl and the unconscious Lydia.

Stig paused at the edge of the jetty. "Everybody back aboard!" he yelled. "Cast off the lines!" Then he too hurled himself into the water in a clumsy dive. The impetus of the dive brought him level with Thorn, and they reached Hal and Lydia at the same time. Lydia was struggling feebly. Like Hal, she had swallowed water when she hit the surface but she was semiconscious. Hal was now ominously still, facedown in the water.

"Take Lydia!" Thorn said, spitting water. "I've got Hal."

He wrapped his hook in the collar of Hal's jerkin and heaved
him upright in the water. Then he took the skirl's arms and draped
them around his own neck and shoulders, striking out in a clumsy
sidestroke for the ship, scissor-kicking strongly as he went.

Stig swam behind Lydia and wrapped his arms under hers, lying on his back to hold her out of the water and kicking toward the
ship as well.

Years before, when they had first formed the brotherband, Hal
had ensured that all members of the crew could swim—a rare
accomplishment among sailors at that time. His foresight now
stood him in good stead—indeed, it probably saved his life.

Thrashing with his free arm, kicking wildly with his legs,
snorting and blowing like a bull walrus, Thorn brought Hal
alongside the ship, where hands reached down to help him aboard.
Ulf leaned far out over the gunwale, held tight around his belt by
Wulf, and grabbed Hal by both arms.

"Pull us in!" he yelled to his brother.

Wulf reared back, assisted by Jesper and Stefan, and plucked
Hal bodily over the railing. He set him down, pale-faced and semiconscious, on the central deck. Ulf reached back for Thorn, but the
old sea wolf waved him away.

"Get Lydia aboard first!" he spluttered through a mouthful of
water—the inlet was still churned up by the constant rain of rocks
and boulders smashing into it from the cliff top above them.

Ulf felt a large body shove him to one side, and Ingvar—of
course it was Ingvar—leaned down to where Stig had brought
Lydia close to the hull. The massive youth grabbed her by the
shoulders of her jerkin and heaved her up and aboard the ship as if

she weighed no more than a baby. Once she was over the rail, he cradled her gently and laid her on the central decking.

Ulf and Wulf had already turned Hal onto his stomach, his hands and arms stretched above his head, and were pumping urgently at his ribs. For several minutes, he remained still, not breathing or showing any sign of life. Then he suddenly erupted in a fit of coughing and spewed seawater all over the deck, and took in a giant, shuddering breath.

Edvin moved in to examine Lydia. She was breathing easily enough, but there was a thin trickle of blood from above her left eyebrow.

"Probably hit by a falling rock," he muttered.

Ingvar moved in to peer closely at Lydia's injury, getting in Edvin's way.

"I'll take care of her," Edvin told him. He pointed to the stern. "You get Stig and Thorn on board."

The two crewmen had swum aft where the rail of the ship dipped down lower to the water. It took Ingvar only a matter of seconds to heave them, dripping wet, onto the deck.

Once he was back on board, Stig took stock of the situation quickly. Hal was sitting up, still dazed, but recovering from his near drowning. Lydia's eyes had opened, and she was responding groggily to Edvin's questions.

"Ulf! Stay with Hal. Edvin, you look after Lydia. The rest of you, get to your oars and pole us out of here!"

The Herons scrambled to do his bidding. The ship was already cast loose, and Stefan and Jesper set their oars against the jetty and the rough walls of the inlet, poling her back toward the open sea. As she began to gather way and the inlet opened up, the others set their oars and began to row, backing the ship out into open water, away from the rain of crashing rocks that was now falling constantly into the inlet, churning the water to foam.

Stig took the tiller, and as they came into clear water, he turned her so she was facing the open sea. Lydia was sitting up now, waving Edvin away. He finished tying a linen bandage around her forehead.

"Edvin! Relieve Ulf!" Stig ordered. "Ulf and Wulf, get the sail on her." He glanced at the telltale. "Port sail!"

Hal rose to his feet, staggered slightly, then took hold of the gunwale to steady himself. He waited several seconds, shook his head to clear it, then moved groggily aft to the steering platform. Stig started to make way for him but he motioned for the first mate to continue steering.

"I'll be all right in a few minutes," he said. "Just give me time to get my head together. Thanks for what you did."

Stig grinned. "Always a pleasure to haul a drowned mackerel aboard," he said. "Although by rights I should make you mop up where you threw up on my deck." As first mate, it was part of his duty to keep the ship spick-and-span.

Hal smiled at the sally. "Is Lydia all right?" he asked.

"Lydia is fine," she said from behind him. "A rock caught me on the forehead and knocked me out after I surfaced. They tell me you held my head out of the water until Stig reached me."

"You've lost your quiver," he said.

She looked down, then nodded. "It came off when I hit the water. I've got a spare in my sleeping berth. Not that I'll need it now," she added.

A thundering roar came from the cliff top, and they all turned to look. A huge eruption of flame, smoke and ashes was pouring out of a massive rent at the top of the cliffs. The hut that had housed the elevator station had long since disappeared. Rocks the size of houses were being hurled high into the air, to come thundering down with massive splashes into the inlet and the waters close to the cliff bottom. As they watched, a twenty-meter section at the very top of the cliff came loose and thundered down into the lagoon. Hal shuddered at the thought of what would have happened to his beloved ship if she'd been under that.

"Looks like we got out just in time," he told Stig.

Stig nodded. The sail was set and drawing strongly in the predawn breeze. "Which way?" he asked.

Hal pointed to a gap between two massive outcrops of rock. So far, the disturbance seemed to be confined to the part of the cliffs where they had been, and all was calm where he was pointing.

"Take us back out the way we came in," he said. "It looks calm enough there."

Stig nodded and called to the crew, "Coming about onto the port tack! Ready on the sails!"

An answering cry told him the sail handlers and trimmers were ready. "Coming about . . . now!" he yelled, and swung the tiller.

The port sail slid down and the starboard sail went up smoothly in its place, with the usual squealing of ropes through blocks and the accompanying groaning of wood and cordage under stress. The ship leaned to starboard and slid smoothly through the water. Hal reached out for the tiller.

"I'll take her now," he said, and Stig handed the tiller over to him.

Hal set his feet and, as always, checked the telltale. The light was growing stronger now and they could see clearly. He glanced astern to where the giant, roiling cloud of ash and smoke, shot through with the flames of the awoken volcano, was staining the morning sky. From time to time, a massive explosion rocked the island, sending more rocks and molten lava high into the air.

"Are we heading back round to the village?" Stig asked.

Hal shook his head firmly. "We're heading for Byzantos. I never want to see this place again." He felt a hand tugging at his sleeve and made a mental note to change his sodden clothes at the first chance he had. He looked down and saw Constantus standing beside him. He smiled at the boy, who looked very serious indeed. Olaf was a few paces away, watching carefully.

"Captain?" said the young emperor. "I want to thank you for getting me out of there."

Hal inclined his head in a self-deprecating movement. "Why, think nothing of it, your emperorship," he said. Like all Skandians—and he considered himself to be one in spite of his mixed parentage—he disdained titles of respect like "your majesty" or "your highness." But Constantus shook his head doggedly.

"No. I am deeply in your debt. You have done me a great service and I will make sure my mother rewards you suitably."

The boy's demeanor was very formal, almost pompous. Hal supposed that came with being royalty, and having everyone around you defer to you and grant your slightest wish. He had a brief moment wondering whether Constantus's mother would be totally delighted to see him again. After all, she would have to relinquish her position as Empress and revert to being Regent when Constantus returned to Byzantos. From what he'd heard of the woman, he didn't think she'd enjoy that. He caught Olaf's gaze and raised an inquisitive eyebrow, but the burly commander didn't seem to be sharing the same thought process.

"I'm sure she will," he said.

Constantus, his duty done, nodded gravely and stepped back from the steering platform. Olaf stepped forward and placed a proprietorial hand on his shoulder.

"Well said, your excellency," Olaf said in a low voice.

Hal smiled to himself. Olaf had been away from home long enough to lose the Skandian reluctance for titles, he thought. Then he sighed.

Home. The thought was a comforting one. This had been a long, hard voyage. He glanced astern to where the cloud of ash and smoke from the awoken volcano was staining the morning sky. As he looked, a massive explosion rocked the island, sending more rocks and molten lava high into the air.

"A good place to be out of," he said to Lydia.

She nodded. "All we have to do now is get Constantus back to his mother, then get us home," she said.

He smiled. "That should be the easy part."

Then the smile faded as a long, low black shape appeared in the narrow channel between the two crags.

The *Vulture* had returned to her nest.

The big black ship was moving fast, under full sail and with her oars pounding the water. Hal had a sinking feeling as he realized she was moving faster than *Heron* could.

And she was blocking their path to the open sea.

Rapidly, he assessed the situation. He glanced at the sail but could see that Ulf and Wulf were wringing every last meter of speed from the ship. He turned to Stig.

"Get for'ard with Ingvar and get the Mangler ready," he said. "If we can knock out a few of their oarsmen, we might have a chance." Stig nodded and called for Ingvar to follow him. They dashed for'ard to where the massive crossbow sat hunched under its canvas covers and began to unlash them.

"Ulf! Wulf!" Hal called, and the two sail trimmers sat up

expectantly, waiting for his orders. Seeing he had their attention, he continued. "I'm going to turn to starboard. The moment the *Vulture* starts to tack after us, I want to reverse the turn. We may be able to slip past if we can out-turn him."

The twins nodded. When it came to sail handling, there were none better and he had absolute confidence in them. Still, he thought, there was always the chance that a rope could jam in a block or a halyard could part at a crucial moment. You could take nothing for granted in a situation like this, where the slightest mistake or delay could be fatal.

"Loki, get us through this," he muttered. He favored the god of tricksters. He seemed a logical choice for someone like Hal, who depended on his wits to defeat his enemies.

Of course, he realized, once he had slipped past *Vulture*—if he *could* slip past *Vulture*—they would still have to outrun her, and that might prove difficult. He shrugged mentally. Time enough to worry about that when he had outmaneuvered her.

The *Vulture* was pounding toward them, closer and closer. He could see the white foam around the ram in her bows as she rose and fell on the gentle waves.

"Coming about . . . now!" he yelled, and threw the tiller over without waiting to see if Ulf and Wulf had responded.

They had. The starboard sail rattled down and hit the deck, billowing and flapping, and the port sail went soaring up the mast, filling and drawing with a percussive *WHOOMP!* as Ulf and Wulf heaved on the sheets. *Heron*'s bow came round sweetly. She crossed *Vulture*'s path with only meters to spare and shot away. Hal heard the heavy thump of the Mangler releasing but had no time to mark the fall of the shot. There was a splintering impact and he knew

Stig had hit something. His first mate was yelling to Ingvar to re-load when Lydia stepped up beside Hal and released a volley of darts at the enemy's steering platform.

Hal watched, eyes squinted in concentration, for Myrgos's next move. This time, learning from his past mistake, the pirate skipper didn't try to tack his square rigger across the wind. He shouted a series of orders, and the sail slid down to the deck as the rowers reversed one bank of oars and went forward on the other.

As the black ship started to turn, Hal shouted his next orders.

"Come about! Port sail up!"

Now their starboard sail and yardarm came sliding down to the deck while all hands, including Stig and Ingvar, heaved on the halyards and sent the port yardarm whipping up the mast, the sail billowing out as it caught the wind.

Not for the first time, Hal blessed the inspiration that had led him to install the fin keel, which allowed the ship to turn so quickly and so adroitly. They shot clear of the *Vulture*, heading obliquely for the gap between the two islands. Looking back over his shoulder, Hal saw the enemy ship complete its turn to port, coming round so that the bow was pointing at them. The sail shot up *Vulture's* mast and filled instantly. The rowers resumed their steady beating of the water, although he could see several gaps in the row of smoothly swinging oars.

With the Mangler no longer able to bear on the other ship, Stig came aft.

"We got a couple of the rowers," he said. "And I saw Lydia hit another. It should slow them down."

Hal was watching the enemy ship as it gained on them, and he shook his head. "Not enough," he said. "She'll catch us before we reach the gap."

Out in the open sea, beyond the gap between the two outcrops, the wind would be fresher and they might regain a speed advantage over the other ship. After all, he reasoned, Myrgos's crew couldn't keep rowing at this muscle-cracking pace indefinitely.

But first they had to reach the open sea, and that was looking doubtful.

"What are you going to do?" Stig asked.

Hal simply shook his head. For once, he had no answer.

"We'll keep on the way we're going," he finally said. "I can't keep dodging and ducking. Myrgos is too good to fall for that again. And if he ever catches us out, that ram will finish us."

The two ships raced across the bay on converging courses. With every meter *Heron* traveled, *Vulture* seemed to go a meter and a half, as she gradually ate up the distance between them. On board the black ship, the pirates could see they were winning the race. They crowded in the bows, yelling and waving their weapons.

Thorn strolled aft and regarded his skirl. "Any thoughts?"

Hal shrugged. "Keep going as we are and kill as many of them as we can when they catch us."

The old sea wolf smiled fiercely. "Sounds good to me." He rummaged in his locker in the rowing wells and sat down, loosening his wooden hook and replacing it with the massive fighting club Hal had fashioned for him. He swung it experimentally, feeling the weight and balance.

"Ah, it feels good to have it back on again," he said.

"Are you always this cheerful before a battle?" Lydia asked him.

He grinned at her. "Every time."

"You realize we don't stand a chance, don't you?"

He shook his head. "There's always a chance, so long as you're alive. You never know what might happen."

"Like what?" she asked. She was prepared to fight, but she wasn't deluding herself with any false hope that they might be successful. There were simply too many men on the other ship.

He shrugged, still grinning. "Who knows? That's what makes the uncertainty so much fun."

The two ships raced on. With every second, *Vulture* came closer. Hal bit his bottom lip in frustration. There was nothing he could do to stave off the inevitable. Still, he thought, he'd play a losing hand out to the end.

"Where are you when I need you, Loki?" he muttered. But this time, there were no saving squalls to conceal him. The sky was clear, apart from the massive pall of smoke and ash that rose from the cliffs behind them. And full daylight was nearly upon them. There was nowhere to hide. Nowhere to escape the grim black ship bearing down on them.

Then it happened.

They felt a massive shock transmitted through the water as it struck the timbers of the hull, making the ship vibrate from stem to stern.

"What was—" Stig started to say, but Thorn cut him off, pointing to the lagoon behind them.

With a massive rumbling sound, a monstrous mound of water erupted from the surface, thirty meters across and rearing up to ten meters above the lagoon. It was white foam, shot through with an unearthly red as the bottom of the lagoon far below opened to the gates of hell.

The crew stood, awestruck, for several seconds as the huge eruption boiled and churned high above the lagoon. Then, as abruptly as it had formed, it collapsed back on itself, returning to the ocean whence it had come.

In its place, as it crashed back to the surface, it created a massive wave, radiating out in a circle, four meters high and traveling as fast as a galloping horse, and pushing a thundering wall of wind ahead of it.

H al was the first on board the ship to recover his wits. The thundering wave could crush them like an eggshell, he realized.

Or it could prove to be their salvation.

"Ulf and Wulf, stay on the sheets! Everyone else, get back aft!" he yelled as an idea struck him.

Because of their relative positions when the eruption occurred, *Vulture* was directly ahead of the speeding wall of water, while *Heron* was angling across its path. If they could maintain their speed and use the massive wind created by the disturbance to keep them moving, they might be able to surf across the line of the wave. If it struck them directly, stern on, it would probably turn the ship head over heels. There was no way they could ride a wave that size if it hit them from behind.

"Sheet home!" he yelled to the twins, and they heaved the sail taut. *Heron*, true to her name, began to fly across the water, throwing spray up to either side of her bow. As the crew came tumbling aft, their extra weight kept the bow high. When the wave hit them, they would need every inch of height they could gain.

Hal looked over his shoulder. The wave was racing toward them. It would hit *Vulture* before it reached them and the corsair was in the worst possible position. *Vulture* had the wave dead astern, rearing up behind her. He could see Myrgos at the tiller, bending forward as he screamed orders at his crew. The oars rose and fell even faster, trying to drive the ship ahead of the wave.

But they didn't have the power to do it. *Vulture*'s bow began to tilt downward as the huge wave overtook her. She faltered, her stern rising higher and higher, causing men to fall from their rowing benches and tumble helplessly into the bow—accentuating her bad position by adding more weight where she least needed it.

The wave picked the ship up bodily, and *Vulture*'s stern came clear of the water at the crest of the wave, while her bow and midships section plunged deeper, in a dive from which Hal's instincts told him she would never recover.

She was an old ship, and a large one, and her keel was never made to support her own weight out of the water. It needed the support of water underneath it, or the sand of a beach. Now, as it hung clear, the weight of the ship proved too much and with a *CRACK* they could hear from the *Heron*, the *Vulture*'s back broke, the rear end of the ship tumbling down behind the wave while the for'ard half plunged underwater and rolled over. The mast went as *Vulture* smashed violently down into the sea ahead of the huge wave. For a second they could see the black hull, with the small figures of her crew desperately scrambling for safety—safety that was nowhere to be found. Then the wave rolled over it, and she was hidden from their sight.

It was a horrifying sight. But there was no time to dwell on it as the monstrous wave hurtled toward them.

"Grab something and hang on!" yelled Hal.

The crew grabbed hold of stays, rowing benches and the railing itself as they waited for the wave.

"Pump the sail!" Hal yelled to the twins, and understanding his order, they quickly eased and then tightened the sheets several times, causing the sail to slacken, then tighten suddenly again. It was an old trick to increase speed and it worked—*Heron* accelerated as the wave thundered down on them.

Hal used the extra speed to swing the bow up the face of the wave, surfing along the face and using the force of the wave itself to maintain their speed and position rather than being lifted helplessly up by it.

He could sense the curl of the lip just behind them and he shoved the tiller over, sending the ship sliding back down the face of the wave, accelerating away from the breaking crest.

Heron trembled with the sheer speed of the ride. The fin keel, secure in its housing, began vibrating as the ship moved faster than she had ever moved before. The vibration set up a humming sound as if the ship herself were groaning in fear.

On and on they sped, alternately plunging down the face of the wave, then using the speed they had gained to swoop back up again, held in place on a knife edge of speed, power and Hal's masterful helmsmanship.

Thorn, crouched in the very stern of the ship, holding on to the backstay, had never seen anything like this in a lifetime at sea. He let out an exultant bellow. Even if they died here today, he thought, it would be worth it to have experienced this insane, rushing, thundering ride.

Thorn stood erect, his beard and hair streaming out in the fantastic wind created by their speed. Lydia, a few meters away, looked at him in amazement.

"Are you mad?" she screamed at him. Her own stomach was clenched tight in terror. The inestimable power of the wave, the headlong rush of the ship along it, the sensation that they were one millimeter away from being out of control and swamped, were almost beyond belief. She knew it was only Hal's remarkable skill as a helmsman, his unequaled *feeling* for the ship, that was keeping them alive.

Thorn turned to her, released his grip on the backstay and stood with his arms spread out to the wind in total abandon as the berserker spirit overtook him. He roared with wild laughter.

"Totally!" he said to her. "This is fantastic! Nobody has ever felt anything like this before!"

The crew heard his words and shook their heads in wonder. Sometimes they suspected Thorn was a little crazy. At other times—such as this—they were sure of it.

But Hal was staring ahead.

Two hundred meters away, the smaller of the two rocky outcrops that formed this entrance to the lagoon was looming toward them. The wave was carrying them at fantastic speed toward it. There was no way he could turn away. If he tried to turn back, the wave would swamp them. But if they continued to rush on like this, they would be driven up onto the rocks. He had to get them off the wave.

"Hold on!" he yelled. It was an unnecessary order. Apart from Thorn, the Herons were gripping tight for their lives. He shoved the tiller, letting the ship angle down, accelerating down the face of the wave, building the speed. Dimly, above the roar of the wave, he heard Thorn's exultant yell. Then he heaved back on the tiller, sending the ship soaring upward once more, using the speed and momentum he had gained to keep her going across and up the wave.

Only this time, he didn't back off at the top. He used the incredible momentum to shoot out and break clear of the crest of the wave.

Heron's bow smashed through the crest, and a welter of foam thundered down onto the crew. She came clear out of the water for half her length. But she was newer than *Vulture*, and better built. Hal himself had selected the timber for her keel and her frames. He had sweated over every rivet that held her together. She hung in the air for several seconds, then smashed down onto the back of the wave, rolling wildly, plunging her bows deep into the water, so that the yardarm pulled clear of its bracket and cracked in half, sagging down against the restraint of the halyards. Then she righted herself, rocking sluggishly, half full of water, and lay in the calm water behind the terrible wave.

A secondary wave caught her. But it was barely half the size of the first wave, no more than two meters high. The *Heron* rose sluggishly to it, half full of water as she was. She rocked and plunged but her watertight central compartments kept her afloat.

Slowly, the crew gathered themselves, looking at one another in relief as they realized they had survived the caldera's onslaught. They released their hold on the ropes and fittings they had clung to through the insane ride across the face of the wave. One or two of them shook their heads in wonder, unable to quite believe that they were still alive. Seawater sloshed thigh deep in the rowing wells, slopping backward and forward with the unsteady motion of the ship.

"Let's get her bailed out," Hal said in the sudden calm that followed the roar of the wave. "Ingvar, Stefan, take down that broken yardarm."

Moving as if they were in a daze, the Herons set about carrying out his orders. Stig stepped up to the steering platform, where Hal sagged unsteadily against the railing, his knees suddenly weak as the adrenaline drained away.

"That was amazing!" Stig said. "I didn't know she could do that." He slapped the oak rail affectionately, then added, "I didn't know *you* could do that."

Hal, his hair plastered down on his head with seawater, grinned in return.

"Neither did I," he said. "Now let's get this water out of her before another one of those waves comes along."

It took an hour's hard work to set the ship to rights. The main task was to bail the water out of her, and the crew set to willingly with buckets and beakers to get it done. Once the massive weight of water was out of her, she rode the water like a seabird once more.

The yardarm was cracked and unusable. Ingvar, Stefan and Hal cut the bindings that held the sail to it and trimmed the ends of the yard itself, putting the two shortened halves into the rack of spare spars. While at sea, they never threw usable timber away.

"Shall we put the sail onto a new spar?" Stefan asked.

Hal shook his head. "Time for that later. For the time being, we'll sail on a foul tack if need be."

A foul tack used the sail on the side from which the wind was blowing. The mast impeded the sail so that it didn't develop its full power. But it would keep the ship moving, albeit at a reduced pace.

Hal looked around the ship. Aside from the cracked yardarm, she had sustained little in the way of physical damage.

"We should go back and look for survivors," he said, remembering the terrible moment of seeing the other ship crack in two.

Thorn shook his head. "There won't be many. Most of them were wearing armor. Not a good idea when you get hit by a monster wave like that."

"Let them drown," said Olaf. "They wouldn't come looking for us if the shoe was on the other foot."

"Which is what makes us different from them," Stig said firmly.

Olaf went to reply, then decided against it.

Hal watched the two of them keenly. "I thought you might want to see if Myrgos survived," he said to Olaf. "You could take him back to Byzantos to stand trial."

That idea appealed to the guard commander. "Good thinking," he said. "I'd enjoy seeing him on the rack."

Hal raised an eyebrow. "Not exactly what I was suggesting."

They sailed back to the point where the wave had overwhelmed

Vulture. The sea was littered with debris—broken planks, hatch covers, oars, casks, clay jars and sections of spars. The surface of the water was also coated with a thick layer of ash from the heaving, belching cliffs behind them.

As Thorn had forecast, very few of the pirate crew had survived—partly because many of them had been wearing armor and partly because very few of them could swim.

They hauled three of them out of the water, more dead than alive, and shoved them roughly into the bow, where Stig and Jesper stood guard over them. But the pirates had no fight left in them. They huddled on the deck, covered in dirty, ash-laden water, and looked down at the planks, not willing to meet their captors' eyes.

"That's about it," Thorn remarked to Hal.

The skirl was drawing breath to give sail orders to Ulf and Wulf when Lydia called:

"Over here! Clinging to that spar!"

Hal swung the tiller and they rowed toward the spot she was pointing to. Thorn gave a mirthless laugh when he saw the hapless survivor hanging on to a section of broken spar.

The wild hair and beard were plastered down by seawater, and the features were half obscured by ash and dirt. But the glaring eyes and snarling mouth were unmistakable. It was Myrgos.

"Up you come, my beauty," said Ingvar, leaning down to lift the pirate captain bodily onto the ship. He set him down and Myrgos slumped against the rail, his eyes alive with hatred, his ugly features contorted by rage.

"Did he say thank you?" Thorn asked.

But then the treacherous Myrgos reached behind his back and drew a long knife from a sheath, slashing at Ingvar.

He caught the big lad a glancing blow on the left forearm, opening a long, shallow cut. Ingvar reacted instinctively. Before Myrgos could recover from the first wild stroke, Ingvar grabbed a handful of his shirtfront and heaved him up and over the rail once more, pitching him bodily into the sea.

There was an ugly thud as Myrgos's head made solid contact with the spar that had so recently saved his life. He let out a short grunt of pain and surprise, then his eyes glazed and he sank back into the water, sliding off the spar and sinking into the dirty, scum-covered water of the caldera.

"Best place for him," said Thorn. They waited a few minutes, but the pirate captain never reappeared.

Finally, Hal put a weary hand on the tiller. "Let's go home," he said.

c h a p t e r   f o r t y

It was mid-morning when *Heron* cruised into the Golden Reach under easy sail, heading for the harbor at Byzantos.

Hal threaded his way skillfully through the bustling traffic on the waterway, realizing after a few minutes that the other craft would come close to him—at times frighteningly close—but would always manage to avoid a collision at the last moment. He grinned to himself. If you didn't have that attitude on this piece of water, you'd never get anywhere. Once he had learned to trust the other helmsmen, and to copy their practice of *close, but not too close*, he found it was a lot more comfortable navigating the Reach.

But then there was one craft that didn't look as if it would give way or shear off at the last moment. A solidly build ten-oar patrol boat heaved to across their path, and sat broadside on. In the bow, a figure in shining armor stood, hand on the hilt of his sword, and held up his hand for them to stop.

"You've seen him, of course?" Thorn said.

Hal nodded. "Wonder what would happen if I just sailed straight into him?"

Thorn grinned. "He'd get that shiny armor all rusty. Don't think that'd make us too popular."

But Hal was already calling orders to Ulf and Wulf. "Let go the sheets. Bring down the sail. Jesper, get in the bow if we need to fend off."

As the sail was released and came sliding down to the deck, the way began to fall off *Heron*. At the last moment, Hal swung her bow to port to avoid contacting the patrol boat and the two craft rode side by side, a few meters separating them, rising and falling on the choppy sea.

He noted that the crew were also wearing armor. Obviously, this wasn't a friendly reception welcoming them back to Byzantos. The armored man's next words confirmed this.

"You left port without permission," he called.

Hal shrugged. There wasn't much else he could do.

"Follow us," the armored one continued, his tone brusque and uncompromising. He pointed across the harbor. "Moor up at the Imperial Wharf."

Hal glanced in the direction he had indicated. The Imperial Wharf was easy to recognize. It was large and solidly built, with several official-looking buildings along its length. Two more patrol boats were moored alongside, and there was room behind them for the *Heron*. Hal waved his compliance and called to Stig.

"We'll go under oars, I think. Too hard to keep station if we sail."

The crew quickly dropped into the rowing wells and ran out their oars, while Ulf and Wulf stowed the sail. The patrol boat waited until they were ready, then gave way, the armored man turning to make sure they were following. Meekly, they processed across the water behind the patrol boat, like a naughty puppy with its tail between its legs. This time there was no need to weave among the rest of the traffic. The other craft gave the official patrol boat a wide berth. Nobody wanted to tangle with them. They all knew from bitter experience that the Emperor's fleet had absolute right of way and any collision would inevitably be blamed on the other craft, and a subsequent heavy fine imposed.

They came alongside the wharf, and the patrol boat sheared off to return to the harbor. The tide was high and the deck was almost level with the wharf. As Hal steered her in, letting the last of her speed die off, Jesper tossed a mooring line to a man on the wharf, who hauled the bow in close to the pilings, creaking and squeaking against the cane fenders that were hung over the edge of the wharf. In the stern, Stig threw another mooring line ashore, and within minutes they were moored securely fore and aft. Hal slipped the retaining rope over the tiller to keep it secure. The rowers ran their oars in and stowed them along the ship's length.

They had barely finished this when they heard the tramp of booted feet on the wharf's planks, and a double file of soldiers—twenty in all—marched along the wharf, coming to a halt opposite the ship and right-turning to face them. Each man was equipped with a shield, spear and helmet, and they all wore short, Toscan-style swords on their right hips. Their commander, a senior officer judging by the amount of gold and silver trim on his armor and cloak fastenings, stepped down from the wharf onto the ship without waiting to be invited.

Thorn raised an eyebrow. "Nice manners they have in this part of the world," he said, not too quietly.

The officer turned an icy glare on him. Then he glanced around the people gathered on the deck and found Olaf. He stepped toward him, his brow furrowed in an angry frown.

"You've got a nerve, Olaf, coming strolling in here calm as you like—"

"We sailed in, actually," Thorn pointed out in a friendly tone.

The officer glared at him. "Shut up, northman."

Thorn's eyebrow, already raised, went a little higher, and his hand dropped to the hilt of his saxe. But the officer didn't notice. He had turned back to Olaf.

"You know the Empress has a warrant out for your arrest," he said. "And she's discovered that the last time you were in port, you escaped from the town prison. Well, you're under arrest now, and this time you won't find it so easy to get away." He called to the men on the wharf, without taking his gaze from Olaf, whose face was slowly reddening with anger. "Corporal!"

"Sir!" a craggy-faced corporal in the leading rank of men responded, coming to attention.

"Take this man's weapon and place him under arrest."

"Sir!" The corporal marched across the wharf and stepped down onto the *Heron*'s railing, then to her deck. Hal eyed his heavy, nailed boots and the marks they had left on the rail with growing annoyance. He stepped forward, blocking the corporal's progress and spoke to the officer.

"You know, I'm getting a little tired of people barging onto my ship without asking permission."

"We don't need your permission. We're on the Empress's business and you are all criminals. It remains to be seen whether or not you'll be arrested with this one." The officer jerked a dismissive thumb at Olaf. As he did, the corporal sidestepped Hal and strode forward to take Olaf's sword from its scabbard.

"And who might decide that?" Thorn asked, belligerently stepping forward to stand beside Hal. On his other side, Stig did the same. Each of them had his hand resting lightly on the hilt of his saxe. The officer noticed this but didn't look intimidated. He glanced at the nineteen armed men on the wharf, then at the *Heron*'s crew.

"Men!" he ordered, and the twenty soldiers came to attention. "Stand by to arrest these criminals if they try to hinder the Empress's justice." He turned back to Thorn to answer his earlier question. "Whether we arrest you or not will be up to the Empress herself. At the moment, we have no orders concerning you." He paused, then added in an ominous tone, "But that can change."

"Excuse me, Colonel." It was a young voice that interrupted him, a high-pitched voice. He turned, annoyance showing in his face, as Constantus stepped up out of the rowing well where he had been watching proceedings. The boy was dressed in clothing contributed by the crew, most of it too big for him and all of it made from common, rough material—nothing like the fine silks and linens he was used to wearing.

"What is it, boy?" the colonel asked dismissively.

Constantus drew himself more erect at the tone. "I'm wondering who is this Empress you keep referring to?" he asked.

The colonel spared him another annoyed glance. "As everyone knows, she is the Empress Justinia, ruler of Byzantos and the eastern empire of Toscana. Now, if you'll shut up and get out of the way . . ."

And that was going too far. Constantus went red with fury. When he spoke, his voice was high pitched and on the verge of breaking.

"I rather fancied that my mother was the Regent, ruling in my name. Not the Empress in her own right," he spat, his voice sharp as a sword blade.

The colonel hesitated at his words, peering more closely at the boy. "Your mother?" he said hesitantly.

"The Regent Justinia," Constantus said. "Ruling in the name of Emperor Constantus." He paused for effect, then jabbed a thumb at his own chest. "Me!"

He spat the last word at the colonel, who now saw past the rough clothes and disheveled appearance to recognize the boy emperor. The man's mouth worked, but no sound came.

Constantus shook his head in disgust, then turned to the corporal. "You! Return Commander Olaf's sword to him."

The corporal also gaped and hesitated.

Constantus's shrill voice cut like a whip. "Do it now!"

The corporal stood irresolute for a second or two, then clumsily held out the sword to Olaf, who took it and returned it, ringing, to its scabbard.

Hal watched in some surprise, wondering where the air of command and the boy's self-assurance had come from.

"These men," Constantus continued, "these men who you call criminals and want to arrest, have just saved me from the pirate

Myrgos. Olaf, commander of my personal guard, recruited this band of Skandians to attack the pirate's stronghold and destroy it. Then they sank his ship and killed Myrgos himself, ridding us of a scourge who has plagued our oceans for years."

"Well, we didn't do it all," Thorn said genially. "The volcano helped a little."

Constantus gave him an angry look. "Be quiet," he ordered.

At that moment, Hal realized it wasn't a natural air of command that gave the boy his self-assurance. It was a matter of upbringing. Constantus had been told since he was a baby that he was superior to other people. Now he was just an arrogant prat with an overblown sense of his own importance.

Still, his attitude and manner had the desired effect on the colonel, who came to attention and hurried to make amends.

"Your excellency," he stammered, "my apologies. I didn't recognize you. I had no idea that you were—"

"If you had looked with a little more care, you might have," Constantus said scathingly. "But you didn't. You were arrogant and high-handed and you jumped to the first conclusion you could see."

Arrogant and high-handed, thought Hal. The boy would know about that.

The colonel bowed his head in abject apology. "Again, your excellency, I beg your pardon. What can I do—"

"You can return to the palace, with your men," Constantus interrupted him. "And tell my mother that Commander Olaf has returned and brought me safely home. Tell her to prepare a fitting reception for Olaf and his men here." He gestured around the assembled crew.

Thorn shifted his feet. "Not sure if I like being referred to as one of Olaf's men," he muttered.

Hal grinned. "Never contradict an emperor. They don't like it."

"Of course, your excellency," the colonel groveled, bowing deeply at the waist. "But perhaps you would allow us to escort you to the palace now—"

"Did you *hear* me?" Constantus interrupted again. "I will come to the palace escorted by my guard commander and his crew. Is that clear?"

"Yes, your excellency. Very clear." The colonel bowed again.

Hal could see that sweat had broken out on his forehead during the exchange. He couldn't help contrasting the young emperor's manner with the way Erak, the Skandian Oberjarl, spoke to and, was spoken to by, his senior commanders. Erak would never treat his commanders with such disdain.

"Tell my mother—*the Regent*—that I will be there in an hour's time," Constantus said haughtily. He laid special stress on the word *Regent*.

The colonel nodded and bowed again. "Of course, your excellency. I'm sure she will be delighted to see you home safe."

Watching the exchange, Thorn rolled his eyes. Constantus's order for him to be silent still rankled. Hal glanced at him and guessed what he was thinking.

"Let it go," he said quietly. "If you throw him into the harbor, it will just get us into more trouble."

The reception hall of the Imperial Palace was crammed with courtiers and nobles eager to welcome their Emperor back from his ordeal.

It was a massive rectangular room with its walls hung with paintings of past emperors, and fantastical scenes from mythical stories and legends, depicting men and exotic beasts, often locked in combat. Thorn studied one of them critically. It showed a muscular warrior, clad in a loincloth, doing battle with a two-headed spotted lion. The warrior's sword was drawn back and his shield held to the side to reveal his muscular bare torso.

"If he doesn't get that shield across quick smart, that big cat is going to do him some terrible damage," the old sea wolf said in a loud aside to Hal.

Hal grinned. Thorn was always unimpressed by rich surroundings like this, he knew.

"Keep it down," he warned. "It's art, and artists always take a lot of license in their work. They're not paid to be accurate."

Thorn shrugged. "Then why are they paid?"

The hall was brilliantly lit by hundreds of candles hanging in four huge chandeliers and in sconces around the walls. Beneath them, the crowds of imperial hangers-on, richly dressed and decked out with fabulous jewelry, swirled back and forth like the sea at the change of the tide. They moved from the massive buffet table—laden with delicacies and surmounted by a gigantic pie constructed in the shape of a volcano, with red-and-orange gravy spilling out of its top and cascading down its pastry sides—to the center of the hall and then to the far end, where the Empress Regent and the boy emperor sat in lavishly decorated thrones on a low platform. Empress Justinia's throne was placed centrally, and was slightly higher than that which bore her son. Constantus, to judge by his sour expression, was less than impressed by their relative sizes, and the fact that his throne was offset to one side—a subservient position.

Hal and the rest of the crew were at the back of the hall, by a side wall. None of them felt comfortable in this sort of formal situation, but they had been commanded to attend and it had been made clear to them that when the Empress Regent Justinia commanded, it was wise to obey.

Olaf stood close to the sycophantic courtiers who were grouped at the foot of the dais, hanging on Justinia's every word. From time to time, Justinia would beckon one of her followers to approach more closely, for a private word. When this happened, the favored one would step onto the dais and drop to one knee as he or she came closer to the imperial presence. In the event that Justinia chose to share a witticism with them, they would throw back their heads and roar with laughter. Immediately, all those around the dais joined in, whether or not they could make out the Empress's words.

"At least Olaf's not primping and preening like a trained monkey," Lydia muttered to Hal. Their one-time shipmate was standing slightly apart from the silk- and satin-clad crowd. He was wearing highly polished dress armor and stood at parade ease. But he was intent on the Empress's every word, and where the others guffawed, he allowed a slight smile to touch his features.

As they watched, Justinia beckoned him forward, calling his name in a clear voice. Olaf stepped to the dais, then sank to one knee in front of her. She held out her hand to him and he took it, letting his lips brush the massive ring on her second finger. Then, at her bidding, he rose and moved to stand beside her throne, between her and the boy emperor.

The crew of the Heron stirred uncomfortably as he went down on one knee. Skandians didn't do that sort of thing.

"Should we kneel down if she calls on us?" Stefan asked in a low voice.

Hal turned to look at him. "We don't do it for Erak. We won't do it for her. We'll bow, that's all."

Thorn grinned. "That should make things interesting."

Now Justinia beckoned to her majordomo, who was standing to one side on the dais. He was a massively overweight man with numerous chins and a receding hairline. He was clad in a silver, shimmering, full-length robe and carried a steel-shod black rod a head higher than himself. He stepped closer to her. He had already made his obeisance earlier in the evening and had no need to continually bob up and down before her. He leaned down as she spoke briefly to him, then straightened, moved a few paces away and banged the heavy rod down on the marble of the dais.

"He'll crack it if he keeps that up," Ingvar murmured.

Hal tried unsuccessfully to hide a grin. His men weren't impressed by pomp and ceremony. Few Skandians were—although it seemed Olaf might have adopted some of the local behavior.

"Silence! Silence for her Excellency the Empress Regent Justinia, paramount ruler of the eastern empire, sovereign of the middle sea, unchallenged ruler of the Northern Massif!"

"She's quite small for all those titles, isn't she?" Jesper whispered.

Hal glared at him. But Jesper was right. Justinia, when she rose gracefully from her throne, could be seen to be quite a petite woman. But she was unquestionably beautiful, with a heart-shaped face, full lips and a small, straight nose. Her hair hung in dark ringlets to one side of her head, and her eyes were dark and flashing. They moved constantly, checking the room and its occupants, never still for more than a few seconds.

She doesn't miss much, Hal thought, as those eyes darted round the room. She held up her hands for silence, even though the hub-bub of conversation had died away at the majordomo's command, and began to speak. Her voice was clear and strong and carried to the far corners of the room, even though she didn't appear to be shouting or straining.

"My lords and ladies, thank you for your presence here tonight. As you know, we are here to celebrate the safe return of my beloved son, the future emperor Constantus."

She turned and gestured to the boy. He had frowned slightly at the words *the future emperor* but he quickly composed his features and bowed his head toward his mother.

The assembled courtiers all applauded enthusiastically in the direction of the boy. He made a graceful gesture with his hand, acknowledging their applause.

"What are they clapping him for?" Ulf asked of no one in particular. "He didn't actually do anything. He just got rescued."

A richly clad noble standing close by shushed him violently. Ulf turned to him and went cross-eyed at him, waggling his head. The noble sniffed haughtily and looked away.

"We are also here," Justinia continued, "to give heartfelt thanks to my faithful guard commander, Captain Olaf Attelson, who planned and executed the successful rescue operation."

Olaf bowed deeply, to more applause, as Justinia waved a languid hand in his direction.

"He planned and executed the rescue?" Edvin said. "I must have missed that part. When did it happen?"

"To accomplish this," Justinia continued, "he traveled far to the north to recruit a crew of brave sailors . . ."

"Because nobody in the south would have a bar of him." That was Jesper again and he earned a shirty look from the man who had shushed Ulf earlier. Fortunately, the man couldn't make out the actual words. He was simply outraged that anyone would speak while the Empress Regent had the floor.

". . . and commanded them in the rescue."

By now the Herons were beyond any further indignant reactions to this hugely inaccurate account of the expedition. None of them saw fit to comment. Justinia turned in her seat and motioned to Olaf.

"Captain, call your men forward," she said.

"His men?" Lydia said indignantly.

Hal shushed her. "You might have known he'd give her a pretty colored account of what went on."

She snorted. Olaf glanced down the long crowded room and saw the Herons standing at the rear.

"Crew of the *Heron!*" he called. "Step forward now!"

The brotherband exchanged a quick glance, then fell in behind Hal, Stig and Thorn as they made their way down the hall toward the dais.

They stopped at the foot of the throne platform. The assembled crowd eyed them curiously. They were used to Skandians, of course. There were several score in the Empress's bodyguard. But they usually wore uniform, and that was styled in keeping with the ornate local fashions. These were sailors, dressed in simple but neat linen shirts and wool trousers, with high leggings bound to the knee. Most of them wore thin leather vests over the shirts. None of them carried a sword, but they all wore heavy, utilitarian saxes in scabbards. Lydia was the exception. She had her long dagger at her side. It had been suggested, when they entered the reception hall, that they might leave these weapons at the door. The suggestion had been ignored.

Olaf indicated Hal to the Empress. "Your serene highness," he said, "this is Hal Mikkelson, skirl of the ship *Heron*. And this is his crew, who served me so well."

A wave of his hand encompassed the rest of the Herons. Hal frowned slightly. He noticed that Olaf didn't identify Stig, or mention that he was his son. The Empress was beckoning, her palm upward, her fingers coiled in a gesture for him to come closer.

"You may approach me, Hal Mikkelson," she said.

Hal stepped up onto the dais and moved closer to her.

The majordomo intercepted him. "It's customary to kneel before her serene highness," he said in a lowered voice.

Hal glanced at him. "So I've noticed," he said. Then he bowed his head stiffly from the neck, keeping his back straight and upright.

Two little vertical lines appeared in the Empress's brow. She continued and her voice was a little colder, a little less friendly.

"You and your crew are welcome in my palace," she said, holding out her hand to him.

Hal took it and bowed once more. He did not raise it to his lips. "Thank you, my lady," he said.

The twin furrows deepened at the form of address, but Justinia decided not to notice it. He released her hand and stepped back half a pace as she continued.

"My commander tells me that you carried out his plan bravely and diligently, and we can thank you for the safe return of our son, and the destruction of the pirates' base."

"Well, we didn't do it all, your empress-ship," said Thorn in a friendly tone. "The volcano did a lot of the work for us."

Several of the Byzantians close to the dais exclaimed at the familiar form of address, and at the fact that this bearded ruffian had dared to interrupt the Empress. Justinia again feigned not to notice, but the furrows, which had smoothed out, returned, deeper than before. The dark eyes darted toward Thorn, registering him for future reference.

This will be a good place to get out of, Hal thought, although Justinia's next words suggested otherwise.

"Captain Attelson also suggested that I might offer you a place in the palace guard," she continued.

Hal smiled briefly. "Under his command, no doubt?"

She nodded. "Of course."

"It's a great honor, my lady, but we'll have to refuse. We have friends and family back in our homeland who will miss us."

He saw the slightest expression of relief cross her face. "I understand completely," she said. "In that case, let me waste no more time, but reward you for your service." She stretched out her hand toward the majordomo, not bothering to favor him with a look. The official reached inside his robe and produced a purse, handing it to her.

"Well, my lady," Hal said, "we didn't do it all. As Thorn has said, the volcano helped a little."

"Nonsense!" she insisted. "You were there to seize the moment and the advantage. And my gratitude is beyond measure. Here," she said, holding a purse out to Hal. "This is for your wonderful crew, by way of thanks."

He weighed the purse in his hand. Her gratitude might be beyond measure, he thought, but her payment was a different matter. He judged that the purse contained a generous, but not excessive, sum of money.

There was a smattering of applause from the assembled courtiers and nobles. Justinia made a small dismissive gesture with her hand, and Hal guessed, correctly, that their conversation was at an end. He bowed once more, then stepped back off the dais. The crew fell in behind him as he led them away to a spot by a side wall.

Constantus now half rose from his throne. "Mother!" he called, and she turned to face him. "Did you remember Captain Olaf?"

"Of course!" she said smoothly, and clapped her hands together. "Captain, stand forward, please!"

Olaf took two paces forward and turned to stand before her. She reached out with a golden pendant, and he bowed his head as she placed it around his neck.

"Captain, you are immediately reinstated as the commander of my son's guard."

"I thank you, your excellency," Olaf said, head still bowed.

"Furthermore, it is my pleasant duty to reward you for your faithful service to our family and to the throne." She turned and called to one side, "Bring the chest!"

Two servants entered, bearing an ironbound chest between them. It was a meter long and half a meter deep, but it was obviously heavy. They placed it down and threw the lid open and the weight was explained. Gold and silver and precious jewels sparkled out of the chest. The room gave an awed gasp of admiration.

"After some consultation, we have decided to award you half the amount that the pirate Myrgos was demanding as ransom," she continued, and again a ripple of applause ran through the room. She made the statement as if it were a recent decision, although Hal seemed to remember that Olaf had been offered that reward previously.

Olaf raised his head and smiled at the Regent. "I thank you, your excellency, although you are far too generous."

"Nonsense!" she gushed. "You brought our son back to us. You have more than earned the reward."

Hal looked at the open chest, with gold chains and precious

jewels spilling out of it. There was a small fortune in there. He glanced down at the comparatively meager purse in his hand and shook his head.

"Let's get out of here," he said to the crew. He turned on his heel and led them out of the reception hall. None of those present seemed upset to see them go.

chapter   forty-two

ater that night, long after the feast had ended and the
guests departed, Olaf was in his suite of rooms—as commander, he was granted a suite. He sat back in a tub-shaped
chair and looked with satisfaction at the rich fittings and
furnishings that went with his position. On a low table to one side,
the open chest of gold and jewels reflected the warm lamplight.

Things had gone well, he thought. Remarkably well. He was
back in a position of power and influence. He was rich—richer
than he had ever expected to be. The reward from Justinia made
him a wealthy man.

And he had the confidence of the Emperor. That, along with
the money, made his future secure. He poured himself a glass of
wine, drank deeply and sighed in satisfaction. For the fifth time
that night, he rose from his chair and walked to the table, running
his hands through the wealth in the strongbox there.

There was a discreet tap at the door. He closed the lid on the chest and moved away from it.

"Who is it?" he called out.

"It's Lacrimus, sir," came the reply. Lacrimus was his personal orderly, a local-born member of the palace guard.

"Come in."

The door opened, and the orderly entered. He was a middle-aged man, tall and stooped over. He was thin—obviously a servant more than a warrior—and his hair was receding from his forehead.

"One of the Skandians is here, sir," Lacrimus said deferentially. "He says he's your son."

There was a question implied in the second statement, but Olaf disdained to answer it. He nodded curtly.

"Send him in. And close the door after him."

Lacrimus bowed and ushered Stig into the room. As ordered, he withdrew again and closed the door.

Stig looked around the spacious living room that comprised a quarter of Olaf's suite. He nodded thoughtfully. "You do well for yourself here, don't you?" he said.

Olaf smiled and nodded. "It's a lot better than a pine hut in Hallasholm, isn't it?"

There was no answering smile from Stig. He moved around the room, taking stock of the furniture and fine fabrics, the thick rugs and ornate wall hangings. He came to rest by the strongbox, laying a hand idly on its lid.

"So I take it you won't be coming home with us?" Stig asked.

Olaf shrugged. "My future is here. There's nothing for me in Hallasholm."

"Your wife is there," Stig said bluntly.

For a moment, Olaf was silent. Then he said, a little awkwardly, "She's better off without me."

"That's a very convenient attitude for you to take," Stig replied, his eyes cold. "Particularly since Constantus has no idea that you deserted her and left her behind when you ran."

Olaf shifted his feet uncomfortably and said nothing. He watched Stig closely.

"You never told Constantus that I'm your son, did you?" the younger man asked.

Olaf went to prevaricate, then realized there was little he could say and replied simply, "No."

"No. Neither did I. But he and I did have a long chat when we were sailing back from Santorillos. He told me the story of how you were shipwrecked on the coast west of Byzantos, and all your shipmates were lost. He told me how you had tried to save them, but couldn't manage it. How you kept your skirl from drowning for three days before you couldn't help him any further and you had to let him go. Then you were recruited into the palace guard."

"I had to tell them something," Olaf said defensively.

"And that's a much better story than the real one," Stig said mildly. "Constantus was very much taken with your loyalty and sense of duty. He said that was why he selected you as his personal guard commander."

"I've served him faithfully," Olaf said, wondering where this conversation was leading. He had an uncomfortable feeling that he knew.

"So you have. And you've been rewarded." Stig flicked open the strongbox lid and looked down at the gleaming riches inside it, saying nothing for several moments. Then he said in a seeming non sequitur, "My mother is a wonderful woman. She's brave and faithful and strong. And she never let anyone down in her life. Particularly not me."

"No," Olaf said carefully.

"When I undertook this quest, it was because I didn't know you. You were my father, but I didn't know what sort of man you are. I wanted to see what sort of man would desert such a wonderful woman and leave her to face the music when he absconded with his shipmates' treasure. What sort of man would subject her to years of shame and misery—and leave her with a young son to bring up alone. I'd hoped there might be some reason that excuses you, that explained your behavior."

He looked up from the treasure chest and locked eyes with Olaf. The older man's gaze held for a few seconds, then dropped away. He couldn't face the accusation and the disdain he saw in his son's eyes.

"Well, I found out. You're a grasping, self-centered person who is always on the lookout for himself, and no one else. And that's not the sort of man I want as a father."

His words were scathing, but there was nothing Olaf could do to counteract them or argue against them. Stig was right. His motives were always self-centered. He had always looked out for himself before all others.

"And now you're a wealthy man," Stig said, reaching down and riffling his hand through the coins and jewelry in the strongbox. "Ironic, isn't it? My friends have pulled your chestnuts out of the fire and you walk off with a big reward."

"I never asked for it," Olaf said weakly.

Stig's hard eyes transfixed him like two spears. "And you're not keeping it. You can keep your fair share as a crew member on the *Heron*. You've earned that."

Olaf was incredulous. "Why should I . . . ?"

"Because," Stig said, riding over his high-pitched query, "if you don't hand it over, I'll have a talk with Constantus and tell him the real story of how you left Hallasholm. How you cheated and robbed your shipmates. How you deserted your wife and child. He might change his opinion of his loyal and trustworthy commander then. Odds are, he'll never trust you again."

Olaf realized he was right. He looked once more at the strong-box, seeing his dreams of a life of idle wealth fading away.

"You're taking the rest for yourself?"

Stig shook his head. "No. Half of it we'll share out among the crew. They have earned it. The other half will go to the men, or their families, who you cheated so long ago."

He slammed the lid of the chest shut and stood challenging his father.

"My mother will finally be able to face those people without the shame she has felt for the past ten years. And that means a lot to me."

He took hold of the strongbox by the handle set into its lid and hefted it off the table.

"But . . . you can't do this. It's . . . it's . . . mine," said Olaf, his voice almost a whimper.

Stig shook his head scornfully. "That's what it always comes down to with you, isn't it?" he said, and strode toward the door. As he went out, he turned back to the stricken figure in the room behind him.

"I'll send you your share in the morning," he said.

E p i l o g u e

The coast of Arrida lay off their port side as *Heron* bowled along under a stiff breeze, heading west in the Constant Sea.

"I thought we might sail across the Constant Sea and up past Araluen," Hal had said as they left Byzantos behind. "I don't know about the rest of you, but I don't fancy those portages up the Dan."

To sail north up the Dan River entailed several backbreaking portages, where the ship had to be hauled bodily overland to handle the rising ground and the resultant fall of the river—not to mention the constant threat of attack from river rats. The crew agreed heartily.

"Well, we're in no rush now that Olaf has had his surprising change of mind over that reward money," Edvin had said.

They all looked at Stig, to see if he'd elaborate. But he'd smiled. "As I said, he decided he didn't deserve all the money. He was just one of the crew. And he wanted to set things right for my mam."

"People are full of surprises," Thorn had commented, with a raised eyebrow. "I'd never have thought he could be so generous. And so unselfish."

And they left it at that. Stig never told them about his final conversation with Olaf, and none of them asked again. But he took to spending long hours standing alone by the rail, watching the sea and the wake of the ship as it streamed out behind them.

On the fifth day, Lydia joined him by the stern rail. Thorn was sitting cross-legged nearby, sewing a new retaining strap onto his hook. He managed the task with remarkable dexterity, considering that he had only one hand.

"I never knew my father," she said to Stig, out of the blue. "I was raised by my grandfather until he was killed in Zavac's raid. I always wondered what sort of man my father might have been."

Stig regarded her gratefully. Somehow, Lydia always seemed to know the right thing to say at moments like this, and he did feel the need to unburden himself to someone.

"Life can be hard," he said with a sigh. "I'd always hoped my father would turn out to be a better man than he was."

"He did save my life," she said reflectively.

He nodded agreement. "He was a fine warrior. But, as a person, he had a lot lacking."

She said nothing for a moment, realizing how difficult it had been for him to say that.

They both glanced across to where Thorn had risen from his

seat on the deck and Hal was helping him with the final piece of stitching—a tricky piece that required two hands. The shaggy head and the young head bent close together over the task, then Hal said something and Thorn threw back his head and laughed.

"The old saying is right," Lydia said eventually. "We can't choose our parents. But we can choose our friends."

Stig slipped a companionable arm around her waist.

"Thank the gods for that," he said.

Turn the page for an exclusive look at

RANGER'S APPRENTICE

THE BEAST FROM ANOTHER TIME

A Short Story

BY JOHN FLANAGAN

1

WILL TOOK A SHIRT FROM THE SMALL HANGING SPACE IN HIS bedroom and held it up to make sure it was clean.

"Three shirts. That should be enough," he said, more to himself than to Maddie, who was leaning against the doorjamb watching him. She raised an eyebrow—an expression she had picked up from him, which he in turn had picked up from Halt.

"How long are you going for?" she asked.

Will thought for a second. "Two weeks. So three shirts will be enough. I'll get two days of normal wear out of each one, then I can turn them inside out for another two days. That'll just about do me."

Maddie frowned at him. His calculation was pretty slap-dash, she thought. That made twelve days, not a full two weeks.

"Besides," he added, stuffing the shirt roughly into the now-bulging saddlebag on the bed, "I don't have room for any more."

"You can't do it like that!" Maddie protested. She moved to

the bed and took the saddlebag from his hands, hauling the bunched-up shirt out again. "It'll be all crinkled and crumpled when you put it on."

Will shrugged. "So it'll be crumpled. I'm a Ranger, not a court dandy."

"You're getting as bad as Halt," she said, pulling the other two equally bunched-up shirts from the bag and laying them on the blanket.

Will grinned at her, and his grim, bearded face was instantly transformed by the expression. "That's the nicest thing anyone has ever said to me," he said.

Maddie tossed her head in mock annoyance. With a few deft movements, she folded the shirts neatly into three flat shapes and slid them into the saddlebag, which was now distinctly un-bulged.

"Now you have room for another one," she said. "And if memory serves me, you'll find there's a perfectly adequate laundry service at Castle Araluen. Just put them out to be washed each day."

"Seems like a waste of soap and water," Will said mildly.

She frowned at him. "That's an excuse you use too often," she said.

He grinned once more. "As you implied, I had Halt to teach me all these good habits. Besides, what is it to you? You're my apprentice. Not my servant."

She folded a fourth shirt and slid it into the saddlebag. "Sometimes I wonder," she said.

Will dropped a hand fondly on her shoulder. "If you have any problems while I'm gone, ask Halt for help," he said.

Maddie nodded, but made a negative gesture with her hand. "I'll be fine."

He smiled, knowing that she would be. She was nearly at the end of her second year now and she was becoming a skillful, capable Ranger. Maddie was a deadly shot with both sling and bow, and her knife throwing was well above average—not that he would tell her that.

In addition, if any sort of trouble or danger did threaten, she had her horse, Bumper, and his dog, Sable, to help her take care of it.

"Make sure you keep busy while I'm gone," he said. "I'll be testing you on your tracking skills when I get back, and we need at least fifty new arrows each." He hefted his two saddlebags over his shoulder and led the way out to the small verandah at the front of the house where Tug stood, waiting patiently for his master. Will heaved the saddlebags over the horse's rump, so that they hung down one on either side. Maddie had brought his bedroll and she boosted it up behind the saddle for him to tie in place. She winced slightly with the movement and he frowned.

"Hip troubling you?" he asked.

"A little. Always does when we've got a change in the weather coming." She'd been wounded by a javelin on her first assignment with Will and still walked with a slight limp as a result. "It'll rain tonight—you should try to find an inn rather than camping out."

Will looked at her with some concern. "Don't suffer in silence," he said. "If it gets worse, we could let Arald's healer have a look at it."

She waved the suggestion aside. "It's not a big thing."

He held her gaze for a few seconds, making sure she wasn't just cracking hardy. Satisfied, he nodded and turned to speak to Sable, who had risen from her spot in the sun at the end of the porch and padded quietly toward them, her tail swishing heavily and an expectant look in her eyes.

"Not this time, Sable," he told her. "You stay here."

He pointed to the ground between them and the dog allowed her front paws to slide out in front of her as she sank to the ground on her belly. She rested her chin on her paws and lay watching him, eyes wide-open and swiveling to match his movements.

Will placed his foot in the stirrup and swung lightly up onto Tug's back. The little horse moved a pace or two to settle his weight, then nickered a farewell to Sable and Maddie. Sable thumped her tail once on the ground.

Maddie raised her hand to wave. "See you in two weeks."

Will nodded. "Take care," he said. He touched Tug's flank with his heel, and the little horse wheeled around and cantered out of the clearing toward the path through the trees that led to the high road.

The following morning, Maddie was sitting on the porch steps in the sunlight, a pot of hot glue and a bundle of unfletched arrow shafts beside her. She slid the fletching jig over the end of a shaft and, dabbing glue onto the spine of a feather vane, put it in position along the guide of the jig, pressing it against the smooth cedar.

She held it in place for some thirty seconds until she was sure it was secure, then repeated the process with another vane. The jig was designed so that it held the feathers at even intervals around the shaft. When the glue had hardened a little more, she would bind the vanes to the shaft with thin waxed thread.

She smiled to herself. The thought of Princess Madelyn, heir to the throne of Araluen, doing manual labor with hot, messy glue would have led her old tutors to throw their hands aloft in horror. But she enjoyed doing this work—she had a keen touch for the skill and the dexterity it required. She went to apply glue to the third vane, spilled the hot liquid on her hand and swore a very un-princessly oath. She looked around for a convenient rag, saw none handy and wiped the hot glue from her fingers onto her jerkin.

"I'm getting as bad as Will," she muttered.

"Hello?"

The voice was querulous and uncertain, with an implicit questioning note to it. She looked up to see an elderly couple emerging from the trees at the edge of the clearing.

Sable, who had been dozing beside her, raised her head and rumbled a low growl.

"Oh, now you tell me," she said. The dog thumped her tail once, then, seeing no apparent danger in the old couple, lowered her head back to the boards.

Maddie set the half-finished arrow to one side and stood up, smiling a welcome. "Can I help you?"

"We want to see the Ranger," the man replied, taking a step farther into the clearing.

His companion matched the movement. "Will Treaty, the Ranger," she added.

Maddie stepped down off the porch and advanced a few paces toward them.

"I'm afraid he's not here," she said pleasantly. "Can I help you? I'm his apprentice."

"You're a girl," the woman said, with a slightly accusatory tone to her voice.

Maddie made sure the smile remained on her face. "I certainly am."

"So how can you be an apprentice Ranger?" the woman continued.

"The usual way. I applied for training and I was accepted. I'm the first girl to be accepted for Ranger training, as a matter of fact."

The old pair exchanged a suspicious glance. "Well, I never heard of that," said the man.

Maddie continued smiling, although it was becoming an effort to maintain the expression. "And now you have," she said. "Can I help you? What did you want to see Will about?"

The man pursed his lips uncertainly. "We wanted to see the Ranger," he repeated.

Maddie finally let the smile disappear. "And as I said, he's not here," she said brusquely. She put her hands on her hips. "So can I help you—in spite of the fact that I'm a girl? Or would you like to come back in two weeks?"

"We've come all the way from the Spiny Mountains," the woman said.

"Walked all the way, we did," the man elaborated. Maddie tilted her head to one side. The Spiny Mountains were a long way away, on the edge of Redmont Fief.

"To see the Ranger. Not a girl," the woman added.

Maddie treated them both to a scowl. "Well, it'd be a pity to walk all that way for nothing," she said. "So you can either tell me what your problem might be, or turn around, go home and come back in two weeks. Take it or leave it."

The couple exchanged a disgruntled look. Finally, the man shrugged.

"Might as well tell you," he said. "Can't do no harm."

"Probably won't do no good, neither," the woman grumbled.

Maddie took a deep breath, let it out in a sigh, and turned away, mounting the low step to the porch. "Then off you go." She tossed the words back over her shoulder. "I have work to do."

She stooped and gathered up the arrows, fletching equipment and glue pot and elbowed the door open. The man spoke just as she was about to step inside and close the door behind her.

"There's a monster. It's taking our sheep."

2

SHE TURNED BACK. THE ELDERLY COUPLE HAD MOVED A LITTLE closer and were standing a few meters from the porch, looking totally forlorn. The man had removed his hat and was twisting it anxiously in his hands.

"How many have you lost?" Maddie asked.

"Two. Two ewes carried off and a lamb injured."

Maddie made a small moue of surprise. Two ewes was a serious loss for a small farm—and she assumed their Spiny Mountain property was a small one. She set her equipment down on a small table just inside the door and held it open, beckoning to the couple.

"Perhaps you'd better come in," she said.

The couple trooped in after her, peering curiously around the interior of the neat little cabin. They stood uncertainly just inside the door until she gestured to the kitchen table and four upright chairs around it. There were only two easy chairs in the cabin, arranged either side of the fireplace.

"Sit down and tell me about it," she said. The pair sat, still looking ill at ease at being in a Ranger's inner sanctum—although anything less confronting than the comfortable little cabin, Maddie couldn't imagine. She offered them coffee, which they refused—somewhat suspiciously—and she realized they had probably never drunk coffee in their lives.

"Maybe we should introduce ourselves," she said. "My name is Maddie."

The farmer bobbed his head, looking as if he was about to rise from his seat, then thinking better of it.

"I'm Hector," he said. "Hec Farrows. And this is my wife, Gert."

Maddie smiled at Gert as the older woman nodded. "Now, tell me about this monster that's taken your sheep."

"Carried them off, it did," said Gert. "Must be a bear, maybe."

"It's not a bear," her husband said doggedly. "It's some kind of cat."

Maddie frowned. "It'd take a big cat to carry off a full-grown sheep."

"Oh, this one is big enough," Hector averred.

Maddie looked keenly at him. "You've seen it then?" she asked.

He hesitated. "Just a quick look when it tried to take the lamb. I scared it off."

Maddie rubbed her chin thoughtfully. She had a sudden sense of déjà vu. When she was first apprenticed to Will, she had helped a couple whose chickens were being killed. But that had turned out to be a marten, not something big enough to carry off a full-grown sheep.

"Did you see it?" she asked the woman, who shook her head.

"Didn't see it. But it'll be a bear sure enough."

"Wasn't no bear," Hector insisted angrily. Maddie had the feeling that they'd had this conversation several times already on their way to Castle Redmont. "I've seen bears. This wasn't one," Hector continued. "Didn't walk upright. Wasn't as heavy in the body as a bear. It moved like a cat."

Gert sniffed disdainfully.

"How big was it?" Maddie asked.

Hector looked thoughtful, then answered. "Big," he said. "Not as big as a bear, but almost. Bigger than a wolf."

Maddie screwed up her lips. That didn't help much.

"Did you see its tracks?" she asked, and they both shook their heads.

"Don't know nothing about tracks," Hec said.

"Did it leave any marks on the lamb?" Maddie asked. She assumed that since the sheep had been carried off, the pair wouldn't know anything about their injuries.

"Claw marks down its right flank," Hector told her. He held up four fingers, spread apart. "Like that."

"Like a bear," Gert said. Hec glared at her.

"Could it have been a wolf?" Maddie asked. It seemed the most likely answer, although it would need to be a very big wolf if it had carried off two fully grown ewes.

Hec shook his head. "Weren't no wolf. As I said, it was a big cat. Bigger than any I've ever seen."

Maddie sat back. "So what do you want me to do about it?" she asked. They looked at her, assessing her.

"We want the Ranger," said Gert.

"We want him to kill it," her husband continued. "We can't afford to keep losing sheep like that. Only got five left."

"Can you afford to wait another two weeks?" Maddie asked, knowing the answer.

Hec looked at his wife, and they both answered at once. "No."

"Then you might have to be satisfied with me," she said. "Why don't you go back home and I'll ask around about big cats in the Spiny Mountains. Then I'll ride out and see what I can do for you."

Hector cleared his throat, reluctant to agree but seeing no alternative.

"Well, all right. But I'm not sure what you can do," he said.

"Being a girl and all," Gert added.

Maddie gave them a thin smile. "I might surprise you," she said.

"They say there used to be big cats in the Spiny Mountains," George said, "hundreds of years ago."

He reached up onto a high shelf in the library, ran his fingers across several old volumes and then brought down a battered, leather-bound book. He set it on his table and began to leaf through the pages.

"How big would they have been?" Maddie asked.

He pouted thoughtfully. "Certainly big enough to take a sheep." He smiled up at her. "Not as big as the desert lions Will said he ran into in Arrida, but quite big."

George had trained as a scribe when Will was apprenticed to the Ranger Halt. Over the years he had served as an attorney, an advocate and a linguist, and in the last five years he had gravitated to the position of head librarian and historian at Castle Redmont. It was a job well suited to his studious nature.

"Aah . . . here we are," he said, finding the page he was looking for and spreading it out for her to see. It showed a sketch of a large catlike creature, with long fangs bared in a snarl, and sharp claws in all four feet.

She read the name under the sketch. "It's called a cuga or cougar."

George nodded. "Of course, it may all be a myth," he said. "But if these things did exist, it's possible there might be one or two survivors in the Spinies. It's a wild area, pretty much uninhabited."

"I wonder why it's suddenly come down into the farmlands there," Maddie said.

George regarded her with an avuncular smile. "That's if it really has," he said. "Remember, nobody's seen a"—he checked the page again—"cougar for hundreds of years. We're not even sure if they really existed."

"Maybe it's injured and can't hunt its normal prey," Maddie

mused. "That's often the reason why wild predators start preying on domestic animals."

"That's a possibility, of course," George admitted. "So what do you plan on doing about it?"

"I might ride out to the farm and see what I can find out," she said.

George raised a warning finger. "You be careful, young Maddie. It may or may not be a cougar, but whatever it is, it sounds dangerous. Are you sure you can handle it?" Rangers and their apprentices, he thought. They were all the same, always ready to go dashing off, putting themselves in danger.

She nodded confidently. "I can handle it," she said.

3

MADDIE RODE INTO THE CLEARING WHERE THE SMALL FARM-
house stood, overshadowed by the Spiny Mountain range
looming in the distance.

The farmhouse was a whitewashed wattle-and-daub construction with a thatched roof. A small barn stood five meters
away, its sides unpainted gray timber slabs. The roof was made
of shingles that had been warped by the weather and would
clearly leak in any sort of rain. In winter, she assumed, the live-
stock would be kept in the barn. Three sheep and two lambs
wandered nervously around the paddock closest to the house. A
milk cow stood placidly by the far fence.

Hector and Gert were busy repairing a fence that surrounded
the home paddock. Though, Maddie realized as she looked more
closely, they weren't actually repairing it. They were reinforcing
it, adding a barrier of spiny thornbushes to the top rail and lashing it in place.

"Good afternoon!" Maddie called.

The elderly couple hadn't noticed her arrival. Now they

looked up and reacted in surprise. Dressed in a gray-and-green Ranger cloak, mounted on what was obviously a Ranger's horse and with a large bow slung across her shoulders, she looked considerably more impressive than she had on their first encounter.

Gert squinted at the mounted figure. "Who is it?" she called.

Hec nudged her with his elbow. "It's the girl from Redmont Castle," he said. "The apprentice."

Maddie noticed that he didn't use the word *Ranger* in his description. Apparently, that was a still a matter of debate.

"Doesn't look like her," Gert said. "She looks like a Ran—" She too stopped short of using the word.

Maddie shifted in her saddle. She had been riding for some hours.

"I said, *good afternoon*," she repeated, with an edge to her voice. The farm couple remembered their manners, such as they were.

"Eh? Oh, yes. Good afternoon," Hec said.

"Better step down," Gert added, without a great deal of warmth.

Maddie raised an eyebrow and swung down from the saddle. The movement caused her a twinge of pain in the hip, and she wondered if she'd ever be rid of the reminder of that old wound.

She led Bumper toward the farmhouse, where there was a spindly hitching rail. Fortunately, Bumper didn't need to be tied, as the rail didn't look strong enough to prevent an elderly vole from escaping. She dropped the rein on the ground and Bumper made himself comfortable, resting his weight on one side and leaning around to snap his teeth at a persistent fly.

Hec finished tying a last bundle of thornbush in place, then stepped back and took off his heavy canvas gauntlets. He and Gert moved to meet Maddie by the door to the farmhouse.

"Better come inside," he said gruffly. Maddie let him hold the door open for her—noting that it dragged on the ground when he did—and entered.

The interior was one room, with a curtained-off section for sleeping quarters at one end. The rest of the space was a combined living room/kitchen, with a crude wooden table and benches to one side and a pair of homemade canvas-and-timber easy chairs by the open fireplace that took up the end wall.

A bread oven was built into the surrounds of the fireplace and a swiveling iron arm held a large black cookpot, which could be moved in and away from the flames of the fire as required. A rack held an assortment of wooden platters, bowls and cups sitting in pairs. The floor was hard beaten earth, with rushes laid over it for warmth and dryness.

The farmhouse was clean enough, but it was small and very poorly ventilated. The air was stuffy and smoky, and there was an overlaying odor that either came from Hector's socks or from Gert's attempts at cheese making. Maddie wrinkled her nose. She wouldn't be sleeping here, she decided.

"What are you doing here?" Gert asked.

Maddie smiled at her, although the blunt tone made her

want to shake the old woman by the shoulders. "I said I'd come out and see what I could do about this monster of yours."

Gert sniffed disparagingly. "Don't see what you can do," she muttered.

Maddie chose to ignore her. She reached into her jerkin and produced a sheet of parchment, onto which she had copied the illustration of the cougar.

"I did a little research," she told them, spreading the drawing out on the table. Hec mouthed the word *research* as if it were totally unfamiliar to him. "The librarian at Castle Redmont showed me this. It appears there might have been creatures like this in these mountains hundreds of years ago. They were called *cougars*."

"We didn't lose our sheep hundreds of years ago," Gert said. "It were last month."

Again, Maddie resisted the temptation to take her by the shoulders and shake her.

"George, he's the librarian, said it's possible that one or two of them might have survived in the mountains, well away from human contact," she said. She looked at Hec and tapped the drawing. "Does this look like what you saw?"

He frowned, turning the sheet toward him to study it more closely. "Could be," he said.

Gert leaned over to look too. "Don't look like no bear."

Hec turned angrily to her. "That's what I said. It ain't no bear." He looked back at Maddie, his mind made up by Gert's disagreement. "Yes. This could be what I saw."

"So what do you plan to do about it?" Gert asked.

Maddie inclined her head. "I thought I'd spend a few nights here and see if it reappeared," she said. "How long is it since it took your last sheep?"

He considered. "Mebbe ten days gone," he said. "Took the first one nine days before that."

"So it should be ready to feed again," Maddie said. "I shot a small deer on the way here and I thought I'd leave it as bait, see if I can draw the beast in so I can get a better look at it."

"Deer belong to the king," Gert said primly. "Common folks ain't allowed to hunt them."

Maddie smiled thinly at her. "I'm a Ranger. We're allowed."

Hec waved a hand round the small farmhouse interior. "Well, you're welcome to bed down by the fire," he said. "Ain't much room but it's warm."

"I thought I'd sleep in the barn," Maddie replied. Normally, she would have camped in the open, but the thought that there may be a large predator in the vicinity meant she was unwilling to risk Bumper, or herself.

Hec shook his head. "Barn's very drafty," he said. "Wind cuts through there like a knife."

Maddie wiped her eyes, which were watering from the smoke and Hec's sock odor.

"That could be a good thing," she said.

For all her disagreeable nature, Gert was an excellent cook. Maddie, knowing how farm folk like this lived hand to mouth,

had brought two chickens and a small sack of potatoes and onions with her. She had no intention to deprive Hec and Gert by
eating their meager rations. Gert quickly jointed the birds,
dipped them in flour and fried the pieces over the fireplace in
clear lard. The onions went in with the chicken, and she boiled
the potatoes separately.

After the meal, Maddie contemplated whether to help with
the clearing up, before deciding against it. Hec and Gert weren't
the most welcoming of hosts and they tended to irritate her.

I've provided the meal, she thought. They can clean up.

She pushed the door open and went outside, sitting down on
a long bench under the eaves of the barn, looking out into the
darkening evening. Several minutes later, Hec emerged, carrying
a bundle of torches under one arm. He set them up on the fence
of the small paddock, spacing them five meters apart. She
watched him curiously, and he turned to explain.

"I keep these lit during the night. It keeps the cat away," he
said. She nodded, though she doubted that the light of the
torches would discourage the cougar if it was hungry enough.
And, she thought, she didn't want to keep it away. But if it made
the old farmer feel his sheep were more secure and kept him out
of her way, so much the better.

"I'll leave a joint from the deer over by the edge of the trees,"
she told him. "That should keep it away from the sheep."

Hec grunted. "Waste of good venison," he muttered to himself. He set the last of the torches in place. "I'll light these when
it gets to full dark."

Maddie nodded. "Good idea. I might get settled in the barn while there's still a little light."

Bumper was still waiting where she'd left him by the farmhouse door. Maddie led him into the small barn and forked hay into a bin. The horse munched it gratefully, then turned his head to one side as he studied her. She forked more hay out of the stack and spread it on the floor for a bed. Not that she expected to sleep for long tonight.

She stowed her belongings, gave Bumper a quick rubdown with several handfuls of straw, then took the rear leg joint of the deer and carried it across to the point she had determined—a young sapling on the edge of the tree line. She wedged the leg into a fork of the tree, then attached a small bell she had brought with her to the sapling itself. She wanted the cougar to have to work to get the meat. That would cause the bell to ring and that would alert her.

An hour later, she was sitting on the bench, rugged up in her cloak, when the farmhouse door creaked open and Hector emerged, carrying a lighted torch. He didn't notice the dark figure by the barn as he moved around the paddock, lighting the nine torches he had left there wedged into the top of the fence rail. Maddie estimated that they would burn for several hours. She wondered whether he would replace them when they burned out. Probably not, she thought. She was about to wish him good night but decided against it. That would lead to a conversation, which would probably be about what she was doing and what she intended to do if the beast showed up. Since that would also probably lead to Hec's decrying her ability to cope with the cougar, she elected to remain silent and unseen.

The brightly burning torches and the relatively early hour would probably dictate against the cougar's making an appearance just yet. Maddie slipped inside the barn and settled into her bedroll on a pile of dry straw as Bumper snorted a friendly good night. She settled herself more comfortably, removing a piece of straw from where it was tickling her neck. The straw and the blankets were warm and toasty, and she soon fell asleep.

4

It was the sheep that sounded the alarm. They were milling nervously in the paddock, bunched together and circling inside the fence in lock step. Something was making them nervous, and she had a fairly good idea what it was.

A second later, Bumper snorted a warning from his stall.

"I heard them," she said softly. She had slept almost fully clothed. Now she sat up and tugged her boots on, then moved toward the door. Her bow and quiver were hanging from a wooden peg and she unhooked them, slinging the quiver over her shoulder and quickly stringing the bow.

She'd found the hinges of the barn door were old and rusted when she'd inspected them earlier, so she had coated them liberally with grease and left them open a few inches to avoid unnecessary movement. Now she peered through the narrow gap and studied the farmyard. Her vision was limited but from what she could see, there was nothing untoward in sight. The sheep, however, continued to run in nervous circles, their little hooves beating a soft tattoo on the hard-packed earth of the paddock. The torches were guttering and smoking and casting an uncertain light across the farmyard. She leaned her shoulder against the door and eased it open another half meter, grateful that her earlier precautions made sure it moved with only the slightest noise.

Maddie slipped sideways out through the door, staying close to the barn wall, under the shadow of the eaves. One of the torches finally went out with a low *pop*, sending a greasy-smelling ribbon of smoke spiraling into the night sky.

Ting!

It was the silvery note of the little bell she'd tied to the sapling. Just a small noise and not sufficiently threatening, she hoped, to discourage the predator. She peered at the sapling, her eyes screwed up for maximum vision. There seemed to be a large form by the base, still in the shadows of the trees. The joint of venison was still wedged in the fork of the sapling.

Then the shadowy form moved, coming out more into the starlight. Her heartbeat accelerated as she saw it more clearly.

It was undoubtedly a large cat—similar to the old drawing George had shown her—and the size of a small bear.

As the beast moved to get a better purchase on the venison, she saw that it was favoring its right forepaw. A glint of metal came from that paw—just above where it joined the leg. Maddie frowned. It was almost as if the animal were wearing a bracelet. Nocking an arrow to her bowstring, she stepped forward silently for a closer look.

Ting! Ting! went the bell as the creature gripped the joint more firmly and heaved at it, using the strength of its hindquarters to gain purchase. She noted that while it exerted more force on the joint, the right forepaw hung limp and useless. And now she could see that the metal bracelet was actually a small trap, clamped on the creature's foot just above the paw itself.

So I was right, she thought. It's injured and looking for easy prey. In the course of their conversations around the fire in their little cabin, Will had told her how his first horse had been injured by a wolf that had been disabled by a trap and had been unable to hunt its normal prey. Instead, it had taken to killing farm animals.

She'd made tentative plans based on this supposition, and they depended on the cat's returning in the next few days. Accordingly, she couldn't afford to let it take the joint. She needed it to be hungry enough to return for it the following night. She took a breath, preparing to shout at it and drive it away, when the situation was resolved by the farmhouse door opening noisily.

As she'd noticed earlier, the hinges on the door had sagged, allowing the bottom to scrape on the earth when it opened and closed. The noise was startling in the silence of the night. Hec emerged, a torch in one hand, a heavy cudgel in the other.

He advanced a pace or two, the torch held high. With the source of light so close to his eyes, it was doubtful that he could see the creature by the edge of the clearing, but he shouted and stamped his foot nonetheless.

"Hey, hey, hey!" he cried, and the large cat instantly let go of the venison shoulder, then turned and disappeared into the shadows under the trees. It moved quickly, but Maddie could see that it was limping, holding that forepaw clear of the ground.

Hec ran to the paddock, holding the torch high, making sure the sheep were unharmed.

"They're all right," Maddie reassured him.

He jumped at the sound of her voice and turned to illuminate her with the burning torch in his hand. "What are you doing?" he asked, although the answer was relatively obvious.

She gestured to the sheep in the paddock, still moving in nervous circles, still bunched together. "Keeping an eye on things. You were right. It was a giant cat."

Hec sniffed derisively. "Why didn't you shoot it then?" he demanded, indicating the bow in her hand, an arrow nocked on the string.

Maddie shrugged. "I was about to when you came blundering out shouting, *Hey, hey, hey!*" she told him. He glowered at her as she moved across the clearing, unfastened the venison shoulder and hoisted it on a rope high into the trees. She didn't want the cougar taking it later in the night. At first, she had thought of keeping the venison in the barn with her, but decided that might be inviting trouble.

In truth, she didn't want to kill the creature. It might well be the last of its kind, and she didn't want to be the one to end that line. She had prepared another course of action and for that she needed the beast to return to the farmhouse in the next few nights. And for that, she needed it hungry.

She watched as Hec renewed the torches around the paddock fence.

"I doubt it'll be back tonight," she said.

Again, the old farmer sniffed disdainfully. "Like you'd know."

She shrugged. It was no good talking to him, she thought. She went back into the barn and rearranged her blankets on the straw, muttering to herself.

Bumper shook his mane. *He's got under your skin, hasn't he?*

The little horse sounded amused. Maddie turned a baleful look on him. "Why don't you keep your observations to yourself?" she said. She was almost certain Bumper grinned at her—if a horse could be said to do such a thing.

Just saying.

"Well, don't."

She tugged angrily at the blankets. One fold was caught under her and it took several tugs to loosen it.

Be easier if you sat up, Bumper told her.

"Be better if you shut up," she said.

He shook his head. This time she was sure he was grinning.

The following morning, Maddie studied the tracks the big cat had left by the sapling.

It was definitely walking on three legs, she thought, favoring one front paw. Then she smiled to herself. It was definite as far as she was concerned, although Will might have had something to say about that. He was at times scathing about her ability to read tracks.

But the impressions in the soft earth around the base of the sapling, coupled with her observations of the creature, made her sure of her facts. She was kneeling by the sapling, lightly tracing the impressions in the ground with her forefinger, when Hec approached her. Gert was a few paces behind him, watching and listening eagerly.

Maddie looked up and greeted them both.

"I was right," she said. "It's injured. There's something that looks like a small trap caught on its right forepaw. That's why it's been attacking your stock."

Hec frowned, not making the connection. "Why's that then?"

Maddie straightened, dusting loose dirt from the knees of her breeches. "With its forepaw disabled, it can't run down its normal prey. So it's gone after your sheep instead. They're an easier target."

"You think it'll be back then?" Gert asked.

Maddie nodded. "I think so. It must be hungry and it didn't get any of the venison last night—just enough of a taste to whet its appetite. Leastways, I hope it'll be back."

"You hope so?" Gert said, moving forward to join them, her voice rising to a shrill note. "You hope that . . . thing will come back here killing our animals?"

But Maddie shook her head. "I hope it comes back so I can deal with it once and for all," she said. Gert looked mollified, although she failed to notice that Maddie had said "deal with it," not "kill it."

Gert nudged Hec with her elbow. "Tell her," she ordered. Hec gave her an exasperated look, then turned to Maddie.

"I was thinking," he said, "with this beast prowling around—"

"You was thinking?" Gert interrupted. "It was me that thought it—as it always is."

Hec hesitated, her interruption disrupting his train of thought. His mouth opened and closed several times as he sought the words he wanted to say. Maddie held up a hand to calm him, then turned to his wife. She had really had enough of the argumentative old biddy.

"Gert, with all due respect and with regard for your mature years, why don't you shut up for once?" she said firmly.

Gert actually recoiled. This girl, this child, this person masquerading as a Ranger, was telling her to shut up.

Maddie forestalled her reply, guessing what was on their minds. "I take it, Hec, you'd like to put the sheep in the barn tonight?" It didn't take a genius to know that was what he was thinking. And it made sense. The barn was there to protect farm stock from the bitter cold of winter—and from predators like the cougar.

"Well . . . yes," he said uncertainly, clearly aware that there would be little extra room in the barn with the three sheep in there. He was less aware of the fact that the atmosphere in the barn would be somewhat . . . close. It would be nearly as bad as the farmhouse.

"Good idea," Maddie said. "I was planning on staying outside anyway tonight, to keep watch. I'll leave my horse in the barn, of course." The second statement wasn't a request, and her tone made sure he knew it. Hec nodded his head several times, pleased that the matter had been resolved so easily.

"One thing, though," Maddie added. "I'd like you to light the torches around the paddock again tonight."

He frowned again. "But why? If the sheep are in the barn, there's no need for the torches."

Maddie smiled thinly. "Humor me," she said.

5

Before she set out from Redmont, Maddie had paid a visit to the apothecary in the little village that nestled under the shadow of the castle, explaining her needs and asking his advice.

"I need something to knock out a large animal," she had told him. "Something to put it to sleep for several hours."

The apothecary sucked in his bottom lip. "How big?" he asked. "And how active?"

"About the size of a small bear," she said. "A wild animal. Not a domestic one."

"Hmm," he said, frowning thoughtfully. Then he led the way to the rear of his storeroom and began pulling down jars and studying them. Finally, he selected one and pried open the lid. A pungent odor filled the air.

"This should do it. Use a gob about the size of your thumb. Smear it on an arrowhead and shoot it into a leg or a shoulder. I assume you'll want to keep your distance while you do it?"

Maddie smiled. "I didn't plan to say *open wide* and put a spoon down its throat," she told him.

He nodded seriously—humor wasn't his strong suit. "Very wise. Use this then. It's a highly concentrated derivative of warmweed. It should take effect a few minutes after the drug gets into the bloodstream."

He measured a small amount of the thick, sticky paste from the jar into a smaller clay pot. He sealed the pot with a cork lid and handed it over.

"I'll charge it to the castle?" he asked.

She nodded. Supplies for Rangers were paid for by the Baron's seneschal. She gathered up the pot, wrapped it carefully in a cloth to protect it and stowed it into her saddlebags. The apothecary followed her out of his store to where Bumper stood, waiting patiently. He noted the bedroll and full saddlebags.

"Going away for a few days?" he asked.

"To the Spiny Mountains," she told him.

"Take care," he warned her. "That's dangerous country."

She nodded in reply, then touched her heels to Bumper's flanks and cantered away.

Maddie remained in the barn for the rest of the day. Hec wouldn't herd the sheep inside until late afternoon, and she wanted to sort out her equipment away from the prying eyes of Hec and, particularly, Gert.

She took the small clay pot from her saddlebag and removed the cork stopper. The pungent smell assailed her senses, and she coughed several times before hastily re-stoppering the pot. Taking two arrows from her quiver, she removed the barbed warheads from them. In their place, she attached to each shaft a lighter length of wood, whose end swelled out into a pointed bulb. There were three grooves running along the bulb, and these would hold the apothecary's paste. When the arrow struck the cougar, the drug would be driven into the wound and then carried into the cougar's bloodstream.

The lighter structure of the arrowhead also meant that the points would break off easily, leaving the cougar unencumbered by a long arrow shaft. Not only would a long shaft be inconvenient, it would move around as the animal ran, catching in the undergrowth and causing further injury. This way, the damage would be confined to a simple puncture wound, easily treated and quick to heal.

She unrolled her standard Ranger's medical kit, making sure she had ample supplies of bandages, needles and thread, and the all-purpose painkiller, a less potent form of warmweed. There was a small flask of potent alcoholic spirit as well, which she could use to clean her knife when she worked on the predator's wounded paw.

Satisfied that she had everything she needed, she set the equipment on a bench in the barn. She would smear the narcotic paste onto the arrows later in the day, leaving it less time to dry out, thus ensuring it retained its potency.

Then she took her sling and pouch of lead shot and heaved the barn door open. Bumper looked up at her curiously.

"Just going to see if I can find some small game," she told him, and he shrugged. It didn't matter to him. He didn't eat meat.

Much as she had been annoyed by Hec's and Gert's cantankerous attitude, she realized that it was probably a result of their living alone, far from other people. She also knew that there would be little meat in their diet. If she could bring back a hare or a rabbit for the pot, it should be a welcome addition—although she doubted that they would show gratitude.

She moved silently through the woods, following a game trail that had been created by deer and smaller animals heading for the nearest water source. En route, she bagged two fat rabbits and a mallard with her sling. She missed a second mallard, overconfidence leading her to attempt an almost impossible shot at one on the fly as it took off. The lead ball splashed just behind the bird, skipping several times across the small lake where it had been resting.

She skinned and field dressed the rabbits, wrapping the entrails in the pelts and throwing them into the lake. The fish would take care of them. The mallard she decided to leave for Gert to prepare. It would be easier to pluck after it had been dipped in boiling water, and Maddie had no way of doing that here in the woods.

On the way back, she picked some wild onions and greens. She still had potatoes in her ration pack, and they, combined with one of the rabbits, would make a decent evening meal for herself.

She dropped the mallard and the other rabbit off at the farmhouse. Gert was a little nonplussed by the generous gesture, while Hec murmured his pleasure at having meat two days running. Maddie brushed aside Gert's awkward thanks and headed back to the barn, where she forked hay into Bumper's feed bin and filled his drinking trough with water she fetched from the well in the farmyard.

Looking around the barn, she took note of the amount of hay that was piled against the walls in one corner. Not the place to light a fire, she thought. She took her cooking kit out into the farmyard and built a fireplace in the open, hauling a small log over from the forest's edge to use as a seat. She gathered kindling and piled it into the circle of rocks she had built, then fetched half a dozen more substantial pieces from the stacked firewood beside the barn.

Gert emerged from the farmhouse, the mallard hanging head down from her hands. She sat on a stool and began to pluck the bird, letting the feathers fly in the breeze. She had obviously scalded it in boiling water to loosen the feathers, Maddie thought.

"You're welcome to eat with us," Gert called eventually. Even she couldn't maintain her unwelcoming ways in the face of Maddie's generosity.

Maddie smiled her thanks but declined. "I'll be fine," she said. "I want an early night. I'll be awake later to see if the cougar returns."

In truth, the prospect of eating with the surly, uncommunicative pair was less than appealing. She was used to eating on her own, or with Will for company. But what she said was true. She planned to eat before sundown, then get a few hours' sleep.

She didn't think the beast would return before the small hours of the morning and there was no point sitting wide-awake waiting for it. If it did return, Bumper would warn her.

She jointed the rabbit and rolled the joints in flour, then heated a large dab of butter in her iron frying pan. Will was an excellent camp cook and he had taught her well. She set several potatoes to boil in a small pot in the ashes at the side of the fire. When they were well under way, she dropped the floured joints into the sizzling butter, watching them as they browned, her mouth watering at the delicious aroma.

She sliced two of the small wild onions and dropped them in with the frying meat. The aromas coming from her little fire became even more mouthwatering. When the food was cooked, she slid it onto her platter and ate quickly. She was hungry and didn't wait for the meat to cool, scalding her mouth as a result. But it was a small penalty for the enjoyment she derived from the meal.

"There's something about cooking in the open," she said to herself as she cleaned her cooking and eating implements and rested them by the fire to dry.

The sun was low over the trees, and the shadows were lengthening. Hec emerged from the farmhouse and walked to the paddock, slipping the gate open and herding the sheep before him toward the barn. She stood and opened the door for him, moving to one side and blocking one of the sheep that seemed intent on escaping. The old farmer shoved the sheep into a stall, putting a beam across the entrance to keep them inside. Maddie watched, wrinkling her nose. She was glad she had decided to stay in the open air. She took her cloak and went back outside, settling down against the wall of the barn and wrapping the cloak around her. She pulled the hood up over her head, aware of Hec's curious gaze, and began breathing deeply. Within the space of a few minutes, she was asleep. She would wake when the moon set, which was two hours away. She was confident that the cougar wouldn't return until much later, by which time she would be awake and on guard. She opened her eyes two hours later, woken by the change in the light as the moon slid over the roof of the barn, throwing long shadows across the farmyard. Hec's torches were still burning brightly, and she slid the barn door open and fetched her bow, quiver and the two specially prepared arrows. She dipped her thumb into the clay pot and smeared a generous daub of the drug onto each of the arrowheads. Then she resumed her position by the wall of the barn and settled down for a long wait.

6

MADDIE WAS COLD AND STIFF, AND HER RIGHT LEG WAS cramping. In addition, the old wound in her hip was aching in the cold.

She longed to change her position, to stretch her legs and relieve the incipient cramp. But she knew any movement would create noise, and if the cougar was in the vicinity, it would frighten him off.

She assumed it was a male, but there was no reason to think that was the case. It could be a female just as easily. Not that it mattered. If there was only one, there was no chance of any further additions. If the cougar had a mate, it wouldn't be hunting for itself. The other big cat would do that.

So the odds were, this was the last of its line—and that was all the more reason not to kill it. It was a magnificent animal and the thought of killing the last of its kind was anathema to her.

If she could render the big cat unconscious, she planned to remove the trap from its paw and treat the wound with a healing, pain-killing salve. Then she would bandage it tightly. If she was successful, the paw would heal and the cougar would be able to hunt its normal prey, far back in the wilds of the mountains. That would leave Hec's sheep safe from the predator in the future.

While the paw was healing, she might have to provide food for the cougar—but that would be easy enough. A large deer or a wild boar would provide enough meat to feed it until it could hunt again.

She sighed inwardly. She was still uncomfortable. But discomfort was a necessary part of hunting. Will had trained her in a hard school. She could sit or lie for hours in the same spot without moving. At some time, her life might depend on the ability to do so. To move was to be heard or seen. She could sit here for hours more if necessary. She had done so before, many times.

Of course, the fact that she *could* do it didn't make it any more comfortable or enjoyable. But that was part of a Ranger's training.

Pop! One of the flares went out, sending a thin spiral of acrid smoke rising into the air. Another was guttering and the remainder were dimming as they ran low on fuel. She scanned the clearing, moving only her eyes, her face hidden in the shadow of her cowl. She knew that if she stared fixedly at the spot where the venison haunch was wedged in the sapling, she might become mesmerized and miss the first sight of the cougar.

If it was coming.

She'd removed the small bell. When she thought about it,

she had decided it was too big a risk. The cougar might associate the gentle *ting!* with Hec's sudden appearance the previous night. It would already be on edge and ready to flee at the slightest noise or movement. When the cougar came—if it came—she would give it several minutes to settle into feeding. Then, when its attention was focused on filling its belly, she would rise and move a little closer before shooting.

She wondered how long the drug would take to act and whether she should shoot both the prepared arrows for a quicker result. She decided against the idea. Too much of the drug might kill the beast, and that was the last thing she wanted. On the other hand, once she shot the drugged arrow and hit the cat, there was always the chance that it might attack her. To that end, her quiver was full of broadhead arrows she could use to defend herself. She would be reluctant to kill the animal, but it might be her last resort if her own life was in danger. It was more likely, she thought, that the impact of the drugged arrow in a non-vital spot would send the cougar running back into the forest.

At least, she hoped that would be the case.

Pop! Another flare went out, and the light was even dimmer in the farmyard. The trees cast weird shadows, and several times Maddie was sure she saw the cougar at the edge of the clearing. Each time, it was just her imagination at work. She blinked several times to ease her eyes. They were starting to blur under the strain of peering through the darkness, trying to penetrate the shadows.

She scanned the clearing again, then concentrated her vision slightly to the side of the spot where the venison was hanging. Peripheral vision was more valuable in reduced light, she knew. Once again, Maddie resisted the almost overpowering urge to move her cramped leg, to ease the ache in her hip. It was all very well for Will to tell her not to move a muscle when she was on watch. He didn't have an old wound that ached in the cold or stiffened if he stayed stock-still for an hour or so. He could—

Movement!

Her eyes shot back to the spot where she had seen it. It was a few meters from the sapling where the venison was hanging. Now there was nothing. The cougar, if it was the cougar, hadn't moved again and was blending into the shadows beneath the trees.

Then, suddenly, it was there, stepping into the clearing, head raised, sniffing the air for any sign of danger. The wind, what there was of it, was blowing from the cat to her, so there was little chance the cat would catch her scent. She froze, holding her breath in case he might hear the slight sound that it made.

Then he moved again, belly low to the ground, padding silently toward the sapling, holding the injured forepaw off the ground as he went. The metal of the trap glinted in the torchlight.

Inside the barn, the sheep sensed the cougar's presence and bleated nervously. She could hear their little hooves rapping on the hard earth floor of the building. The cougar stopped at the sound, raising its head and turning its gaze toward the darkened building. It seemed to be staring directly at Maddie, the torch-light reflecting in its yellow eyes.

She held her breath once more. *Trust the cloak.* It was the first rule of concealment for Rangers. It had been dinned into her brain countless times by Will. *Trust the cloak and remain absolutely still.*

The yellow eyes seemed to be boring into her, but she remained motionless. The sheep inside the barn settled down after a few minutes when they could see no sign of the predator. They could still sense the cougar's presence, but it had come no closer and posed no immediate threat.

All I need now is for old Hec to come blundering out to protect his sheep, she thought. If that happened, she decided she would abandon this project altogether and leave Spiny Mountain farm to the tender mercies of the cougar.

And serve them right, she thought bitterly.

In spite of her fears, Hec didn't appear, and after several minutes, the cougar was on the move again, seeming to flow over the ground, belly low, to the overpowering scent of the venison a few meters away.

It stood on its hind legs to reach the joint, sinking its massive teeth into the meat and using the muscles of its back legs to try to drag the large piece free. But this time, Maddie had tied the haunch securely in place and the cougar couldn't shift it. Growling softly in frustration, the big cat began to tear chunks of meat from the haunch and gulped them down.

The sheep stirred again inside the barn, and the cougar

turned, still balanced on its rear paws, and looked in the direction of the darkened building. Then, after a few seconds, it decided that the sheep posed no threat to it, and resumed feeding. Now the noise of the sheep, and the crunching of the great cat's jaws, would serve Maddie's purpose. They would mask any sound she might make as she moved.

Moving with infinite caution, she rose to her feet, wincing as the strain came on her hip. The cougar continued to feed, its normally acute senses blunted by the pangs of hunger and sheer pleasure of satisfying it.

It was twenty meters away from Maddie and had its back to her as it stood on its hind legs to rend and tear at the venison haunch. Slowly, she selected one of the drugged arrows and nocked it to the bowstring, keeping the other ready between the fingers of her left hand on the bow. Her position wasn't perfect so she moved silently, two long paces to the right, setting her feet down carefully, searching for any loose twigs under them that might snap and alert the feeding animal.

Once she was in position, she would need to draw, aim and shoot in one movement. The bow would creak slightly as she drew it back, and she would only have a second or two before the beast reacted to the warning noise.

Still the big cat was intent on its feeding. Maddie measured the distance between them. At this short range, there would be virtually no arrow drop. She raised the bow, took a breath, then drew and shot.

Thrum-smack!

The noises of the string releasing and the arrow striking home were almost instantaneous. The arrow hit in the heavily muscled part of the cougar's hindquarters, penetrated and stuck. The cat reacted immediately, dropping to all fours—or all threes as it was—and spinning around, snapping its jaws at the sudden pain in its upper hind leg. As it was designed to do, the main shaft of the arrow broke off, leaving the drug-laden head firmly fixed in the beast's flesh.

The cougar growled angrily, trying to bat the short piece of light wood away with its front paw. But Maddie had intentionally aimed at the animal's left flank, so that it would have to support its weight on the injured right front paw when it tried to do so. The right paw, burdened by the trap and badly injured, wouldn't support its weight, and it stumbled, fell, then recovered and bounded away into the forest.

The moment after she had shot, Maddie had nocked a broadhead arrow to the string and had it ready in case the cougar attacked. Now, as it retreated, she started after it impulsively, heading for the narrow game trail it had taken through the trees.

Then good sense intervened and she stopped. It would be foolish in the extreme to go blundering into the forest close behind the injured cat. It could turn on her in an instant. Better to wait a minute or two and allow the drug to take effect, then follow it.

Her heart was racing with the excitement of the moment, adrenaline coursing through her body. Yet she forced herself to remain unmoving for several minutes. Then, carefully, she moved into the forest, stooping to follow the game trail, where branches and bushes grew across it below head height.

Ahead of her, some distance away, she heard an angry growl from the cougar, and the sound froze her in her tracks for a few seconds. Then she reasoned that it was some distance away and continued. The beast was panicked, running to escape, and left a clear trail as it went. Maddie followed it easily, pushing through the close undergrowth, ears and eyes alert for the first sign that the big cat might be doubling back.

Again, she heard the angry growl. It seemed closer this time, and she hesitated, not wishing to run into trouble.

Another growl from close to. But this time it sounded different—less threatening and tailing away into a series of panting grunts. Then there was silence.

Crouched almost double, she pushed on through the bushes, rounding a bend in the trail, bow out before her, arrow nocked and ready to shoot at a moment's notice.

And there, only a few meters away, was the cougar.

7

SHE FROZE, HER HEART LEAPING INTO HER THROAT AS SHE saw the huge, tawny creature lying in the center of the track, belly down, facing toward her.

Then her training took over. The bow came up, and she began to draw back, her eyes fixed on the massive cat. Because, seen this close to, it truly was massive—bigger than the largest wolf she had ever seen, nearly as large as a bear, although not as bulky.

Slowly, she relaxed, letting the string down and replacing the arrow in her quiver as she realized that the big cat was unconscious. Its flanks heaved with its deep breathing, and its eyes were closed. It showed no sign that it had noticed her as she blundered through the low-lying scrub and emerged onto the section of track where it lay.

"Well, the drug works," she said softly to herself. She hesitated still, unwilling to approach the comatose beast immediately. She wasn't totally sure that the cougar was unconscious. It could be a ruse on the animal's part to draw her closer, so those sharp claws and massive fangs could rend and tear at her.

She stood for a full minute, waiting to see if the beast reacted. She shrugged unhappily. She hadn't really thought too deeply about this part of the exercise. Then a further thought struck her. She had no idea how long the beast would remain unconscious, and every minute she wasted standing here took her another minute closer to the time when it might wake up. And if it did so when she was still working the injured paw, the result could be regrettable—to say the least.

Too late, she realized that she should have asked the apothecary for some estimate of how long the animal would remain unconscious.

"This is a fine time to think of that," she told herself. Then, unwillingly, she took a pace forward. Then another. Still no sign of reaction from the cougar. Finally, she covered the remaining distance between them and went down on one knee beside it. She placed the bow to one side and loosened her saxe in its scabbard. Not that a saxe would do her much good if the beast awoke and attacked her. Her breath was coming in short, hard little intakes, and her heart was hammering inside her chest.

The cougar's breathing was long and steady. Its eyes remained shut.

She studied the injured front paw. The trap was a small one—possibly set for rabbits or hares or other small animals. It had snapped shut on the paw, and the cougar had obviously torn it loose from the light chain that would have secured it. It had never been intended to resist an animal as powerful as this. But the teeth of the trap had sunk into the cat's flesh and locked there, and it had been unable to remove it. The area around the trap was matted with dried blood.

Carefully, nervously, she leaned forward and placed her nose next to the injury, sniffing carefully. She was painfully aware that she had placed her head within a few centimeters of the cougar's fangs, and that thought consumed her for some seconds. Then she shook her head, regaining her focus and concentrating on the wounded paw. There was no smell of corruption that she could discern, although the cat was strong smelling in the extreme. No wonder the sheep had panicked, even in the safety of the barn.

Tentatively, she reached out and touched the injured foot, very gently. The cat stirred, but its eyes remained closed. The paw was tucked slightly under the uninjured one, and she would have to move it to work on it. She took hold of the front leg, thirty centimeters above the paw, and gently tugged it clear of its fellow.

The cougar growled as she moved its leg. Obviously, the movement had caused it some pain. Her eyes shot to its face but its own eyes remained tightly closed. The pain had penetrated its drug-fogged senses, but not enough to waken it. Maddie's mouth was dry and she licked her lips nervously. At least now the paw and the trap were in the open and unobstructed so she could work on them.

She opened her medical pack and began to lay out the items

she would need. First was a small oil-fueled lantern with a polished metal reflector behind the lens and wick. She took her flint and steel and struck a flame into a small pile of tinder, then used a wax taper to light the lantern. She settled the lens back in place and adjusted the reflector so that the lantern threw a narrow beam of bright light across the trail. She set it down on a small flat rock, so that it illuminated the cougar's paw. Then she took her canteen, unstoppered it, and poured water over the matted hair and dried blood.

Gently, she used her fingers to loosen the matted fur around the wound, stopping several times to pour more water. Once she had washed away the dried blood and loosened the tight knots of fur, she checked the cougar's breathing once more. It was still deep and even, and the cat showed no sign that her ministrations were causing it any pain.

"That'll change any minute," she muttered.

She sat back on her heels, unwilling to begin the next phase—that of loosening the jaws of the trap and removing it from the cougar's paw. To put off the moment, she checked her equipment once more, making sure she had salves and bandages ready. She had considered stitching the wound but her hands would never remain steady enough for that, and the thought of plunging a needle into the cougar's flesh terrified her.

Taking a deep breath, Maddie committed herself to the task. She took the trap in both hands and tried to pull the jaws apart.

The cougar stirred as she disturbed the trap, and she stopped instantly, checking to see if its eyes were open, but it slumbered on. She reached out for the trap again, then stopped. Her first attempt had told her that she wouldn't loosen it easily. The spring wasn't overly heavy, but she couldn't get a decent purchase on the jaws of the trap.

She sucked in her lower lip, thinking, then drew her saxe from its scabbard. She slipped it between the jaws, holding it flat, then twisted it.

Slowly, the jaws of the trap began to separate. The cougar growled deep in its throat but remained asleep as the steel teeth were slowly withdrawn from its injured paw. Holding the trap open with her saxe, Maddie reached with her left hand and seized the bottom jaw. Then, angling her big knife to gain leverage from the ground, she lifted, opening the trap wider until she heard a welcome *click* and the jaws locked open.

The cougar growled again, but now Maddie knew it was a reaction to the discomfort and not a threat. She set the saxe down and took the trap in both hands, beginning to ease it off the paw.

Some of the blood-matted hair was still stuck to the steel of the trap, and the cougar stirred as she pulled it. She stopped pulling, took up the canteen again and soaked the hair thoroughly. Again, moving with infinite gentleness, she parted the hair and brushed it away from the trap. Then, finally, she took the trap again and slid it free.

The cougar grunted. Maddie took the sound as one of relief from pain, rather than a reaction to it. She set the trap to one side.

Must remember to spring that before I finish, she thought. She didn't want the cougar to inadvertently catch itself again. Then she took the paw in her left hand and raised it into the light. There was a little blood flowing round the edges of the wound, but the wound itself looked clean and free from infection. There was no sign of reddening or swelling in the flesh.

She unstoppered the bottle of spirits she had brought with her and poured a little over the wound. The cougar flinched as the spirits stung the raw flesh and it pulled its paw from her grasp. But, once again, it was an instinctive reaction, not a conscious one. The cat's eyes remained tightly shut.

Maddie took the paw again and began to smear a special healing ointment on the wound. Similar to the sleeping drug she'd used on her arrow, the ointment was derived from warmweed and had a strong odor that set her eyes watering.

The more she used, the less pain the cougar would feel. She slathered it on heavily, spreading it over the paw and the open wound. The cougar grunted, a different sound from the one it had made when she caused it to flinch. Now there was a sense of contentment in the sound as the source of weeks of pain was eased away, leaving the injured paw numb and free of the nagging, throbbing sensation that it had endured.

"You like that, do you?" she said in a crooning tone. She was still nervous about being so close to the wild animal, but her confidence was growing. The difficult part was over now. From this point, everything she did would be making the animal more comfortable, not causing it distress.

And that meant she was less likely to awaken it from its drugged state.

Maddie sat back and studied her handiwork. The wound was well covered with warmweed salve now. The thick ointment would work in three ways. It would mask the pain of the wound, help it heal cleanly and healthily, and its strong smell and bitter taste would discourage the cat from licking the wound. Maddie hoped that four or five days would see the cougar well on the way to a full recovery.

She smiled, satisfied with her work so far, and relieved that the cougar showed no sign of awakening. She took a roll of clean linen bandage from her pack and quickly wound it three or four times around the uninjured paw, pulling it tight and fastening it, leaving the ends of the bandage long and flapping.

Then she used another bandage on the paw she had been treating, working more carefully now. The point of the clumsy bandage on the uninjured paw was to distract the cougar. She knew it would lick and tear at the bandage when it awoke. Her hope was that the flapping, obvious bandage might distract it. After all, there would be little or no sensation in the healing wound, due to the warmweed. This way, she hoped that the cougar would leave the real bandage alone, at least for a day or two, and give the wound time to heal.

Remembering a detail, she leaned to one side and reached for the arrowhead embedded in the cougar's flank, pulling it free and tossing it away into the bushes. Then she moved back to her spot beside the cat's head and began to pack away her kit.

As she did, something disturbed her. Something had changed. She frowned, checking the bandaged paw, making sure the linen was firmly fastened. Then she looked at the cougar's face, and her breath came out in a short gasp.

The yellow eyes were open, watching her. The big predator was awake.

8

MADDIE FROZE. IT WAS AN INVOLUNTARY ACTION. HER MUS-
cles and sinews simply froze. She couldn't have leaped to her feet
and run for her life if she'd wanted to.

She locked gazes with the cougar. She stopped breathing,
stopped thinking, stopped doing anything. Time stood still.

Then the beast dropped its gaze from hers, and it looked
down at the neatly bandaged forepaw, tilting its head to one side.
It was wondering, dimly, why the constant pain from that paw,
which had throbbed unremittingly for weeks, had ceased.

It nudged the paw with its nose and licked tentatively at the
clean linen of the bandage. Its tongue was only a few centimeters
from Maddie's hand as it did so. She remained stock-still. Now
that the initial moment of heart-stopping terror had passed, she
realized that she could move her legs and arms. But there was no
way she was going to. Any movement on her part might be seen
as a threat. So she sat on her heels and waited. The next move
was up to the cougar.

The cougar looked up at her again, its yellow eyes boring into hers. Then, with a low growl, it rose to all four feet, swaying slightly with the aftereffects of the drug, tentatively placing its injured paw on the ground and testing its weight on it. It lifted it once, holding it clear of the ground, then replaced it as the drug started the cougar swaying again.

It thrust its head forward and sniffed at Maddie, its breath hot on her cheek. She closed her eyes. The huge fangs were only centimeters away from her, and there was nothing she could do to defend herself. The cat edged closer and sniffed her jacket and her arms, slowly lowering its head to sniff at her hands, where it could recognize the warm, pungent smell of the salve. Maddie's heart raced in triple time as she endured the cougar's inspection. Any moment now, it could lunge at her and seize her in those powerful jaws, shaking her as a terrier shakes a rat.

Yet she remained unmoving. It was the only course open to her. If the cougar chose to attack, she was dead. She felt its hot, moist breath on her hands. It was sniffing around her head once more, then, finally, it moved away. She opened her eyes.

The cat was sitting back on its haunches several meters away from her, watching her intently. As she looked at it, it raised the bandaged paw and studied it again, then looked back at her, seeming to find a connection between the cessation of pain and the strange two-legged creature in front of it.

Then, in the blink of an eye, it was gone. It rose to its feet, whirling around, and bounded off down the game trail, disappearing round a corner.

Maddie started with the speed of its sudden movement.

Then, reaction set in, triggered by the adrenaline that had been flowing through her body since the cat awoke and the sudden, unexpected release of tension. She sank back onto her haunches, her whole body shaking, her mind numb. Involuntarily, tears began to stream down her face, and she started to shake with delayed reaction and shock.

She knuckled her eyes to wipe the tears away, but they refused to stop flowing. Her nose ran and snot dripped out onto her lap. She could smell the sickly sweet warmweed smell on her hands as she rubbed them against her cheeks.

"Oh my lord," she crooned over and over. "Oh my lord."

Gradually, she regained control of her body. The shaking stopped and the tears ceased to flow. She wiped her nose on her sleeve, the vague thought occurring to her that her old tutor at Castle Araluen would have been scandalized by such common behavior.

She let go a deep, shuddering sigh as she thought of how close she had been to those powerful jaws and huge fangs.

"Well," she said to herself after a long moment, "at least now I know how long it takes before the knockout drug wears off."

She wrapped her medical kit in its pack and climbed wearily to her feet. Her body felt as if she had been beaten all over with cudgels. Her head throbbed—the adrenaline again. Wearily, she stooped to retrieve her bow and quiver. Then, with one last wondering look down the trail in the direction the cougar had taken, she turned and retraced her path to Spiny Mountain farm.

It was well after daybreak when she reached the little farmhouse. Hec and Gert greeted her curiously. They could see from her subdued manner that she had obviously been through some kind of ordeal. Hec stepped forward and touched her arm.

"Are you all right, Ranger?" he asked.

She gave him a tired smile. It was the first time, she realized, that he had acknowledged her status as a Ranger.

"Just tired, Hec," she said. "I didn't get a lot of sleep and I think I might be coming down with something."

Gert reached forward and placed her rough, callused hand on Maddie's forehead.

"You may have a touch of fever," she said. "I'll fetch you some soup, and you get some sleep in the barn." She bustled back to the farmhouse.

Maddie looked after her. Gert had been a prickly, argumentative host. But now that Maddie appeared to need nursing, Gert's maternal instincts seemed to have come to the fore.

In fact, it had been a long time since she'd had a young person to look after. Gert and Hec's children were grown and long gone to their own farms. Both she and her husband realized that Maddie had put herself at some risk, sleeping in the open when there was a chance that the cougar might return. In truth, they were good people at heart, but living in such an isolated location, their social skills had deteriorated. Now they both felt a little ashamed at the way they had treated the young girl in the gray-green cloak.

As Gert bustled off to the farmhouse to fetch the soup, Hec leaned a little closer to Maddie.

"Thought I heard the sheep bleating through the night," he said. "But you told me not to come out. Did the beast return?"

Maddie nodded, then, as her headache throbbed, wished she hadn't. She placed the back of her hand over her forehead.

"Yes. He was here. I took a shot at him and I'm pretty sure I hit him. I don't think he'll be back to worry you. But I'll stay around for a few days to make sure." She didn't meet his eyes as she said it. She wanted Hec to think she'd killed the beast, without her actually saying it. She hoped she was right to assume that when the cougar regained its strength, it would give the farm and its animals a wide berth.

Hec nodded his gratitude. "Thank 'ee, Ranger," he said. "I'm sorry we doubted you. But you know . . . you're a girl and all and we didn't think . . . well, I don't know what we didn't think . . ." His voice tailed off.

She gave him another tired smile. "That's all right, Hec. I get that a lot."

The following morning, Maddie shot a wild sow and dragged the carcass into the forest, following the game trail the cougar had taken the previous night. She continued until she was two kilometers from the farm, and then wedged the carcass in the fork of a low tree—low enough for the cougar to reach but out of reach for smaller predators or wild dogs.

When she returned to the spot that afternoon, the sow had

gone and there were drag marks through the undergrowth, heading deeper into the forest toward the foothills to the Spiny Mountain range.

She waited another two days but there was no sign of the cougar's returning. On the third day, she shot a small deer and took it even farther down the game trail, once again leaving it wedged in the fork of a tree.

"That should keep it busy," she said. Then she set out for home, bidding the old couple farewell.

Will arrived home a few days later and she greeted him cheerfully. She had missed his company. Being alone was all very well, but he was a reassuring presence in the little cabin.

She wasn't sure if he'd approve of her decision to leave the cougar alive, so she glossed over her adventures at Spiny Mountain farm, telling him merely that a large polecat had been raiding the old couple's stock and she had tracked it down and killed it.

Will raised an eyebrow. "*You* tracked it down?" he said, smiling at her. "You must have improved your skills. Or was it wearing hobnailed boots?"

She decided to let his comment pass, and they settled down into the comfortable routine of life in the cabin by the trees.

A week later, they were woken in the middle of the night by Sable's barking, and Bumper and Tug sounding a warning call from the stable. They dashed out onto the little verandah, Will with his bow in hand and Maddie with her sling.

Will took the porch lantern from its hook and held it high, peering into the shadows among the trees.

"Who's there?" he called. "Show yourself!"

"They're not likely to do that," Maddie muttered. "Not with the pair of us armed to the teeth."

"Possibly not," Will agreed. "In any event, they're probably long gone, what with the dog barking and the horses kicking up such a rumpus." He replaced the lantern and reached down to fondle Sable's head. "Good girl," he told her absently, still peering into the darkness. Then he glanced to one side and straightened.

"Hello. What's this?"

At the end of the verandah, two fat, freshly killed hares had been left on the planks. Maddie walked over, stooped and picked them up. They were still warm, and the muscles were limp. They hadn't been dead long.

Will joined her and looked at the hares, puzzled. "Now, who do you suppose left them here?" he mused.

Maddie shrugged, and looked out into the darkness again. As she did, she saw two glowing yellow eyes in the deep shadows, watching them. A low growl rumbled in Sable's throat. Then the eyes blinked shut and they were gone.

"I have friends you know nothing about." Maddie smiled.